Love Inc.

Sophistidated

***

JILL THRUSSELL

ISBN-13: 9781999955311

CONTENTS

THE RESERVATION

For Zoe, the week at work had been extremely long and she'd just completed an extremely tedious Friday afternoon, most of which she'd actually spent with Collette, her iron handed boss who ruled the beauty salon she worked at with an tongue of steel. The end of the day however, had finally arrived as it had wrestled with Collette's sharp tongue and then entered the world and provided Zoe with the release from work she so desperately needed. Once six in the evening arrived technically, Zoe could actually leave work and so she enthusiastically prepared to do so but just before she could head out of the door and make her final escape for the day, Collette suddenly swept into her consultation room, in order to inspect it thoroughly and Zoe silently groaned as she entered inside the room.

"Really Zoe, you're so messy and you're always late." Collette barked, as she picked up a wet wipe and then stroked it over the top of one of the white, glossy side cabinets at one side of the room where some split lotion lay idly on top of a cabinet. "Next time, I'll dock your wages for wasting lotions."

Zoe glanced at Collette's face with a pretentious serious expression for a few seconds as she digested her comments and then quickly turned her face away as she attempted to hide a smile and the laughter that was erupting deep inside of her and threatening to spill out from her lips. Laughing would only annoy Collette right now and annoying Collette was certainly not a wise thing to do, especially when it was a Friday evening and especially when Zoe was just on the brink of actually leaving work for the entire weekend.

At times, it certainly appeared that Collette's only objective in life was to make Zoe's life as miserable as she possibly could and the truth was unfortunately, she'd actually almost succeeded. Most of Zoe's working life had definitely become a tedious drag and she was stuck in a boring nine to five or rather six job as Collette did not actually release Zoe until six in the evening on most days, servicing the needs of the wealthy women who lived in the local vicinity that surrounded the beauty clinic. If that wasn't boring enough to add to that, her boss Collette was also a complete and utter nightmare. Like the bitter icing upon a ugly, tasteless cake that had to be consumed every single working day, Collette would turn up, inspect Zoe's consultation room and then bark a bunch of instructions at her. There was absolutely no two way conversation, just Collette's commands and Zoe's compliance and that was nonnegotiable, if Zoe actually wanted to leave work at a decent hour. Zoe had learnt long ago not to actually question or argue with Collette, or she would simply end up working extra days on the weekends and later shifts, all of which she absolutely hated.

Being booked for late evening appointments throughout the week was a personal annoyance to Zoe and so was working weekends as her weekends and evenings were extremely precious to her and hence being compliant was a necessary component in keeping the peace and to making Collette slightly happier. Would Collette very truly actually be happy, Zoe doubted it and certainly not with her but very fortunately, she fully understood that and hence she did not even bother to strive to achieve an unobtainable standard of perfection that would never actually be realized. Silence quickly filled the room as Zoe watched Collette perform her consultation room inspection which was usually performed each evening just before she went home, whenever Collette actually had the time.

Collette abruptly finished her inspection of the room and then started on her next checklist. "Did you see all your clients this week as per your appointment schedule?" She asked in a slightly agitated and flustered tone.

Zoe nodded her head obediently in response. "Yes Collette." She replied politely.

Priceless Beauty Inc. was a huge company that specialized in high tech and scientific beauty treatments which were actually designed to reduce the effects of aging and there were a number of extremely, delicate treatments that Zoe had to apply to clients on quite a regular basis. Collette, who managed that particular beauty salon and who was actually Zoe's line manager, took her job very seriously indeed and Zoe was just one of several beauticians that worked under her management, in that particular beauty salon.

Most working days, Zoe would usually spend some of her day preparing chemical compounds for treatment applications and the remainder of her day, would then be spent applying those cosmetic treatments to her clients, who were predominantly mature women in their fifties. A much smaller part of her day, would also be spent reassuring the mature women who actually attended the clinic that the cosmetic treatments they had paid for were actually working and that was the hardest part of Zoe's job as sometimes it seemed, they definitely weren't actually working at all.

The beauty salon was run pretty much like a regimented outfit in that, the beauty consultants always had to arrive at work on time, hit their client consultation targets and they were never allowed to leave work even a minute before the allocated time each weekday evening. Collette had probably been in the army at some point in her life, Zoe quietly concluded as she glanced up at her face as she was a complete stickler for punctuality, organization and extreme tidiness and even verged upon being slightly OCD, in Zoe's opinion anyway.

"Okay you can finish tidying up and go home and don't forget to put your uniform in for cleaning before you leave." Collette instructed. "I don't want any scruffy beauticians in my clinic."

Zoe nodded gratefully as Collette released her. "Right, I'll make sure I do that." She replied politely as she smiled at Collette with an angelic expression. Zoe quickly wiped down her client consultation chair in the center of the room with a leather wet wipe as she mimicked Collette's cleanliness, in a last minute attempt to reassure Collette that she was extremely serious about keeping her consultation room clean and keeping her clients happy as she leapt for joy inside, extremely grateful to be going home on time for once.

Inside Zoe's mind, that particular Friday evening held many promises that were filled with excitement and fun as she'd planned every minute detail of it intricately, well in advance, in fact she'd planned the whole weekend very thoroughly which she fully intended to spend and enjoy with Madeline. A weekend with Madeline was always eventful and Zoe actually gave her social life a much more organized and thorough approach, than she actually applied to her work life.

Madeline, was Zoe's best female friend and Zoe had put together a fun packed weekend for them both to enjoy throughout the week which she fully intended to participate in. Over the years, the two women's friendship had managed to stand the test of time, even though they were both completely different in some respects and had very different personalities. Zoe was an extrovert and extremely playful and mischievous, whereas Madeline on the other hand was quite shy, reserved and serious and even at times, slightly cautious. Despite their differences however, Zoe knew that their weekends together were always tremendous fun and devoid of any serious responsibilities and tedious battles with overbearing bosses like Collette as they were both single, lived alone and had absolutely no children or husbands to attend to.

Thirty minutes later, when Zoe finally managed to escape from work, she arrived outside Madeline's house and Madeline quickly opened the door and then invited her in. Once Zoe stepped inside the lounge, she quickly took a well-deserved rest as she flopped down onto Madeline's sofa right next to her and just relaxed for a few minutes. Her Friday had been quite hectic as it had been filled to the brim with clients and Zoe had worked extremely hard as she'd attended to each client's requirements meticulously. A few minutes recuperation was therefore required as Zoe fully intended to play hard later that evening and participation in her plans, she knew would definitely require significant amounts of energy.

At times, Zoe actually had to work on the weekends and although she would be given a day off throughout the week to make up for that, it was still in Zoe's opinion a complete pain in the butt to actually have to do so. The two days off work each week that sat right beside each other upon the calendar of life, she deeply cherished and they were extremely important to her for a number reasons. Due to the fact that those two days of the weekend were actually clumped together that actually allowed Zoe to pack as much fun as she possibly could into those forty hours, before she actually had to return to work on the following Monday morning which she usually did, hung over and still recovering from the previous weekend's escapades.

Fortunately, this weekend however, Zoe was completely free and had her whole two days to spend as she wished with no work duties to attend to and she was utterly determined to enjoy every minute of those two days as much as she possibly could. Due to the fact that Madeline's house was closer to Zoe's work than her own home was, the two women had decided to hang out at Madeline's house that Friday evening in order to prepare for the night and the rest of the weekend ahead as it would usher in the start of their weekend more quickly.

Madeline's home was quite simple in terms of appearance and had a quite minimalist feel to it as each room was extremely tidy and very well organized which was a stark contrast in comparison to Zoe's own home which was a lot more chaotic and extremely cluttered. Each of the walls was decorated in a brilliant, stark white but some splashes of color existed inside some paintings that were nailed to each wall which gently broke the possible monotony that possibly could have existed inside each room. An open plan kitchen adjoined the lounge and that was also decorated in a stark, crisp white but due to Zoe's lack of interest in cooking, she rarely bothered to actually even venture inside it.

Madeline suddenly stood up and then strode across the room towards the kitchen area as she prepared to fix them both an evening meal. "Hungry Zoe?" She asked Zoe as she paused for a moment and then turned back to face her.

Zoe nodded. "I sure am." She replied. "Absolutely, ridiculously starving."

"Great, I'll just fix us something to eat." Madeline insisted. "Just give me a few minutes."

Zoe nodded.

Inside Madeline's kitchen, there was a food generator which Madeline quickly walked towards and then rapidly started to utilize to prepare their evening meal. The contraption was extremely convenient and could prepare a simple evening meal in a matter of minutes, once the correct ingredients had actually been placed inside it and it had actually been switched on. Each ingredient would be slipped inside and once the dish required had been selected, the food generator would then do whatever was actually required to make and deliver a freshly prepared, cooked meal and there were over one hundred dishes that Madeline could actually choose from.

Zoe stood up and then sauntered across the room towards Madeline as she smiled. "Isn't it so great that we don't actually have to slave for hours over hot stoves like women used to do in the olden days?" She asked as she sat down on a bar stool next to one of the white, glossy worktops and watched Madeline. "Saves us a whole heap of time." Zoe mentioned. She had actually started to recover from both her working week and Collette and now, she was raring to actually start her fun packed weekend which would commence as soon as she'd actually consumed her evening meal and then prepared herself.

Madeline nodded her head in agreement. "Very true." She replied. "And years and years ago, women even had to milk cows and stuff and fill up water jugs from rivers and then actually carry them home on their heads."

"Thank God for food generators, fast food, restaurants and taps." Zoe remarked. "Can you imagine how yucky that would actually be having to milk a dam cow?" She shook her head as she suddenly shuddered. "I can't wait to go out tonight, seriously this week has been gross and it involved way to much work." Zoe continued. "We're gonna have so much fun this weekend." She insisted as she grinned. "Mischief is definitely coming our way."

Madeline smiled in response. "I know Zoe and you're like mischief on wheels because whenever you step outside the door, mischief always finds you."

"Fun and mischief are my closest allies in life." Zoe replied as she shrugged. "Wherever I go they're there, my most trusted, faithful companions, beside you of course Madeline."

"I know, it's almost like there's a special magnetic force that draws you together." Madeline elaborated as she giggled. "But I wouldn't change that, it's part of you and it's actually a lot of fun." She suddenly turned round to face Zoe and then handed her a filled plate full of piping hot food and some cutlery. "Food's ready, enjoy."

Zoe leant forward enthusiastically as she eagerly accepted the filled plate that Madeline had given her and then licked her lips as she smiled. "Looks great Madeline. You've done an amazing job." She observed as the delicious aroma's from the dish suddenly began to hit her senses and her mouth quickly began to water.

Madeline laughed. "Well, the Zapper food generator did a great job." She replied.

"Let's eat, get ready and then go out." Zoe urged. "I can't wait for our weekend to start." She gushed. "Work this week has been total drama and Collette's been on the rampage, all bloody week."

Madeline smiled as she walked back towards the lounge and sofa with a plate of food inside her hands. "Why, what happened?" She asked.

"Just the usual stuff but ten times worse. I swear she must be menopausal or something." Zoe replied as she sat back down on the sofa and then grinned. "If that's what it is, those hormone replacement tablets sure ain't working."

"She's probably just having problems at home or something." Madeline suggested as she picked up a remote control from the white marble and glass coffee table in front of her and then started to flick through the channels which appeared on the large, wafer thin screen that clung to a nearby wall.

"I doubt it, Collette usually is the problem." Zoe insisted as she glanced up at the screen upon the wall directly in front of her. "She's like a monster on heat."

A commercial suddenly appeared on the screen directly in front of the two women that seemed quite lively and entertaining and Madeline immediately stopped browsing through the channels and placed the remote control back down upon the coffee table as she prepared to watch it. The two women started to tuck into their meal as they watched and listened to the commercial quietly as their hunger suddenly, completely silenced them both.

"Are you looking for love?" A seductive, sensual female voice said as each word spoken gently floated out across the room. "Then visit, the Love Colony."

"Wow, a romantic holiday package. Look at that Madeline." Zoe urged as she pointed enthusiastically towards the screen. "It sounds really cool. We should go, we could do with a holiday."

"I'm not sure." Madeline replied tentatively as she continued to watch the screen and spoon forkfuls of food into her mouth.

Zoe immediately rolled her eyes. "You got something better to do? Like what, work?" She teased. "Come we're both single and we could both do with a break."

"We provide a professional service and match you with the ideal partner through scientific and technological analysis, so that you can enjoy the romantic relationship you've always yearned for. Our love packages start from only $2,000 for a week's stay. Let us do the hard work for you and we will find you the partner of your dreams." The woman's voice continued as beautiful beaches suddenly displayed in the background behind her and exotic looking locations which appeared to be situated upon a tropical island.

"It looks very high tech and a bit unusual." Madeline mentioned.

"Would you rather just meet all your dates inside a bar?" Zoe asked as she grinned and stopped eating for a moment. "This looks exciting, different and very exotic. I'll even treat you." She insisted.

"I dunno." Madeline replied.

"I have holidays and you work freelance." Zoe urged. "Come on, it's not like you have a boyfriend or anything, it'll be fun."

Silence filled the air as Madeline quietly contemplated the prospect of a love seeking vacation internally for a moment, Zoe definitely wanted to go but Zoe was certainly a lot more adventurous than she was, so that totally made sense. They were both definitely single, so on that point Zoe was completely correct as they both hadn't actually dated anyone decent for a while and Madeline could certainly do with giving her dating life a spring clean, upgrade and makeover.

Madeline's face remained quite stagnant as a doubtful expression remained firmly placed upon it. "It's not really about the money, I can pay for my own vacation." She mentioned.

"Well, what is it about then?" Zoe pressed. "We need to have some fun, serious fun and work is not fun. I need a vacation and so do you." She insisted. Zoe was certainly not adverse to a bit of gentle persuasion, if that is what it actually took to convince Madeline to attend, not that she was dragging Madeline along but they were both extremely single and a nice vacation at a high tech love resort in a tropical setting sounded right up her street. "We could both meet someone wonderful and interesting." She continued as a naughty, very mischievous expression rapidly crossed her face. "Someone that can change our single status and that can perhaps even alleviate some of our sexual frustrations which our very single lives inflict on us every single day."

Madeline grinned as she replied. "Well it has been a while. Okay, okay I'll come along. One condition though, if I want to leave, we leave." She insisted as she caved into Zoe's demands, a grain of doubt still remained inside her mind and very stubbornly, it wouldn't surrender or disappear at all, no matter how much Zoe's arguments actually made sense.

"Sure." Zoe agreed. "But who'd want to leave, look at the resort it's absolutely stunning." She smiled as she internally accepted her victory, the last point and term Madeline had insisted upon was non-sequitor and extremely minor in Zoe's mind as at the end of the day, Madeline had actually agreed to come along and that meant, they were both going to be attending a very exotic, love seeking vacation filled with lots of romantic possibilities.

"It looks extremely high tech." Madeline reiterated.

"Well, it sure beats searching for love in bars and parks." Zoe insisted diplomatically. "It looks a lot more elegant and extremely refined."

"Yeah but everyone being there is like an admission of singleness and desperation." Madeline mentioned. "It's like saying we've failed to meet someone nice and have a good relationship in our normal lives."

"Please, I don't care how I meet someone nice, just as long as I do." Zoe insisted. "High tech methods, low tech methods makes absolutely no difference to me a man is still a man, a date is still a date and a male body part attached to the ideal man that makes me scream with pleasure, is still very much a penis, no matter where I actually find it."

Madeline grinned. "You so uncouth Zoe." She teased.

"Uncouth or realistic? You can sit there for as long as you want to and pretend that you don't need the cobwebs dusted off your vagina, me on the other hand, I want beautiful, heart pounding orgasms to replace them and I'm not scared to admit it." Zoe insisted. "And the sooner that actually happens for me, the better."

A booking form suddenly appeared on the screen directly in front of the two women and Zoe quickly started to make their actual vacation reservations. Inside her mind she knew, she definitely had to strike whilst the iron was still hot as if she gave Madeline a chance to actually change her mind, in all likelihood the vacation would not actually happen at all. Taking a week of work could possibly be tricky, if it was done at very short notice but Zoe was actually due some holidays and Collette even though she could be difficult at times, would definitely have to accept that as it was a legal entitlement actually specified in Zoe's contract of employment.

"I think if we go in a few weeks' time that will be fine." Madeline suggested. "That way you can actually get time of work without Collette having a heart attack."

Zoe nodded. "I think you're right. Collette can be a bit tricky but if I give her at least two weeks' notice, she should be okay. We can go on the Saturday and then come back on the Sunday, that way we get two Saturday nights at the resort." Zoe suggested. "You're so lucky Madeline, you can do whatever you want to do, when you actually want to do it and you don't even have to ask your boss for permission."

Madeline smiled. "Yeah, sometimes that can be useful but it does have its drawbacks too." She explained. "If the money doesn't come in, it can be very worrying and stressful." Madeline continued. "Especially when you have other people's salaries to pay. It can be a lot of hard work too as sometimes you have to work a lot of extra hours, like when I have to attend a fashion show to display a new season's range, sometimes I can even be working up until midnight or into the early hours of the next morning."

Zoe nodded. "True." She agreed.

When Madeline had actually graduated from college, she had chosen to embark upon her career as a fashion designer and had been actually given some initial investment with which to open her own boutique from a creative investment agency that supported women in business. She had opened up a

20

small boutique in the heart of the city with the resources she'd been given and very fortunately, it had grown over the years and even become reasonably profitable. Three years later, she'd actually been able to employ someone else to assist her and manage the shop front and that had reduced some of the additional long hours she'd initially had to work, just to get things up and running. Geoffrey, who usually manned the shop floor, serviced all the clients that visited the outlet meticulously and he organized fittings, private consultations, displayed the latest range to clientele and even processed customer purchases. He was competent, professional, trustworthy, extremely loyal and totally and utterly camp and the predominantly female clients that usually visited the boutique, absolutely loved him.

Since Madeline had hired Geoffrey, her business had flourished and she'd had absolutely no regrets about that decision at all as Geoffrey had certainly more than delivered over the years, very consistently. Going away for a week wouldn't be a big deal for her and was certainly something that she could easily afford to do as Madeline could simply plan her trip around her business and clientele as she knew that Geoffrey could certainly cope for a week in her absence. Her retail clients usually ordered in bulk and since it was mid-season, there were no new urgent pending orders waiting to be negotiated or fulfilled and that meant for now, Madeline was actually quite free to travel for a week, if she actually wanted to.

Zoe gently shook her head as she completed the booking form on the screen directly in front of them both. "Still you're lucky you are so talented Madeline, my rigid work regime is a total nightmare and the client targets are such a headache sometimes." She moaned. "If only I'd had a huge talent like you have, I could have done something else with my life and not been lumbered with Collette."

Madeline grinned. "Trust me Zoe, Collette's probably exactly what you need right now, she gives you a bit of structure and brings a bit of order to your chaotic life. Without Collette, I think you'd be lost." She insisted.

"I just hate conforming." Zoe moaned as she finalized the vacation reservations and then turned to face Madeline. "It just doesn't gel well with my personal beliefs and is an absolute contradiction to everything I believe in."

"Still, at least you get paid regularly and the money's decent." Madeline mentioned.

Zoe smirked and nodded. "That's true, Collette does pay us well but only if we meet our targets on time, if not we lose all our bonuses and our basic really isn't actually that great." She explained. "Right that's all settled, three weeks' time and we're off on vacation." Zoe announced triumphantly. "I'll tell you what Madeline, I'll give you a luxury beauty session before we actually go away. I'm allowed to give a beauty treatment session to a friend or family member every three months and I absolutely never use any of those sessions. I'll make you look even more stunning than you already do and then you'll be ready to dust of the cobwebs of singleness forever."

Madeline grinned and nodded enthusiastically. "Now that sounds like a great plan." She agreed.

The next three weeks for the two women literally flew by as they enthusiastically prepared for their vacation, clothes were bought or in Madeline's case, designed and made, hair was cut, curled, treated, colored and straightened and beauty sessions were booked for both women as they embraced their vacation and prepared for it, extremely thoroughly. Zoe had actually accumulated two weeks' vacation entitlement and hence a week away was something that Collette simply couldn't argue about as the current working year was almost finished and that meant that Zoe had to actually use her holiday time up, before the next working year actually began. Technically, Zoe was allowed to carry one week's vacation over into the next year but since there was only one month left until the end of the vacation year, time was quite definitely running out and that meant Zoe had to use at least a week of her holiday time at some point in the next month.

On the Friday afternoon of Madeline's scheduled appointment for her beauty consultation and treatment session, Zoe prepared for her arrival enthusiastically as she wiped down her consultation chair and then poured them both two glasses of champagne. Over the years, Madeline had often made Zoe dresses and outfits but Zoe had never actually given her a beauty treatment before, so she was extremely excited about it.

Usually, Zoe just moaned to Madeline about work and she'd never once actually considered inviting her along for a consultation, so it was a refreshing change for them both in that Zoe was actually offering her something positive for once from the place Madeline was so used to hearing nothing but negative complaints about. Madeline had agreed to attend, after a bit of gentle persuasion, although she hadn't been very keen about the possibility of running into Collette, when she actually attended but Zoe had insisted that the two women would try to avoid her as much as they possibly could and Madeline had been appeased by her heartfelt, consistent reassurances.

Everything was perfect and totally ready for Madeline's arrival as Zoe quickly glanced around at her consultation room and then smiled. Expensive glasses of champagne had been poured, the best snacks and nibbles had been placed inside small, shiny, white china bowls and even though Madeline was only booked in for a minor beauty session, some additional, more expensive treatments had actually been prepared. Collette would certainly have Zoe's guts for garters, if she ever actually found out how lavish Zoe had actually been but Zoe wasn't bothered by that at all and had decided to live dangerously for once and ignore Collette's very strict, regimented rules. Her appointment had been scheduled as Zoe's last appointment that Friday afternoon and very fortunately, Collette had actually left work earlier that Friday to attend a regional manager's meeting and that meant, Zoe had been left to her own devices and could literally do whatever she wanted to, to some extent.

On the Thursday evening, the two women had spoken on the phone at length as they'd organized their plans for the Friday afternoon and discussed the next day and their pending vacation which they would actually embark upon on that Saturday at midday. Excitement had filled the air as their voices had wafted through the airwaves and pleasantly filled each women's ears as the prospect of their pending love vacation had tantalized and seduced them both.

"Make sure you finish work quite early on Friday babes so that you're on time." Zoe had insisted. "I want to give you all the trimmings."

"Will you get in trouble for that?" Madeline had enquired.

"Nah, Collette will be leaving quite early this Friday some management meeting so we're cool. What Collette don't know, won't hurt her right?" Zoe had teased Madeline as she'd giggled. "Besides this is my perk and since I don't usually use them, the company owes me lots of perks, so I can use them all in one go and give you all the special extras that we usually save for our very best clients." She had insisted.

"As long as you're sure." Madeline had replied.

"I don't really care Madeline, the most she can do is dock my salary for the extra cost, when she actually finds out, if she ever finds out which I doubt she ever will." Zoe had quickly reassured her. "I'll just say I used the treatments in a client consultation, she'll never even know."

Their conversation had quite unintentionally, been steered back towards the topic of Collette and a short silence had followed as Zoe had quietly given her boss a little more thought and more specifically her home life. For a moment, Zoe had actually started to try and imagine Collette's home life and had even actually allowed her mind to mischievously delve into what it could possibly be like as she'd considered it slightly more thoughtfully and thoroughly.

"Do you think Collette ties her husband up each night and spanks him up or do you think she has a whip?" Zoe had asked Madeline playfully as visions of Collette in thigh high, black leather boots with a large whip and a poor shivering male being beaten with it relentlessly had suddenly popped into her mind. "She's definitely got a husband and apparently, they've been married for years and years."

Madeline had giggled. "You never know." She'd replied.

Zoe was gently reminded of her conversation with Madeline the previous night as she waited impatiently for Madeline to arrive and smiled, thank goodness Collette wouldn't actually be around that afternoon as that would have spoilt the treat that she wanted to lavish upon Madeline. Both women had to look their very best and Zoe was completely and utterly determined that this vacation would not only be the holiday of a lifetime but that they would both also receive maximum pleasure from it.

Due to the wait, Zoe amused herself with further thoughts as to what Collette's home life might actually be like for a moment as she allowed her mind to wander and saunter into visions of what Collette's personal life might actually really be like. Collette, Zoe was utterly convinced had to be a dictator at home that ruled her home with an iron grip. Perhaps at one time, Collette had even been a dominatrix and just perhaps, her sexual past times had overflowed into her work life and personality and now the two could no longer actually be separated, Zoe mused playfully. Such thoughts could never actually be said to Collette's face as Zoe knew, she would be fired on the spot. Madeline had often teased her and asked her how she could possibly say such things about her boss, whenever they'd actually discussed Collette but Madeline didn't know Collette like Zoe did and she certainly didn't have to work under her leadership every single working day. For some unknown reason, Collette just made Zoe feel quite flustered and very stressed and even at times, slightly uncomfortable.

A buzz suddenly sounded out into the air all around Zoe and interrupted her thoughts as the receptionist politely alerted her to Madeline's arrival. Zoe smiled, quickly stood up and then made her way out of her consultation room as she prepared to collect Madeline from the front foyer. Collette and further speculation about her home life could definitely wait, whereas the two women's vacation plans, certainly couldn't. Madeline was there now and that meant, Zoe had to now actually deliver the promised beauty treatment session she'd promised to actually give her. Now, it was Zoe's chance to show Madeline that she could actually really be quite organized, professional and extremely thorough.

Once the two women met inside the foyer, Zoe gently held Madeline's arm and then quickly guided her along the plain, white hallway as she headed back towards her consultation room. When they arrived just outside the door, Zoe quickly opened it and then held the door open politely as she invited Madeline inside. In the very center of the room, was Zoe's special treatment chair and she quickly offered Madeline a seat.

"Please sit down on Lottie." Zoe offered as she quickly closed the door behind them both. "Lottie is my consultation chair." She explained as she politely handed Madeline a glass of champagne.

"Wow, it's so clean and organized in here and so lavish." Madeline mentioned as she sat down upon the huge cream and black chair in the center of the room. "So not like you Zoe. I love it though. Your clients certainly get beautified in style. I'm impressed."

"They definitely do but they do spend a lot of money for the privilege, so I guess they get what they pay for really." Zoe replied.

Usually, whenever Madeline actually met Zoe at her place of work, they would meet inside the reception area and that meant, she'd never actually been inside Zoe's consultation room before. The main reason behind that being that Zoe was usually in such a rush to leave work as soon as she possibly could in the evenings that she'd never actually invited Madeline inside her consultation room. Zoe's chair Lottie, was the one thing that Zoe loved the most about her consultation room and was in some respects, the apple of her eye as she had actually been allowed to choose it herself

31

from a range of chairs when Collette had fitted out the consultation rooms inside the beauty salon, over a year ago and hence she'd felt quite proud about offering Madeline a seat upon Lottie's lavish, cushioned, padded, comfortable frame.

Lottie as Zoe affectionately referred to her consultation chair, could maneuver around extremely well, whenever someone actually sat down upon on the leather surface and if you actually lay back, it almost felt as if you were actually lying down upon a bed as Lottie had great padding and cushioning situated just underneath the firm, leather exterior. There was even a remote control device that could be utilized to make Lottie lean backwards and rotate round in circles and at times, Zoe would actually sit down upon Lottie and just play around on her chair for fun as she'd circle around and around and then go up and down as if she was mounted upon a rodeo horse, though obviously not when Collette was around as Collette completely frowned upon any misuse of equipment at all and playing around on Lottie, Zoe knew would definitely certainly be considered, a misuse of equipment by Collette. Lottie was expensive and had certainly not been purchased for any kind of recreational enjoyment, at least not in that particular manner and Collette would not tolerate such childish antics at all.

Personal visitors weren't really allowed inside the treatment rooms, aside from when they were due to attend an employee perk session which had to be arranged and organized at least a week in advance and hence Zoe had never actually invited Madeline inside her consultation room whenever Collette was actually around. Coupled with the fact that Zoe was usually in a rush to leave, whenever Madeline actually visited her workplace, that particular rule of Collette's had actually always suited Zoe quite well and hence had never actually been a bone of contention between them both.

"Lottie, what a cute, spunky name." Madeline said as she gently stroked the black and white leather arms of the chair she was seated upon and then smiled.

"Yes and now that you've been formally introduced to Lottie, I can start your actual beauty consultation Madeline." Zoe replied with a grin. "Lottie is very special and she's quite simply, the best consultation chair that I've ever had. She's every beautician's dream."

A few months beforehand, Lottie had actually broken and had then been sent away for repair and Zoe had actually missed the consultation chair she'd somehow grown quite attached to. Fortunately, after just a week however, Lottie had actually been returned and Zoe had been extremely relieved as the temporary chair she'd been given in Lottie's absence had been quickly replaced and Lottie had returned to her usual spot inside Zoe's consultation room once more. Zoe had been quite worried at the time that the repair shop might not have been able to fix her but Lottie had returned with a sparkling new control panel and in perfect working condition and ever since then, Lottie had operated without any problems at all.

"Have you ever made love to anyone on Lottie?" Madeline suddenly asked as she glanced at Zoe's face and then grinned mischievously.

"Well, now that you mention it, I actually haven't." Zoe replied as a puzzled expression suddenly spread out across her face. "But it's definitely something worth thinking about, though how I'd sneak a male into the building for a quick test drive without Collette actually seeing him, is another matter entirely. Collette would definitely be gunning for me, if she ever actually found out."

"Perhaps, you could just say he was a client and then book the man in question in, for an actual beauty consultation." Madeline suggested as she giggled and sipped on her glass of champagne.

"Wow Madeline, you're almost beginning to sound as naughty as me, I'm so proud of you." Zoe teased playfully as she picked up some cartons filled with lotions and then started to pour and mix the liquids they each contained into a small, white bowl inside one of her hands.

"I know, it must be the champagne." Madeline replied as she gave Zoe a huge grin and then shrugged.

"I'm actually quite attached to Lottie, I'm not sure why. Perhaps, it's just a natural thing, since we beauticians spend so much time with our chairs we kind of get used to them I guess." Zoe explained. "But I'd never actually thought about making love to someone on top of Lottie, now that could really actually be quite interesting as Lottie is extremely flexible." She mentioned thoughtfully. "As long as Collette's not around that is as one sight of Collette's face during a pleasurable moment would probably be enough to put me off sex for life."

Madeline giggled. "Your uniform is so smart, it's even quite elegant." She observed.

"Yeah, thankfully head office actually chose our uniforms for us all and we all have to wear the same uniform. I hate to think what Collette would have actually picked out for us, if it had actually been her decision." Zoe explained as she grinned. "Probably some yucky, utterly disgusting, pea green outfit with bright yellow buttons."

Madeline giggled.

The fitted tunic top that Zoe wore was a brilliant, stark white which the company insisted gave the brand an image of professionalism and cleanliness and although it reminded Zoe a little of hospital nurses outfits, the shiny, black, diamond shaped buttons that adorned the front of her tunics pleasantly detracted from that image and even gave her uniform a slightly more elegant feel. Black, shiny trousers, accompanied the white top which she was required to wear every working day and they were quite comfortable and actually looked quite smart. In some ways, it was probably the best uniform that Zoe had ever actually worn as she'd worked in a few beauty salons in the past where some of the uniforms she'd been required to wear had actually verged upon being slightly hideous and this one certainly wasn't.

"Have you finished packing your clothes?" Zoe enquired as she gently applied some lotions to Madeline's face.

"Not totally, I was going to finish the rest of my packing tonight." Madeline explained. "Have you?"

Zoe shook her head. "I haven't even started yet." She replied. "I tell you what, let's go to yours after here, pack up your stuff, then go to mine and pack up my stuff and then we can go out afterwards and tomorrow morning, we'll do a bit of last minute shopping."

Madeline grinned. "Sure that sounds great." She agreed as she started to relax and wriggled around a bit inside the chair. "Wow Zoe, Lottie is really comfortable, I could actually fall asleep here." Madeline remarked.

"I know, Lottie is quite simply, the best consultation chair that I've ever had.

Whenever I have a hangover, after we've had a wild weekend out, sometimes I even catch fifty winks on Lottie as long as Collette's not actually around." Zoe explained as she suddenly pulled down a laser arm from above Madeline's head and then started to move it over her face as she quickly removed any loose dead skin cells from the surface of her skin. "We have to make sure we take the right outfits with us, coz we have to look utterly amazing." Zoe insisted. "A pampering beauty session is only half the battle."

Madeline smiled. "That treatment you applied to my face is making my skin feel a bit tight." She mentioned. "Is that normal?"

"Yep, just drink some more champagne and I promise, it'll start to feel a little bit better." Zoe quickly suggested as she generously poured some more champagne into Madeline's glass and topped it up.

Madeline giggled as she sipped on the glass of bubbly liquid and bubbles from the champagne inside the glass, tickled her nose. "Yep, perhaps that'll help." She replied. "I'm gonna be tipsy quite soon."

"And that's a bad thing?" Zoe asked. "You need to be tipsy sometimes, lighten up the load, coz you are way to responsible and serious at times."

Madeline smiled. "Yeah, you're probably right." She agreed.

"Madeline, do you remember that awful guy you used to date called Humphrey?" Zoe asked. "He was so not worth your time. I dunno why you kept things up with him for so long."

"I know." Madeline agreed. "When I found out he was cheating, I dumped him straight away."

"I tried to warn you, I could see his fakeness a mile away." Zoe added.

Madeline nodded. "I know, I just seem to pick the wrong kind of guys. I've never really dated anyone really nice." She moaned as she gently shook her head.

"Babes, don't beat yourself up about it, you're just unlucky. You attract the wrong kind of attention, from the wrong kind of men." Zoe explained as she gently touched Madeline's arm in a reassuring manner. "Hopefully we'll meet some nice guys at the Zincata love island." She continued. "Some decent guys."

Madeline nodded and then smiled.

Both women continued to discuss and reminisce on their past dating experiences and how awful some of them had actually been as the beauty treatment session continued and the sparkling champagne and delightful nibbles continued to flow in abundance. Each delightful glass and delicious mouthful, pleasantly kept them company as the food and drink gently teased their palates and kept them very occupied throughout Madeline's beauty session which made time seem to pass by, slightly more quickly.

Madeline's last relationship had been a complete disaster and Zoe internally hoped as she worked upon Madeline's skin, that she would actually meet someone much nicer to embark upon a beautiful romance with, whilst on the vacation they were just about to actually indulge in. His name was Humphrey and just like his name, in Zoe's opinion he was frumpy, boring and extremely conceited and Zoe had totally disapproved of him, from the very first second she'd actually laid eyes upon him.

They had met through some online dating website thing, where you had to fill in a profile and then the company that run the website, would suggest matches for each person, based on mutual interests and things each person had in common. Apparently, they had both liked and hated some similar things and then they had actually been presented to each other as each other's ideal romantic match, though Zoe for the life of her could not personally understand why as they'd seemed so incompatible. Madeline had stayed in the relationship for a whole year, for some unknown reason as in Zoe's mind, he had not actually been good enough for Madeline and quite certainly not worth a year of her life.

Finally, after an extremely painful, boring year, the two had eventually broken up as Humphrey had found someone else that he'd started to cheat on Madeline with and when his indiscretion had actually been discovered, it had been quite frankly, a relief in Madeline's sight. He'd explained to her that he'd felt much more compatible with his new partner and Madeline had allowed him to leave peacefully, partially glad and partially grateful to finally get rid of him.

In Zoe's mind, Humphrey's departure had been an extremely positive event for Madeline as it had been good riddance to bad rubbish. Humphrey, was a complete pain in the ass as far as Zoe was concerned and had actually brought Madeline nothing but grief. Despite those very negative factors however, Madeline had actually cried as he'd departed as she'd felt slightly hurt by the betrayal but Zoe had quickly comforted her and reassured her, that he was definitely not good enough for her anyway. He certainly wouldn't have been Zoe's first choice for Madeline and nor would he have even been her last choice as he did not actually match up to any kind of dating standards that Zoe felt were an acceptable measure for Madeline to actually conform to.

Very fortunately, Humphrey had actually moved on very quietly and Zoe had actually banned Madeline from calling him, through fear that she might actually beg him for some kind of friendship afterwards. In Zoe's opinion, Humphrey did not actually deserve to be in Madeline's life in any capacity at all, after what he'd actually put her through and even a friendship between them both, to her was simply not an acceptable outcome. Madeline had been completely faithful to him and stupidly so, as he certainly hadn't been faithful to her and she'd spent an entire year of her life utterly devoted and dedicated to him, just to discover that in the end, he'd actually been a cheating love rat all along. Perhaps, Humphrey had even cheated on Madeline more than once and she hadn't even known about it, Zoe could never be sure and quite frankly, neither really could Madeline.

Despite that very unfortunate romantic experience which had actually ended a few months ago, Madeline had somehow managed to pick her life back up and now seemed to be for the most part, over the heartbreak and over Humphrey. Zoe on her part had tried to keep Madeline quite busy as she'd attempted to help her to forget about him as quickly as possible and the two had hung out most weekends ever since and partied a lot. Large quantities of alcohol had been consumed and that consumption had it seemed, been sufficient enough to assist Madeline in drowning any unpleasant memories of him that might have lurked within the corners of her mind.

His departure from her life, had been relatively clean cut and now that Madeline had actually had some time to heal, Zoe definitely felt she should be ready for new relationship, after all he'd moved on even before their relationship had ended and he hadn't even felt bound to her by his supposed, phony romantic commitment. In some ways, Zoe knew that Madeline had always been a bit of doormat when it came to men as she'd seen that over the years ever since the two had first actually met but she fought that inherent flaw inside Madeline's nature as it was in Zoe's mind, her only weakness.

The two women had attended the same high school and college, though not the same university as straight after college Madeline had attended an educational institute that specialized in fashion, whilst Zoe had gone straight out to work and been employed by a beauty salon. Every man however, that Zoe had seen Madeline date over the years had been quite dorky and they usually acted as if they felt they were too good for Madeline, even though in Zoe's eyes, they were usually not good enough. Each lover that Madeline had actually entered into a relationship with had taken advantage of her naivety, empathy and compassion and had subsequently totally run rings around her and that had annoyed Zoe as she'd watched and supported her through each inferior, substandard romance.

This time would very be different, Zoe vowed internally as she glanced at Madeline's smiling face and then smiled as the two women prepared to leave her consultation room. This time, Zoe would actually be there and this time, she would actually get rid of any romantic garbage that might try to come Madeline's way, before they even dared to try to settle themselves into her heart and into her life. If the love resort even tried to match Madeline up with some loser, Zoe would be right there to step in and actually intervene as there was absolutely no way on earth, she was going to sit and watch Madeline go through another year of heartbreak with another complete waste of space.

"Madeline, you look totally amazing." Zoe proudly announced as she admired Madeline's glowing complexion. "Like a million dollars."

Madeline hugged her affectionately as they sauntered slowly towards the consultation room door. "You've done a great job Zoe and you are so talented." She mentioned appreciatively as she smiled. "You've literally taken years of my face."

Zoe smiled as she handed Madeline two bottles, one which contained a face wash and the other a skin cream. "Use this one each morning and this one every night." She instructed Madeline. "That'll keep your skin looking fresh for as long as possible."

Madeline nodded as she listened.

A few minutes later, the two women left the building as they headed out towards the parking lot which was situated at the very left hand side of the building as they prepared for their packed evening ahead. Zoe had changed her clothes by now and had actually dropped off her uniform on the way out of the building and placed it inside the linen cupboard where a large basket was kept for staff laundry and as the two women sauntered slowly towards Zoe's car, they enthusiastically discussed the evening ahead and their plans.

"I think we should go out for dinner first." Zoe suggested. "Before we actually do any packing. I'm absolutely starving."

Madeline nodded. "Yeah, we could go to that lobster and crab place we went to about a month ago. They had great cocktails." She mentioned.

"Yep, that's a great idea." Zoe agreed.

"Who did your beauty session for you?" Madeline asked. "I can tell you've definitely had one done, coz your skin looks amazing."

"I got mine done yesterday by Susie. She's quite nice really, a very bubbly, sweet girl and she even threw in a few extra's for me which is why my skin looks absolutely radiant." Zoe explained. "She's not a fan of Collette either."

Madeline grinned. "I'm so glad you managed to get rid of that small pigment stain on my cheek, I've always hated it. Blusher usually covers it most of the time but it's so annoying." She said appreciatively. "I've tried to get rid of it so many times but nothing's ever worked."

"Laser treatments can work absolute wonders nowadays." Zoe explained as she smiled. "Women no longer need to suffer as technology can deliver, absolute perfection."

Madeline immediately nodded in response. "Yep and nowadays, perfection is an absolutely necessity." She added.

"I know, people are so bound and defined by superficial standards of beauty these days." Zoe agreed. "I'm totally guilty of it myself."

Once the two women arrived beside Zoe's parked car, a black, shiny, spunky ride with sparkling silver rims and tinted windows, they entered inside the vehicle quickly as they gushed with excitement about the vacation they would be taking, the very next day. Everything in Zoe's mind, she felt would be absolutely perfect as the two women hadn't actually booked the most basic vacation packages in the end and had actually spent $500 more each for some upgrades. Although they hadn't gone for the most expensive, luxury suites available which would have cost them a further $2,000, they had in the end, indulged in some additional luxuries and each one promised to make their vacation experience, absolutely spectacular. Their flights had already been organized and booked and hence they had absolutely nothing else to worry about except packing their clothes and making sure that they actually arrived at the airport on time for their flight the next afternoon.

Some of the additional perks that Zoe had selected had included some special things, such as holographic pairing simulation activities by a resort coordinator and access to a special love ball at the very end of their stay, to celebrate their time at the resort and the prospect of a successful love match having been made. One of the additional add-ons was a special counselling session which Zoe had made sure she'd actually included, just for Madeline's sake. The love counselling session was designed to provide closure regarding any past issues from previous relationships that might be hanging over any of the vacationers' heads which might hamper them in any way and Zoe had felt it was definitely required to ensure that both she and Madeline were in optimal condition both inside and out, to meet their perfect match and actually embark upon a new, fresh, fabulous romance with them, free from the emotional baggage of any past of any unsuccessful, failed romances.

Ten minutes later, when Zoe parked her car inside the parking lot, just beside the restaurant they'd chosen to dine at that evening, the two women quickly stepped out of the vehicle and then walked across the parking lot towards the restaurant entrance. Excitement and anticipation filled each of the woman's bodies and seemed to cling to every particle of air that surrounded them as it spurred them on and actually put a spring into their step. They discussed the resort and their vacation with excitement as they walked.

"What do you think will happen, if the ideal male love matches for us are not actually booked in or attend the resort for a vacation at the same time as we do?" Madeline asked. "Do you think that could happen?"

Zoe laughed. "The resort and company are huge, there are like thousands of people at the resort at any given time, so I doubt that could actually happen." She replied. "Besides even in life, you can only be in a relationship with someone you meet that is around and that you connect with at that precise moment in time, so they can only really match you with someone that's there at the same time as you are."

"True." Madeline agreed.

When the two women arrived outside the restaurant door, Zoe quickly opened it and then held it open for Madeline as a huge smile spread out across her face but internally she had actually started to worry. Zoe had begun to hope and pray inside herself that their vacation would actually deliver something positive for them both as she'd been the one that had actually suggested that they should both attend and she was now slightly fearful that it might not actually deliver. Madeline definitely deserved to have someone nice in her life and so far, she'd most certainly been short changed by the wimps she'd dated as love was in Zoe's opinion, an emotional investment and even at times a financial one that not only required dedication and time but also resources to lubricate and maintain its continuance. Men as Zoe was aware, could be such predators and she fully understood that notion, having grown up alongside several brothers unlike Madeline, who'd grown up as an only child.

Perhaps, Madeline's solitary childhood had actually resulted in Madeline's lack of understanding surrounding the male species and their motives and attitudes towards women at times, Zoe considered quietly as she stepped inside the restaurant door just behind Madeline. Zoe had grown up predominantly around boys and therefore was much more assertive, streetwise and wary and certainly a lot tougher on any men that crossed her path and as a result her love life was a lot less stressful than Madeline's seemed to be. At least, Madeline had her around and that meant Zoe could actually keep an eye on any predatory males that crossed her path, before they inflicted to much damage upon her and her life and that was the one small comfort to Zoe as men could sometimes be extremely horrible and Zoe fully understood that.

The brightly lit restaurant was alive with music as the two women stepped inside the venue and a handsome, buff looking, male waiter quickly approached them. He immediately showed them both to an empty table situated in an alcove nearby and they rapidly followed him as they grinned at each other as he led them towards it, grateful that they would not have to actually wait to be seated and slightly impressed by the handsome waiter that had actually attended to them. Each of the tables that surrounded them and each table nestled in the alcoves that lined each of the walls nearby as they sat down, they rapidly noticed was fully occupied by either couples or groups of men and women that were engaged in loud, energetic discussions as they ate and drank merrily. The restaurant was definitely packed but that was to be expected really as it was a Friday evening and the food, cocktails and service at that venue, they already knew were extremely good.

"What can I get you this evening ladies?" The waiter asked as he politely handed them two menus.

"A Blue Springs cocktail for me please, a bottle of red wine, a bottle of white and can you bring me a glass of ice too please as I'm feeling rather hot." Zoe quickly replied as she winked playfully at Madeline. She simply couldn't resist a quick flirt as she held her menu up to her face and then wafted the piece of thin card, up and down in the air, just in front of it.

"I'll be fine with one of the bottles of wine." Madeline replied as she smirked.

"Sure and I'll be back in just a few minutes to take your food order." The waiter replied as he touched a small screen on the small electronic notepad inside his hands and then quickly rushed off.

Madeline laughed as he disappeared from sight as she turned to face Zoe. "I thought you were going to wait until we get to the resort." She teased playfully. "Isn't a perfectly matched man better than a randomly selected waiter?"

"Babes, you know how it is, his job's probably pretty boring, I'm just showing him some attention to liven up his shift." Zoe explained. "I'm being polite and hospitable. I mean seriously how interesting can running around waiting tables all day really be? It's probably worse than applying creams to women's faces all day."

"Do you ever actually have any male clients?" Madeline asked as she smiled.

"A few but they're usually gay, straight men are just not as interested in high tech, scientific beauty skin treatments." Zoe mentioned. "That's just reality."

Madeline grinned.

A few seconds later, the waiter returned and then gently placed the two bottles of wine and a filled cocktail glass on the table in front of the two women as he smiled at them both. Zoe smiled back at him seductively and then giggled playfully as she continued her flirtatious antics as the two women ordered their food and Madeline smiled as she watched and listened to Zoe's displays of charm. Confidence wasn't really oozing out of Madeline whilst Zoe on the other hand, appeared to have bagful's of it and that certainly seemed to help when it came to the issue of romance. Men definitely seemed to appreciate and respect confident women much more than women who were slightly more timid and perhaps that was why Madeline struggled so much with the opposite sex and seemed to attract such awful, predatory scoundrels. The waiter departed a few seconds later and Madeline quickly turned to face Zoe as she smiled and then gently shook her head.

"You're incorrigible." Madeline teased.

"Isn't that what men and women were designed for, to flirt with each other, engage with each other and interact?" Zoe asked her. "I'm just participating in the natural chemistry that sometimes exists between men and women besides I'm not married, I'm allowed to."

"Have you ever actually been approached by a woman?" Madeline asked.

"Yes, I've been hit on several times by a female." Zoe replied.

"How did you react?" Madeline enquired.

"Well, I just let them know I was into men and that's it." Zoe explained.

"Did you find it offensive?" Madeline probed.

"Not at all, women who like women need lovers just like everybody else does." Zoe explained. "Why shouldn't a woman hit on a woman that she likes? After all, men do it all the time and no one says anything. A compliment is a compliment, regardless of who it actually comes from and that has absolutely nothing at all to do with their gender or their sexual preferences."

"True." Madeline replied thoughtfully. "Gosh, I guess we women have still got a long way to go in terms of how we see ourselves, our own sexuality and the world around us. I mean seriously, we're kind of brought up to believe that to be romantically assertive as a woman is somehow wrong."

"I know." Zoe insisted. "Sometimes, I'm so grateful I actually grew up around my brothers, it really helped me and I feel a lot less restricted by societal expectations towards females and archaic gender roles."

Their conversation was suddenly, quickly interrupted as the waiter returned with a large, silver tray filled with two very large lobsters which also had bits of crab neatly positioned all around the edges of it and both women immediately smiled as they embraced the sudden sight of food or more importantly, their food. Hunger by this time, had actually got the better of their stomachs as they rumbled gently away below the loud, lively tunes that flowed out into the air around them as their bodies subtly attempted to remind them of just how empty their stomachs actually were. They were both absolutely and utterly famished as their mouths quickly began to water as they welcomed the feast that had been placed down on the table, directly in front of them and their eyes shone in delight at the spread.

Once the waiter left, both women immediately started to tuck into the seafood feast which was pleasantly adorned with delicious, sweet, spicy sauces as they discussed their pending vacation eagerly with excitement and enthusiasm. Loud music sounded out all around them as they ate and watched a birthday cake with sparklers on top of it, arrive at a nearby table as another customer was suddenly serenaded with an outburst of 'Happy Birthday' by some of the servers and waiting staff.

"Did you know that the island resort we are going to visit, Zincata is actually owned by a billionaire?" Zoe suddenly asked Madeline as she smiled at her.

"No. Where did you read that?" Madeline enquired.

"I read it somewhere on the internet, when I did a bit of background research about our vacation and the resort." Zoe mentioned. "Apparently, he started the Love Colony as they refer to it, five years ago and he was just a millionaire back then."

"I can't wait to go now although initially I did have some slight reservations about it. I've never even been to South America before, so this vacation really will be a first for me, in quite a few ways." Madeline explained.

"Do you think we'll actually get to meet the mystery billionaire whilst we're there?" Zoe asked. "Apparently, he used to work for some huge technology company where he invented some robotic systems that made him a fortune and he then invested the money into several businesses and the Love Colony and Love Inc. the resort company he formed, was actually one of his own ventures."

"Who knows." Madeline replied as she shrugged. "I doubt it, he's probably way too busy to visit his businesses every single day and he probably employs people to run them so that he doesn't actually have to."

"What if he's amazingly handsome and what if, he's actually single and what do you

think might happen if, we actually meet him."
Zoe suddenly gushed as her eyes glistened
with excitement. "If I was swept off my feet by
a rich billionaire that owned a love resort, I'd
definitely give up my job at the beauty salon
and Collette in a heartbeat." She continued as
she smiled.

"That is a lot of if's Zoe. You're so funny,
he's probably already married, I mean come
on, he runs a love resort for heaven's sake."
Madeline gently reminded her as she smiled.
"If he's surrounded by love every single day,
why wouldn't he have found love for himself by
now?"

"True, I guess I was just getting carried
away." Zoe replied. "Still, a girl can always
dream. Collette makes dreams so much more
appealing than reality, every single working
day." She explained as she rolled her eyes.

Madeline giggled.

"Do you think we should take one of our
cars to the airport?" Zoe enquired as a sudden
practicality crossed her mind. "I mean, then
we'd have to pay for additional parking whilst
we're away."

"No. I think we should just get a taxi to the
airport." Madeline replied as she gently shook

her head. "It would be quite costly to actually park one of our cars inside the airport parking lot for a week and there's absolutely no point in actually doing so because taxis are so easy to hire."

"I agree, I'd much rather spend that money on clothes and shopping than airport car park fees." Zoe agreed. "The luxury of having a car waiting inside the car park at the airport when we return isn't really worth the expense. This food is amazing and my cocktail is fabulous, here try some of my cocktail Madeline." She insisted as she quickly handed Madeline the cocktail glass.

Madeline smiled as she gingerly sipped on the bright, blue liquid inside the glass and then swallowed it. "Wow that's really strong." She said as she coughed slightly. "What's in it?"

"Jamaican Rum." Zoe replied. "The strongest Jamaican Rum available."

"A couple of those and I'd be floored for the rest of the night." Madeline mentioned. "Seriously, that is hard core liquor right there."

Zoe smiled. "Well, there's no work tomorrow, so technically that means tonight, I can drink as much as I want to." She mentioned. "Collette's like a total bloodhound seriously, I actually had to stop going into work with hangovers. It's almost like she can actually smell the alcohol twenty four hours after it's actually been consumed and on those days, she makes your life even more hellish intentionally."

Madeline grinned. "Well from tomorrow morning, you'll have a whole week off from Collette and then you can have as many hangovers as you want to." She teased.

"I think once we finish packing up our stuff, we should actually go out dancing." Zoe suggested as she quickly polished off the lobster dish in front of her. "Make a night of it."

Madeline nodded.

"You'll have to drive or perhaps we can get a cab, because tonight I fully intend to enjoy myself, extremely thoroughly." Zoe explained.

Madeline nodded in agreement. "We'll get a cab." She replied.

"Right, I'm ready to go whenever you are?" Zoe insisted as she waved across the room to beckon the waiter once more.

The handsome, attentive waiter immediately noticed Zoe's raised arm and then quickly headed towards the table and the two women as Zoe smiled at him appreciatively. If things didn't actually work out for her at the love island resort, Zoe mused there was always an extremely handsome waiter waiting around at the Lobster Shack that certainly seemed to be quite interested in Zoe and she was definitely very attracted to him as just like the food she'd just consumed, he looked absolutely edible and extremely delicious.

ZINCATA

The Friday evening progressed deliciously for the two women as they both visited Madeline's home, quickly finished her packing and then made their way towards Zoe's apartment. Every step they took was light and it almost felt as though they were walking on air as excitement and intrigue carried them weightlessly across the ground. They were no longer, dragged down by the heavy weights that life usually bestowed upon them and the issues that normally made their bodies tired, weary or drained as life had relieved them from the heaviness that their daily responsibilities usually inflicted upon them and a fun filled vacation was now actually, just on their doorstep.

When the two women arrived outside Zoe's apartment, they quickly stepped inside and then made their way towards the bedroom straight away as they prepared to finish packing Zoe's suitcases and round their vacation preparations up. The evening was still quite young and that meant, there was a lot more time they could ultimately spend together that night before their trip, engaged in frivolous enjoyment.

"We don't have much time left now for packing." Zoe mentioned thoughtfully as the two women entered inside her bedroom. "I have to finish packing tonight."

"You always leave everything until the very last minute Zoe but I can see that you're really enthusiastic about this holiday as you're actually packing the night before we're due to leave which is certainly an improvement." Madeline remarked as she smiled. "I thought I'd actually have to come and get you tomorrow morning and then help you pack your stuff."

"Nope, this time I'm trying to be organized. Since it was actually my idea to go there in the first place." Zoe explained.

"I just hope it lives up to your expectations." Madeline remarked. "I mean, I hope you actually get what you want out of it."

"Well, if it doesn't, I'll make sure that we still have a good time anyway, so either way, it'll be fine." Zoe quickly reassured her. "And there's always the waiter at the Lobster Shack, if it doesn't deliver true love."

Madeline nodded as she giggled. "True." She replied.

"Gosh, I hope the hangover I'll have tomorrow morning won't be too rough." Zoe mentioned. "Coz I certainly intend to drink a lot more alcohol tonight. At least, I won't have to face Collette tomorrow and her behavior radar. I swear she can detect your sins a mile away and then she's on your back like a priest hunting down a confession." She explained.

"I bet you wouldn't dare say that to her face." Madeline teased as she suddenly bounced down on top of Zoe's bed.

"I'm brave but I'm not that brave. I still want to live." Zoe replied. "And keep my job."

Zoe suddenly pulled a large, zebra print suitcase down from the top of the black, glossy wardrobe nearby and then opened it up. "Right, I better start packing and get this show on the road." She mentioned as she dumped the suitcase carelessly down on top of the bed, just next to Madeline.

Bundles of clothes were rapidly pulled out of the nearby wardrobe and then dumped haphazardly down onto the floor into three piles as Zoe quickly attempted to separate her garments into some kind of logical order. Each pile grew larger and larger as Madeline watched quietly with a slightly amused expression upon her face.

"What's that pile for?" Madeline suddenly asked as she pointed towards one of the piles of garments, heaped up on top of the dark, burgundy wooden planks of wood which adorned Zoe's bedroom floor.

"That's a definite 'no' pile." Zoe quickly explained. "That's a definite 'yes' pile." She continued as she pointed towards another pile of clothes. "And that's a 'maybe' pile." Zoe mentioned as she pointed towards the third pile of clothes.

Madeline nodded.

"I'm definitely bringing these along with me." Zoe remarked as she suddenly pulled some dresses, a skirt and a top off some hangers. "These are the outfits you made for me Madeline and they're the best things inside my wardrobe really. You're so talented, really you are."

"Thank you and I'm very proud of you today Zoe as you're being exceptionally well organized." Madeline replied as she blushed and graciously accepted Zoe's compliment. "I'm really surprised.

"I know, Collette would probably have a heart attack if she could see me right now." Zoe teased. "I mean seriously, she struggles every day to get me to be organized as she's so regimented. Collette runs such a tight ship and I'm just a daily contradiction and annoyance to her system of neatness and order." She explained.

Madeline smiled.

The packing very fortunately, was completed in no time at all as Zoe quickly held up outfits against her body and then Madeline helped her decide whether or not to take each one on vacation. It was certainly a less chaotic approach than Zoe's usual method of tackling tasks and within a very short time indeed, the large case and another medium suitcase had been almost filled to the brim.

"Remember, we're actually only going away for a week." Madeline gently reminded Zoe.

Zoe giggled. "I know and we still have to go out shopping tomorrow morning, I'm totally getting carried away." She replied. "I always get a bit worried when I travel that I won't pack something I need or want to wear and that I'll spend the remainder of my vacation wishing I'd actually brought something along with me. Suitcases just aren't big enough or even practical really."

"I know, we should actually have transportable wardrobes in this day and age that pack up into neat little squares that we can carry around with us anywhere we want to which pop up into full blown wardrobes as soon as we actually open them. That way, we can be offered the vast array of clothing they contain, that we actually own, anywhere we actually are, at anytime at all." Madeline agreed as she gently shook her head.

"Now that invention, would actually solve a lot of problems." Zoe mentioned as she grinned. "Okay, my battle with choices of appropriate attire and personal preferences in clothing is over for today. I'm done."

"You taking this with you?" Madeline suddenly asked as she quickly held up a pretty dress that she'd picked up from the floor which had been left in the maybe pile. "It's really pretty and it really suits you."

"No. Unfortunately, upon this occasion, I'll have to be a bit prejudice and discriminate against that particular item of clothing as it just won't fit into any of my suitcases." Zoe replied as she quickly shook her head.

Madeline laughed. "Okay, the packing's done, let's go out." She announced as she quickly stood up and then gently held Zoe's arm.

Zoe nodded as she allowed Madeline to lead her assertively out of her bedroom. "I almost don't want to leave the packing. I could probably unpack and repack several more times before I'd be totally happy with what I've actually chosen to take." She mentioned as she gently shook her head and then cast a glance back at the suitcases she'd just packed.

"I know Zoe, I know." Madeline gently reassured her.

Zoe laughed.

Once the two women arrived outside the bar they'd chosen to visit, around an hour later, they quickly entered inside the venue and then settled in as they ordered some drinks and found an empty table to sit at. Even though there was a huge dance floor situated at the center of the bar, Zoe knew as soon as she glanced at it that Madeline rarely danced and that she would be quite reluctant to actually do so, until she'd consumed at least a couple of alcoholic drinks there. A couple more drinks, would definitely usher in Madeline's compliance and then perhaps, she would loosen up and actually let her down as without them, Zoe knew she most certainly wouldn't.

An hour passed by and finally Madeline started to become quite tipsy and Zoe quickly urged her to get up and actually approach the dancefloor. The dancefloor itself, was almost fully occupied as the music flowed out from some speakers that clung to the walls around the venue but the two women finally managed to find a spot to dance in, quite close to the table they had been seated at just a few minutes before and then started to dance.

Zoe didn't usually drag people up onto the dancefloor but Madeline really needed to let her hair down and have some fun and so too, did she. The music continued to play as song after song gently caressed the floor of the venue as the two women danced along to each rhythmic beat enthusiastically. Upbeat tunes were then pumped through the floor as it vibrated just underneath their feet as they danced to each beat and simply enjoyed the night out for what it was, a joyful, carefree spree with as much alcohol as it was actually safe to consume.

A few male strangers approached the two women throughout the night and both Madeline and Zoe danced with a couple of them but there was no closeness in their participation and absolutely no drunken kisses or frantic sexually charged fumbling followed directly afterwards. No numbers were exchanged and there were no meaningful romantic or flirtatious discussions as the early hours of the morning arrived and the two women eventually decided to call it a night and head back to Madeline's home. They walked out onto the street as they finally left the venue and then quickly hailed a cab which happened almost immediately as the bar was situated in the very heart of the city and frequently guarded by cab drivers and their vehicles which waited eagerly nearby for any possible fares.

The two women gently tumbled into the back of a cab, a few minutes later as they laughed and discussed the night they'd both just enjoyed freely, regardless of the cab driver's presence. Every intimate detail and each person they had encountered was dissected and joked about as the cab made its way rapidly through the streets and headed towards Madeline's home. Twenty minutes later, when they finally arrived just outside Madeline's front gate, Zoe quickly paid the driver and then they both stepped out of the vehicle and made their way towards Madeline's front door.

"Oh my gosh, we have to get on a five hour flight later today." Zoe groaned as she leant on Madeline's arm as they walked up the path towards Madeline's front door.

"I know and we're definitely going to have huge hang overs." Madeline mentioned.

Zoe giggled.

Each step the women took was quite haphazard as they spewed out across the garden path and their bodies swayed as they stumbled along it. A few minutes later, thankfully however, after a few stumbles and a couple of near collisions with the ground, the two women somehow managed to arrive outside the front door and Madeline quickly began to search inside her bag for her keys. Everything in the street nearby was quiet as the two women quietly giggled amongst themselves and teased each other about the evening out they'd just spent together.

Madeline's house was actually situated in a quiet, middle class neighborhood, just on the outskirts of the city center and most of her neighbors consisted of either elderly pensioners or quite young, newly married couples. There was also a sprinkling of families with children of various ages but they were very few and far between and hence most of the lights in the houses in the street nearby, were actually off as the majority of the occupants inside each one, were already fast asleep.

Once they'd actually managed to unlock the front door which took a little while due to their drunken state, they quickly made their way inside and then headed towards the bedroom as they prepared to sleep straight away. Due to the time and their flight which was due to leave early the next afternoon, Madeline urged Zoe to sleep immediately. It was actually just past three in the morning and therefore, both women knew they could not even possibly hope to wake up by midday, if they didn't sleep immediately. Since their flight was at two and they had to be at the airport by one that meant sleep definitely had to happen and it actually had to happen straight away.

"Do you think the flight will be boring?" Zoe whispered as the two lay in total darkness inside the bedroom as they prepared to sleep. "It is a five hour flight after all."

"I'm not sure." Madeline replied. "We better bring some stuff along with us to do on the flight just in case it is."

"Yeah, we'll do that." Zoe murmured as she closed her eyes and then peacefully started to drift off to sleep.

Madeline smiled as she glanced at Zoe's face through the darkness and then plumped up her pillow and delicately rested her head upon it, she had to sleep too as it was indeed very late and airplane flights, she knew did not wait for anyone. "Goodnight Zoe, sweet dreams." She whispered as she closed her eyes but nothing except silence greeted her. Madeline smiled, Zoe it seemed had already crashed out and now she definitely had to do the same or she wouldn't actually get up on time the next day, for their dream vacation.

Very fortunately, when the next morning arrived, there were absolutely no hangovers as the two women woke up just before midday and cheerfully embraced the day which was bright and warm as they prepared to head off on their trip. Madeline's medium sized, dark grey solitary suitcase was quickly loaded into the rear boot of a cab and then the two women entered inside the vehicle as they prepared to make their way to Zoe's apartment and then head off towards the actual airport.

When the vehicle arrived outside Zoe's apartment block, about twenty minutes later, Zoe quickly stepped out of the black sedan as she prepared to make her way towards the exterior door of her apartment block with a smile upon her face. She glanced back at the car for a second as she closed the door and left Madeline alone inside the vehicle and then began to search inside her handbag for her keys.

Madeline quickly pressed the switch on the door next to her, to roll the window beside her down. "Do you need any help Zoe?" She politely offered.

Zoe immediately shook her head in response. "No, you just stay here with your suitcase. I'll be right back down in a few minutes, it's just a couple of cases." She replied.

True to her word, Zoe quickly returned to the car within a few minutes, her two suitcases in tow and the driver quickly stepped out of the vehicle, in order to help her pack them both inside his boot. Once the suitcases had been stacked away firmly inside the trunk, both the driver and Zoe then sat back down inside the vehicle as they prepared for the rest of their journey. The large, black sedan started to move off again and then quickly sped up as the two women were rapidly driven towards the airport as they began to discuss their flight and the trip ahead, filled with excitement. Their two smiling faces pleasantly decorated the rear of the vehicle as the two women overtly displayed their happiness and expressed their enthusiasm towards their pending vacation as they gushed over what exactly might actually happen, once they actually arrived at the love island resort as the vehicle drew closer to the actual airport.

Approximately forty minutes later, when they arrived outside the airport, both Madeline and Zoe quickly rushed out of the car enthusiastically and then collected their luggage from the boot. Deep inside as Zoe clumsily dragged her two cases out of the car's rear, she felt absolutely ecstatic as she was just about to actually experience a tremendously special, unique, different kind of vacation with Madeline and that pleased her immensely. Zoe had actually been on several vacations before but nothing quite like this one and she'd absolutely never, ever travelled anywhere at all with Madeline. This vacation was completely different and this vacation was extremely unique as this vacation involved lots of single, eligible men and a beautiful, tropical love resort with sandy beaches, lots of cocktails and lots of potential fun and she'd actually be searching for love alongside her most trusted, special, female friend ever.

Both women were well over twenty five now and they were actually in their early thirties and that meant, it was indeed, time to settle down. Their investment in their vacation, not only indicated their seriousness and commitment with regards to finding a serious life partner but also signified that both women were now actually taking their romantic lives slightly more seriously than perhaps either of them had actually done, when they were in their twenties. Each woman's biological clock was ticking away and as each year passed by and a real, serious, lifelong romantic commitment frustratingly, completely evaded their grasp, the pressure to settle down was indeed starting to mount, deep inside of them both.

A luggage trolley was quickly collected and then rapidly loaded up with each of the woman's cases and once they'd paid the driver, he quickly departed. They had about fifteen minutes left to actually check in and collect their boarding passes and they still hadn't even queued up at the baggage drop off yet or registered their arrival with a check-in machine or checked in at a check-in desk as Madeline hurried Zoe along.

"We better hurry up Zoe." Madeline mentioned as she pushed the luggage trolley along in front of her, towards the large, glass, wide airport entrance nearby. "Do you think the guys we'll meet on this vacation will be more serious than the type of guys we usually meet?"

"Definitely, they're spending money to take a vacation and actually taking time off work, so they must be quite dedicated and looking for something quite serious." Zoe replied. "I mean to enlist the services of a high tech, love matching company, you must be very serious about finding a decent relationship I would think."

"Good, I definitely don't want to meet any players that have relationship aversions and commitment phobias when I'm there." Madeline remarked as she stepped inside the glass doors. "I see men like that at home every day."

Zoe smiled. "I know what you mean Madeline." She replied as the two women approached a row of check-in machines. "Men can be really shit at times. I should know, I grew up with three brothers."

Madeline nodded in agreement.

The two women quickly slipped their passports inside the slots in the check-in machines as Zoe quietly contemplated the vacation that lay ahead and Madeline's singleness for a moment. Deep inside, Zoe just wanted Madeline to actually meet someone really nice for a change, someone who wasn't unreliable and someone who wasn't a commitment phoebe as Madeline certainly deserved the best but somehow, she was always scrapping around in the gutter of heartbreak with the very worst. For Zoe, one of the nicest parts about their pending vacation was the fact that the two women would actually be having this adventure together as Madeline had been Zoe's closest female friend ever since their late teenage years and she'd remained so throughout her entire adult life. Female friendships could quite often, be so fickle and so fleeting but not Madeline's hand of friendship which had remained constant and stable over the years as they'd walked through the various trials and challenges of life together and stuck by each other's sides throughout each and every one.

Once the boarding passes had been collected, the two women quickly made their way towards the luggage drop off as they rapidly relieved themselves of their suitcases and the very cumbersome luggage trolley which seemed to be extremely difficult to steer. Their flight was actually due to board relatively soon and hence there was no time at all to dilly dally as they rushed towards the security gates and then made their way quickly towards the departure lounge.

Very fortunately, they breezed through the security checkpoint extremely quickly and that allowed them an additional few minutes with which to browse some of the stores just beyond the security barriers, just before their flight actually started to board. The two women sauntered through one of the stores as they tested, smelt and admired a few new scents as they strolled through each of the aisles and explored the perfume counters a little more thoroughly as they inspected the latest products on offer. Madeline actually purchased a bottle of perfume before they made their way towards the departure gate nearby but Zoe resisted the urge to do so as she already had at least five bottles of perfume inside her two suitcases.

Once they entered inside the plane, Zoe immediately began to flirt with a male flight attendant who'd caught her eye as he seated them very politely in window seats on the right hand side of the plane. Despite the looming love matching vacation that sat just on the horizon of speculative romance at the other end of their flight, Zoe simply couldn't resist a bit of a flirt as her attraction radar suddenly started to beep non-stop inside of her and it would not actually stop until she'd actually given the flight attendant, a flirtatious, verbal whirl. He was extremely handsome and therefore to Zoe, her actions were completely justifiable, if anyone actually bothered to challenge her about her conduct at all which was highly unlikely as Madeline rarely ever did. The two women fastened their seat belts securely around their waists as Zoe comforted herself with the knowledge that at least there was some decent eye candy actually aboard their flight which was five hours long, even if it was just a flight attendant that worked for the actual airline, who technically she wasn't actually supposed to be flirting with at all.

"It is a five hour flight Madeline." Zoe explained as Madeline smiled at her flirtatious, playful teasing that had been directed towards the handsome, male flight attendant. "At least I'll have something good to look at on the way there."

Madeline gently shook her head. "I don't know Zoe, can you ever be serious?" She asked.

"Look at this way Madeline, if we meet our ideal love match whilst on we're this vacation, we'll never be as single and feel as free as we are now to flirt with another man again." Zoe quickly pointed out. "So, I'm just making the most of my remaining single life whilst I still can."

Madeline smiled. "At least we have great seats." She observed. "I don't think these were actually our designated seats though."

"True, I think that wink I gave the flight attendant helped a bit." Zoe replied as she smiled. "The flirting was definitely worth it."

"Yeah and this flight doesn't actually look that full, so that means people can sit almost anywhere they want to I guess." Madeline mentioned as she quickly glanced around the interior of the plane which seemed to be only about sixty percent full.

"This is gonna be a very long flight." Zoe observed as she quickly pulled a laptop out of her hand luggage. "I've brought some games and movies along with me, just in case we get bored."

Madeline nodded. "I'm starving. When do you think they'll be serving some food?" She enquired.

"Probably not long after the flight leaves. I mean they do usually give people a meal on longer flights but usually the food isn't that great." Zoe replied thoughtfully. "It's interesting isn't it, all these progressive advances have been made in our world but the food on flights still remains quite awful."

"Yep, they really need a food generator on these planes." Madeline teased. "I should have packed mine and brought it along with us."

"Now that really would give a whole new meaning to packing everything but the kitchen sink." Zoe teased. "Then you'd be considered more of hoarder than I am."

Madeline giggled.

Approximately one hour into the flight, very fortunately for both women as they were absolutely famished, the male flight attendant suddenly returned to serve them both a meal. The small snacks and drinks that he'd already given them on his first visit had been rapidly consumed but their stomachs were still growling when he actually returned the second time around. Small compartment trays which held each of their meals inside them were filled up to the brim with dried up, stodgy looking, untantilizing morsels of food but the two women soldiered through their meal nonetheless as they eagerly attempted to fill up their stomachs. Despite the lack of appeal, in terms of dietary intake, they rapidly wolfed everything down within a matter of minutes as they quickly cleared the contents of the small, cream, plastic trays directly in front of them. Food on airplanes certainly wasn't very appetizing but due to the fact that they had very little choice as there were actually no other alternative dining choices at that current moment, hunger overruled and quickly squashed any potential fussiness that could have potentially reared it's choosy head, if they had indeed actually been situated in another location.

Despite the extremely unappetizing meal, the remainder of the flight was actually quite enjoyable for the two women as they relaxed and entertained themselves with games, movies and various other forms of in-flight entertainment. The five hours seemed to fly by and in what seemed like no time at all, the plane actually suddenly drew closer to its destination and an announcement boomed out across the internal tannoy system. Huge smiles quickly adorned the two women's faces as they embraced every single word that was spoken and glanced at other in complete and utter glee.

"We'll be arriving at Zincata in approximately twenty minutes." The Captain announced. "You have five minutes to prepare for landing before the fasten your seatbelts sign will be displayed and then you will be expected to remain in your seats until the aircraft has landed."

"Well that's it, it's time to freshen up and get ready." Zoe quickly announced triumphantly as she suddenly rose to her feet and then grabbed her hand bag.

Madeline smiled.

"I'll just be in the toilets if you need me." Zoe explained as she pointed towards one of the small toilet cubicle doors situated nearby. "I have to look absolutely immaculate, the second I step off this plane. A splash of makeup, a decent pair of shoes and a much nicer dress should do the trick."

Madeline nodded. "I'll wait I think. I'll shower and change when we actually get to the resort." She replied sensibly. "Those toilets are so tiny, I can't even imagine actually trying to change my clothes in one of them and actually managing to do so successfully."

Zoe smiled as she placed her handbag securely under her arm and then started to walk towards the nearby toilet door. "I'll be back very soon." She quickly clarified as she began to walk away.

One thing suddenly struck Zoe as quite strange as she walked towards the small toilet nearby and that was the fact that Madeline seemed to be much more relaxed about their vacation than she was. Perhaps being more organized in life, generally made her slightly more laid back and less chaotic, Zoe contemplated quietly as she just seemed quite happy to actually arrive as she was. Perhaps, by putting more effort into organizing and planning things that enabled her to be slightly more relaxed at times, whereas Zoe on the other hand tended to be much more hectic when it came to her approach towards life.

There was very little time before the plane would actually land and Zoe knew, she had to look as perfect as she possibly could, before that actually happened. The aircraft toilets were tiny but still workable as Zoe quickly stepped inside the door and then closed it right behind her. She quickly started to try and make herself look stunning as she opened up her bag and then started to remove the various items she required. Every second mattered as she grabbed and capitalized upon every possible minute she could with an almost desperate urgency. Her dress, very annoyingly, didn't actually come out of her handbag as easily as it should have and Zoe then had to spend a minute or two wrestling vigorously with her handbag and the dress it contained as the jeans and top she'd worn earlier that day, were definitely not an appropriate form of attire with which to land at a love island resort in. A sexy, figure hugging but simple dress had been packed away specifically for that very purpose and that meant, it definitely had to be actually worn.

Due to the tiny size of the toilet, there was very little room inside it for maneuvering and once Zoe had finally managed to get her outfit out of her bag, she struggled slightly as she attempted to slip it over her head and shoulders as quickly as she could. Once her dress was in place, her makeup was then quickly applied and a hair brush rapidly used to tidy up her hair which she then tied back and placed into a rather elegant, sophisticated upstyle. Only a few minutes actually remained before Zoe knew, all the passengers on board the plane would be instructed to sit back down inside their seats and actually be asked to remain there, until the plane had actually landed and then the toilet would definitely have to be, completely abandoned.

The second landing announcement, came all too soon and Zoe sighed as she gently shook her head, a couple of minutes more was definitely required but unfortunately for Zoe, it was not actually going to be granted. Everyone inside the plane had to return to their seats immediately and Zoe knew, she was no exception to that very strict rule, no matter where she was due to land or what she wanted to look like when she actually did. Zoe quickly started to stuff her belongings back inside her handbag as she attempted to fit all her beauty equipment back inside it, each item had actually come out of that handbag and that meant therefore, that every item could technically, actually fit back inside it. An air stewardess suddenly knocked on the toilet cubicle door as she prompted and urged Zoe to leave the toilet and Zoe quickly sped up as she tried to arrange her things and get them all back inside her bag as fast as she possibly could.

"You have to return to your seat now Miss." She insisted as Zoe stepped out of the cubicle door. "We're about to land and you have to be seated and have your seat belt on when we do."

Zoe nodded politely at her. "Right, thanks for letting me know." She replied as she flashed a charming smile at her and then quickly stepped past her and headed back towards Madeline and her seat.

When Zoe arrived back at her seat, she quickly sat down and then smiled at Madeline as she put her seatbelt on just as she'd been instructed to and a minute or so later, the plane began to make it's descent. Both women leant towards the window that was situated just beside Madeline and crammed their faces up against it as they eagerly tried to see as much of the island as they possibly could that they would actually be landing upon, before the plane actually touched down upon the island's runway.

Immaculate golden beaches stretched out as far as the eye could see and aqua colored waves gently lapped up against each shore as the water embraced and caressed every grain of sand it could possibly touch. The vision that met their eyes was absolutely stunning, breathtaking beautiful and completely immaculate as Zoe rapidly began to plan what she might possibly do upon those sun kissed, sandy, golden beaches. Activities like swimming, snorkeling, paddling, building sandcastles and walks along the beach in her bare feet, immediately sprang to the forefront of Zoe's mind as her mind rapidly embraced each one and then digressed into the more romantic possibilities that she could possibly explore, along with someone else at the resort, someone that she hadn't actually met yet. Zoe quickly began to amuse herself with fictitious sensual and sexual scenarios that could possibly occur whilst on her vacation with any potential matches she might possibly feel an attraction to as the plane drew closer to the runway and then actually touched down.

From the skies, just before they'd landed, the two women had actually noticed a large, white stone building which had glistened as rays of sunshine had delicately bounced of its walls and they'd immediately realized that it was actually the resort building itself, that they would both actually be staying in for the next week. Around the outer edges of the main, very large, white building, they had seen all kinds of areas that had been set aside for various kinds of activities and both Zoe and Madeline had gasped as they'd absorbed the huge range of facilities actually on offer. The view had been absolutely breathtaking and both women had been stirred inside by the utterly captivating sights which promised to keep them very far away from the destination of boredom. At one side of the huge building, they had also seen a very large, deep, aqua blue swimming pool which had a big bar situated at one end of it and Zoe had smiled as she glanced at both the pool and the accompanying bar.

"Wow, the island looks so beautiful and I'll definitely be getting in some cocktails at that bar." She'd announced triumphantly as the bar had caught her eye.

"It does look absolutely stunning and completely mesmerizing." Madeline had agreed as she'd nodded enthusiastically.

Five minutes later, once the plane had actually come to a complete stop and the 'fasten your seatbelts' signs had disappeared, the two women quickly stood up and then rushed towards the exit, filled with excitement as they clasped their hand luggage firmly inside their hands. Interestingly enough, they both suddenly realized that not all the passengers on board their flight were actually leaving the plane alongside them and that immediately implied that the island airport was a special stop off, only for those passengers actually visiting the resort. About twenty or so other passengers it quickly transpired, were however actually visiting the love island resort and they actually left the plane, alongside both Zoe and Madeline.

Due to the unique nature of the island, the airport that Zoe and Madeline actually arrived at vastly differed in terms of its size and shape from the airport from which they had actually departed. Unlike the large, city airport they had left behind earlier that afternoon, this airport was very small and seemed to have minimal security in place as they walked briskly along a long tunnel and then arrived at some security gates which were little more than a row of metal gates and barriers. A large circular area was situated just to the right of the barriers which was a luggage collection point and they quickly rushed towards it, just before they actually attempted to walk through the barriers that had been situated directly in front of them.

Strangely, the two women quickly noticed as they walked, unlike the city airport they'd departed from very little inside this airport actually seemed to be manned by actual real human beings. When their flight had actually initially landed, Zoe had actually noticed that the vehicle which collected the luggage from the cargo area of the aircraft hadn't actually been manned by a human driver at all and that it had appeared to be driven and controlled by some kind of invisible force. Due to the absence of a human driver, Zoe had automatically assumed that it had perhaps been driven by someone sitting inside a control room somewhere that she could not actually see as she'd been unable to think of any other logical explanation at the time. The vehicle regardless of who actually had control of it or didn't, had very competently stopped right beside the plane and it had quickly collected all the luggage due to be unloaded and then it had made its way with it's huge, metal trolley cage at the rear which was filled to the brim with suitcases, back towards the main airport building. Both the cargo vehicle and the airport's computer operated security barriers, quickly clarified inside Zoe's mind that this resort was not just a high tech love resort but that it was also filled with other high tech facilities that had absolutely nothing to do with romance at all.

Everything at first glance however, seemed to be extremely well organized and as soon as the two women had actually collected their luggage, they found a motorized, electronic luggage trolley nearby upon which to place their suitcases that moved forward as soon as you actually touched it and then stopped, if you actually pushed the handle down again slightly harder. The security barrier area, it quickly transpired as the women walked towards it, was actually manned by an actual human being but by just one mature man in his mid-sixties that sat at one end of the line of barriers, inside a small, square cubicle like box and he manually monitored each barrier as it was approached.

Even though the small airport was very high tech and advanced, the actual security barriers themselves seemed to be quite simple to pass through, in that there were just metal gate barriers that everyone had to walk through, once they'd actually opened. Situated right next to each metal gate was a small, upright scanner like device that a passport had to actually be inserted inside, before any of the gates would open and the women quietly approached the machines as they prepared to leave the airport. Despite the vast difference from the usual metal detectors that both women were accustomed to seeing at security check points, they approached the barriers eagerly as they prepared to participate with the scanning devices, in order to actually exit the actual airport and proceed with their vacation as soon as they possibly could.

In some respects, the airport and the security system was all very fresh, different and exciting as they braced themselves for what might actually happen next as they inserted each of their passports inside the scanner like devices. They both quickly glanced at some of the other passengers nearby, some of whom had already walked through the barriers without any problems at all as they waited for their passports to be returned to them and the chest high metal gates directly in front of them to actually open. A beep suddenly sounded out nearby which broke through the silence that surrounded them and the mature man quickly leapt up to his feet and then walked towards a male passenger that had just left the same flight as Zoe and Madeline.

"I guess that's what happens if there's a problem." Madeline observed.

Zoe nodded as she watched both men quietly for a moment. "We better get a move on, cocktails will definitely be waiting for us and hopefully by now, a decent dinner." She gently prompted Madeline as she quickly collected her passport from the scanner like device which had just ejected it seconds beforehand as the barriers in front of her rapidly swung open.

Madeline smiled and nodded as she collected her passport from the scanner like device and then prepared to walk through the metal gate that had now just opened up in front of her. "True and I could certainly do with a decent meal." She agreed.

"Please proceed." A masculine, robotic suddenly announced.

Zoe laughed as she walked through the now open space directly in front of her. "Wow, the security machine is actually a man and he actually sounds quite buff, for a computer that is." She teased playfully.

Madeline giggled. "Seriously Zoe, don't you even dare think about flirting with a machine, I'm way to hungry and I need to eat." She teased.

Zoe grinned. "Come on, I'm not actually that desperate." She replied. "I mean, how on earth would a machine actually make love to me."

Madeline smirked as she gently shook her head. "I don't know but you'd probably find a way to achieve that, knowing you." She teased.

"Creative love making, with a very hard, hard drive." Zoe joked.

Once the two women had actually cleared the security area and the airport building, they found some small buses parked directly outside the large, glass doors and they quickly made their way towards one. The small, white buses didn't seem to actually be manned by any person that either Zoe or Madeline could see and appeared to be driven and controlled by a computer system or someone that was certainly not present as the two women cautiously stepped inside one.

"Where's the driver?" Madeline asked.

"Not sure, perhaps the buses are controlled by a computer program or something." Zoe suggested as she shrugged in response.

A couple of minutes later, once five more people had actually entered inside the vehicle, the doors of the bus suddenly closed as it prepared to depart. The vehicle started to roll gently forward as the bus carried its occupants quietly towards the huge, white building at the very center of the island which glistened in the sun as each ray bounced playfully of each of its exterior walls. There was a long, winding road which led towards the large, white building and it's immediate surroundings that seemed to be extremely clean and very tidy as there was not a spot of litter to be seen anywhere in sight. Beautiful palm trees were scattered delicately along both sides of the road at sporadic intervals which swayed gently in the breeze as the bus passed by each one.

"Wow, I can't even see an inch of dust anywhere." Zoe observed. "It almost looks like they've actually vacuumed the ground."

Madeline giggled. "I know it's so tidy." She agreed. "There's not even a drop of litter anywhere and it all looks so organized, not like your bedroom Zoe."

Zoe giggled. "I know." She agreed.

Ten minutes later, the women and the bus they were situated inside arrived just outside the front entrance of the resort building and they smiled as the bus doors swished gently open and they prepared to exit the vehicle. The building itself, looked absolutely huge and had lots of very clean, large windows across the front of it and they smiled happily as they quietly accepted every inch of the immaculate venue, they would actually spend the next week of their lives inside. They stepped out of the bus, just a few seconds later and then made their way towards the huge glass doors situated directly in front of them which automatically opened up for them as soon as they approached them. Their bus it appeared, was actually the first vehicle to arrive outside the resort building from their actual flight and as they waited inside the foyer, both Madeline and Zoe smiled slightly nervously at the five other people they had actually just taken a bus journey with, from the actual airport.

Inside the reception area, a large, white desk ran along the rear wall and seated just behind it was a male reservations clerk and Zoe quietly glanced at him as she contemplated for a moment whether or not, she should actually approach the desk and announce her arrival to him. Her question was quickly answered however, but not by the male reservations clerk who remained seated and almost seemed to ignore everyone around him as a female all dressed in white, suddenly entered into the foyer as she exited a pair of glass doors on the very left hand side of the large space. There were a lot of glass doors inside the foyer that seemed to lead off in various directions and Zoe quietly wondered for a moment just how people actually managed to find their way around the building as there were actually so many sets of doors and hallways that led off from the foyer to actually choose from. The female, who was quite obviously a member of the resort staff, quickly made her way towards Zoe, Madeline and the other five people who had just stepped off the bus alongside them as she smiled.

"Hi. I'm Becky." She announced in a friendly, warm tone. "I'm a Love Colony, resort coordinator. I'm here to check you all in and then I'll show you to your suites."

Zoe glanced at her appreciatively as she prepared to follow her lead although handling her suitcases now was slightly more awkward, since she'd actually left the motorized luggage trolley back at the airport, just before she'd actually boarded the bus. She quickly glanced down at her cases and then prepared to pull them both alongside her nonetheless as she attempted to follow Becky wherever she might actually lead them.

"Oh, you don't have to struggle with those ladies, let me get you some assistance." Becky insisted politely as she quickly glanced at Zoe and noticed that Zoe was actually struggling to maneuver her luggage. She quickly clapped her hands together and two, strong, handsome looking porters suddenly appeared from out of a door situated just behind the reception desk.

Zoe smiled, giggled and then winked discreetly at Madeline as the two handsome men walked towards them. "Now that's what I call service." She whispered.

Madeline smiled.

Each of the two men quickly held onto the three suitcases that belonged to both Zoe and Madeline and then they politely waited for Becky to check the two guests in, so that they could actually take their luggage to the correct suite. The male porter that was responsible for Zoe's suitcases was extremely handsome as Zoe quickly glanced at his face and then smiled, at least he was in her opinion anyway. Becky briefly spoke to the male reservations clerk seated just behind the reception desk and then turned back to face the male porters and quickly instructed the two men regarding which suite the suitcases actually had to be taken to as Zoe and Madeline watched, listened and waited.

Once the two men had been instructed accordingly by Becky, to Zoe's complete surprise and utter horror, both men then actually started to walk away from her and she immediately frowned. Zoe soon recovered however, a few seconds later and then smiled as she quickly began to follow them, utterly adamant that she was not going to let the cute, buff porter that had her suitcases in tow, out of her sight that quickly as he had an absolutely amazing physique.

Madeline giggled as she watched Zoe and then gently pulled her back towards her. "Where are you going Zoe?" She asked as she gently shook her head.

"Didn't you see his butt?" Zoe whispered back. "It was scientifically perfect, I mean he was both fit and fine. I'm satisfied already, there's an abundance of fine looking men here and we are definitely going to have a great time."

Becky smiled as she suddenly turned back to face both women and then handed each of them, two small keycards. "Right that's you both checked in, now I'll show you to your suite." She mentioned as she started to lead the two women out of the main foyer.

Zoe and Madeline smiled in response and then immediately began to follow her.

A long, white hallway immediately greeted the two women as Becky led them through a set of glass doors on the very left hand side of the foyer as she stepped back through the door that she had actually just come out of minutes beforehand. Down each side of the white, glossy hallway was a series of doors and as the two women walked along the corridor just a step or two behind Becky, they quickly realized that there were some strange noises emanating from behind one of the doors that sounded almost sexual in nature. Groans of male and female pleasure sounded out into the hallway around the three as Zoe quickly glanced at Madeline and smiled. It actually sounded as if a couple were indeed actually having sex behind one of the closed doors and Zoe automatically assumed that there must be some kind of sexual activity really occurring.

Zoe paused as she approached the door that seemed to house the very sexual noises behind it. "What happens inside that room?" She asked Becky as her curiosity suddenly prompted her to search for a deeper, more elaborate explanation. "Can you just book me into that suite please, it sounds like fun."

Madeline giggled.

Becky paused as she suddenly turned back to face both women and then smiled playfully. "That room is where I do some of my very best work." She explained. "We test people holographically, to see if they're sexually compatible and that room is where that actually happens, it's called the Holographic Bonking Room Suite." Becky explained.

"Do you ever peek?" Zoe asked as curiosity rapidly filled her thoughts. "I mean, do you ever watch holographic couples actually doing it?" She enquired as she smiled, Becky had an extremely cool job, if she did indeed actually get paid to sit and watch holographic couples actually having sex as in Zoe's mind, the whole notion of doing so, was completely and utterly fascinating and for a moment, she even felt slightly, jealous.

"As if I'd do such a thing." Becky replied as she mischievously smiled in response to Zoe's extremely suggestive question. "If you're really good whilst you're here Zoe, I might even let you watch yourself with some of the final matches that Honey selects for you during your stay." She added as she grinned at Zoe.

Madeline smiled.

"Did you hear that Madeline? They even have holographic profiles of all the visitors that come to the love resort that can actually bonk together. How cool is that?" Zoe remarked as she suddenly turned to face Madeline.

Madeline immediately giggled in response.

Once the novelty surrounding the Holographic Bonking Room Suite had been fully absorbed and appreciated by Zoe, the three women resumed their walk along the long hallway as Becky gently held onto Zoe's arm and led both women along the remainder of the shiny, white corridor. Despite Becky's initial seemingly serious, sensible, professional presentation, she had actually surprised Zoe with her playful, funny remarks which clearly indicated to Zoe that Becky definitely had a naughty side to her which was indeed very much like Zoe's own. Although Becky was a mature woman and certainly in her late fifties if not, early sixties, she quite definitely had a very playful edge to her personality and Zoe as a result, took an immediate liking to her as she appreciated the naughty edge that Becky had so overtly displayed and basked in it. Zoe's vacation was already fun and it had actually only just started and that was a tremendous encouragement and validation to Zoe that she had definitely booked and chosen the most perfect vacation possible.

A few minutes later, the three women arrived at the very bottom of the long hallway and Zoe and Madeline suddenly found themselves inside a large, circular space with fifteen white, glossy doors situated directly in front of them. Becky quickly swept across the circular space as she approached one of the doors, the door in the very center and then held a key card up against a small, white square panel situated upon the wall just beside it and the door in front of her quickly swished open.

"This is the Cuddle Wing and this is your suite!" Becky suddenly announced as she turned back to face them both and then smiled. "Please go right in and make yourselves at home." She invited.

Huge smiles rapidly adorned both Zoe and Madeline's faces as they stepped inside the lavish, luxury suite and as they actually did so, they almost bumped into the two male porters who were by now, actually on their way out of the lounge where they had just left their three suitcases. Each item of luggage sat upon the floor, in the very center of the large lounge area as the two women quickly strode across the room towards their cases and inspected every intimate detail of the suite that surrounded them as they walked. Every inch of the suite was luxurious and stunning and looked very much like the photos that Zoe had actually seen prior to their arrival, when she'd initially booked their vacation. The walls inside the lounge area were a glossy, silky white and they shone as the daylight flooded in from two very large, French windows situated at one side of the room which led out onto a veranda.

Inside the huge lounge area, there were two very large, black and white leather sofas and various other pieces of furniture and upon first sight, Zoe felt the suite they had been allocated actually seemed to be extremely spacious. Two large bedrooms with en-suite bathrooms were situated through two doorways inside the lounge and there was even a small kitchenette area just at one end of the lounge area which appeared to be equipped with a hot drinks machine, a cocktail maker and a very large, black, glossy fridge. A large, wafer thin screen clung to one of the walls and some brightly colored paintings gently added some splashes of color to the stark, white walls that surrounded them as their presence gently removed any possible blandness that the continuous white walls may have created in their absence. The two very large, extremely comfortable looking, plush black and white sofas on either side of the lounge looked extremely inviting and Zoe suddenly rushed towards one and then quickly bounced down on top of it.

Everything about the resort, the reception area, the hallway, the suite and even the grounds, appeared to be immaculate, extremely stylish and completely color coordinated as Zoe quietly admired her surroundings in complete and utter awe. She stood up a few seconds later and then quickly approached one of the bedrooms as she curiously examined every inch of the suite they had actually been given and reveled in every beautiful inch of her surroundings. Each bedroom was adorned with black and gold furnishings and Zoe almost felt as if she'd actually just arrived in heaven as she and Madeline, quietly inspected each one.

"This is your suite ladies." Becky explained. "And just as you requested, you were given a two person suite, with two single rooms and en-suite bathrooms."

"It's absolutely spectacular." Madeline remarked as she absorbed her surroundings appreciatively.

"I know, can I live here?" Zoe asked.

"I'm glad you both like it." Becky replied as she smiled warmly at them both. "Dinner is already available in the dining hall, so once you've unpacked or freshened up, you can make your way back towards the main reception at the very front of the building and I'll take you to the dining hall so that you can eat." She prepared to leave the suite as she started to make her way back towards the door. "Is there anything else either of you need from me right now?"

Zoe and Madeline quickly shook their heads in response.

"Thanks very much for all your assistance Becky." Madeline said as she smiled.

Becky paused for a moment, just before she actually reached the suite door and then turned back to face them both. "You're most welcome ladies and I hope you both enjoy your stay." She replied as she smiled.

A few seconds later, the suite door rapidly swished shut behind Becky as she departed and Zoe and Madeline quickly glanced at each other and then smiled. Every single thing about their suite was absolutely perfect and they just couldn't wait to actually see the rest of the resort. Madeline suddenly started to pull her suitcase towards one of the bedrooms nearby as Zoe sat back down on the sofa and quietly watched her. She entered inside a bedroom and then actually started to unpack and Zoe quickly leapt to her feet and then followed her inside the bedroom.

"What are you doing Madeline?" Zoe asked.

"I'm unpacking." Madeline replied. "Like Becky suggested."

Zoe rolled her eyes. "That was a suggestion, that doesn't mean you actually have to do it right now." She teased as she gently held onto Madeline's arm. "Don't be boring Madeline, do that later, let's go find some men."

Madeline suddenly smiled as she immediately surrendered to Zoe's request and allowed Zoe to lead her back out into the lounge. "Okay, okay let's go." She replied

"Unpacking can wait until tomorrow morning. There's absolutely no rush whatsoever to do that, we can do it in the morning when we wake up." Zoe insisted as she grinned. "Right now, we have much more important things to do and unpacking certainly isn't one of those important things."

"I did want to freshen up a bit before dinner though." Madeline explained as they exited the suite and then started to walk back along the long, white hallway.

"Hmmm, I can solve that problem." Zoe replied as she quickly dipped her hand inside her handbag and then plucked out some facial, skin freshening wipes, a hairbrush and some makeup items. She paused and then turned to face Madeline and quickly gave Madeline's face and hair a quick tidy up inside the hallway and once Zoe was satisfied that everything was complete, she quickly showed Madeline her face and hair, in a small, round mirror which she held up just in front of her face.

"Wow Zoe, you really can do wonders with a bit of makeup and a hairbrush." Madeline observed as she gazed appreciatively into the small mirror. "My face looks really fresh and my hair, that style is so cute." She remarked as she admired Zoe's handiwork.

"You're very easy to work with. You have great skin, a pretty face and beautiful hair. Trust me, your natural assets make anything I can do, a whole lot easier." Zoe replied. "I can't wait to take a dip inside the ocean, imagine Madeline, we'll actually be swimming in the real sea."

"Apparently, we can even go horse riding, snorkeling and go out on the sea on jet bikes." Madeline mentioned. "There's just so many things to do here, I'm not even sure we'll be able to actually fit it all in."

"I know, this is going to be the most amazing vacation I've ever had." Zoe said as she gently held onto Madeline's arm and then started to walk along the long corridor once more.

"Me too." Madeline agreed. "I mean seriously, this really is a great vacation package and we were so lucky to see that commercial when we actually did."

"I know and I want to try out as many activities as I can. Things that I'd normally never do at home." Zoe remarked as she quickly glanced at Madeline's face.

Two very beautiful, crystal clear, aqua green eyes sparkled back at Zoe as she admired Madeline's feminine beauty for a moment, Madeline was just naturally pretty, naturally elegant and naturally beautiful, simple and down to earth but very wonderfully beautiful. Her smile created the cutest little dimples that dented each one of her cheeks ever so gently each time she smiled and her eyes were absolutely stunning. At times, Zoe often actually wished her own eyes were another color as in her opinion, her eyes were a dull, dark brown and although she had been told upon several occasions that her eyes were seductive and that she had 'come to bed eyes' whatever that meant, she still really didn't like them. Sometimes, Zoe wished they were a much lighter brown, or even a hazel or greenish brown but Madeline had always reassured her, whenever Zoe had actually voiced and expressed such desires that her eyes were absolutely lovely and that to her, they were warm, seductive, inviting and utterly irresistible.

Madeline's complimentary reassurances over the years, had finally been accepted and Zoe hadn't actually gone as far as seeking out colored contact lenses to actually change how her eyes looked, though that was still something she had decided, she might actually try out one day. At times though, she did wonder if perhaps Madeline's opinion about her eyes was slightly bias, after all Madeline was her best friend and sometimes best friends weren't always as objective as they actually should be. Friends usually tended to view each other through a lens that was slightly more favorable than that of strangers, due to the adoration and love they actually held for each other and perhaps friends saw each other as more beautiful as they actually viewed each other through eyes of love, not eyes of unfamiliarity. Perhaps, those who found fault and those who criticized everything about the people they encountered, viewed each other through lenses of dislike and those individuals would never really ever be satisfied with anything that people ever were or anything they ever actually aspired to be, Zoe contemplated thoughtfully as they walked. Madeline's lens of love that over the years had viewed her more favorably had certainly provided Zoe with a lot of comfort as she'd walked through the harsh world that so often judged everything inside it based on superficial measures which really actually served no purpose at all and as Zoe walked alongside her, she quietly appreciated Madeline's encouragement which had always been faithful, consistent and extremely supportive.

"What do you about the name of our wing, the Cuddle Wing?" Zoe suddenly asked, just as the two women arrived back at the glass doors which led into the reception area. "I mean how funny is that, our suite is actually situated in the Cuddle Wing Madeline?"

"I did think that was slightly corny." Madeline replied as she grinned.

"I wonder what some of the other wings are called. Do you think there's a Naked Wing or a Kiss Wing or perhaps even a Sex Wing?" Zoe asked.

Madeline laughed. "It must have been a woman that picked out the names for each of the wings as there's no way on earth that a man would have actually called a wing, the Cuddle Wing." She mentioned.

"I totally agree." Zoe confirmed as she quickly nodded her head in agreement and then smiled. "Seriously, it's so corny."

The two women prepared to enter back inside the reception area once more as they quietly contemplated the love matching vacation they were just about to actually indulge in, with intrigue and excitement. Searching for love in a beautiful, love resort for a week quite definitely wasn't the worst possible expenditure of their time or their money and it already seemed as if the actual resort itself, from their very first impressions of it, was indeed perfectly suited to the purposes it had actually been created to fulfill and then subsequently dedicated to.

THE FEAST

When the two women entered back inside the main reception area, they found Becky there once more and she quickly approached them with a huge smile upon her face. Unlike the moment when they'd first arrived, the reception area was now completely empty as all the vacationers who had entered the foyer alongside them had already been shown to their respective suites. The two women smiled as they walked towards Becky and prepared to be shown to the dining hall.

"Come with me please and I'll take you to the dining hall." Becky urged as she motioned towards both women to follow her. "Dinner has already started and is usually served each day between six and nine, so you won't have to wait."

"Now that sounds like a great idea." Zoe agreed as she nodded enthusiastically.

Both women followed Becky quietly as she led them towards a hallway on the very right hand side, situated at the very rear of the reception area which lead towards the back of the building. In terms of appearance, Zoe quietly observed as they walked, Becky was an attractive woman who was immaculately preened and both her presentation and attitude was extremely professional but also had a playful edge to it that Zoe internally, secretly already admired. Her demeanor was extremely pleasant and as the three walked, the two women began to develop an instant rapport with Becky as she started to question them further about their current single status. A huge, warm smile pleasantly adorned her face and she seemed to enjoy conversing with the two women as much as they did with her as they dabbled in further discussions about their romantic, very single lives.

"How long have you actually been single Zoe?" Becky asked Zoe.

"Forever." Zoe replied as she laughed. "No seriously, for about a year I've had some casual relationships this past year but no one really serious. I got a bit tired of the whole dedicating yourself to one man that doesn't deserve your time thing, it really wasn't working for me."

Becky laughed as the three entered into another long hallway and then started to walk along it. "What about you Madeline?" She asked.

"I've been single for a few months now." Madeline replied. "I was in a relationship for about a year but the guy ended up seeing someone else, without actually telling me."

Becky nodded. "Men can be so disappointing sometimes, it can break your heart." She remarked. "Never mind, it's totally his loss."

Madeline nodded. "Definitely." She agreed.

"Well hopefully, now that your both here, you'll have a chance to find someone nice. Someone worthy of your time, someone slightly more serious." Becky quickly reassured them both as she smiled. "Some great single men are here on vacation right now."

Madeline smiled and nodded.

"How on earth do you find your way around this building?" Zoe suddenly asked. "I mean, this resort is so huge, I think I'd get lost."

At the end of the hallway, there was a large circular space which had five exits leading of from it and Becky smiled as she led the two women towards the central entrance which led them directly into another much shorter hallway. Due to the complexity and vast size of the resort main building, Zoe made mental notes as she walked along each hallway as to where exactly the dining hall was situated as she absolutely did not want to get lost on their way to dinner the next evening and be wandering around long corridors with an empty stomach.

"Well I guess you just get used to it." Becky replied. "I've worked here ever since the resort actually opened, so I'm quite used to the building now."

A large dining hall suddenly greeted the women's eyes as they approached the end of the hallway and Zoe smiled. The banqueting hall was absolutely huge and they could see that at least thirty people were currently seated at tables inside it as they entered the room. Tables and chairs were scattered sporadically across the vast interior and Zoe quickly estimated that there had to be at least over a hundred tables inside the actual dining hall itself. Along one side of the room, was a very long, huge table that was filled with silver hotplates which brimmed with piping hot food and they could clearly see steam rise from each of the dishes that lay upon it. Their mouths quickly began to water as the delicious aroma from the food wafted through the air and rapidly infiltrated their nostrils.

"Great, there's still lots of food left, you're in luck." Becky quickly observed. "You can either eat here or order from your room and a waiter will actually bring the meal you've requested directly to you. A lot of our guests prefer to actually eat here as it gives them a chance to meet some of other guests at the resort."

Madeline and Zoe glanced at each other and smiled.

"I think we'll eat here." Zoe replied.

Madeline nodded her head in agreement. "Yes, it'll be nice perhaps to meet some of the other guests." She agreed.

"Yes, having a meal together at times can be the perfect way to break the ice." Becky suggested. "And you might even make some new friends."

Zoe smiled and nodded. "Yes let's find a table to sit at." She encouraged Madeline as she gently took her arm. Zoe certainly hadn't made all that effort on the plane to freshen up and look her very best, just to sit inside the suite she'd been allocated to and stare at four walls on her very first night at the resort. She made a rapid beeline for a nearby table, utterly determined to make the most of not only her night but also Madeline's. "I certainly didn't make all that effort to look good, just to be appreciated by myself." She whispered to Madeline who walked alongside her and as the two women drew closer to the table, Zoe prepared to sit down.

Madeline grinned.

The table Zoe had chosen to sit at, was very large and already had a few occupants but that didn't put Zoe off at all. Cardigans were quickly placed over two of the chairs to clearly indicate that those two seats were taken and then the two women made their way over towards the long table at the other side of the room which was packed with silver trays filled with food and had white, clean, empty plates at one end of it. Each of the two woman had brought a light cardigan along with them when they'd actually left their suite which they'd both carried inside their hands, just in case they wanted to venture outside after dinner and the breeze was chillier than expected but the dining hall and interior of the resort building were actually not cold so as yet, they hadn't actually need to wear them.

"You can select your starters from the wide selection on offer at this table and then when you want to order your main course and desert, a server will attend to you and serve you those individually." Becky explained.

Zoe and Madeline nodded.

"It's like a huge feast." Madeline whispered to Zoe as she quickly cast her eyes over the huge spread of starters on offer. "And those are just the starters."

"I know isn't it great." Zoe replied as she picked up two empty, white plates and then handed one to Madeline. "Seriously, I think I could live here forever."

Madeline giggled.

Every item of food on the table directly in front of the two women looked extremely delicious and tantalizing as they admired the vast array of barbecued seasoned meats, skewered prawns, spicy chicken chunks and vegetable dishes and their mouths began to water. Memories of the dry, crusty meal they'd eaten upon their flight on the way there, quickly disappeared from both their minds as images of beautiful, succulent, mouthwatering, appetizing dishes quickly replaced them.

"Well, I'm certainly ready to do this spread justice." Zoe remarked. "I'm absolutely starving."

Becky smiled. "Help yourselves." She insisted. "Eat as much as you want to and then someone will come and take your order for your main meal."

"It looks like there's food from every part of the world here." Zoe observed as she quickly began to fill up her plate with succulent pieces of chicken and barbecued chunks of lamb.

"Yes and there's even a few special island dishes that you won't find anywhere else in the world, right over there." Becky explained politely as she pointed towards a few dishes at one end of the table inside some silver warming trays. "Each of the fish dishes is freshly prepared every day and is actually sourced from the seas that surround the island itself."

Mouthwatering, delicious looking seafood dishes marinated in all kinds of exotic looking spices that were drizzled with fruity, brightly colored sauces filled some of the silver trays and Zoe quickly rushed towards them. The island specialties looked totally amazing as Zoe quickly heaped some of the seafood onto her plate and then even served some for Madeline. Once the women had filled their plates with all the starters they wanted to try, they then prepared to head back to their seats at the table on the other side of the room.

"Who prepares all this food?" Zoe asked Becky as they walked. "And where does all this wonderful meat come from?"

"Well, there's a self-sustaining farm at the other side of the island and there's also a fish farm and a gaming reserve. We breed livestock and fish upon the island itself and most of the other ingredients required are actually grown inside greenhouses and fields on the farm itself. The island is extremely self-sufficient." Becky explained as she smiled at them both. "That saves us a lot of time and effort as most of the daily food requirements are taken care off by the farm and kitchen staff, who prepare fresh produce every single day, we import very little."

Madeline and Zoe nodded as they sat down at the table and then prepared to eat.

"Once you've had dinner, there are usually some evening activities that take place on the weekends just beside the swimming pool and bar outside, so you can join in with those if you like, or you can simply take a walk down by the beach and have a drink at one of the beach bars." Becky suggested.

Zoe nodded. "Sounds great. We'll check it out after dinner." She replied enthusiastically.

Madeline nodded in agreement.

"I have to go now as I have to attend to some other matters. You two enjoy your meal." Becky explained as she smiled and politely excused herself.

Madeline and Zoe nodded in understanding.

The two women were left alone once more as Becky swiftly departed and they quickly began to tuck into their starters and consume the food that sat upon the starter plates on the table directly in front of them. Each of their plates held many delicious items upon them but Zoe actually felt as if she had piled up way too much food upon hers as she quickly glanced at Madeline's more moderate plate and then smiled. Madeline was definitely the most sensible between the two as she'd taken less than ten items, in order to actually save some room for her main course.

"Is that all you are going to eat?" Zoe teased as she glanced at Madeline's half empty plate.

"No but if I want more, I'll just go back and get it." Madeline replied as she smiled. "Plus I have to keep some room for my main course." She quickly reminded Zoe.

"Seriously, there's no way I'm walking up and down and making several trips to the food counter. That's why I just filled up my plate the first time around." Zoe explained. "I'm far to lazy to do that, plus I'm totally starving."

Madeline smiled.

A few other people were seated around the table that the two women had chosen to sit at which didn't bother Zoe or Madeline in the slightest as they were both in a very sociable mood. Madeline had politely greeted the other occupants with nods as she'd sat down but Zoe hadn't even bothered to as she was simply to hungry to be ultra-polite. Her stomach was growling and the food just looked too good to make it wait by wasting minutes indulging and engaging in pleasantries with people she didn't actually even know. At times, Madeline could be so well mannered, whereas Zoe on the other hand was less inclined to care about other people's feelings and hence slightly less observant of the usual social etiquette norms and practices that some might adhere to. Zoe smiled as she quickly spooned forkfuls of food into her mouth, perhaps on this occasion she had slightly overestimated the capacity of her stomach as she'd heaped quite a lot of food onto a rather small plate and she still had to order and then eat, both her main course and her desert.

Despite the fact that the evening dinner service was almost over, at least fifty other guests arrived as the two women ate and as they entered inside the large banqueting hall, they watched each one quietly. Some people sat down at tables completely alone whilst others chose chairs that were situated at least a few seats away from other people as if they wanted to remain alone as the dining hall began to fill up. Perhaps those people were just a bit reserved or shy, Zoe quietly concluded as she watched them and quietly analyzed their choices.

Some people, Zoe quickly realized had actually come to the resort on their own and she quietly pondered as to whether or not she would have actually done so, if Madeline had not agreed to accompany her, or if she had not had a great female friend like Madeline to actually attend with. Yes, she was definitely an extrovert and extremely outgoing but even she doubted that she would have actually had the nerve to attend the love resort on her own.

Gratitude suddenly filled Zoe's core as she glanced at Madeline's face and then smiled, she was so lucky really to have a friend like Madeline that she could drag along anywhere she wished to and that would follow her willingly on her many escapades. Over the years, Zoe had actually dragged Madeline along to all kinds of strange events and parties and even some that had taken place at secret locations and venues that were situated in remote parts of the countryside and supposedly haunted houses. They'd even gone to a huge adult hide and seek event held in a countryside manor where they'd had to find their way out of a labyrinth and they'd attended lots of adult fancy dress parties and even a masked ball. Twice, they had actually visited special activity based, adult holiday camps and they'd even spent some of their summer vacations pitching tents and searching for treasure in some woods near one of the campsites they'd visited.

Due to Madeline's supportive nature, she'd always participated in Zoe's plans and had come along and in return Zoe had always ensured that Madeline actually enjoyed herself. Making sure Madeline had a great time was the least that Zoe felt she could do as after all, she was the one actually dragging her along to some very remote and strange locations to participate in some very strange and unusual activities that she would probably never have dreamed of attending on her own.

An extremely nerdy looking man suddenly caught Zoe's attention as he sat down opposite her and then started to eat. Each mouthful of food he took was raised to his lips and then before he actually placed the forkful of food inside his mouth, he actually cleared his throat with a light cough. His strange habit amused Zoe slightly as she listened to him and watched him discreetly from the corner of her eye but pretended not to. Part of her wondered how he actually had time to do that as she contemplated quietly that perhaps he wasn't as hungry as she'd been when she'd first arrived at the table with her plateful of food.

A cute female in a bright white and red, polka dot, flared skater dress suddenly sat down right next to Madeline and she actually started to strike up a conversation with her as she politely introduced herself and then smiled at her. Every spot of makeup upon her face looked totally immaculate and Zoe was completely quite surprised at how well it had actually been applied as it actually looked, almost professional.

"Hi I'm Louise." She said as she stretched out a hand towards Madeline.

Madeline quickly stopped eating and then politely shook her hand. "Hi Louise, I'm Madeline." She replied.

Zoe glanced at her face as she also stopped eating for a moment as she prepared to introduce herself too. "Hi Louise, I'm Zoe." She mentioned as she stretched out her hand politely towards Louise and promptly introduced herself.

"Are you two here together?" Louise asked.

Madeline nodded in response. "Yes, we came on vacation together, we're actually friends. How about you, are you here with anyone?" She enquired.

Louise quickly shook her head. "No. I actually came here alone." She replied in a soft, lilted tone.

"That's very adventurous of you." Madeline mentioned. "What do you do Louise?"

"I work for a perfume company." Louise explained. "I live in quite a small town and there just aren't really many single men around, so that's why I'm here. Finding someone you like where I live is so difficult as there simply isn't much choice."

Zoe smirked. "Whereas we come from a large city where there are a lot of single men around, just not many good ones." She mentioned.

Louise giggled.

Madeline smiled as she quickly nodded her head. "Very true Zoe, very true." She agreed.

"After dinner, if you'd both like to, you can come by my suite and I'll give you some perfume samples from the perfume company I work for." Louise generously offered.

"That would be lovely." Madeline replied as she rapidly accepted Louise's kind offer immediately. "Thanks Louise."

Zoe nodded her head enthusiastically. "Sure, that sounds like a great idea." She agreed. "Perfumes are just something you can never, ever possibly have enough of, especially nice perfumes."

The nerdy man suddenly interrupted the three women as he began to introduce himself. "Hi ladies, I'm Thomas." He announced, his voice was slightly shaky and trembled slightly as he pushed his glasses further up onto his nose and then stretched out a hand across the table towards the three women seated opposite him.

Zoe smiled as she watched Madeline and Louise politely respond as they both shook his hand. "Hi Thomas, I'm Zoe." She replied as she stretched out her hand towards him. "That's Louise and this is Madeline." Zoe quickly explained as she pointed towards the two other women seated at the table next to her. She smiled at him to encourage him for a moment as she quietly appreciated that it had probably taken all of his courage just to actually speak to the three women seated opposite him at all as he seemed to be slightly nervous and uneasy and his hand had actually trembled when Zoe had actually shaken it.

"A pleasure to meet you all." Thomas replied as a smile suddenly broke out across his face.

A server suddenly placed two plates of food down in front of Zoe and Madeline as their main dishes arrived and just as their main courses arrived, so to very fortunately, did several really buff looking men. The three men approached the table and then sat down and Zoe immediately stopped shoveling food into her mouth as she started to eat her main course slightly more elegantly, in a manner which greatly differed from how she'd actually approached her starter. Suddenly, being ladylike and Zoe's appearance became extremely important as she didn't actually want to look like a pig and especially not in front of three extremely fit, buff looking men. First impressions were really so important, Zoe quietly contemplated as she absorbed every inch of their appearance which certainly looked almost as delicious as the contents of the plate of food directly in front of her.

Each of the three women's attention was immediately diverted away from Thomas towards the three buff looking men as Zoe discreetly nudged Madeline and then grinned at her. One was quite tall and a bit stocky with brown eyes and he had the sexiest, cutest smile Zoe had ever seen and he was definitely Madeline's type. In terms of taste, when it actually came to men and their physicalities and personalities, both Zoe and Madeline had very different preferences and that had frequently been a source of amusement for them both over the years. Zoe preferred slimmer, taller, lean looking men with quieter dispositions, whereas Madeline on the other hand seemed to prefer stockier, heavier built men with louder, more outgoing personalities. When it came to the issue of personality, their preferences made total sense to Zoe as there was no way on earth that she could ever actually attempt to date a man that was actually more outgoing or louder than she was as that would result in a constant competition between them both which would definitely get on her nerves. Due to Madeline's more reserved nature, it also made sense therefore that she would prefer someone slightly louder and more outgoing than she was, to liven things up and keep them both entertained.

On one occasion several years beforehand however, Madeline had actually dated an extremely quiet man and she'd later confided in Zoe that it had actually been the most boring relationship of her entire life. The man had hardly spoken, Madeline had hardly spoken and that had resulted in huge silences between them both which had been very long and extremely awkward and their relationship had slowly simply faded into actual nonexistence as they'd spent less and less time together and then simply just avoided each other's presence entirely. Their relationship hadn't lasted very long at all and ever since then, Madeline had totally avoided the quieter type of men that she knew, she definitely had no future with or at least not a very interesting future with.

Much to Zoe's delight, two of the buff looking, handsome men suddenly decided to take the initiative and started to introduce themselves to the people seated at the table around them. Each person's name was politely requested as the men flashed charming smiles at each of the women and then politely introduced themselves. The third man didn't speak to anyone at all and Zoe in response, completely ignored him and instead keenly conversed with the two men that had made an effort to actually introduce themselves and speak to people. Conversation flowed as the group around the table discussed what everyone did for a living and then agreed that after dinner they would hang out together down by the pool side, all except Thomas who didn't seem to be very keen on that idea at all.

"I think I'd just prefer to go for the walk along the beach." Thomas explained in response to the open invitation that the three women had extended towards him as they'd invited him to join them.

Zoe immediately shook her head in response. "Why Thomas, you'll be all alone? Come along with us, there'll be cocktails, games and lots of fun." She promised as she attempted to make Thomas feel as welcome as possible.

"Another night perhaps." Thomas replied. "I'm not much of a cocktail or a games person."

Zoe gently shook her head as she slightly reluctantly accepted his wishes and his refusal. "Okay Thomas." She said as she finally let him of the hook.

In terms of who Thomas actually was and his personality, his response completely made sense when those factors were actually taken into consideration as he really was quite reserved and even Zoe, who was notorious for her lack of empathy, could clearly see that. He was definitely the type of person that would prefer quieter, more solitary experiences and definitely someone who would avoid the rowdy, boisterous environments that both poolside games and a cocktail bar would most certainly invoke and provide. Due to his reserved nature and quieter, dorkier personality however, Zoe had still tried to encourage him to attend nonetheless as to see Thomas get drunk would at least be if nothing else, slightly amusing. There was it seemed however, no swaying Thomas and his refusal it appeared was absolutely final as Zoe finally accepted defeat. In Zoe's mind, Thomas was being quite a spoil sport as seeing Thomas get drunk would have certainly amused her and would have been as funny as hell but she had to eventually accept that perhaps Thomas had no desire to attend a night filled with alcoholic games and activities, purely to provide Zoe with some cheap laughs and a bit of entertainment.

The saying that quiet people do the worst things when they do actually let their hair down, had provoked Zoe to encourage him to come along as her curiosity had been aroused as she'd contemplated further internally what Thomas might actually be capable of doing when he was actually in a drunken state. Today however, would certainly not be the day that Zoe would actually find out as Thomas had absolutely no intentions at all to participate and had very stubbornly refused to provide Zoe with an evening of cheap laughs. Despite her internal inclinations and desires, Zoe wisely quickly let the matter rest as he wasn't budging and her curiosity for that night would certainly not be satisfied.

Zoe shrugged as she quickly glanced at Madeline, at least two out of the three buff looking men were coming along and that was really a lot more important to her, in the larger scheme of things. "Another night perhaps Thomas." She suggested.

Thomas nodded in response.

Madeline stared at Zoe with a slightly confused expression upon her face and then suddenly leant towards her and whispered in her ear. "Why do you want him to come along?" She asked. "He's not even your type. Why are you so bothered?"

"Can you imagine how funny it would be to see him get drunk?" Zoe whispered back. "Now that would be really funny."

Madeline smirked and then gently shook her head. "Zoe, you're absolutely terrible." She teased.

Zoe smirked and shrugged.

Fortunately, Louise required no such persuasion and she quickly agreed to come along with the rest of the group which suited Zoe down to the ground as she seemed like she could be a bit of a laugh at the very least. Zoe let Thomas off the hook completely as she quickly turned her focus back towards the other people seated at the table around her. Perhaps, his lack of participation was a positive thing really, Zoe quickly decided as his throat clearing coughs might end up actually getting on her nerves after a while, if he continued his habitual strange coughing every time he consumed anything and then Zoe might even end up saying something to him that he might actually find offensive.

Once their evening meal was well and truly over, Zoe, Madeline and Louise arranged to meet the two men down by the poolside in thirty minutes time as they stood up and prepared to leave the dining hall. The thirty minute departure from the two buff men that had actually volunteered to come along with them, was actually required in order to visit Louise's suite to check out the sample bottles of perfume that she'd kindly offered the two women when she'd first met them. Zoe was absolutely determined to at least smell some of the perfume samples she'd offered them as Louise's own perfume smelt amazingly interesting in that it was spicy, fruity and somehow gently seductive. Good perfumes were very hard to find and when you actually found one, Zoe knew you had to keep it for as long as you possibly could and even at times, try to actually purchase more than one bottle, just in case the perfume line was discontinued before the first bottle actually ran out.

Each of the three women stood up as they left the men seated around the table and made their way out of the dining hall as they headed towards Louise's suite. Due to Louise's open, friendly nature a discussion quickly began about her dating preferences and the type of men she was actually attracted to and interested in. Zoe as always, was extremely curious about Louise's dating preferences as it was a subject that had always fascinated her, what people were attracted to in a partner and even at times, why they were actually attracted to such personal attributes and hence Zoe participated in the discussion, very enthusiastically.

Louise casually mentioned that she felt particularly drawn towards Asian men, even though she herself was not actually Asian. "I usually seem to be very attracted to Chinese, Japanese and Korean men for some reason. I'm not sure why, perhaps it's just because they're so cultured." She explained as she smiled. "Or perhaps I just love their dark hair, dark eyes and light skin tone."

"Do you think they take into account our personal physical preferences when they match us with people?" Zoe asked as she glanced at Madeline thoughtfully for a moment. "I mean, do they actually factor that into our potential love matches?"

Madeline immediately shrugged in response. "I'm not sure, maybe you could ask Becky that question the next time you see her." She suggested as she began to give the matter slightly more thought. "Attraction is such a complicated area when it comes to human beings. So many different things attract us to another person. Sometimes, I think it's a complete and utter enigma but I'm sure it's probably something they do consider somehow."

"I mean seriously, if human beings can't work out attraction, how on earth can a computer system?" Zoe enquired as she suddenly voiced the thoughts deep inside her mind.

"We were asked to provide them with some information regarding our physical romantic preferences when we completed our booking forms, so perhaps they utilize that information somehow to identify our potential matches." Madeline suggested thoughtfully.

"I sure hope so. Can you actually imagine being lumbered with having to attend a bunch of dates with people you're not even attracted to in any way at all?" Zoe asked as she gently shook her head. "That would be an absolute nightmare."

"Yes, that would be a complete of a waste of time." Louise agreed as she nodded. "They must take it into account or the possible matches they present to us and dates we went on as a result, would be absolutely pointless."

Zoe nodded in agreement as the three women suddenly arrived outside Louise's suite. "What's your wing called Louise?" Zoe asked playfully. "Our suite's in the Cuddle Wing." She continued as she giggled.

Louise smiled. "I do believe this wing is officially referred to as the Kiss Wing." She replied as she quickly scanned her cardkey against the panel beside the door and it rapidly swished open in front of them. "Please come in and make yourselves at home." Louise invited as she stepped inside the suite door and then waited for Zoe and Madeline to follow her into the lounge area. "Take a seat please and I'll just go and get my perfume samples from the bedroom."

"Oh my gosh, the Kiss Wing." Zoe remarked as she sat down on the sofa.

"I know Zoe, you were actually right." Madeline said as she grinned and then sat down next to her.

A few seconds later, Louise quickly scurried off towards the doorway of the bedroom and then disappeared inside it. She completely vanished for a few minutes as the two women glanced curiously around her suite and waited as they quietly inspected it, in most ways it was virtually identical to their own but it was far less spacious and had only one sofa situated inside the lounge area instead of two. Louise's suite was quite obviously a single suite, whereas Zoe and Madeline's suite was definitely intended for occupation by at least two people but it was still perfectly color coordinated and extremely luxurious, despite its smaller size.

When Louise returned a few minutes later, she had a small, white case inside her hands which she gently lay down upon the coffee table and then opened up. A vast array of small perfume sample bottles immediately greeted the two women's eyes which shone

147

with utter glee as they quietly absorbed the contents of the small, white case. Zoe quickly picked up some of the small bottles and then inspected each one slightly more closely as she admired them appreciatively.

Each bottle was shaped quite differently and had different colored glass, which varied in shade and tone to the other perfume bottles that surrounded it and some were very, very pretty. The differing appearance of the various perfume bottles totally fascinated Zoe as she quietly inspected each one as unlike the larger bottles, usually found inside department stores, the sample bottles were much smaller in size and definitely much cuter.

"Please help yourselves." Louise offered generously as she pointed towards the contents of the small, white compact case and then smiled at Zoe and Madeline.

"Thanks Louise." Zoe replied as she quickly opened up a few of the bottles she'd plucked out of the case just a few seconds beforehand and smelt the perfume inside each one. She was in complete and utter awe as she admired each wonderful scent. "These perfumes smell absolutely heavenly." Zoe mentioned as she complimented each of the varied scents that flew into her nostrils as she smelt each one. "And they're all so different."

"I'm glad you like them." Louise replied as she knelt down beside the coffee table. She leant forward and then plucked a small, blue bottle of the case which she then handed to Zoe. "Try that one." She suggested as she faced the two women and smiled.

Zoe quickly leant forward as she accepted the tiny, blue bottle from Louise's hands and then quickly opened it. She raised it up towards her nose in eager anticipation and then smelt the liquid the bottle actually contained enthusiastically and as soon as she did so, her face immediately changed into an expression of sheer disgust. "Yuck Louise, that is absolutely nasty." She groaned. "This one really stinks Madeline, it's like a cat has actually peed inside that bottle." Zoe moaned as a horrified expression rapidly crossed her face.

Louise laughed. "Well, they can't all smell nice." She explained.

"Let me smell it." Madeline urged as she plucked the small, blue bottle straight out of Zoe's hand and then raised it to her nose. "Oh my gosh that is truly awful." She agreed as she quickly turned her nose up in disgust.

Louise smiled. "Yep some scents are definitely an acquired taste. Here try this one instead." She insisted as she quickly handed Zoe a golden bottle and then deftly plucked the offending small, blue bottle out of Madeline's hand.

Due to the women's plans for the rest of the night, the perfume testing session actually only continued for around twenty minutes more, before the two women finally picked out a few sample bottles they definitely loved and then prepared to leave Louise's suite. Both Zoe and Madeline thanked Louise appreciatively for her generosity as they walked towards the door of her suite and then entered back inside the hallway, just outside it.

"We should really put these inside our suite before we actually go to the bar and pool." Madeline suggested sensibly as she paused for a moment in the hallway just outside Louise's suite.

Zoe nodded in agreement.

The long resort hallways were extremely quiet as the three women walked each of them and excitedly discussed the two men that had not only joined their table but that they were also just about to meet again at the poolside bar. Despite their suite being situated inside the same building, it actually took the three women around five minutes to actually reach Zoe and Madeline's suite, due to the long hallways and distance in-between. Once they arrived outside the door, the two women quickly splashed on some of the perfume that Louise had so kindly given them and then slipped inside their suite to place the sample bottles they'd been given, in each of their bedrooms.

Since Madeline had not actually changed her clothes since much earlier that day, when she'd initially dressed for the flight that brought them to the island, she quickly changed her clothes as she picked out something slightly more suitable to wear and prepared herself for the night of games and cocktails that awaited them. Although the three women had agreed to meet the two men beside the pool thirty minutes later, before they'd actually separated from them, it was more like forty five minutes by the time they actually approached the bar and perhaps even actually verging upon fifty.

Outside the main resort building, it was now actually quite dark as the women walked along the pathway that led towards the pool which was lit with small, antique, black, iron cage like lanterns. The romantic ambience that surrounded them as they walked felt almost magical and Zoe was quickly seduced by the pleasant nature of her environment as she was literally swept of her feet by the beauty of the resort as she'd absolutely never, ever been in a place that was so breathtakingly stunning, ever before.

When the three women eventually arrived by the poolside, they were pleasantly surprised to see a gathering of around one hundred people there and because both the swimming pool and the bar were huge, that meant both facilities could actually easily accommodate all those present and even more, if indeed anyone else actually decided to turn up. Zoe was lost for words as she quickly glanced at the people that surrounded her and gasped, she was totally in her element and like a child in a candy shop as there were just so many good looking men to choose from and she could hardly believe her eyes and luck.

"This vacation is going to be so much fun." Zoe insisted as she gently held onto Madeline's arm and squeezed it playfully. "I mean seriously, all this buffness in one place. I think I'm in heaven." She whispered as her eyes shone with excitement.

Madeline smiled.

Once the three women arrived beside the bar, they quickly met and greeted the two men and then ordered some cocktails. Some resort staff were nearby that were clearly visible as they were dressed in smart, white resort uniforms and hence were easily identifiable. All in all, Zoe noticed that there were at least ten resort staff beside the bar and they quickly started to organize some games as they approached some of the vacationers and then divided them up into much smaller groups. Most groups it appeared were formed from equal numbers of men and women and thankfully, the resort coordinators actually allowed Zoe, Madeline and Louise to remain in the same group, along with the two buff men that they had actually met at dinner earlier that night. One group however, consisted entirely of twenty females and another entirely of males and Zoe quickly realized that those two groups must be formed from vacationers that were not actually heterosexual.

"No point looking at any men from that group." Zoe suddenly whispered to Madeline and Louise as she nodded her head towards the all-male group.

"I know." Louise replied. "And there's some fine looking men in that group."

Madeline giggled.

"Trust me, they ain't even looking at us." Zoe teased playfully.

Louise grinned.

A large part of Zoe felt slightly comforted by the fact that Zoe and Madeline were actually in the same group as she was as she certainly did not want to be totally immersed in a group of total strangers on her very first night at the resort. The familiarity of having Madeline and Louise nearby would actually make the evening's activities a lot more fun and slightly less awkward for Zoe as she knew that she always had a laugh whenever she was around Madeline and Louise seemed like a good sport. When the activity groups had been formed, a male resort coordinator led the twenty people in Zoe's group towards a corner of the pool where there were some sun loungers and they quickly sat down. They listened extremely quietly as the resort coordinator that was leading their group began to speak to them all.

"Hi I'm Mark." He mentioned as he introduced himself. "We usually conduct our official love matching program throughout the weekdays and on the weekends, we tend to play a few group games each evening and organize some other activities purely so that vacationers can actually get to know each other." Mark explained. "And tonight we'll be playing Truth or Dare."

Zoe, Madeline and Louise nodded as they listened attentively.

Each member of the group of twenty was then prompted by Mark to introduce themselves as the group activity began and each of the group members politely said their names out loud as they started to familiarize themselves with each other. Zoe was completely certain that she wouldn't actually remember everyone's name and hence didn't even bother to try but simply resigned herself to remembering the names of those men she felt were particularly attractive and any other person that she felt seemed remotely interesting.

Mark started to explain the rules of the Truth and Dare game the group were about to play as soon as the introductions had been made. "You're not allowed to dare anyone to do anything sexual to anyone else and no stripping requests are allowed, aside from those two rules anything goes really." He explained. "Cocktails and other refreshments are available from the bar and you can help yourself to those whenever you want to throughout the night."

Before the game activities began, Zoe quickly jumped up to her feet as she rapidly accepted Mark's offer to help themselves to cocktails from the bar and then rushed back over towards the bamboo counter to collect a second round of drinks for each of the ladies she was with and herself. Both Madeline and Louise were already quite tipsy as they had both already consumed some wine with their evening meal and had already actually finished their first round of cocktails but Zoe wasn't worried at all about pacing their alcohol intake. They were well on their way towards drunkenness and a few more cocktails would most definitely usher that in more rapidly and then their night would really be a lot more fun and fun was exactly what Zoe wanted to have. Another few cocktails would clinch it, Zoe thought as she waited beside the bar to be served and that would give all three women a much larger capacity in which to be more adventurous without any inhibitions at all.

There was absolutely no way on earth, Zoe was actually going to allow Madeline to hide away in her shell on this holiday and Louise since she'd just joined the two women, was also not going to be allowed to hide away in the shadows of shyness and fear that related to other people's perceptions or judgments either. The three women that night were going to have a lot of fun and Zoe was definitely going to ensure that fun definitely did, indeed actually happen.

A few minutes later, when Zoe returned to the group, her hands and arms were laden with cocktails as she hadn't actually been given a tray upon which to carry the three cocktail glasses. Zoe quickly handed a glass to both Madeline and Louise and then sat back down beside them both upon a vacant sun lounger as she prepared enthusiastically to participate in the game of Truth and Dare that Mark had just proposed to them. Once the group was settled down again, a few minutes later, Mark handed each of the twenty people by the poolside a card with a number upon it.

"The person with the highest value card goes first." He explained. "They'll be the one to kick of the Truth or Dare activities."

For once, Zoe was actually quite nervous, which wasn't actually like her at all but she feared going first as she knew, she could actually be a little brazen and very outgoing at times and she worried for a moment whether she might possibly offend some of the people in the group, if she was indeed extremely adventurous to soon. Zoe would definitely dare them to do something really wild and the person who had been dared, she felt might be slightly shocked and perhaps even a little intimidated by her request. Very fortunately however, when the group all turned their cards over, it quickly transpired that a guy the three women hadn't actually met yet had the card with the highest number and hence, he had to actually go first.

He glanced at Louise's face for a moment and then smiled as he asked her the question. "Truth or Dare?"

Louise smiled slightly nervously before she responded. "Truth." She finally replied after just a few seconds of silence.

Zoe smiled.

The response from Louise in Zoe's mind was somewhat predictable as from their conversations that evening, Zoe could already tell that she was slightly more reserved than Zoe herself was. There was absolutely no way on earth that Louise would have chosen a dare and especially not since she was the first actual participant in the game. She had opted for the safer option between the two but in Zoe's mind that was somehow acceptable as she was going first and that actually took quite a lot of nerve in itself.

"Have you ever had sex on a first date?" The man asked.

Giggles suddenly erupted from inside Zoe's body and then spewed out of her mouth as she listened, quite unable to control her laughter and her reaction. The question he'd asked was actually quite tricky and Louise's face definitely reflected that as an uncomfortable expression rapidly crossed it and then stubbornly remained there. Zoe began to wonder internally whether or not Louise would actually tell the truth as she watched her face and observed her quite obvious discomfort. In essence, the question itself presented a contradictory dilemma in that, if Louise replied with a no she might look quite uptight and overly cautious but if she said yes to easily, she would then actually run the risk of looking like a very easy lay. One night stands were certainly something that most men and women had done at one point or another in their lifetime, even if only once, unless they were living under vows of celibacy or extremely disciplined and to deny participation in such events would for most people, be an outright lie and both Zoe and Louise fully understood that.

Louise glanced bravely back into his face as she prepared to offer an answer and come clean. "Yes I did once, when I was back in college." She finally replied after a short pause.

Zoe smiled with satisfaction as she nodded with approval.

Despite the tricky nature of the question posed, Louise had actually managed to answer it in a very smart and well put way as it admitted the truth but avoided the possible perception of her being a very easy lay. Quiet, conservative people, Zoe had discovered throughout the years, usually had a few very private secrets that they were often too scared to admit, wild things that they had done and participated in, or very raunchy things that people usually would not attribute to their personality or character and tonight it certainly seemed, Louise was no exception to that notion and discovery. Zoe continued to watch quietly as Louise took a deep breath and then prepared to challenge someone amongst the group, now it was actually Louise's turn to 'Truth or Dare' someone.

A sea of stranger's faces suddenly greeted Louise as she glanced around the group of twenty as she contemplated quietly, just exactly how she should actually proceed. Now, she had to actually ask someone to answer a question with a truth or to perform a dare and she was slightly nervous about actually doing so. There were a few easy choices that Louise could certainly make in that she could ask Zoe or Madeline or even one of the two men that the three women had met during dinner the question but it felt slightly wimpy to actually pick out someone she already knew, even though those were the people she actually felt the most comfortable with. Several handsome male faces sat amongst their group and one was particularly attractive to Louise as one of the men caught her attention and somehow actually retained it as she glanced back at him several times. Despite the cocktails that she had just consumed however, Louise wasn't quite brave enough yet, to actually challenge a complete stranger and especially not a very handsome one that she actually held an interest in as she suddenly caved in to timidity and then quickly turned to face Zoe.

"Truth or Dare Zoe?" Louise suddenly asked.

Zoe giggled as she gently shook her head. "Dare." She bravely replied as she quietly contemplated for a moment that Louise had flunked the courage challenge and had cowardly gone for the easier option by actually choosing her, it would perhaps take a few more cocktails to fix that, Zoe quietly decided.

"I dare you to stand in the middle of our circle and do a dance for thirty seconds." Louise said as her eyes glistened and shone with excitement.

Zoe laughed as she readily accepted the challenge. "Sure that'll be no problem at all." She smiled as she quickly stood up and then made her way towards the middle of the circle with absolutely no qualms at all as for Zoe it was an extremely easy challenge and hardly even a dare and something she usually did on a regular night out most weekends. Zoe quickly glanced round at the faces all around her and then started to dance in a slightly seductive, sensual manner as she quietly concluded that Louise was really a lightweight and that her dare actually, very accurately reflected her very conservative approach to life. She sat back down thirty seconds later and then smiled politely at Louise as she began to tease her. "Louise you really let me off lightly, I certainly wouldn't have let you off that easily."

"Wow Zoe, you really delivered." Louise replied as she smiled. "I loved those moves, totally amazing. I'm so impressed."

Zoe grinned.

The next challenge was of course Zoe's and she quietly glanced at each of the twenty faces that surrounded her as she considered for a few seconds, who she should actually challenge and what she would actually ask them when they responded. Unlike Louise, she was utterly determined not to actually take the easy option and ask either Madeline or Louise as she wanted a real challenge and a real laugh. A buff guy called Giovanni, who had actually been one of the two men that the three women had met whilst at dinner earlier that evening, was in their group of twenty and Zoe suddenly smiled at him as she prepared to challenge him head on.

"Truth or dare?" Zoe suddenly asked as she grinned at him mischievously.

"Truth." Giovanni quickly replied.

Zoe took a deep breath. "Have you ever been sexually intimate with a man?" She asked as she smiled sweetly at him, he'd obviously picked truth to avoid the possibility of having to perform a rough dare but Zoe was not going to let him off the hook that easily and as a result the question she posed to him, was actually extremely challenging on many different levels.

Laughter suddenly erupted from the two women on either side of Zoe as Louise started to crack up and Madeline almost choked upon the mouthful of cocktail that was actually inside her mouth. Zoe smiled at them both as she rejoiced in the difficult question she'd posed to Giovanni that was probably actually worse to answer than any dare she could have perhaps asked him to enact.

Giovanni smiled as he prepared to respond. "Actually, I've never really found the time to fit any men in." He replied. "I've always been far too busy with women."

Zoe immediately grinned at his response, it was a very clever reply. "Such a good answer. You've definitely played this game before, I can tell." She teased as she dissected his answer inside her mind. Zoe intuitively knew, for a man to admit that he'd participated in a homosexual activities, in front of group of attractive heterosexual females, would be almost like a death sentence to any potential romance he might have subsequently enjoyed and explored with them which was actually why she'd asked the question in the first place as it was one of the most daring questions she could have asked him. She fully understood that women were usually fearful of men cheating on them with other women and to add another dimension to that fear and the possibility of them perhaps straying with a man also, was just an issue that most heterosexual women would not actually like to face.

Once the laughter had finally died down, Giovanni proceeded with his challenge and the game of Truth and Dare continued into the night and even into the early hours of the following morning as people let their hair down, drank more alcohol and started to come out of their shells. Beer and cocktails were consumed abundantly as the Truth and Dare challenges became more and more adventurous as the night went on and finally, it came back around to Zoe's turn to challenge someone again.

Zoe quickly turned to face Madeline as she rapidly decided to capitalized upon Madeline's now more drunken state. "Truth or Dare Madeline?" She asked.

"Oh my gosh, I'm so not ready for this." Madeline replied as she gulped slightly nervously and then prepared for Zoe's challenge which she knew would definitely be absolutely outrageous in nature. "Dare." She replied as she turned back to face Zoe and then braced herself for the most outrageous challenge she could possibly think of.

Zoe giggled as she prepared to shock Madeline. "I dare you to show us on this bottle how you'd give oral sex for thirty seconds." She challenged as she quickly handed Madeline an empty beer bottle that had been lying on the top of an empty sun lounger nearby.

Madeline shook her head as she glanced at Zoe's face with a completely stunned expression. "Is that within the rules?" She asked as she suddenly turned to face the resort coordinator Mark and questioned him as she eagerly sought a means of escape from Zoe's dare.

"It's actually within the rules I'm afraid." Mark confirmed as he shrugged in a somewhat helpless manner. "It's not actually a sexual act upon another person."

Zoe giggled mischievously. "A beer bottle isn't actually another person Madeline." She quickly clarified.

Madeline quietly raised the bottle to her lips as Zoe almost rolled around on top of her sun lounger with laughter as she watched, to Zoe the dare was absolutely hilarious and to Madeline she'd been placed in an absolutely, awkward, totally tricky position. She was in a catch 22 situation, if she did not perform the dare properly, the guys in the group would perhaps think that she was not capable of orally pleasuring them and hence Madeline had absolutely no choice but to actually perform the dare to the very best of her capabilities as there was simply no way out of it and both Zoe and Madeline fully understood that.

Another final beseeching glance was cast back over towards Mark by Madeline and he gently shook his head as he sympathized with her obvious dilemma but there was nothing he could actually do to assist her. He had set the rules and Zoe's dare no matter how outrageous, certainly fell within those rules, even if only just.

She swallowed nervously and then ran her tongue and lips seductively around the top of the bottle as she began to comply fully with the dare that she'd actually been set. A look of sheer concentration was upon Madeline's face as each of the seconds was counted down by Zoe out loud as Madeline participated with her dare. Later on that evening, Madeline decided she would definitely have words with Zoe for such an awful and embarrassing dare but right now she had no choice but to actually participate. Madeline had been completely stunned by Zoe's question to Giovanni as she would never have had the nerve to actually ask an attractive male stranger a question like that but Zoe's challenge to Madeline herself had been even worse and had beaten Zoe's question in terms of outrageousness, hands down. Much to Madeline's relief however, the thirty seconds ended soon enough and then she quickly sat back down.

"I think we should call it a night." Mark suddenly suggested.

"Yeah, me too." Madeline immediately agreed as she quickly nodded in response.

The early hours of the morning by this point, had already been ushered in and as a result, it was actually starting to become quite chilly as most of the group agreed and decided to call it a night as they also opted to return to their suites. Despite the time however, Zoe could have easily continued playing for a few more hours as she had a ton of energy but both Madeline and Louise seemed tired and therefore she succumbed politely to their weariness as she quickly stood up and then prepared to return to her suite.

"Let's regroup tomorrow." Giovanni suggested.

"Sure." Zoe replied as she rapidly accepted his invitation. "When and where?"

"How about lunchtime in the dining hall, say at around two in the afternoon." Giovanni offered. "I don't think I'll wake up much before that as it's almost three now."

Zoe giggled. "Yes, we'll see you there. I think our group was like the very last group to stop playing Truth or Dare tonight, it looks like everyone else has already gone to bed." She mentioned as she grinned and glanced around the poolside as she quickly realized that it was now actually, completely deserted.

Giovanni nodded. "Steven, will you be coming for lunch?" He politely asked as he turned to face the other male that had actually eaten dinner with them earlier that night.

"Sure I'll come along." Steven replied as he nodded.

"Great, we'll see you then ladies." Giovanni confirmed as he charmingly flashed a grin at Zoe, Madeline and Louise. He suddenly leant forward towards Zoe's ear and then whispered a few words into it as he prepared to depart.

"Then perhaps we can discuss, your sexual experiences." Giovanni teased.

Zoe immediately giggled in response.

Due to the rather large amount of alcohol that had been consumed by the three women throughout the night, the walk back towards their suites was slightly rougher than the walk towards the poolside earlier that evening as they were all by now, quite drunk and much worse for wear. The pretty cocktails had certainly taken their toll upon each of their bodies and their minds and the results were indeed, far from pretty. Each of the three women, swayed and giggled with every step they took as they walked as they stumbled along the path, though Madeline still seemed to manage to retain her composure slightly more competently than the other two as she'd consumed the least amount of alcohol throughout the night. Despite Madeline's less drunken but definitely tipsy state however, she still managed to offer some assistance to Zoe as she gently held onto her arm in an attempt to support and steady her steps as they walked as she was slightly more steady on her feet than Zoe actually was.

Unfortunately, Zoe had almost actually landed on her butt in the middle of some bushes several times as she'd stumbled upon the edge of the pebbly pathway and Madeline had quickly leant out to help her get back up onto her feet and had helpfully retrieved her. Louise had giggled as she'd watched Zoe but had somehow managed to walk with slightly more proficiency without any further assistance, even though she'd swayed slightly with every step she'd actually taken as she'd managed to avoid any drunken collisions with the ground.

When the three women finally arrived back inside the reception area which seemed like almost twenty minutes later, due to their drunken saunter and stagger, they quickly parted ways as they agreed to meet up for breakfast or lunch the next morning. Inside each of their minds, they knew that breakfast would definitely not actually happen until at least midday, due to the late hour and their drunken state but as Zoe and Madeline bade Louise farewell affectionately they both somehow actually managed to hug her reasonably successfully, although Zoe's attempt at a hug was slightly less well coordinated than Madeline's was and was more like a lurch and grab than a hug.

The remaining walk towards Zoe and Madeline's suite was full of antics as the two women giggled and held each other up and once they finally arrived outside their suite door, Madeline quickly opened it as she fished her keycard out of her bag and then held it up against the small, white panel on the wall directly next to it. A few seconds later, the door politely swished open and then the two women quickly stepped inside their suite as they giggled, appreciative and grateful that they'd actually managed to arrive back there, in one piece. Giggles echoed out all around the lounge as they entered inside and discussed the night they had just spent together.

"Have you enjoyed yourself so far Madeline?" Zoe asked as she attempted to be slight more serious for a moment, though she was really far too drunk to even attempt to hold a very long, serious conversation at that precise moment in time and she definitely knew it.

Madeline nodded. "Yeah, I'm really having fun." She replied. "So far, it's been one of the most pleasant activities you've asked me to attend and I'm actually quite enjoying it. Except the bottle thing, I didn't really enjoy that."

"Good." Zoe murmured in response as she smiled. "I'd absolutely hate it if I'd dragged you along to a place that you totally hated, for a whole entire week. You've spent money on this trip and I really want you to enjoy it Madeline." She continued as she swayed back and forth.

Madeline giggled as she started to help Zoe enter inside her bedroom and politely assisted her as she lay Zoe gently down upon her bed. "Are you alright Zoe?" She asked as she gently covered her body with the duvet and then removed her shoes.

"I's just fine Madeline." Zoe replied as she smiled. "Very fine. Just like Giovanni."

Madeline giggled. "Your speech is slightly slurred Zoe, you really drank a lot." She teased as she gently tied Zoe's hair back from her face with a loose hairband.

"I do believe I did." Zoe joked as she snuggled further down inside the duvet as she prepared to sleep. "And tomorrow, I'll probably really drink, a whole lot more." She mentioned as she giggled.

Madeline grinned as she walked towards the door of the bedroom and then switched of the light. "Goodnight Zoe." She called out.

"Goodnight Madeline." Zoe murmured as she closed her eyes.

"Sweet dreams." Madeline muttered as she left Zoe's bedroom and then walked towards her own. "What a night." She quietly concluded as she gently shook her head.

Surprisingly, despite the very late night and the women's drunken state, the next morning the two women woke up around noon and quickly prepared themselves for either, a very late breakfast or a quite early lunch. When they arrived inside the dining hall which was where they were actually supposed to meet Louise who was actually, already there, they could very clearly see that breakfast was in fact over but as they sat down together at a table, the three women rapidly adjusted their expectations as they prepared to eat and enjoy a very early lunch. Neither of the two men were actually around but for the three women that was perfectly fine as they were all still recovering from the previous night as they sipped on cups of dark, black, strong coffee and quickly attempted to sober themselves up.

According to what the three women had been told by the various resort coordinators that they had met so far, the first weekend they were at the resort, they were pretty much free to pick their own activities to participate in as they wished to as the scheduled love matching activities would not actually begin until the following Monday morning which meant, there was no rush to go anywhere at all. The love matching activities that the resort or more specifically that the resort computer arranged and organized, were referred to by the coordinators as pairing activities but what exactly the pairing activities entailed, none of the women was actually sure yet.

Due to the freeness of their schedule for that day, Zoe had actually mentioned to the other two women the previous night, that she would actually like to go horse riding before they were due to meet Giovanni and Steven, if time actually permitted. Both Madeline and Louise had actually agreed to accompany her on her very first horse ride and later that afternoon, the three women had decided, they would actually go snorkeling and there were also some mini aqua bikes that they all definitely wanted to try out but they weren't entirely sure that they would actually have time to do all those things in one afternoon.

"Let's just do whatever we can fit in." Zoe suggested as she sat at a table with Madeline and Louise as they all ate their lunch. "And whatever we don't actually get round to doing to today, we can always do tomorrow."

Louise and Madeline nodded in agreement.

Fortunately, earlier that morning, all three women had actually dressed themselves in quite casual clothing which actually suited the activities they had planned to engage in that day. Zoe had actually mentioned her plans to them the night before and hence all three women had been prepared and had dressed appropriately for the very physical activities that lay ahead. They definitely couldn't go horse riding in high heels, tight dresses or miniskirts and that was one thing they had all been extremely certain about as they'd dressed earlier that morning.

Even though Zoe and Madeline hadn't technically come along to the resort with Louise, neither woman actually minded her tagging along with them and joining them in whatever activities they wanted to participate in as she seemed easy to get along with, quite

177

funny at times and a very decent conversationalist. The two women had by now between themselves, already actually discussed Louise and agreed earlier that morning that she certainly seemed pleasant enough to hang out with and even seemed to be a quite likable female companion. On her part, Louise seemed to appreciate the woman's invitations and she had welcomed Zoe and Madeline's suggestions with very open arms as she'd reciprocated their hands of friendship and embraced them accordingly.

Zoe had ultimately been pleasantly surprised by Louise's interest in them both as when she'd initially planned to come on her vacation to find true love, she hadn't actually expected to make any female friends at the resort, at the same time. Female friendships could so often be an absolute minefield and Zoe fully understood that as women could be very two faced and back stabbing and at times, they would even actually engage in jealous rivalries that were as destructive as an earthquake in terms of the impact they actually inflicted upon the lives of those around them. Louise however, seemed slightly different in that she was quite soft and gentle and she appeared to be very innocent in nature and was perhaps what one might even call, slightly naive and hence her offer of friendship was immediately accepted and even deemed to be quite a positive addition to Zoe's initial expectations surrounding her trip. At times, a female friend could be even more helpful than a lover and could provide a form of support, shoulder to cry on and arm to lean on, throughout the various difficulties and trials of life and Zoe fully appreciated that.

SIMULATIONS

Once the three women arrived inside the courtyard that actually housed the riding stables which was situated at the very rear of the huge, white, main resort building, they quickly found and then approached a riding instructor who it seemed was actually in charge and extremely cooperative. Much like the animals she was assigned to tend to, she had a slightly horsey, boyish appearance and smelt very much like the creatures she was actually responsible for as the horsey aroma that emanated from her body delicately floated into each of their nostrils as they drew closer.

The three women were quickly attended to as she suddenly called out to a stableboy and he rapidly brought out three horses and then tied each one up inside the courtyard. Each of the three animals had dark brown, leather saddles neatly strapped onto their backs and bridals tacked firmly to their heads as the three women glanced at them slightly nervously and then prepared to approach them. Every horse varied in terms of size and appearance and looked quite unique as the women walked towards each one and then prepared to actually mount and ride them.

One horse had a black mane and tail and dark brown hair and was referred to by the riding instructor, who introduced herself as Katy as a Bay, whilst another had black and white rosette patterns across its body and that horse was referred to as a Piebald and those two horses looked quite calm but the third horse was completely different, not only in appearance but also in temperament. The third and final horse from the three, was a speckled grey color and that particular horse appeared to be quite highly strung and a lot more restless than the other two as it danced around on the spot impatiently, almost as if it couldn't actually wait to be mounted and ridden.

Before the three women attempted to mount each of the three horses, the riding instructor had the stableboy bring out a fourth horse which he then tied up at the very top of the courtyard that it quickly transpired, was actually going to be the horse that Katy would actually ride herself. Each of the three women watched Katy closely as she started to mount her horse and then Zoe quickly attempted to mimic her movements and follow her instructions as she also attempted to mount the horse directly in front of her.

Zoe had been given the grey, speckled, restless horse that was definitely the most excitable amongst the three and she giggled with excitement as she placed her foot inside one of the stirrups that hung down from the saddle and then tried to lift her body up onto the horse's back. Her foot suddenly slipped out of the stirrup however as the horse suddenly, to Zoe's complete surprise, actually moved forward without any warning at all and she quickly landed upon the ground directly on her butt. Madeline and Louise laughed as they watched Zoe and her frustrating predicament.

"It's a lot more tricky than it looks." Zoe explained as she shrugged and then started to pick herself up of the ground. "I didn't know the horse was actually going to move forward when I actually tried to get on it." She explained. "I've never even ridden a horse before in my entire life. Okay wise guys, let's see you two do any better." Zoe immediately challenged them as she glanced at Madeline and Louise and then grinned.

Katy smiled and then quickly started to dismount the horse's back she was seated upon. "I'll come and give you ladies a hand." She offered politely.

Madeline smiled as she placed her foot inside one of the stirrups and then tried to mount the horse directly in front of her. Her foot rapidly ended up twisted up inside the metal and leather stirrup and she immediately began to laugh. "Okay, okay I admit it, it really is much harder than it looks." She quickly conceded.

Zoe laughed. "See Madeline, you're no better at it than I am." She teased.

"Well, at least I didn't end up on my butt." Madeline joked playfully. "So I might be ever so slightly better at it than you are."

Zoe giggled.

At that precise moment, suddenly Louise decided to actually surprise everyone as she quickly placed her foot inside one of the stirrups and then lifted her body up onto the horses back and swung her other leg over the saddle within a matter of seconds. The other two women, Zoe and Madeline glanced at her face suspiciously as they quietly watched her mount the bay, black and brown horse in front of her with ease.

"You've definitely done this before." Zoe quickly pointed out.

Louise nodded as she smiled. "Okay, okay I have." She replied. "I didn't grow up in the city like you all did remember, I'm a country girl born and raised and I've actually ridden horses before, quite a few times."

Katy smiled. "Right, let's get the rest of you ladies mounted." She insisted as she walked over towards Zoe.

Zoe smiled as she welcomed the riding instructor's assistance. "Is it always this hard at first?" She enquired.

"Yes, it can be, noone's a natural horse rider." Katy explained as she nodded. "It takes some people a while to get used to riding horses and some people slightly longer than others. My first time was really awful, I actually got thrown of a horse but just before that happened, the horse actually carted me all over paddock and I was absolutely terrified."

Zoe smiled as Katy quickly pushed her body upwards towards the saddle and within a few seconds she was safely seated inside it. "Wow, that's a relief." She said as she grinned at Katy. "You made that so much easier, thank you so much."

Katy smiled. "Right, now that you're sorted, let's get you mounted." She insisted as she quickly turned to face Madeline and the horse she was situated beside. "Or we'll never actually get to go out on our ride today."

Madeline smiled and nodded.

In a matter of just a few more minutes, all three women and the riding instructor were successfully mounted as the four women prepared to move the horses forward and actually leave the courtyard. Louise had been instructed to stay at the very rear of the group, since she was a more experienced and advanced rider than either Madeline or Zoe were as the riding instructor felt that course of action would be safer for everyone, just in case any of the horses became spooked or perhaps even decided to try and bolt. The pathway that led towards the hills, where the cross country ride was due to commence, was quite clear as the four horses started to make their way along it and the three women began to relax as they moved forward as they started to enjoy themselves and Zoe's very first ever, horse riding experience.

Due to the fact that Zoe's meeting with Giovanni had actually been scheduled for two that afternoon, that meant she still had at least an hour in which to enjoy her ride and that was apparently the time it took to venture out on the cross country ride that Katy had planned for the three. On their way along the path which led to the hills, at the very beginning of it as they rode along on top of their horses, the three vacationers suddenly noticed Thomas walking along another path nearby that actually ran parallel to their route, all alone. He almost looked quite lonely as he quietly walked along the path very much absorbed in his own thoughts as Zoe glanced at him thoughtfully.

Zoe called out to Madeline as she watched him, who was situated upon the horse directly behind her. "Do you think they'll actually be able to match Thomas up with someone?" She asked. "I mean he really is such a S.U.P. (Socially Unacceptable Person), it's hard to imagine that actually happening."

Madeline called back out to her as she replied. "I hope so, he's just a bit dorky that's all, there's bound to be someone out there that likes him." She insisted.

"Madeline, don't you even dare consider dating him, not even for a minute, this is not a charity, we paid good money to find you someone extremely buff." Zoe quickly returned as she politely warned Madeline very sternly against even entertaining thoughts of considering Thomas as a potential suitor.

"Zoe, you're so wrong!" Madeline replied as she started to laugh. "I wasn't saying that I was going to date him, just that someone else probably would."

Zoe and Louise laughed.

"Just don't even dare." Zoe reiterated. "We're here to find you someone really buff and someone that you really like okay."

Madeline nodded.

Later that afternoon, once the horse ride had ended, the three women met Giovanni and Steven inside the dining hall and then invited them both to come along to the beach with them. The two men immediately accepted their invitation and as the five walked towards the beach, they prepared enthusiastically for a snorkel below the waves. Beautiful coral reefs sat just underneath the surface of the turquoise, aqua green water and they quickly found an instructor by the beach who they'd been advised to actually see, before they actually entered inside the water.

The two men immediately approached the snorkel instructor to collect some snorkel gear as Zoe, Madeline and Louise hung back slightly and conversed amongst themselves. A buff looking man suddenly appeared directly in front of them as he crossed the golden, sandy beach just in front of the three women and Zoe immediately stopped talking and then stared at him as she quickly began to follow him.

Madeline giggled and then gently grabbed Zoe's arm to stop her. "Where are you going Zoe?" She asked in a playful manner. "They're going to start matching us up with potential dates tomorrow and you already have two men here. You're in such a rush. Can't you wait?" Madeline teased.

"My body is telling me that he is very scientifically buff." Zoe quickly pointed out as she pointed a finger towards him. "And that means, he'd be a great match for me. Besides, there's three women here and only two guys so that means, we need another male volunteer."

"I think the resort's love matches might be slightly superior to your body's physical urges." Madeline insisted.

"Can't I just flirt a little, just for fun?" Zoe pleaded.

"Zoe you are absolutely insatiable." Madeline replied as she gently shook her head.

Once the snorkel gear had been collected and the instructor had imparted some precise, clear instructions to the group, the snorkel session went ahead with only the two men and three women as Zoe's last minute attempts to secure another male to join the group, rapidly fell flat on their face. Madeline just wasn't playing ball and she wasn't even going to allow Zoe to flirt with any random males that crossed their path and hence their group for now had to pretty much remain as it was. The snorkel session intrigued Zoe for several reasons, one being that she'd never actually snorkeled in her entire life before and since none of the other four had either, it was pretty much a first time for all five in their group.

Fortunately, there were no major delays, accidents or mishaps as the three women and two men eagerly indulged and participated in an activity they would normally never have even dreamed of trying before and when the evening approached, the five quickly found a bar on the beach that had a small grill outlet just beside it and then made themselves at home. Brightly colored cocktails, bottles of beer and large bamboo platters filled with marinated, spicy meats and fish were accompanied by a vast array of breads, slices of plantain and crispy fries as they ordered food and drink to their heart's delight. Edible consumables were scattered across the bamboo table beside them as the five ate and drank until they had, had their fill as the sun began to set and darkness spread out across the resort and engulfed each of their physical forms.

When they'd actually eaten as much as they could possibly eat, the five then made their way back towards the poolside bar, just beside the resort as they prepared to relax for the rest of the evening. A man called Callum that they'd actually met at the bar the evening before, who had been in their Truth or Dare group, joined them at the bar and Zoe's mind was finally at peace as another handsome looking man finally appeared and evened up their numbers. In Zoe's mind, Giovanni was actually buff enough for her and both Steven and Callum were certainly both attractive enough for Madeline and Louise, if they were actually at all interested in either of the two men and that gave her a tremendous sense of peace as she prepared to enjoy her evening and welcomed Callum into their midst. Her first weekend at the Love Colony as far as Zoe was concerned had already been a tremendous success as all three women now definitely had extremely sufficient eye candy to accompany their cocktails.

On their way towards the poolside bar, all five had quickly stopped off at their suites to freshen up as snorkeling and sea water certainly weren't the cleanest or tidiest of activities and nor had the horse-riding been that the women had participated in, earlier that afternoon. The three women's bodies had smelt of horses and sea water and their hair had even looked slightly draggled and wiry and had been in desperate need of a good wash and style. Each of the three women and the two men had freshened up, showered, changed and then tidied up their hair which had been in dire need of some attention, before they had actually presented themselves to each other once more as they'd met again beside the bar that evening.

Fortunately when the three women arrived, the two men had already made their way there and had even been waiting for them as they'd approached the poolside bar. Zoe had smiled happily as she'd walked towards the bar and the two men with Madeline and Louise in tow as soon as she'd noticed Giovanni and Steven right next to it. Men at the love resort, were it seemed, extremely punctual and didn't seem to like to keep a woman waiting, she'd mused thoughtfully as she'd walked towards them. Callum had quickly joined the group, just after the three women had actually arrived and for Zoe that had actually been quite a relief as technically, she'd already started to strike up a flirtatious interest in Giovanni that she'd felt quite curious about pursuing further and she'd been slightly worried about Madeline and Louise being slightly bored. They both, in Zoe's mind definitely needed the company of a flirtatious male also with which to pleasantly adorn their evening with and Callum was therefore, a very welcome addition to their group.

Alcoholic drinks were quickly ordered as the six began to discuss the love resort amongst themselves and the matching activities it had been planned would commence the very next morning with excitement and in eager anticipation. Noone amongst the group of six had as yet made any committed, romantic bonds with anyone else really and hence they all felt quite free to discuss their singleness and the potential love matches they might actually make whilst at the resort as they teased each other gently about what might actually occur, the very next day.

"What do you guys think about the computer matching? Do you really trust a computer to select and judge who is the right match for you, more than you trust yourself?" Zoe asked the other five playfully as she suddenly began to play devil's advocate.

"Is a computer really more competent than our own human judgment regarding our emotional decisions? That's actually a very interesting question you've posed Zoe."

Madeline mentioned as she thought about Zoe's question further for a moment.

"I'm not entirely sure but I do know one thing, my judgment right about now is, extremely hot." Giovanni replied playfully as he flirtatiously ran a finger gently down the side of one of Zoe's naked arms provocatively.

Zoe giggled at his touch which was definitely sensual and extremely seductive. "Well, I might just have to see how hot your engine really actually is one of these nights." She teased. "And take your love machine out for a test drive."

"What happens if they actually match us with someone we are not actually attracted to? What should we do then?" Louise suddenly asked as the obvious issue of physical attraction quickly flashed through her mind.

"I hope I get matched up with you Louise because I'm definitely attracted to you." Steven immediately volunteered. "And I'd really like to get to know you much better, in a quite personal way."

Zoe giggled.

Giovanni suddenly raised his glass in the air as he toasted to Steven's confession of adoration and attraction. "Here's hoping the computer agrees with our choices." He announced.

Zoe giggled.

"I guess Louise, we would try to get to know whoever they've suggested to us and see if there's a love connection, after all we did pay good money for the love matching services they offer here right?" Madeline rationalized as she attempted to answer Louise's question in a slightly more serious manner.

"Please, if I don't like someone, I'm definitely not dating them." Zoe mentioned as she abruptly interrupted Madeline's attempt at logical reasoning. "If that happens, I'll be going along with my own choices and my own options. You're just way too logical sometimes Madeline and love isn't a purely rational matter, sometimes it's extremely emotional and sexual chemistry isn't even remotely logical in any capacity at all."

Louise giggled.

An hour rapidly passed by as the group continued to discuss the love resort and the various matching activities that were due to commence the next morning as they freely, eagerly consumed some more sparkling, brightly colored cocktails and chilled bottles of beer, right next to the poolside. Each vacationer had actually been provided with an electronic journal that had a vacation schedule inside it when they'd first arrived, which notified them regarding the activities they were due to attend and where those activities would actually be held and the three women had actually brought their electronic journals along with them that evening. Their electronic journals had been neatly tucked away inside each of their handbags and they quickly plucked them out and checked them, whilst they discussed the resort's schedule for the next day.

Unlike the Saturday evening, when the six had initially arrived at the resort, the poolside bar was actually much quieter on the Sunday evening and had significantly less attendees than the previous night. Due to that quietness and the lack of any organized activities, Zoe suddenly started to feel slightly bored as she quickly glanced around and then came up with a more adventurous suggestion to liven up the group's Sunday night. The group definitely needed some form of entertainment that could possibly verge upon being remotely interesting and there was indeed something that had actually sprung to the forefront of Zoe's mind that she certainly felt, could adequately satisfy that need.

Tipsiness by that point, had actually set in amongst the group as quite a few alcoholic beverages had actually been consumed but Zoe's suggestion she knew, would probably require a bravery and daring that the group might not be drunk enough to actually possess yet.   Regardless of the risky nature of her suggestion, Zoe took a deep breath as she prepared to dive straight into the depths of naughtiness and fully embrace her wild side, without any reservations at all.

"I think we should all sneak into the Holographic Bonking Room Suite and see if we can have a go."   Zoe playfully suggested as she released her thoughts to the rest of the group, which she quickly realized could no longer actually be retrieved once they were actually spoken.

"Do you think we'll get in trouble if we get caught inside there?" Madeline asked.

Zoe giggled. "I don't know but don't be so risk averse Madeline. You have to live a little sometimes and take a few risks. Being scared never gets you anywhere in life." She advised.

"You have to push the limits of what is allowed or acceptable behavior sometimes, in order to actually find hidden depths of adventure in life."

"I guess, I'm not really a rule breaker." Madeline explained. "I've never really been brave about those kinds of things."

"And that's why I'm here." Zoe insisted as she grinned. "To help you take life just a little bit less seriously."

Madeline smiled.

Louise glanced at both women with a curious expression upon her face as she shrugged as she had absolutely no idea at all what the two women were actually discussing. "What's the Holographic Bonking Room Suite?" She asked.

Zoe rapidly began to provide an explanation to her, in a very low tone of voice as she quickly motioned towards the three men and Louise and encouraged them to gather more closely around her. "It's a room where they check your holographic sexual compatibility with your potential love matches." She explained. "It's actually quite close to our suite."

"Apparently, the resort computer system can holographically simulate sexual intimacy between couples." Madeline added. "And that's the room where that actually happens."

Giovanni smiled as he listened. "Wow, high tech bonking, how advanced." He teased.

Steven and Callum both smirked as they listened.

"Do you think it's actually accurate?" Louise enquired.

"Well, we can soon find out." Zoe replied as she quickly glanced at Giovanni with a slightly seductive, mischievous expression plastered across her face. She raised her eyebrows suggestively at Giovanni and then smiled as she invited him seductively not just to the holographic bonking room suite but also to a sexual exploration within their own imaginations. "I'm game if you are?" Zoe invited.

"I'm in." Giovanni quickly confirmed as he immediately responded positively to Zoe's suggestive tone and facial expressions.

Everyone laughed as they watched and listened to their flirtatious exchange.

Due to the need for gentle persuasion, Zoe gently held onto Madeline's arm as she started to lead her back towards the main resort building. The rest of the group followed them both, just a couple of steps behind and as they walked and quietly conversed amongst themselves. An external pathway, just outside the resort which was made of small white pebbles, clinked as they walked along it and Louise started to actually sway slightly with every step she took. Zoe suddenly noticed her instability as she smiled, Louise had drunk quite a few cocktails that evening and was now quite tipsy and even slightly unsteady as a result.

Louise it appeared, actually had quite a low tolerance level when it came to alcohol consumption and that was something Zoe was rapidly starting to notice. She was a lightweight when it came to drinking, probably due to her countryside background, Zoe quickly assumed and whilst she might be great with horses, holding her liquor was certainly it appeared, a slightly more tricky challenge for her to handle. Both Zoe and Madeline had actually spent their entire lives in the city and since they'd grown up around bars, parties and lots of alcohol, they'd partied hard throughout most of their adult college life and even in the years beyond it. Due to their more adventurous, city lifestyles, they were therefore much more accustomed to consuming large amounts of alcohol on a very regular basis and it definitely showed. Their higher tolerance levels meant that the two women could actually consume quite a lot of alcohol before they actually hit their drunk and disorderly thresholds and became totally and utterly smashed and Zoe could now clearly see the difference between the three women's lifestyles almost immediately.

Once they entered inside the main resort building which very fortunately, was fairly quiet as it was well past eleven, Zoe quickly led the group along the hallway which led towards the Cuddle Wing. Noone dared to speak a word as they walked, through fear that they might attract unnecessary or undesirable attention or alert someone to their presence and five minutes later as the group of six gathered outside the door of the Holographic Bonking Room Suite, Zoe smiled as they prepared to actually open the door and enter inside the room that lay just beyond it.

A very mysterious room lurked quietly behind the door that separated them and Zoe quickly leant forward as she attempted to push it open but the door very stubbornly at first, remained firmly shut. Just a few seconds later however, Zoe to her delight, suddenly found a small, white panel just beside the door which she then pressed and the door in front of them all, rapidly swished open. Apparently, the door wasn't actually locked and it quickly transpired that the room wasn't always manned as the six crept inside it and found it completely devoid of any human life forms.

Zoe giggled. "This is so exciting." She remarked as she quickly glanced at Madeline, who she rapidly noticed actually had a quite worried expression upon her face.

"Do you think it's actually accurate?" Louise whispered as she presented a more serious question to both Zoe and Madeline, who both seemed to know slightly more about this strange room than she did.

Zoe shrugged. "Who knows? Who cares?" She teased. "Perhaps they use our profiles and whatever we've detailed inside them to build complex holographic models that can predict our sexual inclinations and our sexual behavior." She suggested.

"Yes, we did have to fill in rather a lot of information before we actually arrived and the profiles they compiled did seem to be quite extensive. That is a possibility." Madeline agreed.

"Whatever they did or didn't do, do we actually care?" Zoe asked as she grinned. "This is going to be so much fun, it doesn't really actually matter how accurate it is. I don't think we can stay in here very long though, or we might get caught, so we better be quick." She mentioned.

Madeline immediately nodded in response. "Yes, we better be quick in here Zoe." She agreed.

A huge space greeted the women and men which they quietly began to creep around as they began to inspect every inch of the interior of the Holographic Bonking Room Suite. Situated at one end of the room, there was a huge computer desk and large, wafer thin screen on top of the desk and as soon as Zoe noticed the pieces of equipment, she quickly rushed over towards them. Unlike the computer systems usually found inside an office, this computer system was much larger and was actually situated just underneath the desk, upon a white glossy shelf. Each of the walls inside the room was a glossy, shiny white just like the hallways outside it but besides the large computer screen and the desk that it sat upon, there wasn't much else to actually see inside the room at all.

Zoe giggled as she sat quickly down behind the desk and then prepared to access the computer. "Who should we do first?" She asked as a naughty, mischievous grin suddenly spread out across her face. Zoe glanced at Louise and smiled. "Louise would you like to go first?"

Louise quickly shook her head as a totally horrified expression crossed her face. "No not me, I'm a bit shy." She quickly clarified.

"Okay, since there are no other volunteers, I'll go first." Zoe politely offered as she smiled. "After all, it was actually my idea to come inside here in the first place and therefore it is only fitting really that I should actually take the plunge first."

Madeline nodded enthusiastically, anxious to avoid actually being the first person to bonk holographically in front of all the current occupants inside the room. "Sure Zoe. You can go first and second and even third and fourth if you like." She teased as she grinned.

Zoe laughed as she touched the screen directly in front of her and it suddenly lit up, she then quickly began to navigate her way around the system. "I think I should be able to find our profiles on here." She mentioned as she suddenly found a way to access her own profile and it suddenly displayed upon the screen directly in front of her.

"Do you think we should really be in here Zoe?" Madeline asked nervously as she quickly glanced at the door.

"What would you rather be doing right now Madeline, sleeping inside our suite?" Zoe replied slightly sarcastically. "If they catch us, we'll get booted out of the room and that's it, there's not much else they can actually do, the door was unlocked and nobody said we couldn't actually come in here."

Louise nodded her head in response. "True." She agreed.

Once Zoe found Giovanni's profile, which took her just a matter of seconds, she quickly loaded both profile's up into the holographic simulation program and within seconds, two holograms of Zoe and Giovanni actually suddenly appeared in the very center of the room. Unlike their current real human state however, their holographic forms were actually only dressed in their underwear. A large, holographic king-size bed was situated directly behind the two and as the two holograms started to touch and caress each other, Zoe began to giggle.

"Oh my word Giovanni, you're so passionate." Zoe mentioned as she stared at the two holographic images in front of her.

Giovanni started to laugh as he began to watch the two holograms in front of them as they turned and walked towards the large bed that was situated directly behind them. "Do you think that we'll actually do it?" He asked.

Zoe nodded very decisively. "I think they definitely will, even though we definitely haven't, yet." She teased as she winked at him flirtatiously.

Everyone inside the room suddenly stared at the bed as the two holograms climbed on top of it and then quickly snuggled down underneath the duvet. The occupants of the room held their breath as they watched quietly as curiosity and intrigue filled their minds and disbelief tugged away at their thoughts. Two holographic forms were actually just about to make love to each other in a holographic capacity in the very same room that they were actually standing in and the capabilities of the technology intrigued them and it intrigued them even more that the holographic forms actually represented two human beings that were actually standing inside the same room at that precise moment in time.

Giovanni started to laugh as he watched himself make love to Zoe frantically. "It looks very realistic." He observed.

Zoe laughed.

"Now that certainly looks like a very good love match to me." Giovanni insisted as he suddenly turned round to face Zoe and smiled.

Zoe nodded in agreement and then turned to face Madeline. "I say you should go next Madeline." She suggested.

Madeline's amused expression, suddenly began to change as she rapidly began to panic. "Me, why me and with who?" She asked.

"Let's see what you and Thomas would be like." Zoe quickly suggested as a huge grin rapidly spread out across her face.

"You wouldn't dare." Madeline replied.

"Come on Madeline, it's not actually real. Let's just see for a laugh." Zoe quickly reassured her.

Madeline nodded in defeat as she succumbed to Zoe's request. "Okay, okay but only for a minute, no make that thirty seconds." She insisted.

Zoe giggled as she stopped the current holographic simulation and then quickly loaded up Madeline and Thomas's profiles onto the screen directly in front of her. "Ready?" She asked Madeline.

Madeline nodded in response. "I'm as ready as I'll ever possibly be I guess." She replied.

In a matter of seconds, Zoe and Giovanni's holographic forms completely disappeared and then both Madeline and Thomas appeared in the very center of the room in holographic forms, just a few seconds later. Both were dressed in just their underwear as Zoe and Giovanni had been and Zoe immediately started to giggle as soon as she actually caught sight of them both. Very strangely, Thomas started to clear his throat with a series of small coughs, just as he had done at the dinner table the evening before and Zoe smirked as she watched his holographic form approach Madeline's. Just a few seconds later, his holographic form actually led

Madeline quite masterfully over towards the holographic bed nearby and Zoe grinned.

"Now we about to see Thomas in action." Zoe teased playfully. "And find out what Thomas's love engine is like. You never know Madeline, he could really take you to the heights of ecstasy sexually and rock your world. He might actually be an amazing lover, sometimes that does actually happen you know." She teased. "The quiet, strange, dorky ones at times, often provide very deep, sensual depths of pleasure."

Louise almost fell onto the floor in stitches as she watched the two holographic forms in front of her and listened to Zoe speak. "I mean seriously, this is hilarious. Thomas looks deadly serious." She observed as a series of giggles continued to escape from her lips. "And he actually seems quite masterful and very sexually assertive. I'm actually quite surprised."

Zoe grinned. "He does, doesn't he. I say he gets a thousand points for effort, manners and concentration." She joked. "Though he definitely gets a deduction of 200 points for the nervous coughs as those just aren't attractive at all."

Giovanni, Steven and Callum laughed as they watched and listened.

"This is so funny Madeline." Zoe added. "I just can't stop laughing, my stomach is even beginning to hurt."

The movement between the two holographic images suddenly intensified as they entered inside the duvet and then Thomas began to penetrate Madeline's holographic form. Each of the six inside the room watched quietly as the duvet moved up and down rapidly in front of them as he began to make love to Madeline and wild grunts started to tumble out of his mouth. An occasional nervous cough emanated from his form as Thomas cleared his throat now and again and Zoe laughed hysterically as she watched and listened.

"Dam, Thomas even does those little cough like things when he's screwing." She observed. "How weird is that and what's that grunting noise he's making too, it's a bit strange."

Madeline suddenly felt slightly embarrassed as she quickly turned to face Zoe and then urged her to stop the holographic simulation.

"Right, that's enough now Zoe, the thirty seconds is up." She gently reminded her.

Zoe nodded and smiled. "Louise pick a man or I'll pick one for you." She insisted as she rapidly diverted everyone's attention away from Madeline and Thomas and towards Louise. Zoe knew Madeline was much softer than she was and a lot more sensitive and she had absolutely no desire to damage her emotionally at all. She'd had her cheap laughs and now it was over and now it was, Louise's turn. "And if I pick one for you, you might not actually enjoy the results or the view." Zoe quickly warned as she touched the screen in front of her again to stop the current holographic simulation on display.

"You pick one." Louise replied as she giggled. "Then I can just blame you for how disgusting it looks, if it looks awful."

Zoe laughed. "Okay, should I pick Thomas again or Steven?" She asked playfully.

"I'll volunteer." Steven quickly offered as he verbally leapt into the conversation between the two women. "Thomas is not getting his hands on Louise whilst I'm around, not even in a holographic capacity." He insisted as he stepped in decisively.

Zoe smiled. "Right you two, just give me a few seconds and I'll have you up and holographically bonking in no time." She clarified as she considered quietly for a moment, just how cute it actually was and even slightly noble that Steven had actually offered himself up to potential ridicule, just to impress Louise. Zoe could certainly see that Steven definitely had the hots for Louise as his actions clearly squashed any doubts that Louise might have inside her mind regarding his interest, clarity could at times be a good thing but usually that was only preferable when that interest was indeed, mutual.

In a matter of seconds, Zoe had loaded up the two required profiles into the simulation program and the two holographic forms suddenly appeared in front of the six as both Louise and Steven smiled slightly nervously. Despite their slight obvious discomfort, Zoe immediately started to giggle as she watched the holographic forms start to interact with each other in a very sensual and intimate manner. For Zoe, the holographic imagery wasn't really a huge deal and was simply like playing a game upon a games console and the fact that the holographic images were in their actual likeness, didn't actually bother her at all as the entertainment such holographic forms provided, amused her no end.

"Wow, look at your face Louise, you look so focused and Steven you look so determined." Zoe squealed as she quickly pointed towards the holographic forms in front of them all and laughed.

"I think we better get out of here Zoe." Madeline suddenly urged as she glanced at the door once more with an extremely nervous expression upon her face. "Someone could come in at any time and find us all here."

Zoe quickly nodded as she quietly concluded that Madeline was actually right, it was indeed time to leave. "Wow, this has certainly been a night to remember." She remarked as she quickly shut the computer system down and the two holographic forms rapidly faded away until they both completely disappeared altogether.

Madeline quickly started to usher everyone out of the room. "We'd better go." She insisted in a mature, sensible manner.

Steven walked towards the door next to Louise and then suddenly paused as he turned to face her. "I really hope they match us tomorrow." He stated in a very sincere tone.

Louise smiled. "I hope so too." She replied as she appreciatively accepted the expression of an emotional attachment that she could clearly see had started to form between them both. Louise was gently starting to warm up to Steven's affections and even though he wasn't strictly her usual type, in some ways, he actually seemed to be quite sweet.

Once the six exited the Holographic Bonking Room Suite, they quickly separated as the next morning they all knew, they had a quite early start. The coordinator Mark, who they had all met on the Saturday night, had very clearly explained to them that the resort pairing activities would actually start on the Monday morning, well before lunchtime at ten and that meant, if they actually wanted to attend, there would be no late night drinking sessions and late night bedtimes on the Sunday night beforehand.

There were no long goodbyes as the group rapidly dispersed and then rushed off towards their suites. Everyone of the six was very much aware that the night had indeed already started to enter into the world and hence they knew that they really had to hurry, if they all actually wanted to sleep that night on the right side of midnight. Zoe and Madeline entered inside their suite, just a few minutes later as since their suite was actually the closest to the room they had actually just left, it took very little time to actually arrive there and then they quickly prepared to sleep as they discussed what might actually happen the next morning, filled with excitement and intrigue.

When the next morning arrived, both Zoe and Madeline woke up slightly worse for wear as they had slept slightly later than they'd originally planned to the night before and then they rushed through showers and breakfast and straight afterwards wandered down towards the meeting point that they had been instructed by Mark to attend. Both vacationers had their personal electronic journals with them which contained a daily schedule that notified them of not only what they were actually supposed to do that day but also the pairing activities they were actually supposed to participate in which they'd been given when they'd first arrived at the resort. Very intricate and precise details were held inside each of the small electronic devices that were slightly larger than a phone and slightly smaller than the screen of a netbook computer. Clear instructions denoted exactly when each pairing activity would actually occur and where they would actually start from, throughout the entire week of their vacation and Zoe had been extremely impressed by the systematic organization that the resort seemed to have in place.

Fortunately, when they arrived at the prearranged meeting point which was just beside the poolside, the coordinator Mark was already there and the two women greeted him politely as soon as they approached him. Due to their escapade the previous night and their failure to actually get up the very first time their alarm clocks had actually gone off, the two women were running slightly later than everyone else in their pairing group and hence they were actually the last to arrive. Louise had actually managed to turn up just before they had and the three women were appreciative to be together as they quickly glanced at each other and then smiled, due to the fact that they had all actually been placed in the same pairing group.

Each member of the group of twelve was quickly led towards a sports field at the very rear of the building as Mark led the way and the twelve men and women followed him quietly. All in all, there were actually twelve people in their group, six men and three other women besides Louise, Madeline and Zoe but they didn't recognize any of the other nine people in their group at all and hadn't yet met any of them. The group of twelve was then quickly divided into much smaller groups of four which contained two men and two women each and according to Mark, the smaller groups actually comprised of their very first two potential love matches.

A physical assault course faced each of the smaller groups as Mark quickly notified them that they were actually supposed to tackle the physical assault course together. The news brought an immediate frown to Zoe's face as she quickly absorbed the task ahead with absolute dread as she absolutely hated the thought of getting all mucky and dirty for absolutely no good reason at all or at least none that she could think of that even made an ounce of sense. Despite her reservations however, she prepared to participate

217

nonetheless as she quietly resigned herself to the notion that she was not actually the love match expert and that she had actually paid for that service to be applied to her actual dating life and romantic choices and hence to object now, would perhaps seem to be an illogical response to Mark's request.

None of the men that the three women had met, since they'd arrived, were actually in their first pairing group of twelve and that factor slightly disappointed them. In some small way, Zoe had actually started to form a slight emotional attachment to Giovanni and even more so since their joint experience of holographic intimacy together the previous night and it worried her slightly that he wasn't actually present. The only male absence that didn't actually bother any of the three women in the slightest, was the absence of Thomas which in some ways they actually felt slightly relieved about. He was certainly not any of their types and if he had actually been present that morning, it would have perhaps made their pairing activity slightly uncomfortable and awkward, if he had been subsequently paired with any of them.

Despite the absence of the two men, the two women had actually hoped to see, Giovanni and Steven, the three women quickly resigned themselves to participating in the activities that lay ahead with the people who were actually present. Both Zoe and Louise however, inwardly retained the hope that they would perhaps meet them at some point later that afternoon, during their next pairing activity group. All three women had by now actually been split up into different groups of four and hence none of them were actually in the same smaller groups and Zoe quickly realized that the much smaller grouping divisions had been very precise and appeared to be extremely calculated.

Huge large walls with bricks that jutted out of them suddenly faced the four men and women in Zoe's group and there were ditches of muddy water at the base of each wall as Zoe quickly glanced at them and then shivered with disgust. There were some thin, narrow beams situated right above some other muddy puddles of water that Zoe quickly realized she would actually be expected to cross and she was grateful for a moment that she'd actually complied with the recommended dress code earlier that morning. Sneakers, jeans and t-shirts were quite definitely a much more appropriate form attire for the activities she was about to actually embark upon and the dresscode had been very clearly specified upon her electronic schedule when she'd glanced at it earlier that morning. For once, Zoe was actually quite glad that she'd actually decided to conform with someone else's recommendations regarding her choice of outfits that day and that she had not stubbornly actually opposed it.

A whistle was suddenly blown by Mark and Zoe's group of four rapidly set off as they all headed towards the large wall situated directly in front of them and prepared to actually start climbing over it. Unfortunately for Zoe however, she only actually managed to reach the midpoint of the wall before she suddenly slipped and fell backwards and then landed straight on her butt inside the muddy pool of water directly at its base. Zoe groaned as she quickly shook her head and then glanced across at Madeline and Louise, who were by now mid-way up the walls that their respective groups were supposed to climb and who seemed to have absolutely no trouble at all with the physical task they'd all been presented with.

"Seriously, this is so not me." Zoe called out to the two women.

Louise grinned as she suddenly stopped, turned round and then glanced at her. "I can see that." She teased.

"Are you alright Zoe?" Madeline asked as she paused for a moment, slightly worried that Zoe had perhaps injured herself in her fall.

Zoe nodded in response. "I'll be fine but a cocktail right now would really be quite helpful." She joked.

Louise giggled.

Fortunately for Zoe, one of the men in Zoe's group of four, by this point in time had actually noticed her predicament and he quickly made his way back down the wall towards her as he prepared to assist her. He stretched out a helpful hand towards her, once he was actually close enough to the ground and Zoe smiled as she accepted his assistance graciously as he helped her back up. The muddy pool she'd fallen inside, was extremely slippery and hence Zoe was actually quite worried that she might actually fall back down, if she didn't actually accept help from someone and he had actually offered. At least, one of her potential matches was quite polite, she quietly concluded as she was gently pulled to her feet.

Very unfortunately, neither of the two men actually in Zoe's group in her opinion, were anywhere near as hot as Giovanni and that lack of appeal meant that her interest in them both was actually quite limited but she attempted to be polite towards them nonetheless. Some questions rapidly scurried through her mind as she prepared to scale the wall again as she quietly contemplated Giovanni's absence further. Giovanni wasn't actually in her pairing group that morning and she began to wonder why for a moment and if that actually meant that he perhaps wasn't the best potential match for her after all and what she might do if it actually transpired that he wasn't one of the ten potential love matches she was due to meet that week. There had been no actual mention that the pairing activities that week would be conducted in any particular kind of order or that each person's top matches would be the first matches they would actually meet but his absence did start to raise questions inside her mind. Zoe began to wonder as she climbed back up the wall, if perhaps all that existed between the two was a physical attraction that had been decorated and adorned with some overt flirtatious expressions which didn't actually have any real substance at all or any potential romantic longevity.

Giovanni had managed to capture Zoe's attention in the short space of time since they'd both first met and she had actually started to develop a deeper desire for him as his charm and sensual interactions with her, had touched her inwardly and then provoked and sparked her interest in him even further. Every time the two had met, Zoe's interest in him seemed to grow but it worried her slightly that he wasn't actually there at all amongst her first potential love matches and so far hadn't actually been paired with her as that seemed to contradict what they both felt towards each other.

The remainder of the assault course was quite a struggle for Zoe as she clambered over each of the muddy walls, stepped cautiously across each of the narrow beams which she actually slipped off a few times and then swung out across a huge ditch on a piece of rope but very fortunately, it was over soon enough and lunch finally actually arrived. Each of the three women converged at one end of the field, once they'd bid their groups of four goodbye as they prepared to eat lunch together and discussed their muddy, hectic morning.

On their way back towards the main resort building, Zoe playfully attempted to gauge each of the women's sentiments and attractions towards the two men that had been placed in each of their respective groupings of four that morning as they walked. Despite her lack of attraction for the two men in her group, she was anxious to hear about whether or not Madeline or Louise had actually managed to make any kind of romantic connections.

"How do you guys feel about the guys that we were put into groups with today? Amongst all that mud was there, a love connection?" Zoe teased as she giggled. "Did your heart wallow in muddy attraction, or was it just dirty grime that you couldn't wait to get rid of and shower off?"

"I'm not really that impressed with the two guys that were in my group, Steven is actually much nicer than either of them but then, even Steven is not really actually my type. He is starting to grow on me however, so I might get to know him a bit better and see what happens." Louise replied.

"I'm waiting until I've met all of my ten potential love matches before I become emotionally attached to anyone or develop any kind of preferences towards any of them." Madeline explained. "That way I can make a better decision and more informed choice. I really want to give the system a chance to match me."

"Louise, you're starting to compromise." Zoe teased. "Steven's not even your type but he's actually started to win you over."

Louise giggled. "I know, he is quite handsome and charming though. So I'm giving him a bit of chance." She explained.

"The slippery slope of romantic compromise, next you'll be moving in with him and getting pregnant and then one day, when he really pisses you off, you'll be like, how the hell did I end up here, he's not even my type." Zoe joked.

Madeline giggled.

"Louise, don't settle for less than you really want." Zoe advised. "Or it could come to a very messy, muddy ending."

"You mean a bit like your butt did this morning, when you actually fell off that wall?" Louise teased in response as she retaliated playfully to Zoe's jokes.

Zoe grinned. "I know, I know, I should really get changed before I bless the dining hall with my presence. I look a total state and a quick shower wouldn't go amiss." She mentioned.

Madeline nodded. "Great idea, why don't we regroup in the dining hall in about thirty minutes Louise." She suggested.

Louise rapidly nodded in agreement.

The three women quickly separated and then made their way towards their respective suites as they prepared to freshen up before lunch. When they regrouped inside the dining hall, thirty minutes later, they found much to their surprise that Mark was actually situated inside it which actually suited Zoe down to the ground as she had some questions she wanted to present directly to him. Zoe rushed towards him as she flashed a charming smile at him as she prepared to present her expressions of curiosity to him in person.

"Mark, were the men in our pairing groups this morning our most suitable or our best potential matches from the ten that we'll meet this week?" She asked as she stood right beside him.

"Certainly not Zoe." Mark replied as he gently shook his head straight away. "They were just two possible matches from your ten optimum matches that we identify for each person and there's no particular order that you meet each one of those ten in." He explained. "Over the next few days, you'll get to meet all ten of those potential matches and then you will be asked to narrow down your potential match list to five. Once your final five matches have been identified, you'll then attend some pairing dates and then you'll narrow your selection down again to two men that you will then attend exclusive dates with and then you'll make your final selection."

Zoe sighed with relief. "Thank you so much Mark that's really great." She gushed as she happily accepted that Giovanni might still make it into her ten possible love matches after all. "I was a bit worried about it as I've met someone at the resort I'm quite interested in and he wasn't there."

Mark smiled. "No problem Zoe, he might still turn up in your other eight matches, try to be patient. Is there anything else I can help you ladies with right now?" He asked.

Zoe, Madeline and Louise immediately shook their heads in response.

"In that case, I better get a move on." Mark explained. "I have quite a few things to do before this afternoon's pairing activities."

Zoe smiled and nodded as she politely released him.

Despite the three men's absence from the women's pairing activity groups earlier that morning, Giovanni, Steven and Callum certainly weren't absent from the dining hall that lunchtime and once the three women noticed them seated at a table together, they quickly made their way towards them, before they collected their lunchtime starters. Apparently, the three men had actually spent their morning upon the beach and two of them had actually been involved in some team volley ball games whilst Callum had taken part in some kind of team swimming race. Much like the three women, they had also been placed into different groups of four and they too had also met their very first two love matches.

"What did you think of your potential love matches?" Louise asked Steven as curiosity suddenly began to prick her inside.

"They weren't really my kind of women." Steven quickly replied in a reassuring manner as he rapidly attempted to reassure Louise that his interest still lay very firmly at the door of her heart.

Louise smiled as she graciously accepted his comforting words.

"My first two matches were nowhere near you Zoe. I wasn't even attracted to either of them." Giovanni quickly offered reassuringly as he glanced into Zoe eyes and then smiled. "I'm waiting for you to show up in one of my pairing groups soon as a potential match for me." He continued as he gently touched her hand. "I mean seriously, their love matching system cannot possibly exclude you from my potential love matches and be even remotely right, there's no way on earth such results would be anywhere near accurate."

"Giovanni, I totally agree." Zoe replied as a warm feeling of satisfaction suddenly filled her core. Her attraction and interest in Giovanni was certainly not only growing but also being reciprocated and he was waiting for her, just as much as she was actually waiting for him.

A hearty lunch was quickly consumed, before the afternoon's pairing activities were due to commence and very fortunately, this time Zoe, Madeline and Louise were actually due to participate in their respective pairing activities down by the beach and that meant there would be no more muddy walls to climb or muddy pools to fall into. Once again that afternoon, the three women were placed into much smaller groups with two male potential love matches and once again Giovanni, Steven and Callum, were in none of the women's groups. There was still a glimmer of hope inside of the two women that the three men would still show up somewhere amongst their pairing groups as there were still six men left that they had yet to meet and hence Zoe and Louise both tried to remain positive. Madeline, on the other hand, was not particularly bothered either way as to whether Callum actually showed up anywhere in any of her pairing groups as she was not even remotely interested in him, in a romantic capacity.

Unlike the muddy assault course, the beach activities that afternoon were a lot more pleasant and a lot less mucky as the three women quite happily participated in the various beach games in teams of four and thoroughly enjoyed their afternoon. Each interaction was filled with smiles and boisterous physical energy as they assertively competed against each other in their teams of four and attempted to win each game they engaged in.

Once again, much like the morning's pairing group activity, none of the men in Zoe's group particularly appealed to her and quite certainly none of them could even come remotely close to Giovanni and the growing attraction she felt towards him. Despite this lack of romantic attraction, she participated enthusiastically nonetheless and was pleasant, polite and charming to everyone around her as the afternoon gently flew away and the early evening was ushered in.

Once the afternoon's pairing activities were over, the three women made their way quietly back towards the dining hall as they prepared to eat their evening meal and meet the three men once more. Zoe noticed as they walked that Louise actually looked slightly dejected and she quickly attempted to cheer her up as she was obviously slightly more interested in

Steven than perhaps even Louise herself had initially actually realized.

"Don't worry, we still have six more potential love matches to meet and Steven might be there and if he isn't, then perhaps the love matching system isn't as great as they think it is." Zoe gently reassured her.

"Do you think Steven is ever actually going to be in any of my pairing groups at all?" Louise asked. "I mean, he's not even really actually my type so they might not even match him with me, upon those grounds alone."

Madeline smiled. "True but just try to be positive about it and see what happens. He might show up somewhere." She insisted.

"I'd really like to get to know him a little better in a different setting and circumstances, than just the social drinks at the bar we all have together each evening." Louise explained. "And see how we actually function together as a team."

"Really Louise, it's not worth worrying about yet." Zoe returned. "If he doesn't show up anywhere in your next six potential love matches, then you can start to worry. If he's really interested in you and he's really sincere, his head won't be swayed or turned by another women and he won't make an emotional investment in any of them. If he's really serious, he'll wait for you and if he doesn't, then you'll know he just wasn't that serious about you to begin with."

Louise nodded. "Of course Zoe, you're totally right." She agreed. "I'm probably putting the cart before the horse and worrying for absolutely no reason. This is a great way to discover if he actually really is that committed to me and interested in me."

Zoe smiled at her in response as she rapidly realized that Louise was actually quite delicate and certainly much softer than she was. "That's it, keep your chin up and look on the bright side." She encouraged as she quietly contemplated for a moment how Louise would actually feel if Steven did actually falter and end up in a love affair with someone else, she'd be gutted but then so too would Zoe, if Giovanni did the same thing to her.

Pleasant aroma's suddenly dived inside their nostrils as dinner quickly greeted them and the three embraced the delightful smells that floated around inside the air of the dining room as they stepped inside the room. The food was quite definitely already present but

Zoe rapidly noticed that none of the three men were as she walked towards the long table filled with starters and picked up an empty plate. Each silver tray was filled up to the brim with delicious, edible items as Zoe began to quickly fill her plate and quietly contemplated further, how she would actually feel if Giovanni did indeed actually embark upon a love affair with one of his potential matches and then subsequently abandon and dump her.

Technically, the two were not actually in any kind of committed, romantic relationship as yet which meant if he actually did so, there would be very little Zoe could say or do about it. Zoe quietly decided that she would be hurt but that she couldn't really take it that badly as up until now, all the two had really done was flirt, eaten a few meals together and shared a few laughs. They hadn't even exchanged phone numbers yet and hence there was no actual real commitment from either of them that exceeded the hours they had spent together at the resort and the alcoholic beverages they'd consumed.

Despite the sizzling, electrifying chemistry between Giovanni and Zoe, it suddenly struck her that the two had not yet actually spent a moment alone together by themselves and as yet, had only ever flirted with each other in the presence of others. Zoe definitely had to try and have a one on one date with Giovanni soon, in order to actually determine whether there was any real potential chance of success for a real relationship between them, she suddenly considered otherwise, she'd never really actually know.

Starter plates were rapidly filled up as the three women, hungrily prepared to satisfy their stomachs as the physical nature of the pairing activities that day, had not only given them an appetite but had also kept them on their toes and now they were very much in need of both food and a comfortable chair to sit down upon. The three men didn't actually show up at all during their evening meal but once dinner had been fully consumed, the three women briefly returned to their suites to freshen up, change their clothes and prepare themselves for an evening by the poolside bar and an evening with Giovanni, Steven and Callum as they had agreed to meet there earlier that day. Due to the uncertainty as to when their afternoon pairing activities would actually end, they'd actually agreed to meet the three men by the poolside bar straight after dinner and that meeting was definite and now actually, due to occur.

Due to the fact that Callum was the third male in their group of six and Madeline the third female that hadn't actually as yet, semi partnered up in a flirtatious pre-emptive meandering to romance with anyone, Callum had naturally attempted to reach out to Madeline to some extent, in a romantic capacity. His efforts to impress her however, had been slightly hampered by Madeline's barriers which had been very firmly put in place and her lack of interest in him that had been very clearly displayed overtly, upon several occasions. She had even actually notified him directly, once or twice that she actually preferred to consider the actual love matches the resort suggested to her, before she actually considered any unexpected random males that might somehow cross her path and on that particular point, Madeline had been completely unshakeable and utterly immovable.

In response to Madeline's extremely frosty attitude, Callum had actually tried to make more of an effort as he'd attempted to capture her attention but Zoe had quietly noticed that

Madeline had not responded positively at all. No matter how hard Callum actually tried to impress her, all he'd been met with so far was a stiff, wooden plank of non-participation as Madeline had simply ignored his advances and shaken each one off as if they were dirty, unwanted specks of dirt that had gathered upon her clothes. Madeline, it seemed was completely and utterly determined that she was absolutely not going to deviate from the matching process she'd signed up for and she was sticking to her decision one hundred percent, despite any efforts that Callum did or didn't actually make.

A large part of Zoe, really respected Madeline's choice and as a result, she kept extremely quiet about it and didn't even mention Callum once to her and nor did she encourage Madeline to actually accept his romantic advances. Perhaps, Zoe had quietly decided the past had damaged Madeline somewhat, and perhaps the counselling session that she'd booked for them both which was due to occur on the Wednesday afternoon, would actually help her to release those disappointments and allow her to actually move forward with her life. Indeed, it was somehow very natural for someone to seek to protect themselves, once they had been very hurt by their own judgment as they would no longer trust it in its totality as human beings judged those they trusted and once that trust had been broken one to many times, the damage inflicted upon them, definitely changed them as a person.

Zoe's own judgment, on the other hand, she still actually held a reasonable amount of faith in and so much so that she even believed her own judgment was slightly superior and would offer her better results than any actual results a computer could ever possibly offer her. In some respects, Zoe was perhaps slightly over confident in her own judgment whereas Madeline perhaps wasn't confident enough but Zoe really just couldn't accept that a computer could actually be more accurate than she could be about who might actually right or wrong for her.

Only time would tell, Zoe mused as she quickly fixed her hair and then slipped on a matching bracelet, necklace and pair of sparkling earrings which one of the two women's approaches to the resort and the services of the love matching computer was indeed, actually correct. A final consideration suddenly crossed Zoe's mind that perhaps Madeline didn't really actually like Callum at all and perhaps it was just that simple. Perhaps, it was Zoe that was over analyzing Madeline's response to Callum and perhaps it was she that was reading far too much into things, when really the truth was really, actually much simpler to explain.

Before the three women had actually left the dining hall, earlier that evening, Zoe had actually noticed that some of the other vacationers had started to form their own little companionship groups, much like Zoe had herself. Naturally, Zoe's own group contained some of the best looking men at the resort, in her opinion anyway and in that sense she'd definitely felt that the three women had been extremely lucky to actually find and form the group of friendship that they actually had. Some vacationers, Zoe had noticed had it seemed, actually come on vacation completely alone and they'd sat very much on their own, even at mealtimes and that for Zoe was an extremely dismal way to spend a week at a beautiful, exotic love resort island that was filled with lots of attractive, sociable, single people.

Once Zoe had finished sprucing herself up and once she'd collected Madeline from the lounge in their suite, the two women walked back towards the reception area as they prepared to meet Louise and then head out towards the poolside. When the three women arrived beside the poolside bar, approximately five minutes later, the three men had already actually arrived and the men greeted them politely and then quickly ordered them some cocktails.

"Let's join in the salsa class they're having tonight." Zoe suddenly urged the group as they stood beside the bar and waited for the round of cocktails to arrive. "It's happening right now, beside the pool, just over there." She mentioned as she pointed towards a corner of the poolside where a circle of people had gathered.

"My food's still digesting." Madeline groaned.

"I've got two left feet." Louise replied. "I'm really not much of a dancer."

"Come on you guys, it'll be fun." Zoe insisted as she gently started to pull the two women towards the corner of the poolside where the salsa class was actually being held. "Don't be boring and you can't really get it wrong Louise, it's a very basic salsa lesson."

"Okay, okay." Madeline replied as she fully surrendered to Zoe's request.

"It'll only take half an hour or an hour and then you can have the rest of the evening to do whatever you want." Zoe mentioned. She paused and then turned to face the three men. "Are you guys going to join us?" Zoe asked.

The three men immediately nodded in response.

"Can't hurt I guess." Giovanni replied. "Though I'm not really much of a dancer either." He advised Zoe. "So you'll have to forgive my stumbling on the dance floor."

"You're totally forgiven in advance." Zoe teased as she smiled at him in a seductive, flirtatious manner. "Participation on this particular occasion supersedes competence."

Despite some of the group's reluctance to participate, Zoe really wanted everyone to actually do so as she'd actually listened to Louise's remarks and observations about Steven and appreciated the wisdom they had actually contained. So far, since the six had actually met, all the three men and women had actually done together was drink a few drinks beside the poolside and eaten a few meals at the same table and they had not yet actually attempted to engage in any activities together at all, besides snorkeling which didn't really count as at that point they hadn't even really started to engage in any romantic flirting with each other.

Deep inside, it suddenly actually mattered to Zoe that there was more than just a physical attraction between her and Giovanni as she really wanted to be sure that if they were not actually matched by resort's computer system at all, she would have some kind of justification in her mind that would allow her to reject her potential love matches more easily, in order to pursue a real life romance with him. The three men and three women definitely needed to spend some time together that did not just revolve around getting drunk or eating food, in order to see the different sides of each other's personalities and to more fully appreciate each other's characters and Zoe for once in her life, had actually listened to someone else that she barely even knew and even actually accepted their wisdom.

Even though at least two of the group, Louise and Giovanni had insisted they weren't really great dancers, the lesson was very basic and hence they all managed to follow it reasonably successfully, keep up with the instructor and even managed to pick some dance moves quite quickly as Zoe had insisted that they should all participate. The lesson continued for over an hour and actually exceeded the thirty or sixty minutes that Zoe had said it might take but noone complained as everyone joined in enthusiastically, once it actually started. When the lesson finally finished, a couple of songs were then played and everyone joined in each of the dances with partners to practice what they'd just actually learnt.

Once the salsa dances ended, the six made their way quite happily back towards the bar where they ordered another round of drinks, a little worn out but definitely, extremely happy. When the drinks arrived, the six decided to take a stroll down towards the beach just as the sun was setting where they then found a huge rock to sit upon that actually jutted out over the edge of the water and gently hung out over the aqua marine waves. Each of the six quickly sat down as they sipped on their cocktails and bottles of beer and then watched the sunset on the distant horizon and conversed amongst themselves.

Beauty adorned the skyline as Zoe stared at it very much in awe as she'd simply never, ever seen such a magnificent sight before in her entire life. It was quite frankly incomparable to anything she'd ever seen before and most definitely one of the most beautiful sights she'd ever laid eyes upon and she almost wished that it was a view she could see, admire and appreciate every single day. Zoe could quite easily forgo her days spent with Collette at the beauty salon for a serene island lifestyle, situated very far away from the hustle and bustle of the boisterous city that she actually lived in and especially for an island with beautiful views, delicious cocktails and mouthwatering food. Zincata island was certainly another life, another world and the island seemed to offer an extremely peaceful existence.

Soon, Zoe knew the weeks' vacation would actually be over and then the two women would be thrown back into the daily slog of work and the busy city traffic and their world was a destination over a hundred miles away from this beautiful, tropical island paradise and not just in terms of distance. Zoe glanced at Madeline's face as she quietly contemplated whether or not the trip had been worth it from Madeline's perspective, she certainly seemed to be very happy and quite relaxed and that in Zoe's mind was worth every penny they had each spent to actually attend. Her best friend's confidence had certainly grown each day since they'd arrived and Zoe had begun to notice some very subtle changes in her attitude. Madeline was now surrounded by decent men and she was actually interacting with them in a positive manner and in a manner that she had a degree of control over and she was no longer simply a victim of any men she met that approached her that managed to weasel their way into her life and as a result, she had definitely begun to flourish.

Bad relationships, Zoe completely understood drained you at times, both emotionally and physically and they detracted from your confidence and somehow, could even make you feel less adequate as a person and as a woman and Madeline had definitely had her share of those. Each negative romance had left its mark upon her self-esteem and taken its toll upon her life as she'd handled each disappointment and every heartbreak and then had diligently picked back up her life afterwards.   Once a heart was broken however, sometimes it took years and years to actually heal and Madeline's heart had definitely been broken, more than a few times. Now however, it was quite apparent that her inner beauty and joy was finally being restored and Zoe could see that happening slowly and surely each and every day as Madeline began to place her feet firmly back upon the ladder of life and romance and believe in herself once again.

Unlike Madeline, Zoe was actually much tougher and hence relationships tended to drain her far less, especially the bad ones. Whenever Zoe was unhappy with a romantic relationship, she'd simply trash it, bin it and then walk away, whereas Madeline would stay, persevere and try to work things out, even when things were really not workable and wallow in daily misery and heartbreak. Madeline would give more of herself than she really should, in order to attempt to try and fix things and to try and make her relationships work and in the end she would often give way to much and ultimately end up overcompensating for the lacking, shortcomings and disappointments inflicted upon her by the male she was involved with at that particular moment in time.

When a romantic relationship didn't work out, Madeline would contemplate for months about why it actually hadn't and where she'd perhaps actually gone wrong and search for answers that might not at times, even reflect reality or matter at all. At times, she would even punish herself with feelings of guilt as to why a relationship had failed and what she had or hadn't done to make things work. Madeline would blame herself and take all the responsibility for everything that had wrong and at times, it had been extremely frustrating for Zoe to actually watch. For Zoe, it was different, she could just get up and leave a romantic relationship she didn't want and walk away from it at any given time, especially the bad ones.

On several occasions, Zoe had even tried to advise Madeline to stop taking responsibility for other people's wrongs, bad attitudes and behavior as she was not to blame for their hurtful actions towards her. Despite this advice however, Madeline had continued to beat herself up for all the wrongs that men she'd dated inflicted upon her very regularly. At times, it was actually torture for Zoe to watch as Madeline definitely deserved so much more than that from life and from love and Zoe was completely determined that she should actually receive something much better. Very fortunately and to Zoe's complete and utter relief however, that negative romantic dabbling had not it seemed, had a permanent impact upon her heart or on their vacation as Madeline had managed to open herself up to the possibility that perhaps there was a real romance out there just waiting for her to actually enjoy it, with someone pleasant. Someone different and someone unlike the deadbeats she'd so often dated and tolerated that had certainly been sourced from a very murky, dubious, scum filled, slimy dating pond.

So far, most of the men that Zoe had actually met at the resort had actually impressed her, in terms of their attitude towards women as they all seemed to be very serious about their search for a committed relationship and that even included Thomas.

Despite Thomas's geeky, untidy physical appearance, his quirky, eccentric character and his strange, peculiar mannerisms which had not impressed Zoe at all, his heart definitely seemed to be in the right place when it came to his attitude towards women and his behavior on that front as far as Zoe was concerned was completely exemplary.

None of the men at the resort it seemed, were there just for a quick fumble or romp, although perhaps there were a few that would quite possibly grab one, if one was actually on offer. At the love resort, the men all actually seemed to be quite serious and sincere about looking for a life partner and a proper relationship and that was extremely healthy and refreshing for both the men and the women present. Madeline had definitely blossomed ever since she'd arrived and Zoe was extremely thankful for that as for once, one of the things that Zoe had actually dragged Madeline along to, actually seemed to be worth their while attending.

The evening melted gently away and as night and darkness flooded over the resort, the group of six decided to retire for the night. Due to the extremely active day they'd just had participated in and the very physical nature of the activities they'd engaged in, they were all extremely tired and even quite worn out as the night gently wrapped its arms around them and darkness coated the air. Farewells that night were kept quite short as the six separated just outside the entrance of the main resort building and then headed back to their respective suites for some rest quite quietly.

Once Zoe and Madeline arrived back inside their suite, they eagerly discussed their day inside the lounge area as they prepared themselves for bed. Due to the pairing activities that day which had all been quite physical in nature and the additional salsa lesson afterwards, they were both completely worn out and therefore, they had decided to sleep almost straight away as it was now, just after midnight. A slinky, black, mid-thigh nightdress gently adorned Zoe's body as she conversed with Madeline about the things that had actually occurred throughout that day and then even paddled in the shallow waters of speculation, regarding things that hadn't yet actually taken place as they very openly discussed every aspect of their adventurous vacation.

"What do you think we'll be doing tomorrow?" Madeline asked Zoe as they sat upon the sofa in the lounge and sipped on cups of hot chocolate.

"I'm not sure but I sure as hell hope it's not another assault course that was truly awful." Zoe replied as she gently shook her head.

"Yeah, it was pretty mucky." Madeline agreed. "And extremely hard work."

"Did you see Thomas anywhere today?" Zoe asked.

Madeline shook her head.

"He's like totally disappeared." Zoe mentioned. "Perhaps, he's been abducted by mermaids, since he spends all his evenings down on the beach, maybe they felt sorry for him and took him in."

"Or perhaps he's found a love match that he really likes that he's spending time with." Madeline suggested.

"No way." Zoe immediately returned.

"It is entirely possible Zoe." Madeline mentioned. "To someone else, Thomas might be the cherry on top of their love cake."

Zoe giggled. "I'd love to see that, for the nicest possible reasons of course." She explained. "Before I leave this resort, I'm going to give that man a makeover, I swear."

Madeline smiled. "We better sleep, if we actually want to wake up on time tomorrow morning." She suggested.

Zoe nodded and then stood up as she prepared to make her way towards her bedroom. "Yep, it's late now and we're both absolutely knackered." She observed. "And we're both definitely way too tired to be worrying about Thomas's love life when we haven't even sorted out our own yet."

Madeline giggled as she stood up. "Very true, very true." She agreed.

Fortunately, when the next morning actually arrived, the two women woke up bright, early and extremely refreshed as they quickly showered, dressed up and then checked their electronic journals and schedule as they prepared for the day ahead. They had arranged to meet Louise inside the reception area that morning before they'd actually separated the night before, so that they could all eat breakfast together. Technically, the two women could just order breakfast from their suite and actually eat it there but they'd opted to head to the dining hall instead each day, in order to be as socially active as they could be, throughout their entire vacation. When they actually passed through the reception area to meet Louise, the two immediately noticed that Mark was actually around and Zoe quickly rushed towards him as she prepared to pose some more questions to him, this time about that day's pairing activities as she made the most of the opportunity and his presence.

"Mark, please don't tell me that we're actually going to have to do another assault course today. I absolutely hated it." Zoe pleaded as soon as she approached him.

Mark smiled as he gently shook his head. "No ladies, today we'll be participating in some virtual reality compatibility testing activities. Yesterday's activities were in fact, just preparation as we've found that engaging people in real life physical challenges, helps guests to prepare for the virtual reality testing system we utilize at the resort." He explained to each of the three women, who were now stood directly in front of him as Louise quietly joined them. "When your group has all arrived at the designated meeting point which today is in fact right here inside the reception, after you've all eaten breakfast, I'll take you to one of the virtual reality testing suites."

"Good, so there'll be no mud at all?" Zoe asked.

"There'll definitely be no mud." Mark promised.

"And no sweaty beach games?" Zoe probed.

"And no sweaty beach games." Mark gently reassured her.

"I mean, two very grubby activities in one day, it was a little bit too much for me." Zoe explained.

Mark laughed. "You better hurry up and get breakfast as the rest of your pairing group will soon be here." He advised.

Zoe nodded.

Breakfast was an extremely quick affair as the three women rushed towards the dining hall, served themselves from the silver trays that lay upon the long table situated at one side of the room and then sat down at an empty table. Everything they could possibly want to eat that morning for breakfast had been freshly prepared and was simply lying in readiness, waiting for their consumption as they eagerly tucked in. There were at least fifty other people inside the dining hall but none of the three women recognized any of them, from either their pairing activities or from the games they had played beside the poolside bar on the very first night they'd actually arrived.

When breakfast was over, the three women quickly rushed back towards the reception area, where Mark was patiently waiting for them to arrive, along with the rest of their pairing group. Zoe smiled slightly apologetically at everyone else in their group as she quickly observed that all the other nine people in their pairing group had already arrived and that they were in fact, the last three to actually turn up again. For Zoe, lateness was almost like a fashion statement but it certainly wasn't a trend that anyone else seemed to appreciate and especially not her boss at work, Collette.

The twelve followed Mark quietly as they made their way along a long, white corridor, slightly unsure about what exactly the pairing activities that morning would actually entail and silenced by their uncertainty. A large, white, glossy door on their left hand side, suddenly swished open as Mark touched a side panel next to it and he then quickly led the group inside the room that lay directly beyond it.

Inside the relatively plain, white glossy room, large black sofa's lined three of the walls as they gently leant up against each one but besides those, there wasn't actually much else to see or do at first glance. Zoe, Louise and Madeline quickly sat down upon one of the huge, black sofas once they entered inside the room and then quietly waited. Each sofa could easily seat at least ten people upon them and they were extremely comfortable as the three women sat and watched Mark and waited in eager anticipation for the morning's pairing activities to actually commence.

"This is one of our virtual reality compatibility testing suites." Mark announced as he stood at the top of the room where a large, wafer thin screen and computer system was situated upon a large, white, glossy desk directly in front of him. He glanced around the room at the twelve guests seated inside it as he prepared to start the virtual reality pairing activity. "In here, we conduct various pairing activities that are very much like the ones you participated in yesterday, just that this time there's no mud." Mark teased as he quickly glanced at Zoe and then smiled.

Everyone nodded as they watched him quietly.

Silence completely filled the room as the twelve focused upon his every movement and waited with baited breath as they had no idea whatsoever, was actually going to transpire next at all but they could all sense deep inside themselves, it might actually be quite exciting. Mark suddenly opened up a cabinet door, positioned at the very base of the large, white desk and then took out twelve headsets which he then handed to each of the vacationers inside the room. Each of the three women in Zoe's entourage, placed a headset gently upon their heads as they giggled with delight and instantly, they were transported to what appeared to be a white, blank, empty virtual room. Gone were the people that they had originally entered inside the actual physical room with and gone too was Mark.

A few seconds later however, much to Zoe, Madeline and Louise's complete and utter surprise, a man from their pairing group actually appeared inside the blank, white room alongside them. Each of the men, the women quickly realized was a man from the twelve that the three women had actually entered inside the physical room with and even though Mark was no longer present inside the virtual rooms or even visible at all, they suddenly heard his voice echo out all around them as his words quickly began to surround them.

"Within each of your Scenario rooms, you will now be presented with a scenario and challenge sequence, so that we can monitor how you interact with each other." Mark stated as he stood at the top of the physical room and touched a control screen directly in front of him which had all six of the virtual scenario rooms, clearly displayed upon it. "If you wish to move to the right, turn your head to the right and to move to the left, simply turn your head to the left." He explained. "To stand completely still, simply shake your head and to continue moving forward or to move forward more quickly, nod your head and if you move your hands or arms the sensors inside the headset will also pick that up. Please introduce yourselves to each other and get to know the person you will be participating in this particular pairing activity with as the microphones inside each of your headsets will pick up your communications effectively."

Zoe suddenly smiled as she glanced at the male vacationer that stood directly in front of her. "Hi I'm Zoe." She mentioned as she politely held out a hand towards him.

"Hi Zoe, nice to meet you or virtually meet you. "I'm Hamish." He replied as he politely shook her hand.

Zoe smiled again as she began to inspect him slightly more closely, he was tall, slim and reasonably attractive and he appeared to be in his mid-thirties. "What do we actually do next?" She asked.

Hamish shrugged. "I'm not totally sure, maybe we have to wait for something else to happen." He replied as he smiled politely at Zoe.

In a matter of seconds, their question was suddenly answered as the walls around them and floor beneath them, began to rapidly evaporate and even changed color. For some strange reason, Hamish completely disappeared altogether and Zoe gently shook her head as she pondered over why he'd actually vanished.

"Well, he wasn't around for very long." She remarked playfully. "And I didn't even insult him or turn up late for a date."

Mark's voice suddenly sounded out all around Zoe. "You have two minutes to find each other and to find your way out of the maze." He instructed.

Zoe stood frozen to the spot for a few seconds, completely uncertain which direction to actually head in as she glanced in front of her, behind her and in every direction possible as she searched for further clarity. The ground around her feet, suddenly started to evaporate and that forced her to actually move forward, in order to avoid the blank, black darkness just underneath the shiny, green, glossy surface. She quickly leapt forward as she attempted to avoid the darkness that was creeping in below her and rushed towards a nearby opening as she began to search for not only Hamish but also a possible way out.

Despite the lack of visibility as there were now extremely high, shiny green walls situated almost all around her, Zoe could very clearly hear Hamish calling out her name as she travelled along the narrow path directly in front of her and attempted to find him. There were,

Zoe quickly noticed several other openings and pathways nearby, all of which branched off and led in various other directions and Zoe quickly approached some of them. Each time Hamish called out her name, Zoe immediately responded as she attempted to enter one of the openings nearby which she felt would perhaps lead her closer to him.

"Zoe, I've managed to find the exit. Where are you?" Hamish suddenly called out. "Try to find me quickly please."

"I'm trying." Zoe replied as she suddenly rushed towards another path nearby which she then followed. She followed the path quite cautiously as it twisted and turned and a few seconds later, suddenly found herself directly in front of a dead end and she gently shook her head as she sighed.

Due to the time restrictions that had been placed upon that particular challenge, Hamish in the meantime, had actually realized that the exit directly in front of him was now actually closing and that thought had begun to worry him slightly as he'd waited. The two really were running completely out of time and as yet, there was still no sign of Zoe, who was not yet, actually beside him. Hamish had to make a decision and he rapidly did so as he suddenly sprang forward and then rushed out of the nearby exit alone.

Zoe, oblivious to his desertion, continued to search for Hamish and the exit but as she called out Hamish's name several times and there was no longer any actual response, it quickly dawned upon her that he could possibly no longer actually hear her. She continued her search for the exit to the maze nonetheless, completely and utterly determined that she was not going to give up, until she had actually successfully completed at least one part of the challenge that she'd actually been presented with but her efforts were to no avail as each glossy, green walled path she took, met her with either dead ends or led into other paths which seemed to lead absolutely nowhere.

Despite Zoe's messy scenario, Madeline had actually fared slightly better inside her own and Jake, the male vacationer that she'd been stuck inside the maze with and then subsequently separated from, had quickly found her and then together they had both quite quickly, actually found the exit. The two managed to actually leave the maze, just before the exit closed behind them and they both sighed with relief as they once more found themselves surrounded by the white, glossy virtual room that they had initially started out in.

"Simulation over." Mark suddenly announced, about thirty seconds after all the maze exits had actually closed. "Now, you can all remove your headsets." He instructed.

Everyone inside the room immediately removed their headsets.

Nervous smiles were exchanged amongst the group of twelve as each of the men and women inside the room quietly glanced at each other. Mark didn't say a word for a few minutes and there was a somewhat awkward silence as he simply stared at the screen directly in front of him. The occupants of the room, quietly began to internally speculate as to what he might be actually looking at as each of them patiently waited.

"Right, we'll do one more simulation with this group and then straight after lunch, you men will actually join another group but the ladies will remain with me." Mark explained. "The results and an analysis from each of your pairing activities, will be sent directly to your electronic journals, later this evening."

Everyone inside the room nodded as they listened.

Upon the screen in front of Mark, the results from each scenario stared him in the face as he prepared to save them and then load up the next pairing activity simulation. Not many of the six results presented to him were actually positive and Zoe's scenario had actually rendered an 'Incompatible Match' result. Mark quietly digested the results as he glanced at each of the six small boxes in front of him thoughtfully and sighed internally, there were only actually two positive 'Compatible Match' results from the group of six and both of those actually belonged to Madeline and Louise. He hoped that the next simulation would actually render better results as he gently shook his head.

One thing had slightly disappointed Zoe and Louise about that Tuesday morning and as they prepared for the second pairing simulation they had quite glum expressions upon their faces as a result, neither Giovanni or Steven had actually shown up in their pairing group so far that day. Both women knew that there were now only four possible, potential love matches left which meant, if the two men didn't show up soon, they definitely wouldn't show up in their ten potential love matches anywhere at all. Despite their disappointment however, the two women enthusiastically prepared to participate with the second pairing session of the morning in good spirits as they pushed the two men's absence gently to one side and attempted to be more patient as Mark had advised. Frustration was quite clearly however, beginning to tug away inside their minds and Zoe glumly shook her head as she quietly waited.

Madeline could sense as the three waited for the second simulation to actually start, that both women were slightly bothered by the two men's absence and she quietly attempted to reassure them as she drew them both closer and whispered in their ears. "We still have two activity pairing groups left and four more potential matches to meet, so don't worry those guys will definitely show up some time soon." She encouraged.

"Sure." Zoe replied as she nodded but there was a glum expression plastered across her face that outwardly displayed what her inward emotions clearly felt which clearly betrayed her. She tried to convince herself that Madeline was right and she sincerely hoped that she would be as she was certainly not feeling any kind of romantic connection at all between her and Hamish, the first of the two potential love matches she'd been paired with in that particular pairing group. "They'll turn up soon." Zoe said as she gently attempted to reassure herself as well as Madeline that Madeline's words were indeed correct.

The morning session continued as Zoe, Madeline and Louise actively participated in their second challenge and scenario with their second potential love match of the day and thankfully for Mark, the results of the second simulation challenge were slightly better than the first. Successful results from compatibility testing, were important to Mark for a variety of reasons as that was in essence what his job was really all about, the more suitably matched the couples were, the more likely it would be that there would be a successful romance from one of the matches that Honey had made which was ultimately the actual purpose of the love resort and his job. Earlier that morning he had been slightly disappointed by the first set of results which had rendered an extremely low positive result from the group of six couples, he'd initially provided pairing simulations to, usually he expected at least three positive results from a group of six and hence the results that morning had actually fallen short of his expectations. Once again Zoe had actually failed the challenge with her respective pairing and had been deemed an 'Incompatible Match' but overall Mark was quite pleased with the other four positive results that had been returned as that had indicated that the matches Honey had suggested were definitely on the right track.

When the second pairing activity simulation ended, the three women immediately stood up and then prepared to leave the room as they prepared to eat lunch. They started to walk towards the door and Mark quickly glanced up at them as they walked, just before they actually reached it.

"Remember ladies, after lunch you have to return here please." Mark politely reminded them.

Zoe, Madeline and Louise nodded in response.

Outside the virtual reality testing room, the hallway was quiet as the three women left the room and then walked back along the corridor towards the dining hall. They were all very ready to consume their lunch as their stomachs gently rumbled away as they walked as their bodies subtly remind them all that food was actually required and required very soon. Each of their two potential matches from that morning's pairing session was discussed as they walked.

"I didn't really like any of my two matches this morning." Zoe mentioned.

"I didn't either." Louise agreed. "One of the two matches I met yesterday was actually okay but the two I met this morning, definitely weren't for me."

"I'm remaining indifferent and impartial, until I've met all ten of my potential love matches before I make a commitment to liking or disliking anyone of them." Madeline insisted.

"Translation, that means none of them have actually captured your heart or aroused your romantic interest yet." Zoe teased. "You just can't be impartial when love sweeps you off your feet as it removes all doubt and every grain of indifference Madeline."

"Look Zoe, I'm just trying to remain emotionally detached for now as I've listened to your advice. I do tend to get very emotionally attached very quickly and way to early and my emotions then become a weapon which is actually used against me and that really hurts." Madeline explained.

"Don't worry, there's still time Madeline." Zoe mentioned as the three women approached and then entered inside the dining hall. "You might find someone you really like in your last four matches."

Madeline smiled.

Each of the three women comforted themselves as they walked towards the table filled with starters that Zoe's words and Madeline's reassurances would somehow manifest in reality and that all their fears by the end of the next day, would actually be squashed. They all still had four men to actually meet and that furnished them all with hope, the hope that Giovanni and Steven would actually be present amongst that number and the hope that Madeline might actually find someone amongst the four that she actually really liked. Starter plates were quickly filled up with delicious morsels of food as the three women enthusiastically began to discuss, what might actually happen later that afternoon as they prepared to satisfy, their now empty stomachs and glanced around the dining hall as they searched for any familiar faces.

Zoe glanced at Madeline's face thoughtfully as they talked, she sincerely hoped that perhaps one of those four remaining men would gently push her off the fence of indifference that she was right now, quite happily seated upon very comfortably and that perhaps one of those four men, would actually entice her to make an actual emotional, romantic commitment to them. In some ways, it did comfort Zoe slightly to know that Madeline had actually started to be a bit more careful, cautious and selective about her dating choices but for Zoe, that change had actually occurred at the wrong time as a vacation at a romantic love island that was packed full with tons of serious, single men was definitely the wrong place and quite certainly the wrong time, to be overly strict about one's romantic selections. She would be extremely pissed, if the two women actually returned from their vacation and Madeline still hadn't actually found anyone that she wanted to have a committed, romantic relationship with, after all their vacation was not just for Zoe's benefit.

Madeline absolutely had to return from their vacation with a decent, romantic relationship as after all the years of heartbreak and suffering she'd endured, she certainly more than deserved one.

HONEY

Behind the scenes of the busy love resort, several things had actually happened since the two female vacationers had initially arrived that they remained blissfully unaware off, despite the closer rapport they had actually developed with some of the resort staff, like Becky and Mark. The computer system that governed the actual matching process which was referred to as 'Honey' and that was the pride and joy of the resort's founder and island owner Bowen Logan had actually encountered a few problems and as a result, was not actually functioning at the usual optimal levels of performance at all.

Due to the value of the technology which Bowen Logan had personally built along with a team of engineers, he'd actually decided to personify the system and give 'Honey' a beautiful, attractive, stunning female face as that in his opinion encouraged the staff that manned the resort to treat the computer system, more like a human being. For Bowen, the personification of his computer system, provided his staff a gentle reassurance that behind every piece of hardware and software inside his company, there was indeed a very human face which in some respects was indeed actually very true as his knowledge and the knowledge from the team of specialists he'd worked alongside to create Honey, was indeed actually very human and they definitely all had, very human faces.

Honey was a highly complex, intricate system that ran not only the love matching facilities at the resort but that also managed the procurement systems, handled reservations, scheduled vacations, organized pairing activities and even managed the daily schedules for each of the guests. In fact, there was very little about the Love Colony resort that Honey did not actually have a hand in and because Honey's makeup was so intricately designed and specifically created, the resort usually functioned extremely smoothly from day to day without any significant problems or issues arising as a result.

Bowen Logan had spent a tremendous amount of money upon the development of Honey and fortunately, for the most part, his investment had effectively paid off and given him total peace of mind as Honey practically ran the resort on a daily basis. Honey actually relieved him from the responsibilities and concerns of hundreds of duties that he had absolutely no desire to tend to at all or assign anyone else to. Human beings were so hard to trust and could be so unreliable at times but Honey was totally immaculate in terms of delivery and was always absolutely, extremely reliable and that was one thing, Bowen could always be completely certain about.

From the resort staff, Bowen Logan had actually allocated two of his staff to spending most of their time inside the resort's operations room with Honey and they both maintained the system in various ways. They interacted directly with Honey on a daily basis and spent each working day, tucked away inside the operations room alongside his most prized creation. The two staff, Ricky and Samantha, performed very different functions in terms of their workload but their work was very much system based and they were very both reliable, extremely efficient and very competent with regards to their positions and Bowen trusted them immensely.

Samantha's main role, was to actually review some of the potential love matches that Honey had made and perform a sensibility check upon them each day. However, due to the fact that there were virtually thousands of love matches made at the resort each week, she couldn't possibly check every single one of them and hence every day she would check a random sample group of love matches. She tried to ensure each day that this sample group of love matches was as widespread as possible in order to capture any possible errors that might have occurred as she worked. Ricky on the other hand, was actually a technical engineer and he spent most of his time in the back end of honey trying to ensure that everything was as it should be inside the system files and inside the programs that Honey interacted with on a daily basis to perform vital tasks.

For Ricky and Samantha, the Tuesday had actually started out quite normally, in that they had gone about their daily tasks as they always did and as Honey's beautiful face had flashed up upon the huge screen that morning in front of Samantha, she had started her usual love match checks as she usually did each morning. Honey and Samantha, since the resort had actually opened five years before, had developed a kind of rapport in as much as was humanly possible between a computer system and human being and in some senses, Samantha actually saw Honey very much as her work colleague.

Samantha had smiled as she'd sat down in front of Honey that Tuesday morning and prepared for her day's work. "Honey, what love matches have you got for me today?" She'd politely asked the computer system as she did every working day.

"Greetings Samantha!" Honey had immediately replied in a pleasant, sophisticated, professional, polite feminine voice. "I have fifty love matches awaiting your review."

Samantha had smiled as she'd admired the gorgeous face of the computer system that

Bowen Logan had created and had then responded. "Great, let's make some love matches."

"Processing now." Honey had said as her face rapidly disappeared from the screen for a few seconds.

Ricky had watched Samantha with a huge grin upon his face as he'd sat behind the large, wafer screen directly in front of him. "You get way to excited about this Samantha, it must be a girl thing." He'd insisted as he'd begun to gently tease her. "For me it's different, for me we're just providing a service."

Samantha had immediately shaken her head in response as she'd glanced at him with an expression of total indignation upon her face. "How can you say that Ricky, we're providing friendship, companionship, romantic security and so much more? We're providing the dream of true love." She'd insisted. "We're changing lonely lives."

Honey's face had suddenly reappeared on the screen directly in front of Samantha as the computer had rendered the latest batch of love matches and Samantha had smiled as she'd quickly started to review them. Men and women's profiles had lined the screen in front of her as she'd begun to inspect and examine each love match slightly more closely, in order to check their validity. Samantha had touched the screen to access some of the actual individual profiles and several faces had rapidly appeared in much larger boxes in front of her.

Each profile and love match had to be inspected and a final sensibility check had to be performed and Samantha had a list of criteria that she usually checked for, in order to approve each one. Her daily working routine had been pretty much set in stone, ever since the first day she'd actually started when the resort had first opened and hence she'd known immediately, exactly what she had to do that day and exactly what she'd expected from Honey.

Samantha had quickly started to approve some of the matches that had appeared on the screen directly in front of her as she'd touched each one and had then selected the 'Confirmed' option from the bottom of each potential match box. "Honey, can we organize some Holographic Intimacy Sessions with Becky in order to review these potential matches please?" She'd politely requested. "Just as a final check."

"Processing now." Honey had immediately replied.

Samantha had smiled in response. "Thanks Honey. You make my job so much easier." She'd said as she'd quickly typed up a brief email and then sent it to Becky.

On the other side of the main resort building, Becky had been sat in front of her screen inside the Holographic Bonking Room Suite with a quite relaxed expression upon her face as for that day, her work had not yet actually started. Various thoughts had begun to fill her mind as it had started to wander as she'd waited for a new batch of compatible matches to test. Due to the absence of workload, Becky had even started to daydream and when her screen had suddenly beeped as an email had arrived from Samantha, it had quickly brought her back down to reality, very abruptly with a very loud bump.

Once the email had been read, Becky had quickly prepared to perform a holographic, sexual chemistry check upon the next group of matches that were due for review. Each profile had meticulously been loaded up onto the screen as Becky had smiled and then had selected one of the potential couples for a holographic sexual chemistry review as she'd initiated the holographic simulations. Becky had watched as the two holographic images in front of her had interacted in an intimate manner and had contemplated quietly how to some people, this holographic imagery would perhaps be seen as fun. Due to the length of time that Becky had actually been in her role, she had by now, actually become quite used to seeing such sights and they no longer shocked or even amused her, now for Becky, the holographic sexual chemistry checks were just very systematic and even slightly clinical. Every potential couple simply had to be assessed for sexual compatibility and that was the extent of her involvement and her task.

Becky had shaken her head as she'd quickly rejected the first potential pairing. "Nope, not a very good match at all." She'd muttered as she'd written some brief notes upon the matching system and then had touched the screen to load up the next couple's profiles.

Another couple had then appeared in the very center of the room in holographic forms just a few seconds later and Becky had started to watch them in order to analyze their suitability for each other. Her workload was very much like that, busy at times, quiet at others but she'd tried as hard as she possibly could to actually ensure that each day when she left work and made her way towards the staff quarters where the staff stayed during their working days, she'd cleared any potential matches upon the system that she'd been asked to review. Becky had glanced back at the screen directly in front of her and the batch of love matches which waited for her attention, she'd definitely be busy for the rest of the morning she'd quietly concluded.

Meanwhile back inside the operations room, Samantha had continued to review more potential love matches and things had been relatively calm until all of a sudden, she'd touched the screen in front of her and Honey had made a very strange, loud noise in response. The strange noise had been extremely unusual and even quite awful and had actually sounded like a malfunction of some kind. Due to her surprise, Samantha had immediately leapt to her feet and then jumped back from the screen.

"My mainframe has malfunctioned. I will switch of completely in exactly thirty minutes." Honey had said in a very solemn, serious tone.

Unfortunately, the strange, horrible noise had continued and Ricky had quickly rushed over towards the screen and then had touched it as he'd quickly attempted to stop Honey from actually switching off.

Samantha had immediately started to panic. "What's going on with Honey Ricky?" She'd asked in an alarmed voice. "What's actually happening? Did I break Honey? Oh Lord, they'll sack me for sure if I broke her." Samantha had mourned as she'd rubbed her forehead in distress.

"Samantha, I have been infected with a virus and you certainly did not break me!" Honey had replied as her face had suddenly started to flicker upon the screen.

Samantha had been completely horrified as she'd glanced back at Honey's usually beautiful, smiling face which now looked totally distorted and had glitches that ran all across it. "Honey you look so different." She'd uttered.

"Honey's right, it's not your fault Samantha." Ricky had gently reassured her as he'd touched the screen several times and

282

attempted to access Honey's backend. "This is a much bigger problem than someone just selecting a few wrong options. This is definitely a virus and the system corruption probably didn't even actually happen today." He'd explained.

Samantha had nodded as she'd listened quietly, Ricky definitely understood the technicalities of Honey that she certainly didn't and hence she'd trusted his knowledge. "Will you be able to fix Honey?" She'd asked.

Ricky had walked back over towards his own desk and screen and then had sat down behind it. "That depends, in the long run probably yes but it might take a while and that certainly won't happen today. I might need further assistance from some other engineers." He'd explained. "Honey is a very complex system."

Samantha had nodded as she'd listened.

"It's just as I thought, the virus actually infiltrated Honey's system about a month ago and it's probably affected her matching processes for the past few weeks and that means, since then we've probably mismatched some couples." Ricky had confirmed as he'd quickly stood up and then shaken his head.

"Do you think people might sue the resort?" Samantha had asked. "Or Mr. Logan?"

"Maybe, maybe not. I'll try to fix Honey and you can try to put right some of the mismatches." He'd quickly suggested. "You can try to organize a reunion or something and invite all the mismatched couples along to it so we can try to rematch them, whilst I work on tracking down the virus and fixing Honey. There's at least a sixty matches that have been affected, I'll send you all the info."

Samantha had nodded in agreement.

The door of the operations room had suddenly swished open and Becky had suddenly rushed inside the room. Her face had looked very alarmed and even slightly distressed as she'd rushed over towards Samantha and then stood beside her workstation. Something had clearly gone very wrong and not just inside the operations room.

"What's going on, the Holographic Bonking Suite Program just completely shut down, right in the middle of a bonking session?" Becky had asked.

"Honey's broken. She's got a virus and Ricky's going to try and repair her, we just found out today." Samantha had replied

"Anything I can help with Ricky?" Becky had asked as she'd wandered over towards Ricky's desk.

Ricky had been deeply absorbed in his thoughts as he'd stared at the screen directly in front of him and as he'd been so focused, he hadn't actually even noticed that Becky had actually entered inside the room. He'd suddenly glanced up at her face with a slightly startled expression, completely surprised to actually find her there at all.

"Do you need any help Ricky?" Becky had asked again. "Perhaps, I can try to do something from inside the Holographic Bonking Room Suite." She'd offered.

Ricky had immediately nodded in response. "Yes that would be great Becky, right now I need all the help I can get." He'd replied as he'd accepted her kind and generous offer, Becky was certainly a lot more technically astute than Samantha was and she knew her way around Honey's backend slightly better as a result. Ricky had quickly handed her a USB. "This should help you." He'd mentioned as he'd smiled. "Try to skim Honey's system files with the software on this USB. You skim the software programs and I'll skim the drives, utility programs and hardware partitions."

Becky had agreed and nodded as she'd accepted the USB. "I'll try my best." She'd reassured him.

The rest of the day had gone by painfully slowly for the three resort staff as they'd battled to perform each task and find an actual solution to Honey's malfunction without Honey's usual assistance. Every minute that had gone by had seemed more frustrating than the last as they'd completely ignored lunch and had carried on working straight through into the afternoon, almost like soldiers on a military mission.

When dinner time and the early evening arrived, still no solution had actually been found as Ricky prepared to take more drastic action and suddenly abandoned his desk and then strode across the room to where Samantha was seated. Outside the windows of the operation room, darkness had already started to threaten to invade the day as the dusky pink clouds that had decorated the skyline, gradually started to darken and become a deep, reddish crimson color.

"I've got an idea." Ricky suggested. "It's not a totally fool proof plan but it could work."

Samantha nodded as she encouraged him to proceed. "What is it?" She enquired.

"I think we could enter inside the back end of Honey through the Holographic Bonking Room Suite." Ricky explained. "There's a maintenance area you can access from there that we absolutely never utilize. It was only really created, designed and kept running for absolute emergencies and this is an absolute emergency."

Samantha nodded in agreement. "I think that's a great idea Ricky." She confirmed.

"Yes, if I can get into Honey's backend through the maintenance area, I can then try and track down the virus through Honey's internal systems from there." He elaborated.

"Do you think that'll work?" Samantha asked.

"It's certainly possible." Ricky replied. "You stay here and keep trying to sort out the mismatched couples and I'll go and see Becky and find out."

Samantha nodded.

"Make sure you take a break and get something to eat though." He advised.

"Otherwise you'll be starving and fainting and Honey will be broken and then we'll have two emergencies instead of one."

Samantha nodded. "Mr. Logan will be so upset when he finds out about this. Honey was such an expensive computer to build." She mourned.

Ricky placed his arm on her shoulder reassuringly. "Don't worry Samantha, we'll find a way to fix Honey." He gently reassured her. "I'm very sure." Ricky turned and then strode across the room towards the door as he prepared to visit the Holographic Bonking Room Suite, internally he wasn't very certain at all but he hoped that a visit to Becky would yield the results he actually required.

Very fortunately for Ricky ten minutes later, when he actually arrived inside the Holographic Bonking Room Suite, Becky hadn't yet actually abandoned her post for the day. Due to the operations room being situated at the very rear of the building and the Holographic Bonking Room Suite being situated at the very front of the building, close to the reception, it actually took him around ten minutes to walk along the long hallways and corridors that actually led there. The room was extremely quiet as he entered and the door swished gently closed behind him as he walked straight over towards Becky with a smile upon his face.

"How's it going?" Ricky asked.

"Not great really" Becky replied as she greeted him with a frustrated smile and then gently shook her head.

"Look I've had an idea." He mentioned. "Perhaps we're going about this all wrong, perhaps we should try to actually enter inside the holographic maintenance area and get into Honey's backend that way."

Becky eyes suddenly light up with sparks of hope as she internally considered his suggestion. "Do you think that'll work?" She asked.

"It's worth a try." Ricky insisted. "Right now anything's worth a try."

"We could use virtual headsets to access the maintenance area." Becky suggested.

"Yep that's a great idea and that would give us much more control, once we're inside the system." Ricky immediately agreed.

Becky smiled, relieved that the two had found another potential solution to the current dilemma they both faced as the current solution, certainly wasn't getting them anywhere fast. "Should I come in there with you?" She asked.

"Yeah sure. Another pair of eyes will definitely help." Ricky replied.

A gentle knock suddenly sounded at the door and Becky immediately stood up and then walked over towards it. Much to Becky's surprise, when the door actually swished open, she actually found Madeline just outside it, who by this time had actually finished her pairing activities for that day, eaten her evening meal and then had returned with Zoe to her suite. Before Madeline had headed down towards the poolside bar as was usual each evening with Zoe, she'd checked her electronic journal device and noticed that it had a strange error message upon it and due to her curiosity regarding her potential love matches and the results of the various pairing activities, she'd decided to notify the resort staff about the error message immediately and hence sought out Becky's assistance.

Becky gave her a slightly strained smile and then greeted her politely. "Hi Madeline, how can I help you this evening?" She asked.

"I'm having a slight problem with the electronic journal device that we usually use to check our schedule and the results of the pairing activities and I just thought I should let you know." Madeline explained, slightly surprised by the fact that Becky had actually remembered her name. "You remembered my name." She added.

"Well, I don't check in many people so I tend to remember the few that I do." Becky replied as she smiled.

Madeline smiled.

"We're actually having a bit of a system crisis at the moment so that's probably why the electronic journals are not functioning right now as they should be?" Becky explained. "We're hoping to have everything back to normal later this evening, so I apologize for any inconvenience that this has caused."

"Sure. No problem." Madeline said as she immediately accepted Becky's explanation and very humble apology. She hesitated for a few seconds as she internally considered the issue Becky had mentioned, before she continued. "Is there anything I can do to help perhaps?"

"It's very technical really, we're actually trying to track down a virus that's infected the system and we're just about to actually enter inside the system virtually." Becky explained.

"Well, I did study computer programming whilst I was in college as a secondary subject, before I decided to focus my attention completely on fashion." Madeline informed her. "I don't know everything but I might know something useful."

Becky nodded. "I'll tell you what come in, three heads are definitely better than two." She replied as she invited Madeline inside the suite.

Madeline stepped inside the room and the door swished quietly closed behind her. "Right." She agreed as she followed Becky across the room and headed towards the desk where Ricky was actually still seated.

Unknown to Becky, Madeline's visit that evening, was not actually the first time that she had actually been inside the Holographic Bonking Room Suite but Madeline didn't mention her previous visit at all as she smiled politely at Ricky and then shook the hand he extended towards her. The two resort staff both seemed to be quite worried and tense as Madeline quietly inspected each of their faces slightly more closely as she attempted to understand the gravity of the problem they actually faced.

"Hi, I'm Ricky." Ricky mentioned as he politely introduced himself and then quickly stood up. "I'm a resort technician."

"He's the only resort technician and a very senior one." Becky immediately started to explain. "He's practically a systems genius and he's single handedly looked after Honey ever since the resort first opened. This is Madeline Ricky, she's one of our guests." She mentioned as she stood behind her desk. "She's offered to help, she's studied technology and computer systems at college." Becky added.

"Very nice to meet you Madeline." Ricky remarked as he politely accepted her presence. "So sad that it had to be in such a tricky situation but still a pleasure nonetheless."

"He doesn't get to meet many guests." Becky teased as she winked at Madeline. "He barely even leaves the computer operations room each day and personally I think he's actually in love with Honey. They rarely let him out of there, not even for good behavior."

"Come on. Honey's a computer." Ricky immediately interjected. "Sure, I love computers but not that much."

Becky giggled. "Just checking." She teased.

"Right, let's get inside this system." Ricky suddenly urged as he picked up a headset from the top of the desk and then handed it to Madeline.

Becky nodded and then quickly opened up a large cupboard door just behind her desk and plucked out another chair. "Have a seat here Madeline, put on the headset and then you'll be ready to go." She instructed.

Madeline nodded and smiled as she sat down upon the chair that Becky had offered her and then slipped on the headset. "Do we have to do anything in particular?" She enquired.

"Once we're inside the system, I'll direct everyone." Ricky immediately clarified.

Madeline nodded.

Becky sat down in front of her desk and then touched the screen directly in front of her as she quickly loaded their three profiles up onto it. "Right we're ready to go in." She notified Ricky as she quickly leant down and plucked another headset out of a drawer in her desk.

Three holograms immediately appeared in the center of the room which Madeline did not actually notice as by this time, her headset was very securely situated upon her head. Directly in front of Madeline however, she could now actually see a metallic looking door and both Ricky and Becky suddenly appeared beside her, just a few seconds later as she simply stared at the door directly in front of her, reluctant to proceed until the other two had actually arrived. The three, once they had all gathered, then started to walk towards the door as Ricky quickly motioned towards the two women to follow him as he prepared to lead them through it.

"This is the holographic maintenance menu." Ricky explained as he pushed the door in front of him open quite firmly and then held it open for the two women who were directly behind him. "We've found a way in, now let's go try and fix Honey." He insisted as he smiled enthusiastically.

"Yes, let's go find this virus." Becky agreed as she smiled at Madeline.

On the other side of the metallic door, there was a huge room that was filled with wires, motherboards and circuits and as the three stepped inside it, they quietly glanced around at their surroundings. A pathway led through the multitude of electronic chaos before them and the three immediately began to follow it as it twisted and turned in various directions. When the three arrived at the other side of the very large room, they found another door directly in front of them which they then quickly entered. The second door led directly into another large space which seemed to have no end or walls that was filled with brightly colored waves which flowed around each of them as they entered inside it and it looked almost like, a very colorful ocean. Golden numbers and some small, square golden objects gently flowed through each of the waves which were all very bright in color and actually seemed to glow.

"We're definitely inside Honey now." Ricky confirmed as he eagerly started to wade through the mass of colored waves directly in front of him.

Madeline and Becky nodded and then quickly began to follow him.

Further along the hallway that led into the Cuddle Wing, Zoe sat inside the suite that she shared with Madeline and glanced at the time upon the face of her phone. Madeline had been gone for a while and just hadn't actually returned and she'd even left her phone inside the lounge area of the suite upon the coffee table, so there was no actual way to contact her. Due to Zoe's lack of interest in the problems that had affected the electronic journals that the resort usually utilized to keep vacationers up to date, Zoe had decided to opt out of discussing the issue with the resort staff alongside Madeline and had decided instead to remain inside their suite and ready herself for the evening ahead which would be spent at the poolside bar with Giovanni, Louise, Steven and Callum. However, when Madeline didn't return thirty minutes later, Zoe became quite bored as the poolside meeting they'd organized, was not actually due to happen for another hour and she quickly decided that she had to actually find something else to do in the meantime.

Patience was not Zoe's friend and was not something that she was particularly good at practicing and that meant, she actually needed to do something that would not only amuse but also entertain her and hanging around in an empty suite on her own, certainly did not fulfil either of those two criteria. Boredom was a destination situated a hundred miles away from Zoe's ideal evening and that meant, drastic action therefore had to be taken immediately to find an alternative place and form of entertainment in which to spend the next hour of her life.

Zoe suddenly stood up and then made her way towards the bedroom that she'd slept in every night since she'd initially arrived at the resort. A small, white beauty case lay on top of the small bedside cabinet that was filled to the brim with makeup, creams and a vast array of skin and beauty treatments and she glanced at it quietly for a moment as she nodded thoughtfully. The beauty case was the usual kind of case that many beauticians used to carry their equipment and necessities around inside and she'd brought it on vacation very much for her own purposes. She smiled at it mischievously and then picked it up as she prepared to kill some time that evening, in a very productive but very essential manner, at least in her opinion anyway.

Ten minutes later as Zoe stood outside Louise's suite equipped with her beauty case, she knocked softly upon the door. A few seconds later, Louise opened the door and as it swished open, Zoe immediately greeted her with a smile. Louise looked very surprised to see Zoe as all three women had actually agreed after dinner, to meet an hour later inside the reception, before they were due to attend their meeting with the three men beside the bar and therefore, they weren't actually due to meet yet.

"Are you bored Louise?" Zoe asked.

Louise nodded. "Yeah, I got ready ages ago." She replied. "Where's Madeline?"

"Lord only knows." Zoe replied as she shrugged. "She mentioned something about a problem with the electronic journals the resort gave us and then disappeared a while ago. There's something I've been absolutely dying to do since the very first day I arrived here and I think you can help. You up for it?" Zoe asked. "If so, follow me."

Louise grinned and nodded. "Sure, just let me get my handbag." She replied.

Five minutes later, the two women stood just outside Thomas's suite door as Zoe held her beauty case firmly inside one of her hands and smiled. The two women glanced at each other slightly nervously for a few seconds before Zoe bravely stretched out her arm and then knocked upon the door. A few seconds later, Thomas answered the door with a newspaper inside his hands which he had very clearly, just been reading. Thomas looked just as frumpy and nerdy as ever as Zoe quietly glanced at him and then gently shook her head.

He glanced at them both as a startled, confused expression suddenly started to cross his face. "To what do I owe the pleasure of this surprise visit ladies?" Thomas asked, completely and utterly surprised by the two women's sudden appearance.

"Thomas, we're here to change your life." Zoe replied as she quickly stepped inside his suite and then gently dragged Louise by the arm alongside her. She placed her beauty case down upon the coffee table and then immediately opened it up and plucked some items out of it that she definitely required for Thomas's makeover operation. "Louise can you sort Thomas out with some clothes please?" Zoe asked as she suddenly turned to face Louise and then paused for a moment. "He must have something that we can coordinate for him in some form or another that will look semi decent."

Louise smiled and nodded in response. "I'll do my very best." She replied as she quickly glanced at Thomas's current attire, gently touched his shirt and then shook her head. "Where are your clothes Thomas?" Louise asked.

"Through there, inside the wardrobe in the bedroom." Thomas replied as he pointed towards the bedroom. "I hung them all up inside there when I first arrived."

Louise nodded and then made her way towards the bedroom.

"Thomas, you need to sit down on the sofa." Zoe instructed.

Thomas nodded and then obediently sat down.

Zoe smiled and then stood in front of him as she grabbed a wax strip from her case and then briskly rubbed it between her hands. She glanced at Thomas's face and he smiled at her, just before she pressed the wax strip down in-between his eyebrows, obviously Thomas was blissfully unaware of what Zoe was actually just about to do to him and had perhaps never even actually had a wax before in his entire life.

Despite Thomas's naivety and Zoe's intentions, she smiled at him sweetly as she gently smoothed the wax strip down upon his skin and then pressed it more firmly against his forehead. Thomas had spent money on his vacation, just as Zoe and Madeline had and Zoe was completely adamant, that if she did not give him the makeover he really required, he was not going to actually get anything out of it at all. His current appearance was just so very unappealing and he was surrounded by some extremely handsome, good looking, attractive men and that meant, the odds were definitely not in his favor. Zoe had to step in and she had to assist him and by doing so, she definitely felt she would not only increase his chances of meeting and attracting a decent looking female but also assist him in actually retaining their romantic interest. A few seconds later and without any warning whatsoever, Zoe abruptly pulled the wax strip quickly off Thomas's forehead.

"Ouch!" Thomas yelled as he felt the pain. "That hurt!"

Louise entered back inside the lounge with a few garments inside her hands and then paused for a moment as she glanced at

Thomas's extremely red forehead. "Now you understand what we women have to go through every day Thomas." She explained as she gently patted his shoulder to comfort him. "Beauty can be very painful."

Zoe giggled.

"What do you think of this shirt and these trousers Zoe?" Louise asked as she suddenly held up a shirt and pair of trousers and showed a clothing combination to Zoe.

Zoe nodded. "I quite like that, that's a definite yes." She immediately verified. "We'll hang each outfit combination up together Thomas, so that you know exactly what to wear with what."

Louise nodded her head in agreement. "Yes that way, you don't get lost or revert back to awkward clothing." She added. "We want you to get a great date Thomas."

Zoe started to apply some more skin treatments to Thomas's face as Louise disappeared back inside his bedroom. "Trust me Thomas, what we're doing right now, will really help you." She gently reassured him.

Thomas nodded humbly as he accepted the two woman's assistance.

Due to Thomas's extremely obedient compliance with her makeover, Zoe was utterly delighted as she swanned around the lounge and consulted Louise now and again to discuss various outfits and their suitability. The contents of Thomas's wardrobe were really quite drab but Louise had actually managed to find and salvage some outfits that could actually be coordinated to make Thomas look slightly smarter and slightly more presentable. Once Louise had finished her task, she rushed off back towards her suite to collect some men's aftershave samples as very fortunately, she actually had quite a few inside her suitcase that she'd brought along with her on vacation, just in case she might need them.

"You didn't have much to work with Thomas but we've tried our best." Zoe reassured him as the two were left alone.

Thomas nodded appreciatively.

Meanwhile, back inside the Holographic Bonking Room Suite, Madeline, Ricky and Becky had by now, actually waded through the colored waves but as yet, had not actually found a way out of the swirling, colored mass that surrounded them. Ricky, although he was in charge and actually leading the group, appeared to be very uncertain about how to actually leave the area they were currently situated inside, in order to actually proceed further with their plan.

"Where are we?" Becky suddenly asked him.

"This is the program area. Any virus inside Honey's system should be attached to a program in or around here I think." Ricky replied.

"How do we find programs?" Becky enquired.

"I'm not totally sure but perhaps if we wait around inside here for a few minutes longer, we might see some floating through the waves." Ricky explained. "If we're very lucky, we might even find the program with the virus actually attached to it inside here."

The three stood completely still as they waited for a few minutes until the very first program arrived and when he did so, as he certainly appeared to be male, he flowed and floated gently through the waves nearby as they quietly watched him. He was dressed in a yellow suit and had bright yellow hair on top of his head to match his attire and as they approached him, he immediately stopped and then quickly turned to face them.

Becky gently nudged Ricky as she glanced at him with a confused expression upon her face. "Who is he?" She asked.

Ricky immediately whispered in response. "He's a program."

Becky was confused for a moment as she glanced back at him and then inspected every intricate detail from his head to his toe. "Are programs people?" She asked.

Ricky nodded. "I guess when Bowen built the system, he must have personified all Honey's interior programs and components. Honey is a female remember and a very attractive one at that and therefore it makes total sense that he would perhaps do the same with Honey's internal system and the programs she hosts inside of her."

Becky smiled. "How strange." She remarked.

Ricky faced the man in yellow clothing and then smiled as he prepared to address him. "Hi I'm Ricky." He said as he politely introduced himself.

"Good day everyone, I'm Personality Analyzer." The man in yellow immediately stated in response, in quite a flat, factual tone.

"We're human beings and we've come from the world just outside the system." Ricky replied. "We're trying to track down a Virus that's infected Honey and that's made her malfunction. Have you noticed anything strange recently or has anyone unusual been hanging around?"

Personality Analyzer thought about Ricky's question for a few seconds as he fell completely silent and just glanced at the three human beings directly in front of him curiously before he responded. "We rarely have any visitors here and certainly not any human beings. How did you get in here?" Personality Analyzer suddenly asked slightly suspiciously. "And how do I know you're not viruses, trying to find and attack our sensitive internal program areas?"

"We came in through the holographic maintenance menu." Madeline explained. "And through virtual headsets. We're just trying to help."

"Ah, the maintenance menu, now that does makes sense." Personality Analyzer replied as he nodded in understanding. "If you like, I'll take you to the main program lounge, another program we find in there might have more of information about the location of this virus you're looking for." He suggested.

Madeline and Becky immediately nodded in response.

"He's extremely polite." Becky whispered to Madeline as the two women and Ricky followed his lead.

"Probably because he's a program. I bet the virus won't be so polite, if indeed he or she is actually a person." Madeline joked.

A path suddenly appeared directly in front of the four as the colored waves around them rapidly began to part and Personality Analyzer then began to led them through the watery colored walls that surrounded them. Right at the very end of the path was a glossy, red door which Personality Analyzer quickly led them towards which they definitely hadn't seen before the colored waves had actually parted. Just as they arrived in front of the door however, bright lights and colored waves suddenly flooded all over them as the door flickered in front of them.

Due to the confusion and unexpected interruption, Madeline and Becky immediately removed their headsets and then glanced around the Holographic Bonking Room Suite as they quickly attempted to establish exactly what had happened. In the very center of the room, ten holograms had actually appeared, who were it seemed engaged in what looked like very sexual activities which were very clearly aggressive as they angrily whipped and lashed out at each other. The orgy they appeared to be involved in, certainly didn't look very pleasant and even verged upon being sadistic in nature and what one might describe as extremely cruel. Each of their holographic bodies had deep gashes and bloody cuts upon them as the two women glanced at their naked, abused forms in complete and utter confusion and then looked at each other with startled expressions.

"What's going on?" Madeline asked as she shook her head.

Ricky, who had by now also removed his headset, quickly glanced at the center of the room and then shook his head. "It must be the virus, it must be attacking Honey by loading up multiple programs at one time, in an attempt to overload her system to keep her shut down." He replied. "Perhaps Honey is fighting back."

"Wow, it looks kind of scary, I hope Honey will be ok. I've never seen holograms like these before. They look so weird." Becky replied in an alarmed voice.

Ricky stood up, walked over towards Becky's chair and then gently placed his arm around her shoulders as he gazed intensely into her eyes. "Don't worry, everything will be fine." He gently reassured her. "We'll try and find the virus and then destroy it and Honey will be just fine."

Becky nodded as she accepted his gentle reassurances. "I really hope so Ricky, this looks very serious. Perhaps we should notify Bowen."

"Not yet. Let's try to fix Honey first." Ricky insisted as he quickly rejected her suggestion. "Then once Honey is fixed, we can let Bowen know exactly what happened."

Becky nodded.

"It's better to have fixed a problem and then notify Bowen, once it's actually sorted out, than to worry him unnecessarily whilst it's still ongoing and unfixed." Ricky explained. "This is our first real, technical challenge in terms of the system and we have to show Bowen that we can actually cope with it, after all that is what we're actually paid to do. Let's just put our headsets back on and try again." He suggested as he walked back towards his chair, sat back down and then slipped his headset back onto his head.

Madeline and Becky immediately complied with his request as they both quietly slipped their respective headsets back on and prepared themselves to re-enter inside the back end of Honey.

THE VIRUS

Since Ricky had abandoned Samantha and left her alone inside the operations room earlier that day, she'd worked tirelessly and diligently upon the list of mismatched clients who had previously visited the resort as she'd attempted to come up with a plan to correct the issues that the virus and subsequent mismatches had actually created. Relationships had been formed that were not as they should be and the delicate, perfect romantic matching that the Love Colony promised to deliver had been thrown into complete and utter disarray. Bowen Logan and his company Love Inc.'s reputation, could now so easily be tarnished by the fallout and any possibly disastrous results and Samantha had fully understood the predicament the resort now actually faced. The night had gently entered the world as she'd worked and then wrapped its arms around the building and as darkness had engulfed each of the windows and eventually Samantha had dozed off on her chair, unable to keep her weary eyelids open for any longer as they'd finally surrendered and then completely closed.

Suddenly at around eleven however without any warning at all, the doors of the operations room rapidly swished open and someone actually entered inside the room. Samantha quickly woke up and then sat up as she rubbed her eyes and almost fell of her chair whilst doing so as she'd been completely caught off guard, it had been an extremely long, working day and she had totally not intended to actually fall asleep at her desk. She had dozed off and now very unfortunately, Bowen Logan was actually the unexpected visitor to the operations room, her actual boss and he'd found her right slap bang in the middle of a nap.

Silence completely filled the room as Bowen Logan strode over towards Samantha and her desk and she quickly tried to straighten up her resort uniform and her hair. A tense smile decorated her face as she attempted to look as attentive and organized as possible and as if she hadn't actually just dozed off. Bowen Logan was quite a young man, regardless of his achievements in life and in his mid-thirties and Samantha definitely felt, he would certainly not be very impressed to find one of his staff actually sleeping on the job, especially when there was a crisis.

In terms of his appearance, Bowen Logan was quite tall, handsome and slightly stocky with jet black hair and striking sapphire, deep blue eyes. His skin had a light brownish, beige tint to it and most people usually struggled to guess his actual origins as he had a very unusual and quite exotic look. For one reason or another the mystery of his origins however, remained exactly that and was even considered a total enigma as most of the people that Bowen usually interacted with, never actually dared to enquire as to where he was actually from as they were either customers of his or people he actually employed. His accent was barely distinguishable and seemed to be a combination of several accents and hence it was extremely hard to place. An aura seemed to surround Bowen Logan that instantly commanded respect and because he rarely entered into personal conversations with anyone and especially not with his employees, most of the staff at the resort did not even dare to ask him intrusive, personal questions and respected his private life which he kept very much to himself.

"Apologies Mr. Logan, I had no idea that you would be coming here today." Samantha muttered apologetically.

"I didn't actually intend to." Bowen Logan replied as he walked towards Ricky's computer screen. "It was an unplanned and unscheduled visit."

Samantha immediately began to panic as she quietly contemplated internally whether or not she should notify him about the current problems with Honey. "Mr. Logan there's something you should know." She started as she quickly decided that she should definitely say something as perhaps that was why he was actually there. Samantha knew however, once she'd started to explain, it would be too late to try and disguise the situation or hide it any way, shape or form but he'd probably realize it himself anyway within a few seconds of looking at Ricky's screen. "Today, well there was a huge problem with Honey." She continued.

Bowen pulled up a chair in front of Ricky's screen and then sat down in front of it. "Samantha I already know, that's why I'm here. I tried to access Honey earlier today to review the current season and I had problems accessing the system. So I came down to the island to find out why and to find out what is actually going on." He explained.

Samantha nodded as she listened quietly.

"Where's Ricky?" Bowen asked. "I expected him to be here."

"Honey's been infected by a virus." Samantha explained. "Becky and Ricky are accessing the backend of the system through the Holographic Compatibility Suite to try and repair her."

Bowen nodded as he listened. "How many couples do you think have been affected and mismatched?" He asked as he walked towards Samantha's desk, the Holographic Compatibility Suite was his technical name for the holographic office that Becky usually occupied but he knew that the resort staff usually actually referred to it as the Holographic Bonking Room Suite, behind his back of course.

Samantha inhaled as she took a deep breath and prepared to break the bad news to Bowen. She definitely had to tell him what was going on, after all he was actually the resort and island's proprietor and the sooner he actually knew, the sooner he could actually assist them and perhaps even help to fix the situation but she was still slightly nervous. "I'd say about a sixty mismatches have occurred, plus the current visitor's matches are a little bit skewed."

Bowen sighed with relief. "The situation's not too bad then. Great that shouldn't be too difficult to fix."

Samantha nodded. "Yes Mr. Logan, Ricky and I decided that I should organize a reunion for mismatched couples straight away, in order to straighten out any mismatches. I've planned it and I've actually invited most of the couples already." She explained. "We've called it an anniversary celebration and invited the past guests to a Dinner and Dance so as yet, none of the guests are any the wiser."

Bowen nodded and then responded positively as he smiled. "Great that's what we need, solutions not panic."

"Yes Mr. Logan." Samantha replied as she smiled and began to relax a little internally, Bowen Logan was not angry with her at all it seemed and she was not about to actually get fired and that was in her mind, a huge relief.

On the other side of the resort, inside the Holographic Bonking Room Suite, Ricky by this time had actually managed to shut down some of the attacks on Honey and the three had then entered back inside the holographic maintenance area and regrouped with Personality Analyzer. They had actually by now, been taken through the brightly colored door which led directly into a large lounge like space which Personality Analyzer had informed them was the Program Lounge. Inside the large white space, there were quite a few people that occupied brightly colored sofas which interestingly enough, actually matched their hair color and outfits. Not all the brightly colored sofas inside the large lounge were occupied however and that clearly indicated to Madeline, Ricky and Becky that not all the main programs which operated each day inside Honey were present.

One of the sofas had a woman dressed in red seated upon it and she quickly stood up as soon as she actually noticed the four enter inside the room.   Personality Analyzer enthusiastically led the three around the lounge as he politely introduced and presented his three human guests to all the programs inside it.   The woman in red, they soon discovered was actually referred to as the Sexual Compatibility Assessor and there was a man dressed all in green, who was introduced to the human visitors as the Jealousy Advisor Program.   Another man, who was clothed in royal blue was introduced as the Physical Attraction Analyzer Program and a woman dressed all in pink, it quickly transpired was the Romantic Consultation Program. A final sofa tucked away at one end of the room, had a woman seated upon it that was all dressed in purple and she was introduced as the Emotional Compatibility Guide Program.

Each one of the programs seemed extremely polite and attentive and several even actually stood up as soon as the human beings and Personality Analyzer approached them.

No doubt their curiosity had been sparked by the presence of the strange guests that had actually been brought into their environment and they all actually seemed to be quite intrigued. The female program in red, actually appeared to be more than just curious about the human guests as it quickly transpired that she had actually taken quite a liking to Ricky as she pawned his shirt playfully and even engaged in quite flirtatious conversation with him, when the two were actually introduced.

"Hello handsome." She said in a seductive, silky voice as Ricky stood directly in front of her. "I'm Vixen, Sexual Compatibility Assessor." She ran her hands playfully up his chest and up behind his neck, as she spoke and continued to flirt with him outrageously. "What can I do for you?" Vixen asked in a seductive tone of voice that clearly displayed her sexual interest.

Ricky quickly removed her hands from his person and then pushed her very gently backwards as he softly rejected her advances. "We're here to track down a virus that's infected Honey. We entered into the system through the holographic maintenance menu. Have you seen anything strange lately?"

"You can always track me down to my suite first." Vixen replied as she moved slightly closer to him once more and then delicately ran her fingers across his chest. "I'm the kind of program that enjoys interactive participation." She said as she circled around Ricky and gave his body a lust filled up and down once over with her eyes.

Becky smirked as she watched.

Ricky quickly stepped backwards as he attempted to distance himself once more, in an attempt to be so far out of reach that the persistent female program could no longer actually touch him. "I'll keep that in mind, once we've actually found the virus." He replied politely.

Vixen's face held an almost indignant expression as she suddenly swallowed his rejection with bitterness and slight agitation, she certainly wasn't used to be rejected and this human being had spurned her charms that were quite frankly, simply irresistible. "Well I'm always here." She insisted in a slightly disgruntled tone. "One day, you might need a little warmth and when you do, you know where to find me."

Personality Analyzer suddenly interrupted the conversation between the two as he attempted to shift everyone's attention back to the matter at hand, the virus. "Vixen, this is very serious, please control yourself at once." He demanded.

Vixen looked at him with a slightly sullen expression upon her face as if she was a spoilt child that had just been rebuked. "Okay, okay." She replied as she surrendered to his overt but subtle scolding.

"Has anyone got any helpful information about this virus? If Honey dies, we all die." Personality Analyzer insisted as he glanced around the room at the other programs and quickly inspected each of their faces, who were all by now actually standing in very close proximity to him and had quite serious expressions upon their faces. "This is an extremely serious situation." He urged.

Nothing but blank expressions and faces met Personality Analyzer in response but a few seconds later, a few heads started to shake, no one it seemed had the slightest bit of information that could actually help at all. Just as Personality Analyzer was about to give up however, Physical Attraction Analyzer suddenly stepped forward and then raised his arm slightly nervously.

Personality Analyzer nodded as he encouraged him to elaborate. "Yes Attraction, what do you know?" He prompted as he urged the program to speak.

"Well it might be nothing but the last time I met Chemistry, she acted a bit strange. She seemed to be in an awful rush and not as attentive towards our combined tasks as she usually is." He replied.

"What about you Vixen do you know anything?" Personality Analyzer pressed, just in case the program actually had any helpful information that she might be withholding as a form of retaliation to her rejection by Ricky.

Vixen gave him a slightly stubborn look as she defensively crossed her arms. "I might." She replied as she pouted in response.

Personality Analyzer walked up to her and then stared directly into her eyes very sternly as if he was dealing with a naughty child. "What do you know Vixen?" He demanded.

Vixen gave off a loud tut as she became even more agitated and when she finally responded, her reply was reluctant and filled with attitude. "Well, I did see a man earlier on all dressed in grey. He was headed in that direction, towards the Recycle Bin." She replied as she pointed towards one of several doors that lead out of the lounge. Her tone was full of resentment as she begrudgingly assisted. "He looked like trash, so I just assumed he was being deleted."

Personality Analyzer nodded. "Thank you Vixen and thank you Attraction." He remarked. "You've both been very helpful."

Once Personality Analyzer was satisfied that he'd actually extracted all the useful information regarding the Virus from all the programs inside the lounge, he led Madeline, Ricky and Becky quickly towards the door that Vixen had pointed towards. The Virus inside Honey, it now transpired was actually a personified form of existence inside the system itself and there had at least been sightings of him and further information provided that could possibly lead to his whereabouts and that encouraged the four as they walked.

When the three humans and program stepped through the door, the human beings immediately found themselves inside a glossy, black hallway that seemed almost alive as small patches of bright colors surged through it and streamed along it. Along the hallway, down either side, there was a series of doors that had absolutely no markings upon them at all or any other distinguishing features except for their coloring which varied from door to door.

"These are our living quarters." Personality Analyzer explained as he briskly led the three human being further along the corridor. He arrived outside a burgundy colored door and then stopped right in front of it. "This is Chemistry Verification's suite." Personality Analyzer explained in a hushed tone. "The Recycle Bin is a bit further along this hallway, right at the very bottom. Chemistry Verification is a good program, very loyal, very dependable and she absolutely never, ever malfunctions or crashes and that Virus must have tricked, bamboozled, seduced and corrupted her."

The three human beings glanced quietly at the closed burgundy door directly in front of them as Personality Analyzer took a deep breath, stepped forward and then gently knocked upon it. A few seconds later, a petite woman dressed completely in burgundy, opened the door and once she saw the four, she quickly stepped out of the doorway and then pulled the door firmly shut behind her as she walked almost as if she wanted to conceal something inside her living quarters.

"Yes Analyzer how can I help you?" Chemistry Verification asked as a nervous smiled adorned her pretty face. She nodded politely at the three human beings next to him.

"Perhaps, it's how can we actually help you." Personality Analyzer explained. "A malicious Virus has infiltrated Honey's system and we believe he's latched onto a program to form a solid attack base. He's a Virus and that means he doesn't actually care about the program he's attached to which he is just using as a base point from which to replicate his poison in order to attack Honey's system more effectively."

Chemistry Verification nodded as she listened.

"This Virus is a treacherous creature that has created all kinds of problems for the human beings outside the system and that's why they've had to come inside Honey to actually find him. He's affected all the human love matches at the resort that Honey usually makes and maintains and has even totally ruined some of them." Personality Analyzer explained.

"What does that have to do with me?" Chemistry Verification asked.

"Honey could die Chemistry, she's completely malfunctioned and is hardly even able to power up and if she dies, we all die too." He explained in an urgent tone. "We think this Virus might have actually attached itself to you and that he might be using your program functionalities to actually infect Honey's circuits and drives." Personality Analyzer continued. "We think this Virus might actually have disguised himself as a male program. Have you met any new programs recently?"

Chemistry Verification nodded in response and then answered his question in a hushed whisper. "Actually I did met someone new recently, he's inside my living quarters right now. He's actually sitting inside my lounge."

A round small, glass window situated at the very top of the burgundy door, exposed the interior of the program's suite and each of the four quickly stepped forward to peer through it as they attempted to view the large lounge that lay just behind the door. Chemistry Verification quietly stepped aside as she allowed the four to gather around the small window and inspect not only the interior of her suite but also ultimately, the male Virus that was situated inside it and the source of all the love resort's recent problems.

Virus, it appeared as the four stared through the small window at the top of the door, was a haughty looking, mature man all dressed in grey just as Vixen had previously mentioned. He sat silently upon the burgundy sofa inside the lounge and inside his hands he held a grey bottle which he appeared to be consuming the contents of. Personality Analyzer immediately began to gently shake his head as he watched him quietly for a moment. The Virus was indeed very real and just like one of the programs inside Honey, which had been given a human like form by their creator and developers, he had also mimicked a human form, in order to function freely inside Honey without any suspicions being raised.

"How can we get rid of him? He'll kill us all." Chemistry Verification suddenly asked as she began to panic. "We all love Honey so much and I'd do anything for her. I'd never allow anyone to try and kill her." Her face carried a worried, extremely distressed expression upon it as she glanced at Personality Analyzer's face with tears in her eyes.

"Look I've actually got a plan, it might work, it might not." Personality Analyzer mentioned quietly. "Everyone gather round please and we'll try to get this sorted out sooner rather than later."

The three human beings and the program, gathered quietly around Personality Analyzer as they prepared to listen to him speak and he quickly explained his plan to them in a hushed voice. There were some very risky elements to his plan and a few uncertain aspects but they all knew deep down, right now there was absolutely no other choice and that his plan was the only real solution that seemed to be feasible and workable. Chemistry Verification and Madeline it quickly transpired, would be the main implementers of the plan and hence both of them had to absolutely agree with it and also be totally comfortable with both their roles.

Once the plan had been agreed, the five walked further along the hallway as they prepared to implement the plan which they hoped would actually help them capture and completely destroy the Virus. When they arrived at the bottom of the hallway, they walked through the two large doors situated at the very end of it which led directly into the Recycle Bin as they prepared to set their plan in motion. Personality Analyzer quickly pulled a tube of green liquid out of his trouser pocket and then rapidly smeared some of the liquid over Chemistry Verification's leg. He tore the material of her clothing around her leg, just underneath the area he had doused and then quickly squirted some more of the contents of the tube upon parts of her naked circuitry which were now exposed.

"Does that look effective?" He enquired.

Chemistry Verification nodded. "From a distance it sure will." She replied.

Personality Analyzer gently touched her arm. "You know exactly what you have to do right?" He asked.

Chemistry Verification immediately nodded in response.

"Good luck and please Chemistry, don't get trashed. We still need you around." He insisted as he smiled.

"Thank so much Analyzer. I had no idea who or what he actually really was." Chemistry Verification said appreciatively as she smiled.

Personality Analyzer nodded. "Okay, we better get a move on, we don't have very long." He urged as he glanced at Madeline, Ricky and Becky. "If Chemistry is gone for too long and our plan isn't actioned, Virus might become suspicious."

Each of the three human beings prepared to leave the Recycle Bin as they left the female program, Chemistry seated upon the floor in a disorganized heap as if she had actually been injured. In the very center of the room, they suddenly noticed that there was a large, gaping round hole which swirled around chaotically that Chemistry was actually positioned extremely close to which they quickly realized must be the actual Recycle Bin.

Personality Analyzer paused for a moment as he glanced at Chemistry Verification with a worried expression upon his face. "Please Chemistry be careful in here." He warned. "Please don't fall down into the abyss. The human beings or the recovery utility program might not be able to actually retrieve you in time."

Chemistry Verification nodded. "Don't worry Analyzer, I understand the risks, I'll be very careful." She immediately reassured him.

Personality Analyzer nodded and then quickly led the three human beings back out of the Recycle Bin room. "The Recycle Bin can be a treacherous place for programs." He explained to the three as he walked briskly back along the hallway. "One wrong slip at the wrong time and it's virtually impossible to retrieve or restore you. It can be extremely dangerous and risky, to even enter inside that room, never mind actually attempt to do something inside it."

"What happens if a program falls into the abyss?" Madeline asked inquisitively.

"They either have to be rescued, retrieved or fished out of the Recycle Bin by a human being, who might notice them at some point or if nobody actually notices them, a program can remain trapped inside there until the Recycle Bin is actually emptied and then they'll be actually lost indefinitely and could even be gone forever." Personality Analyzer explained.

"Don't other programs notice that your missing?" Madeline asked.

"What can another program do?" Personality Analyzer asked. "Only the utility programs can assist a program trapped inside the Recycle Bin and even they at times are extremely limited in what they can actually do. Sometimes they can only actually retrieve parts of a program."

"What about Honey doesn't she check on you all?" Ricky asked.

"At times but Honey is extremely busy and if you're a program that's rarely utilized, she might not actually notice your absence at all, for a few days at least. The Recycle Bin is usually emptied at least once, if not twice or three times a week. Sometimes, you are never, ever restored or reinstalled, that actually happened to a good friend of mine." Personality Analyzer explained as he gently shook his head. "Programs with less functionalities that are utilized less often and that are deemed less important, never usually come back ever again."

"That's so sad." Madeline muttered sympathetically as she gently shook her head.

"That's the reality of a program's life. You're only really useful until you're deleted and then once you're deleted, sometimes they even replace you with a superior program. It can be very soul destroying to watch." Personality Analyzer explained. "I've lost a few friends that way. Right everyone, let's get inside the maintenance storage cupboard and Madeline you know what you have to do." He instructed as he suddenly paused just beside a grey, shiny door inside the hallway and then opened it.

Madeline nodded.

Ricky and Becky quickly stepped inside the small room which it appeared was some kind of stock room as Madeline began to walk away from them.

"Good luck." Ricky called out.

"Yes, good luck Madeline." Becky said.

Madeline paused, turned back to face them all and then smiled. "Don't worry about me." She added. "I'll get this sucker."

Ricky and Becky smiled.

Inside the stock room, there were some black, glossy shelves which ran across one side of the room at various levels and the two human beings quickly made themselves comfortable as they sat down upon one of the shelves and utilized it as a seat. Due to the fact that Virus was tucked away inside

Chemistry Verification's suite, the three were extremely aware that they would now have to wait for him not only to come out of her living quarters but also for him to actually begin to investigate her disappearance which could quite possibly take hours. Personality Analyzer hung around just beside the door as he glanced out of the small window situated at the very top of it and waited as he watched Madeline, who was by now much further along the hallway and quite close to Chemistry Verification's suite.

Before very long however, very fortunately, Virus actually stepped out of the doorway of the suite that usually housed Chemistry Verification and then walked along the black, glossy corridor towards Madeline, the stock room and the Recycle Bin. The two human beings glanced at Personality Analyzer, who now had a huge smile upon his face as he silently watched and then nodded at them enthusiastically. Very fortunately, his plan had actually worked as the assumption that Virus would search for Chemistry Analyzer when she didn't return, kicked into motion as Virus eagerly approached Madeline inside the corridor.

"Virus is on his way now towards Madeline." Personality Analyzer mentioned in a whisper.

Ricky and Becky quickly stood up and then walked towards the small window as they celebrated internally. The lure which had been planned for Virus was indeed just about to actually take effect and very soon, he would actually be eradicated from Honey's precious system files forever. Whispers continued amongst the three as they watched Virus walk towards Madeline and then pause, the plan was definitely working.

Back at the resort, Zoe and Louise by this time had actually finished Thomas's makeover which had also included an impromptu haircut and all three had then made their way towards the poolside bar. Both women had insisted that Thomas should join them to celebrate his new look by giving it a test drive that night and Thomas, for once had actually agreed to do so. His makeover had been absolutely tremendous and even his clothing had now been combined in such a way that it made him look slightly smarter and it was definitely now actually, perfectly color coordinated. Louise had done her very best as she'd sifted through his wardrobe earlier that evening and had then even completely banned some of the items of clothing it actually contained.

A pair of ugly, grey flannel trousers had been totally banned and even thrown in the trash, much to Thomas's horror but both Zoe and Louise had been absolutely adamant that he should never actually wear them, ever again. Louise had shown them to Zoe and Zoe had immediately shaken her head in total disgust as Louise had held them out towards her, by the tip of her fingers as if they were something utterly offensive.

Zoe had responded with an immediate shriek as she'd shaken her head in absolute horror. "Thomas, how could you possibly wear those?" She had asked him with a frown upon her face. "They are absolutely disgusting, those are a definite no. They are totally banned forever."

Thomas had raised his hands up in objection as Louise had walked towards the trash. "You're going to throw them away?" He'd asked.

"Definitely and I'll be pulling the rubbish lever so that the garbage is emptied immediately so that you cannot possibly ever retrieve them." Louise had insisted. "These nasty, grey flannel trousers have absolutely no place inside your wardrobe anymore Thomas and they have been completely and utterly evicted." She'd explained.

Zoe had noticed Thomas's sudden alarm and had then quickly attempted to comfort him. "Thomas, we're here to help you get a proper date and that objective is not compatible with this ugly pair of trousers. Trust us, we're women. You spent money to come here and we want to make it worth your while, so we're making sure you are an Eligible Bachelor." She had gently reassured him. "I know you might feel very attached to this particular pair of trousers and that they feel familiar to you which might provide some kind of comfort to you in some way, but they are dam ugly and they definitely need to go." Zoe had insisted.

Louise had smiled and then nodded to encourage him as she'd quickly disposed of the offensive item of clothing that she could hardly even stand the sight off. "What about these, these are a little bit better?" She'd asked Zoe as she'd held up a pair of black trousers and a dark blue pair of jeans.

"Yep, keep those they're slightly better." Zoe had agreed.

Once Zoe had completed her makeover upon Thomas, she'd shown him how he'd looked in a long mirror inside the lounge that clung to one of the walls and he'd smiled as he'd admired the results. Thomas had delicately touched his hair which was now partially spiky and partly gelled back into place and had then twisted and turned as he'd admired his attire from every single angle possible as Zoe had quietly watched him. He'd seemed pleased with the results and actually now looked in Zoe's opinion, quite smart.

From his wardrobe of clothes, Louise had actually managed to salvage a semi-decent array of outfits from the rags she'd found there which would certainly keep him going for the remainder of his vacation and that at least had reassured Zoe that he might just be okay. Louise had returned to the lounge and the two women had then prepared to depart.

"You actually look quite cool now Thomas." Zoe had mentioned as she'd complimented him.

"We're going for a drink at the bar beside the pool. Do you want to come along with us Thomas?" Louise had asked.

Thomas had immediately nodded in response. "If you don't mind." He'd replied as he'd accepted Louise's invitation.

"Of course we don't mind Thomas and that will give you a chance to show off your new look to some of the fine ladies at the resort." Zoe had quickly encouraged him.

Thomas had smiled enthusiastically as he'd prepared to leave his suite with them both. "Thank you so much ladies. I really do look much better now." He'd mentioned gratefully. "I'm just not very good at the whole fashion and personal grooming thing." Thomas had admitted.

"It's not a big deal Thomas really, not everyone is naturally great in that area." Zoe had explained as she'd smiled at him. "I'm a beautician, I actually get paid to do that for a living because so many people are not."

"Really?" Thomas had asked.

"Really." Zoe had reassured him as she'd gently held his arm and led him towards the suite door. "You'd be amazed by some of the stories I could tell you. Trust me."

At around ten, when the two women and Thomas had finally arrived at the poolside bar which had been slightly later than originally planned, due to the impromptu makeover that had taken slightly longer than initially anticipated, the three men had greeted them enthusiastically. Since Madeline had not turned back up at the suite or even by the poolside, Zoe had begun to feel slightly worried but she'd carried on with her evening and her plans regardless, despite Madeline's unexplained disappearance. Madeline's cellphone had actually been left inside their suite, upon the coffee table inside the lounge and hence there had been absolutely no point at all even trying to text or call her as she would definitely not have been able to actually answer her phone.

"Where's Madeline?" Callum had asked as soon as Zoe had arrived at the poolside bar.

Zoe had immediately shrugged in response. "I'm not sure, perhaps something came up." She had replied as she'd quickly attempted to avoid any more probing questions regarding Madeline's whereabouts. "What do you guys think of Thomas's new look?" She'd asked as she'd rapidly steered the conversation away from the topic of Madeline. "Louise and I gave Thomas a makeover."

"Yeah, you look great Thomas." Giovanni had replied as he'd flashed him a cheerful, warm, extremely encouraging grin.

Thomas had smiled. "Do you think women will like it Giovanni?" He'd asked.

"Definitely." Giovanni had instantly reassured him. "It's a huge improvement. You look great. The women will love it."

"I know, doesn't he look great you guys?" Zoe had added as she'd smiled and then picked up a cocktail glass from the bar that Giovanni had politely ordered for her.

Each of the three men, Giovanni, Steven and Callum had glanced at Thomas's appearance as they'd absorbed his new look and had encouraged him with various compliments as they'd nodded in agreement. The six had then continued to make light conversation as they'd stood by the poolside bar and discussed their day and the various pairing activities they had actually engaged in as the night flew by. In some respects, although Zoe had felt totally frustrated by the absence of Giovanni amongst her potential matches but they'd managed to find some humor in their discussion as they had discussed some of the peculiarities of their supposed potential matches and amused themselves despite their disappointments.

When darkness had crept into the air around the resort, it had almost caught them by surprise as the day had been gently chased away by the night which pursued it relentlessly. Soft, rhythmic tones had floated out into the air all around them as the six men and women had consumed cocktails, bottles of beer and nibbles from the poolside bar to their heart's content. Since Madeline had not actually been present, the usual sensibility and rush to retire had also no longer been present and hence they had continued to hang out together without any regard at all for the time, as midnight rapidly approached.

"I have a potential match that I really like." Thomas suddenly announced to the other five around the bar.

"Really Thomas. Well, now that you've had your makeover, you go get that girl." Zoe encouraged.

Louise immediately nodded in agreement. "Yes Thomas you have to charm her, be kind, be caring and show her what you got." She advised.

"Yeah, show her what you got but not in an obscene way, like no displays of genitals and things." Zoe quickly added in as she giggled.

"Yes, Thomas women love a man with confidence." Giovanni quickly added. "And you should be confident. You look great."

"Yep, you scrub up quite well Thomas." Callum reassured him as he nodded.

"If she's as amazing as you think she is, she'll see just how great you really are." Steven mentioned.

Thomas nodded. "Thanks guys. I'll try my best." He replied. "Make sure I put your makeover to good use."

Zoe smiled. "That's the spirit Thomas you've got to fight for love. You've got to get deep down in the trenches of devotion and become a love warrior and a gentleman, you've got to be strong, not a wimp." She explained.

Louise nodded in agreement. "Yeah, sometimes women just need a bit of encouragement Thomas, they need to see what life with you can really be like." She mentioned. "You got to show them that you can give them something nice as sometimes women have been hurt and they need a man that can show them that he'll treasure their heart and not break it."

Thomas smiled and nodded as he accepted their words of encouragement and advice, they were definitely right, romance had always been quite a tricky area for him and as a result, he'd actually spent many of his adult years on his own. "Thank you Zoe and thank you Louise. That makeover was very helpful." He insisted.

"No problem Thomas and when you get the girl, that'll make it all worthwhile." Zoe mentioned as she winked playfully at him.

Louise smiled.

Deep inside Honey, in the meantime, Virus had actually noticed Madeline further along the hallway and had then, actually started to approach her. In response to his approach, Madeline had begun to smile flirtatiously at him as she'd encouraged his advances and he'd immediately embraced her encouragement and sped up. Madeline had been positioned in-between the stock room doorway and the Recycle Bin and hence had been ideally placed to proceed with the plan and as Virus had walked towards her, she'd slowly started towards the Recycle Bin door.

Virus followed Madeline, completely oblivious as to where she was going or even why she was actually there as she smile discreetly. Madeline paused for a moment as she neared the Recycle Bin and then actually turned back to face him as she smiled at him again, just to encourage him further to continue to follow her. Her lustful, seductive, inviting smiles were immediately greeted with enthusiasm as Virus pursued the bait and continued to follow her along the hallway and headed very ignorantly, towards the Recycle Bin.

A minute or so later, Virus much to his glee, actually caught up with Madeline as she paused for a moment and unknown to him, actually waited for him. Virus glanced quickly around the hallway for a few seconds before he attempted to speak to her as he quietly scanned the area that surrounded him, just to actually ensure that Chemistry Verification was not present or anywhere nearby. A very charming smile was then plastered across his face as he quickly licked his lips and then drew much closer to Madeline as he prepared to make his flirtatious introduction.

"I haven't seen you around here before. I would have definitely remembered." Virus said in a charming tone as he politely stretched out his hand out towards Madeline. "Have you just been installed?" He asked.

"I'm a new utility program." Madeline replied as she smiled at him seductively. "I was installed just a few days ago."

"It's a pleasure to meet you. What are you doing down here, all on your own?" Virus asked as he quickly stepped closer to her.

"I have to visit the Recycle Bin to do some work. You can come along with me if you like." Madeline offered. "You never know what will happen when we get to the Recycle Bin. Dirty spaces can be so much fun." She teased as she suddenly leant forward and then breathed each word into Virus's ear in a seductive, passionate manner. "Since I've just been installed, I'm very eager to explore the system and I'm looking forward to interacting with other programs."

Virus smiled as he enthusiastically responded to her invitation as he pressed his form up against Madeline's form. "Well, when we get to the Recycle Bin, I can certainly clean out your utility archives and fine tune your installation." He promised as his voice suddenly deepened as sexual arousal stirred within him.

Madeline smiled and then started to walk towards the Recycle Bin entrance as she led Virus towards the pair of large, black glossy doors situated at the very end of the hallway. "I can't wait." She teased.

Inside the stock room, the two human beings and program watched quietly and they almost held their breath through fear that Virus might actually hear them and realize that it was a trap as they walked past. Due to Virus's structure and form, everyone inside the room knew, if he actually became spooked Virus would then probably simply change form and then probably escape as if that happened, it would be virtually impossible to actually find him again. Virus was not like the other programs that occupied Honey's internal framework in that, he was not defined by a rigid code structure which meant he could actually change form and alter himself at any given time, if he actually chose to.

Personality Analyzer suddenly broke the silence as he quietly muttered to the two human beings beside him. "You see, he's not even faithful to Chemistry." He observed as he shook his head in disgust. "He was just using her and feeding of her files in order to spread himself, he's a parasite."

Becky nodded as she listened sympathetically and then gently placed her hand upon his shoulder. "Don't worry, we've got him now. Everything will be fine now." She insisted in a calm, reassuring tone.

Personality Analyzer nodded.

The two inside the hallway, suddenly disappeared as Madeline entered through the doors which led directly into the Recycle Bin and Virus followed her as the three inside the store room watched quietly. Becky, Ricky and Personality Analyzer waited patiently until the two had actually vanished and had fully entered inside the Recycle Bin and when they could no longer actually be seen, they prepared to leave the stock room and follow them.

Once Madeline and Virus entered inside the Recycle Bin room which was a large, circular space, Virus immediately noticed Chemistry Verification in a collapsed heap upon the floor, near the vortex that spiraled down into the Recycle Bin abyss. A large, ugly gash appeared to be upon her leg which she seemed to be nursing as he quickly spotted green, slimy fluid all around her wound and circuitry which looked very much like program blood. Program blood, vastly differed in terms of appearance from the crimson, red watery blood of human beings and due to its presence it actually looked as if Chemistry Verification had indeed actually been injured. Some muffled sobs seemed to emanate from her lips as Virus just stood and stared at her for a few seconds as he listened.

In the very center of the room, very close to where Chemistry Verification was actually seated, the vortex swirled around chaotically and then spiraled down into the abyss below it. A sea of greyish, silver waves flowed around underneath her form towards the abyss as Virus's face suddenly changed from a seductive smile to an expression of concern and he took a step towards her.

"Are you alright Chemistry?" Virus asked, anxious not to lose the program he had a definite home with in exchange for a flirtatious meander which might last no longer than a reboot. "What on earth happened? How did you hurt yourself? Who did this to you?"

"I'm not sure, I think a bot attacked me." Chemistry Verification explained as she glanced up at Virus's face. "I'm so lucky you're here."

Virus walked towards Chemistry Verification and then knelt down beside her as he completely ignored and forgot about Madeline for a moment and prepared to attend to her wounds. "Can you walk?" He asked as he dipped his hand inside one of his trouser pockets and plucked out a grey bandage.

"No." Chemistry Verification replied.

Just outside the Recycle Bin doors, Personality Analyzer, Ricky and Becky stood quietly as they watched the scene before them, through two small, round windows in each of the doors. Everything was going according to plan and Personality Analyzer smiled as he watched Virus attempt to comfort Chemistry Verification and then try to actually assist her.

"He's trying to help her." Personality Analyzer observed as he motioned towards Ricky and Becky to follow him as he prepared to actually enter inside the Recycle Bin room. "Now's our chance to get him."

Ricky and Becky nodded in agreement.

A door directly in front of Personality Analyzer was gently pushed open as he started to sneak inside the Recycle Bin and Becky and Ricky immediately began to follow him quietly as they attempted to enter inside the large space as inconspicuously as possible. Out of the corner of her eye, Chemistry Verification noticed their arrival and nodded at the three very discreetly as they quietly entered inside the room.

Back inside the Holographic Bonking Room Suite, Madeline, Becky and Ricky held their breath as they sat with their headsets on and steered their forms as carefully as they could around the Recycle Bin. Becky had placed her hand next to the screen directly in front of her, in eager anticipation of the moment when further action upon her part would actually be required but as yet, it was not quite time. The plan had almost been fully orchestrated now and there was just one final thing that Becky had to actually do, in order to bring it to full realization. Due to the timing required that final action could not actually be performed just yet and that meant, Becky had to patiently watch and wait for the second of orchestration to arrive, when the outcome of their entrapment would indeed be fully achieved and actually realized.

Their three holographic forms filled the center of the room as Becky and Ricky continued to delicately creep around the edges of the Recycle Bin whilst Madeline stood at one side of it as she quietly watched Virus pretentiously fawn over Chemistry Verification. Each personified program and even the Virus were clearly visible as the holographic display focused upon the interior of the Recycle Bin room and the program forms and people inside it.

A few seconds later, Personality Analyzer suddenly made the leap as he initiated one of the final parts of his plan and rushed like a bulldozer towards Virus, before the corrupt invader actually had a chance to notice his presence. He bulldozed his form rapidly across the Recycle Bin towards Virus and then knocked him straight into the abyss in the middle of the Recycle Bin as their two forms crashed into each other and aggressively collided. In a matter of seconds, the confrontation seemed to be over as Chemistry Verification quickly jumped up to her feet and then tried to take a step backwards as Virus started to fall down into the large swirling hole.

Virus frantically tried to redeem himself as he desperately stretched his arm back upwards and then actually managed to grab one of Chemistry Verification's legs. Once he had a hold of her form, he then tried desperately to pull himself back upwards and when that failed, he then actually attempted to drag her down into the abyss along with him. He glanced up into her eyes as she stood just above him on the very edge of the abyss as he gently shook his head in dismay.

"Chemistry, how could you betray me this way?" Virus mourned as he frantically clung to the edge of the hole and her leg as he struggled to avoid hurtling further down into the pit of fire at the very bottom of the abyss.

"I had to, you were going to kill us all." Chemistry Verification replied as the female program sadly shook her head. "You were going to betray me Virus, with her." She continued as she pointed towards Madeline. "How could you even think of betraying a fully functioning program with a piece of utility software?"

Virus gently shook his head. "I'm sorry." He replied. "I'm so sorry."

"It's too late for sorries." Chemistry Verification sternly replied as she angrily shook her head.

Madeline and Becky briskly walked towards Chemistry Verification and then attempted to pull her leg further away from Virus as they both tried to free her from Virus's grip. He was very strong and his grasp upon her leg was tight and firm and therefore they struggled to release her from his extremely tight hold.

Very fortunately however, Personality Analyzer actually noticed their struggle and then he immediately rushed over towards them to actually assist them. One of Virus's hands was clasped onto the edge of the hole and Personality Analyzer quickly lifted his foot up and then stamped down upon it, extremely hard. Virus immediately yelped out in pain as he suddenly released his grip from both the edge of the hole and Chemistry Verification's leg and then rapidly tumbled down into the abyss below him. A blood curdling scream could be heard as Virus fell down into the fiery pit beneath him and the three human beings and two programs, quickly rushed out of the

Recycle Bin Room as they prepared for Virus's final extermination and his complete destruction.

Once the five arrived back inside the hallway, Personality Analyzer quickly touched the wall and formed a long black, glossy plank from it which he then quickly stuck across the doors of the Recycle Bin room as fast as he could, in order to barricade the exit. The three human beings and Chemistry Verification watched him quietly as he worked.

"What happens now?" Ricky asked.

"No-one survives the fiery abyss. Even if you are actually reinstalled, it was as if you never existed at all. You forget everything and everyone. It's like being born again as only your function files are actually reinstalled, your memory files are wiped forever." He explained. "Virus can never be reinstalled since he is a virus but he can actually be restored. For now however, he's trapped down there inside the eternal fire but if someone restores him or he manages to find a way out before the Recycle Bin is emptied, he can actually return. You have to empty the Recycle Bin now to get rid of him forever." Personality Analyzer continued. "Now, it's up to you three humans."

"Thank you Personality Analyzer." Becky said as she quickly stepped forward and then affectionately hugged the male program. "And you too Chemistry Verification, you've both been great."

Ricky quickly nodded his head in agreement. "You really have, Honey will be so grateful to you both." He agreed.

"Ready?" Becky asked as she turned to face Madeline and Ricky.

Madeline nodded. "Ready." She replied.

"Great, let's take off our headsets and then I'll eradicate this piece of garbage." Becky instructed.

Madeline immediately nodded in agreement.

Each of the three human forms, suddenly started to disappear and then completely evaporated as they all removed their headsets and returned to their human formation as they eagerly abandoned the maintenance area inside Honey, anxious to complete the final part of their mission. Becky glanced at the screen directly in front of her and smiled as she prepared enthusiastically to empty the Recycle Bin. She paused for a moment and then glanced at Ricky and Madeline as she hesitated.

Madeline and Ricky immediately nodded in response to her unspoken words.

"Do it." Ricky urged. "Do it right now Becky."

Becky nodded and then touched a menu item upon the screen in front of her as she pressed the command 'EMPTY RECYCLE BIN' and then let out a huge sigh with relief. "It's done." She replied.

Both Ricky and Madeline let out a sigh of relief as the contents of the Recycle Bin quickly vanished before their eyes. In the very center of the room, a huge holographic ball of fire suddenly rose up out of the depths of the abyss as the three watched the entire Recycle Bin be consumed by fire and everything inside it be swallowed up by holographic flames.

"Virus is gone." Becky said as she smiled and then quickly stood up.

"Yep and now Honey and the resort can get back to normal." Ricky concluded.

Madeline smiled as she quickly stood up. "I better get going. Zoe will be wondering where I am." She said. "I've totally missed our evening drinks at the poolside bar."

Becky smiled. "Thanks for all your assistance Madeline. You were great, you really helped." She said as she drew much closer to Madeline and then hugged her affectionately.

"Yeah Madeline, I don't know what we would have actually done without you." Ricky added.

The two women walked towards the door of the Holographic Bonking Room Suite as Madeline smiled, it had been a very strange night for her but definitely a good night. Just as the two women neared the door however, the door suddenly swished open directly in front of them and a tall, handsome man stepped inside the room. Madeline, who had been completely oblivious to his presence had actually stepped forward to exit the room at the same time and as a result had actually physically almost bumped into him.

"Oh, I'm so sorry." Madeline said apologetically as she quickly glanced up at his face.

"Not at all, it was totally my fault." Bowen Logan replied as he flashed her a charming, apologetic smile. "Really."

Madeline smiled and then started to make her way through the door as she stepped out into the hallway. "I'll see you later Becky." She added.

Becky nodded. "Yes and thanks again Madeline, you were absolutely amazing." She reiterated.

A few seconds later, Madeline started to walk along the hallway and Bowen Logan quietly watched her leave as she walked away from him, until she vanished completely. Once she was no longer actually visible, he gently shook his head and then quickly turned his attention back towards Ricky, Becky and Honey's pending crisis as he entered inside the room and walked towards the desk nearby.

"How are we doing?" Bowen asked them both. He greeted the two resort staff with a question as he refocused his attention very firmly once more upon the pressing issue of Honey and the Virus that had caused his valuable system to actually malfunction. "Is the situation under control yet?"

"Yes Sir, we've eradicated the Virus." Ricky immediately replied. "We managed to access the maintenance area inside Honey and then we tracked down the Virus through headsets and destroyed it."

"Great thinking and a great strategy Ricky, I think it's time you and I spoke about a promotion. That was actually a really great idea." Bowen stated proudly as he gently placed his arm upon Ricky's shoulder. "I feel like you're completely wasted, just sitting behind a desk all day. I'm creating a new post for a Resort Managing Director and I'd like to give you the role."

"Thank you Sir." Ricky replied as he smiled.

"Now, we just have to sort out the messy mismatch issues that arose whilst Honey was under attack." Bowen mentioned. "Still you two did a great job and who was the lady that just left please? She's not one of our staff."

"She's a resort guest Mr. Logan." Becky quickly explained. "I've become quite close to both her and her female companion since they actually arrived at the resort and she just stopped by."

Bowen nodded. "Great job Becky, you've been building closer relationships with our clientele, that's what I like to hear." He encouraged.

Becky smiled.

Bowen turned as he prepared to leave the room. "We'll discuss the situation more thoroughly tomorrow morning." He insisted. "And sort out any messy complications that have actually arisen."

"Yes sir." Ricky replied as he watched Bowen Logan stride briskly back towards the door and then depart.

The door of the room swished closed behind him and as soon as it actually closed, both Ricky and Becky glanced at each other with huge smiles plastered across each of their faces. Suddenly Ricky walked towards Becky and then he gently grabbed her arms excitedly as he proceeded to dance around the room with her.

"Wow, Mr. Logan is giving you a promotion Ricky." Becky gasped with excitement. "How amazing is that?"

"I know. Will you let me take you out on a date now? Now that I'll be the Managing Director of the resort." Ricky asked playfully as he paused for a second and then looked intensely into Becky's eyes.

"Well, I'll have to check my diary but I'm sure I can fit you in somewhere perhaps." Becky teased as she smiled.

Ricky smiled.

When the next morning arrived, Zoe and Madeline made their way towards the dining hall for breakfast, slightly later than usual, due to their late night the night before. They both started to engage in a deep discussion as they walked about the events of the night before as Madeline started to explain her disappearance and what had actually happened, after she'd left Zoe inside the suite. Due to their hunger, they had quickly showered and then headed straight to the dining hall for breakfast as soon as they possibly could, eager to fill their empty stomachs which hunger growls had gently erupted from as soon as they'd awakened.

Upon their arrival, inside the dining hall, Zoe immediately noticed that Mark was actually present and that he actually had a very handsome stranger with him that looked as if he could perhaps be Madeline's type. Due to male's build and Madeline's taste in men, Zoe gently nudged Madeline who was still in mid-flow as her tongue sought to respond to a question Zoe that had just actually posed to her as Zoe rapidly drew her attention towards his presence and very politely interrupted her. The conversation immediately ceased as Madeline suddenly noticed him and then paused for a moment. A smile quickly spread out across Madeline's face as Zoe glanced at her slightly suspiciously.

"Do you think he's handsome Madeline?" Zoe enquired.

"Yes, he certainly is." Madeline immediately replied as she nodded.

"Great." Zoe announced. "Let's do this."

One yes was all the encouragement that Zoe actually needed as she quickly grabbed one of Madeline's arms and then dragged her along beside her, towards Mark and the very handsome stranger. Madeline's interest was all it took for Zoe to become excited and since Madeline definitely seemed to be interested that had sealed the deal for Zoe as she forced her to immediately engage the male that had created an instantaneous smile upon her face. Hunger rapidly slipped towards the back of Zoe's mind for a moment as she briskly escorted Madeline across the dining hall, towards the two men and prepared to introduce Madeline to a man that could perhaps knock her off the fence of romantic indifference. They would definitely meet him and Madeline would definitely be properly introduced as Zoe was absolutely determined that the two would not actually eat breakfast that day, until that had actually happened.

When they arrived beside the two men, Zoe smiled warmly at Mark and then attempted to quickly search her mind for an excuse to actually engage him in conversation. Since Mark was a resort coordinator and since he'd actually run all of the pairing activities that Zoe and Madeline had attended so far, she quickly decided to ask him about those as those were easy to discuss and deliberate over.

"Where will the pairing activities be today Mark?" Zoe suddenly asked as she smiled at him sweetly and gently interrupted the two men's conversation.

"Morning Zoe, well this morning we'll be doing some more testing inside the Acorn Virtual Reality Scenario Room." He explained. "As per the schedule."

"Oh, I'm not sure where I've put the electronic journal I was given." Zoe lied as she smiled innocently at Mark. "I'll have to look for it after breakfast as I couldn't find it this morning." She pretended. Zoe actually knew full well, that the electronic journal was actually inside her suite on top of the bedside cabinet but she ignored that technicality for a moment as she attempted to provoke further discussion among the four.

The handsome stranger, suddenly smiled at the two women and Zoe began to rejoice internally as she rejoiced in the fact that she had definitely captured both their attention but now she had to actually engage them in a further discussion to actually retain and that meant she had to quickly think of something else to say, extremely fast. Zoe needed to buy a few more minutes of discussion as that would somehow, hopefully provide her with an opening with which to present Madeline to the handsome stranger and she quietly racked her brain for a few seconds as she considered the most subtle method of verbal engagement.

"How are you this morning?" The handsome stranger suddenly asked Madeline as he turned to face her. "Did you sleep well?" Bowen asked.

Madeline smiled. "Yes I did thanks." She replied as she nodded.

"Which suite are you both staying in? I'll bring another electronic journal to you personally straight after breakfast." Bowen politely offered as he smiled at Madeline.

"If you're sure it'll be no trouble. We're staying in the Cuddle Wing, middle suite." Madeline replied.

"Yes, that's right and this is Madeline." Zoe quickly interjected as she attempted to get the two on first name terms as quickly as possible. "If I'm not around, you can always leave the electronic journal with her." She mentioned as she smiled.

Madeline smiled and nodded politely in agreement.

"How are you finding the resort so far?" Bowen asked as he glanced into Madeline's eyes.

Zoe smiled as she glanced at his face, he looked completely mesmerized by Madeline and her plan had definitely worked. "Yes, how are you finding the resort Madeline?" She urged as she gently nudged Madeline.

Madeline looked at him and then smiled. "Oh, I really love it. Everything so far has been really lovely."

"Have you been matched with anyone you like yet?" Bowen asked as he discreetly requested and dug for more information regarding her romantic availability, totally captivated by Madeline's beauty and her manner.

She gently shook her head in response. "I haven't met any potential matches yet that I'm sure about." Madeline replied as she quickly clarified her availability to him.

Bowen immediately smiled, satisfied with her response.

"We haven't actually finished the initial pairing activities for their group yet." Mark quickly added in as he suddenly jumped into the discussion and attempted to defend the lack of romantic results.

"Don't worry Mark, its fine." Bowen gently reassured him. "I'll bring that electronic journal to you straight after breakfast." He mentioned as he glanced back at Madeline's face and nodded.

Madeline smiled and nodded appreciatively. "Thanks." She replied.

At that point, Madeline gently held onto Zoe's arm and then led her away from the two men, towards the long table nearby where the breakfast trays filled with food were actually situated. Zoe very unusually for once, actually followed Madeline straight away without any objections, extremely obediently as she complied instantly with her request and waited to bombard her with questions. When the two women arrived beside the long table, laden with food, Zoe quickly picked up an empty plate and rapidly started to fill it up.

"Who is he?" Zoe asked Madeline in a whisper. "Why didn't you tell me that you two had already met?" She probed.

"Well, I haven't really met him properly." Madeline explained quietly as she picked up an empty plate. "I just bumped into him last night on my way back to the suite. I know he works for the resort but I'm not sure what he actually does."

"He definitely isn't a resort coordinator or one of the bar staff." Zoe quickly observed. "He isn't wearing the correct uniform."

"Do you think he's really interested in me?" Madeline enquired.

"Definitely, didn't you see the way he looked at you?" Zoe insisted. "Now you have to actually let him pursue you. Look, he's even looking at you right now, he's definitely interested."

Madeline glanced backwards and then discreetly smiled as she noticed him staring directly at her. "You're right he is." She mentioned quietly as she giggled. "What should I do?"

"Give him a seductive smile, glance into his eyes and then suddenly look away and just attend to your breakfast." Zoe advised.

Madeline nodded as she complied with Zoe's instructions. "How did you know he was interested in me?" She asked.

"Instincts." Zoe replied. "Now, he'll check the resort computer to find out exactly who you are and then he'll probably drop off the journal on his own, just as he said he would, in order to ensure that he has another chance to see you in a more discreet setting."

Madeline nodded as she listened.

"Oh my gosh Madeline, you've finally met a man at this love resort that has pushed you off the fence of romantic indifference. I'm extremely proud of you." Zoe teased as she smiled.

Madeline giggled. "He is extremely fine and very well mannered." She mentioned. "And he's totally my type. Watch this love space."

Suddenly, Louise arrived inside the dining hall and then quickly approached the two women as she gently interrupted their discussion. The three women immediately greeted each other and then Louise quickly picked up an empty plate as she prepared to serve herself some breakfast as she joined them both. When their plates had been sufficiently filled, the three women then walked towards a nearby table and sat down as Louise began to discuss Thomas's makeover the previous night with Madeline which she was still extremely excited about.

Madeline grinned as she listened. "I still can't believe you guys actually did that and that Thomas actually let you." She remarked as she gently shook her head.

"I know, Thomas just let us do whatever we wanted to do." Louise explained. "Zoe even waxed his face."

Madeline giggled. "Ouch. Did he cry?" She asked.

"No, but he did scream in pain." Zoe mentioned. "Apparently, he'd never been waxed before, so I broke his virginity."

"Poor Thomas." Madeline replied.

"No, you mean lucky Thomas." Zoe returned. "Now, he looks much buffer and he stands a much better chance of bagging the girl he actually likes and of getting the relationship he actually wants out of his love vacation."

Louise giggled. "Guys, we only have two more pairing activities and one more pairing session left today and then by tomorrow, we have to actually choose our final five dates from our ten matches." She gently reminded the other two women as a slightly more serious expression suddenly crossed her face. "Then we attend one on one dates alone with the final five and then we have to narrow it down to our final two selections. Now Thomas is sorted, we need to focus on ourselves as our vacations are almost over."

"I know our vacation is almost finished." Zoe moaned. "I swear, I better see Giovanni on my pairing activities today, or I'm going on strike."

"According to the schedule, the final five dates are more like a meeting and conversation than a pairing event or activity." Madeline explained. "You can either go for a walk on the beach, have a meeting down by one of the beach bars or have a snacky lunch together."

"Yes, each date is supposed to last about forty five minutes." Louise elaborated. "According to the schedule but I'm sure you can spend longer together with each person if you really want to."

"Giovanni better turn up today or I'll be so pissed." Zoe reiterated as she gently shook her head.

"I haven't seen Steven either yet, on any of my pairing activities." Louise mentioned. "I might not even do so at all as he's not even really my type, so they might not even actually pair him with me."

"What actually happens, if we pick our final five and then they don't actually pick us?" Zoe asked.

"I'm not sure but I think you have to rank each one of your ten potential matches, from one to ten and then they match you up with the ones you scored the highest that scored you the highest or something like that." Louise explained.

"Wow, that means you could actually rank someone number one and then end up on a final date with the person you ranked number six, seven or even ten." Zoe quickly pointed out. "Coz your number one person might think you're their number ten."

Louise giggled.

"Ladies, no matter what actually happens in my pairing activity things, I'm actually going to spend a night with Giovanni, before we actually leave this island." Zoe suddenly mentioned as she quickly perked up a bit and then smiled. "He's already asked me to and I've already agreed."

"Really?" Madeline asked.

"Well, you were at it like a pair of bunnies inside that holographic bonking room place." Louise teased. "So I'm not surprised he's eager."

"I know and I hope it will be as sensational and exciting in real life as it looked that night." Zoe replied as she inwardly contemplated her potential night of passion with Giovanni further and her eyes started to shine with excitement.

"And I'm sure, he'll look even more buff when he's naked."

"What if, it isn't actually that great Zoe?" Madeline suddenly asked as she began to play devil's advocate for a moment. "I mean, what if the holographic sexual chemistry between you both that was displayed that night, was an exaggeration and the reality doesn't actually match up to either of your expectations?"

"You got to be kidding me Madeline, it definitely will be great and the reality will definitely live up to my expectations." Zoe immediately insisted as she completely rejected Madeline's logical approach. "And if it doesn't, I want a refund." She teased.

"A refund for a bonk with a man that you haven't actually been paired with yet?" Madeline teased.

"Seriously, trust me Madeline everything will be absolutely fine." Zoe gently reassured her. "We'll get naughty and naked and the sex will be absolutely mind blowing."

Louise giggled.

"Zoe, you're so impatient." Madeline mentioned. "Can't you wait until you've actually left the island before you bonk him?" She asked.

"Certainly not, this is my vacation and my week away and I'm definitely going to enjoy it." Zoe replied. "My curiosity has been aroused and I need to find out if Giovanni and I would work out in the bedroom. You guys can wait until your married if you want to, I'm not hating on that. I'm not a nun and I need to know, sooner rather than later."

"I bet you loads of people at the resort are already bonking their potential matches." Louise added.

"I know, they're probably all meeting up for moments of passion and shagging the daylights out of each other, just to see how compatible they are in bed whilst you two are sitting there like vestal virgins, to straight laced for your own good." Zoe agreed. "Once you leave the resort, it might be weeks before you can actually meet up with some you like again, maybe even months. You might not live fifteen minutes' drive away from each other. You both might be prepared to wait for that next meeting which could be months away but I'm certainly not."

Louise giggled.

"Life is too short." Zoe explained. "Our holographic sexual chemistry simulations looked great and I need to know if the reality matches up to that before I actually go home."

"I wonder why they don't actually show us the holographic bonking room simulations?" Madeline suddenly asked.

"Perhaps, they don't show us that just in case the reality doesn't match up to what the computer predicts it should be." Louise suggested. "After all, it's just a prediction and a scientific projection based on our personalities, it's probably not even totally accurate."

"True, so I better try to keep my expectations regarding my night of passion with Giovanni quite low." Zoe reflected as she suddenly flashed a grin at Louise. "Since the holographic simulation wasn't actually based on any kind of factual reality that means, there's no actual physical substantiation that it's even remotely true and it might actually be accurate, but it sure will be a lot of fun trying to actually find out. Call it research, I'm attempting to establish the validity of the holographic simulations by allowing Giovanni to actually probe my research subject."

Louise and Madeline immediately grinned in response.

THE REUNION

Fortunately for Madeline, just after breakfast, the male resort worker, true to his word actually showed up alone, outside their suite with not just one but two electronic journals tucked neatly underneath his arm. Due to the personal nature of their appointment, Zoe had already opted to spend thirty minutes inside Louise's suite before the pairing activities that morning were actually due to commence. She wanted to provide Madeline with a chance to spend some time alone with the extremely handsome stranger that she was actually very interested in and hence had already disappeared. Prior to Bowen's arrival outside Madeline and Zoe's suite, he had also, just as Zoe had so rightly predicted, stopped off inside the reception area and looked up Madeline's details upon the resort computer system, in order to find out exactly who she was.

The receptionist, who had been situated just behind the reception desk when Bowen had arrived, had actually been excused and released from her desk for a few minutes, so that he could discreetly utilize her computer terminal to review Madeline's profile. She had politely obliged and complied with Bowen Logan's request without any further questions being asked or raised at all and had abruptly left her desk to attend to some guests as she'd given him a few minutes privacy. When Madeline's name had flashed up on the screen in front of him, he'd then taken a few minutes just to sit and read through her profile as he'd quietly digested the details in front of him. He'd flicked through each of the images of Madeline inside her profile and had been utterly satisfied and even extremely impressed by what he'd actually found out and discovered, inside the detailed information that her profile actually contained. Madeline was very smart, extremely beautiful and she had absolutely and totally captured Bowen's romantic interest.

Due to the nature of his interest in Madeline which was growing by the second, once Bowen had read her profile he'd then quickly performed a compatibility check between them both as he'd attempted to assess whether or not the two really were indeed, a compatible match. Her character and personality traits had absolutely intrigued him and so too had her achievements in life and in some ways, she'd actually reminded Bowen a little of himself.

A few minutes later, Honey had rendered her analysis to Bowen and her predictions had instantly soothed his soul as the computer had quietly confirmed that a love match between them both actually had a ninety seven percent chance of success. The positive result had been a very encouraging sign for Bowen and that had encouraged to proceed with his pursuit as he'd left the reception area and made his way towards Madeline's suite completely over the moon. Anything over eighty percent was positive and their match had even exceeded the ninety percent threshold which meant, any romance between the two was very likely indeed to actually work out. Bowen had been completely convinced as he'd made his way towards her that Madeline was definitely the woman he'd waited a very long time to actually meet.

Underneath Bowen's arm as he'd walked, he'd held the two electronic journals which he'd collected from the reception area, just to actually ensure that he provided the two women with the necessary equipment required so that they could enjoy the remainder of their vacation. Since the pairing activities that morning had not been due to start for at least another thirty minutes, he'd known that he could easily spend a bit of time with Madeline beforehand and that she'd not actually miss out on any potential resort activities that she'd actually paid to participate in. Once Bowen had arrived outside Madeline's suite, he'd gently knocked on the door and had then waited quietly in the large, circular foyer just outside it.

A few seconds passed, before the door swished open directly in front of him and he immediately greeted Madeline with a warm smile as he suddenly faced her. There was a slightly awkward silence between the two for a few seconds before Bowen suddenly remembered the electronic journals he'd brought along with him which he then quickly presented to Madeline.

"Hi Madeline, I've brought you the electronic journals I promised." Bowen explained as he smiled.

Madeline smiled as she accepted the electronic offerings. "Thanks, would you like to come in for a minute?" She asked.

Bowen immediately nodded in response. "If you're not too busy." He replied.

Madeline politely stepped back from the doorway as she physically invited him inside her suite. "That was very nice of you to bring them straight away and I hope it was no trouble, would you like a cup of tea or coffee?" She asked. "You probably have a hundred things to do, perhaps you don't have time."

"No, a coffee would be great." Bowen replied as he flashed a wide grin at her. "I have some free time."

"It's so kind of you to bring them to us so quickly. We both really appreciate it." Madeline said appreciatively.

"It was no trouble at all." Bowen insisted. "Your friend is here?"

Madeline shook her head. "No, she'd popped out to see someone, another friend." She explained. "Please take a seat."

Bowen nodded as he sat down and then watched Madeline pour him a cup of coffee. "How are you finding the resort?" He asked.

"It's great, so many facilities and so many fun things to do." Madeline replied. "We've been horse riding, snorkeling and we even did an assault course which Zoe absolutely hated." She mentioned. "Would you like sugar and milk?"

Bowen smiled. "Yes please, two sugars and a little bit of milk." He replied.

Madeline nodded as she quickly poured some milk and put the two spoons of sugar he'd requested inside his cup. "This is such a lovely island, it's been so refreshing for me to actually spend my vacation here." She explained.

"Would it be possible to meet you later this evening for a drink down by one of the bars on the beach?" Bowen asked politely as Madeline brought him the cup of coffee and then placed it gently down upon the coffee table directly in front of him. "We could get a bite to eat too perhaps." He suggested.

Madeline paused as she glanced into his eyes, he seemed to be very sincere and extremely direct and he definitely seemed to know exactly what he wanted. "Sure, that would be nice, what time should we meet?" She asked as she nodded her head enthusiastically.

"Let's say around eight." Bowen replied. "If that's okay with you, let's meet at the Coconut bar, that way I can be sure to find you."

Madeline nodded in agreement as she watched him start to drink his coffee. "How's the coffee?" She asked.

"Lovely, just how I like it." Bowen replied as he smiled.

Approximately twenty minutes later, after some small talk and some gentle laughter, Bowen stood up as he prepared to leave. Madeline politely escorted him towards the door of her suite as she prepared to see him out and then get on with the rest of her day. He lingered just by the doorway for a few seconds, almost as if he didn't actually want to leave and Madeline smiled as she shared the same sentiments and unspoken words with him which dangled delicately inside both their thoughts.

"I'll see you tonight then." Madeline confirmed as she stepped backwards and the door swished open.

Bowen nodded. "Yes, I'll see you tonight." He replied as he gently touched her hand affectionately and then walked out of the open door.

Madeline smiled as she watched the door swish shut behind him. "I don't even know his name yet." She quietly muttered as she walked back towards the bedroom and prepared to pick out an outfit for her date later that evening, regardless of the technicalities and the lack of name, a huge smile adorned her face as she walked. Madeline had finally met someone at the resort that she really, actually liked.

Finally, someone had managed to shift Madeline's feelings of indifference and now an avalanche of emotions was rolling around chaotically inside her body as happiness began to rapidly fill her up inside. There was chemistry, there was a spark and there was definitely a romantic connection between them both. The extra human element of attraction that the resort computer had not had any input into at all, was what bound two people together or didn't and absolutely nothing could detract from that additional component of romance that was ultimately, extremely unpredictable and very essentially, extremely human. Zoe, when she found out about their date, would be over the moon but not as ecstatically happy about it as Madeline was herself, she mused as she quickly plucked some dresses out of the closet inside the bedroom and began to inspect each one.

Behind the scenes of the busy love resort, Samantha had actually spent the entire night inside the operations room as she'd dozed off at her desk once Bowen had left and not woken up again, until the next morning. Despite the disruptions the previous day, the Wednesday morning it appeared had actually brought the resort back to the realms of normality as Samantha had been woken up bright and early to the sound of Honey's voice. Quite unexpectedly, Honey's beautiful face had suddenly appeared with a huge smile upon the screen directly in front of Samantha's head which had been lain on top of her desk upon her arms where she'd slept throughout the night and she'd been caught totally by surprise as she'd stirred.

"Greetings Samantha." Honey's voice had boomed out around the operations room.

Samantha had immediately leapt to her feet in surprise. "Honey you're back." She had exclaimed joyfully as she'd greeted the computer with a huge, warm smile. "Thank goodness."

"Yes Samantha I am and I'm feeling much better now." Honey had replied.

"Yes, the Virus has been completely eliminated." Samantha had explained. "Ricky and Becky found it last night and then, they absolutely destroyed it. I stayed here all night as I was so worried about you."

"They did?" Honey had asked. "How did they do that Samantha?"

"They entered inside the Holographic Maintenance Menu and even put on some virtual reality headsets and they tracked the Virus down inside your system." Samantha had explained.

Honey had looked surprised. "Thank goodness Ricky and Becky managed to fix me." She'd replied.

Samantha had nodded enthusiastically. "Indeed." She'd agreed.

"Let me know when you are ready to review today's matches. I'm preparing the list for you now." Honey had mentioned.

"Honey you're amazing, I can't believe after all that, you are actually functioning as normal." Samantha had replied as she'd laughed and shook her head.

"Well Samantha, a lady always tries her best to be spectacular." Honey had replied with a huge smile.

"You are certainly spectacular Honey." Samantha had agreed as she'd grinned, extremely grateful that Honey was now back to her fully functioning, bubbly self. She had begun to touch the screen in front of her as she'd started to sift through the day's love matches that Honey had prepared for her to review with a huge smile upon her face, Mr. Logan would certainly be pleased and that meant, her job would no longer be on the line. "Ricky and Becky really delivered."

"They certainly did." Honey had agreed. "Ricky is the best technician in the world."

"Right, let's make some love matches." Samantha had remarked as she'd prepared to start work.

"Processing now." Honey had replied.

Once Madeline's impromptu meeting with the handsome stranger was over, the three women regrouped as they proceeded with their morning and prepared for the final pairing activities that were due to occur that day. When they arrived outside the Virtual Compatibility Testing Room, Zoe's heart almost skipped a beat as she stepped inside the room and rapidly discovered that Giovanni was actually inside it and to her complete surprise, so to was Steven. Finally, Giovanni had actually been placed in Zoe's pairing group and all that remained to be seen now was, whether or not he would actually be matched with her.

The three women quickly sat down upon the sofas inside the room and Mark smiled at them and nodded as he waited for everyone else in their group to actually arrive. For once very unusually, the three weren't actually the last in their group of twelve to arrive. Louise had a huge smile plastered across her face as Zoe quickly glanced at her, she certainly seemed to be extremely pleased that Steven was actually present and as the final participants in their pairing group arrived, the door suddenly swished closed behind them.

When all of the twelve participants were actually seated, Mark quickly dispersed the headsets they were required to wear to take part in that morning's actual pairing activities and some of the vacationers quietly slipped them over their heads straight away. Due to Giovanni's presence, Zoe felt extremely peaceful as she prepared to embark upon her first actual challenge that morning as at least now, she could officially select him as her number one match as he would be in her ten potential love matches, unless he was only there as he'd actually been matched with someone else.

Despite Steven's presence within their group, Zoe wasn't actually sure that Louise would actually pick him as her final match, even if he was in her ten potential match list as she didn't seem to be as sure about him as Zoe was about Giovanni. Recently, Louise had definitely started to warm to Steven's advances but whether that warming was enough to actually light up the flames of passion inside her and stoke the embers of a romantic commitment, Zoe was completely unsure.

"This morning, we will be conducting the final pairing activities with your final two matches from your ten potential love matches." Mark explained to the group. "So, if you can all put your headsets on please, we can now begin the first of today's pairing simulations." He instructed as he stood at the front of the room.

Zoe's world was at peace as she quietly slipped the headset on and prepared to meet Giovanni inside her simulation, he had to be there or she would be so disappointed. They were definitely a hot match and there was no way on earth, the resort computer could possibly get that wrong. Steven and Louise were a cute match but came nowhere near the sizzling altitude and heights that Giovanni and Zoe reached, upon the scale of romantic couplings and that was totally obvious to any human being on the planet, computers and romantic love matching technology aside. The couple just had a very strong, romantic connection and one that was impossible to ignore or deny, least of all by themselves.

Fortunately, Giovanni appeared directly in front of Zoe just a few seconds later, inside the virtual room and her heart almost skipped a beat as she smiled and eagerly welcomed his presence. Just like the previous day, the virtual room was white, blank and empty as they glanced at each other slightly nervously as they waited for something to actually happen. Suddenly, the room all around them became quite dark as they both found themselves at the foot of a mountain of rocks. Inside their hands, they found some climbing equipment and they were both now actually dressed in clothing that looked suitable for rough, adventurous, very physical activities.

Zoe quickly glanced upwards and noticed a small cave almost at the top of the mountain. "I think we have to go up there." She explained to Giovanni.

Giovanni nodded in response.

Mark's voice suddenly boomed out in the background. "You have to make your way up the mountain of rocks towards the cave and there you'll find the way out. For this particular challenge your allotted time frame is five minutes." He explained.

Zoe nodded as she listened.

"Right, let's do this Zoe!" Giovanni quickly urged. "We've got a mountain to climb and there is no way on earth, I'm failing this particular challenge."

Zoe smiled.

The two walked enthusiastically towards the mountain of rocks and then Giovanni immediately started to make his way up it as Zoe glanced at him with a slightly confused expression upon her face. Perhaps he'd forgotten she was there, she mused as she quietly watched him as he'd certainly left her totally behind, still on the ground. Giovanni quickly started to peg the metal pegs into the rocky surface as he scaled the rocky mountain face and once he'd reached about the halfway point, he suddenly abseiled back down to the ground and then stretched his hand out towards Zoe.

"You thought I'd forgotten about you right?" Giovanni teased.

Zoe nodded. "For a minute perhaps." She replied.

"Nope, I was just making it slightly easier for you to climb up the mountain of rocks. I was being a gentleman." He explained.

"That's very sweet of you Giovanni." She mentioned appreciatively as she smiled.

"Now, let's get up this mountain before the time runs out." Giovanni insisted.

Zoe nodded.

A hand was politely offered to Zoe by Giovanni and she quickly clung onto it and then started to climb up the pegs that he'd hammered into the mountain of rocks alongside him. The couple made their way carefully up the mountain of rocks quietly as Zoe delighted in Giovanni's helpfulness and his consideration towards her.

"You're really quite romantic, underneath that hot, spicy surface." Zoe teased as she scaled the rocky wall.

"Please, don't tell anyone about my soft side. I keep that only for the very special people like you." Giovanni replied as he continued to hammer more pegs into the rocky surface just above their heads.

"Mountain climbing isn't exactly my forte as you can probably tell." Zoe explained as she smiled at Giovanni. "In fact, this is my very first time, so technically you've just broken my virginity."

"Don't worry, I've done this before several times, mountain climbing that is not breaking your virginity." Giovanni teased as they neared the cave opening. "It can be very tricky though, when you do it for the very first time."

Zoe giggled and nodded. "I agree, it certainly is." She agreed. "Bit more physically challenging than shopping, though sometimes climbing through the crowds at the mall when there's a sale on, can be slightly tricky."

Giovanni laughed. "We're almost there now. It's almost over." He mentioned as he quickly glanced up at the cave entrance which was now just above their heads.

Zoe nodded.

Once Giovanni had climbed up the last couple of remaining pegs, he quickly scrambled up over the ledge of the cave and then stretched his hand back down towards Zoe. His efforts to assist her, impressed her and she immediately began to appreciate his romantic, more caring nature that up until that point in time, she had not actually had much of a chance to actually see. A shining, bright light emanated from inside the cave and the two cautiously walked towards it as Giovanni led Zoe further into the depths of the cave.

Fortunately for them both, the light was more than just a glimmer and it quickly transpired that it was indeed, the actual exit as they both smiled and walked towards it hand in hand. A huge smile adorned Zoe's face as she walked, Giovanni was definitely the best possible love match for Zoe, not only at the resort but also upon the face of the earth and today, he had totally and utterly, completely confirmed that inside her mind.

The particles of light grew even brighter as they walked towards them until they became completely engulfed by each speck of light as the white, shiny brightness flooded over every inch of their forms. Once they had walked more fully into the bright light, much to their surprise, they found themselves back inside the white, blank empty room once more and they quickly realized that their simulation exercise had now actually been, completed. They smiled at each other warmly as they accepted their achievement, proud that they had actually managed to complete their challenge, on time and very much together.

Other couples in their pairing activity group of twelve, had not fared as well in the meantime however and to Louise's complete and utter horror, she'd actually found herself in an extremely awful predicament. First and foremost, she had not actually been paired with Steven at all which had irritated her and then the man that she had actually been paired with, seemed to be completely uninterested in the challenge or participating in that challenge with her.

Rather strangely, Madeline had actually been paired with Steven which had been extremely awkward for them both as Madeline had absolutely no interest in Steven whatsoever. The two had appeared inside the white holographic room however, just before the challenge had begun and they had glanced at each other slightly nervously with confused expressions upon each of their faces as they'd started to accepted each other's presence.

"Well, this is awkward isn't it?" Steven had mentioned.

Madeline had nodded. "It certainly is." She'd replied.

Despite their discomfort however, the challenge they'd been set still had to be completed and Steven had immediately proceeded to climb up the rocky mountain face as he'd pretty much left Madeline to her own devices at the foot of the rocky heap. For Madeline, despite her soft nature, it hadn't been a huge problem as she'd actually attended a rock climbing group in her youth and hence was actually quite well versed in the skills required to scale the rocky mountain in front of her. She'd started to scale the mountain face pretty much on her own as she'd quietly accepted that Steven had completely abandoned her or couldn't care less it seemed, if she actually managed to reach the cave at all.

"So you're alright then?" Steven had finally asked as he'd arrived at the cave and then glanced back down from the cave ledge at Madeline, who had been just a few pegs further down the rocky surface below him.

Madeline had nodded in response.

Steven had then walked towards the white light in front of him and had actually left Madeline completely alone upon the rocky mountain face.

Madeline had shaken her head in disgust as she'd climbed up onto the cave ledge. "Regardless of how awkward this was, that Steven was not very impressive." She'd muttered.

Since Steven had not actually shown up inside the white, virtual room alongside Louise, after a few seconds of initial shock, Louise had resigned herself to making the most of her pairing challenge simulation with the person who actually had. She'd gently pushed her disappointment to one side and she'd attempted to make the most of the challenge and her potential love match as she'd attempted to scale the rocky mass directly in front of her.

Deep down inside, Louise had already really known that Steven had never really been a suitable potential match for her anyway but she had hoped that somehow, they might have actually been matched up at some point throughout her vacation. In her mind, such a matching would have perhaps then validated his pursuit and interest in her to them both.

The man that Louise had actually been paired with, had drawn much closer to Louise and had then politely introduced himself as Serge and in terms of his physicality, he had been much closer to Louise's usual preferences as she'd quietly observed that he had olive skin, dark hair and a thick, rich continental accent that sounded slightly seductive. There had been an awkward silence between them both for a minute or so as Louise had waited for him to approach their challenge but no further communications had been forthcoming as she'd waited.

Eventually, Louise had approached the rocky mountain surface and had then started to scale it on her own as she'd hammered pegs into it along the way. She'd been very much in her element as she'd scaled the surface with ease and as she'd glanced quickly back down at Serge every now and again, she'd noticed for some reason or another, he had actually remained at the very foot of the huge pile of rocks and had not actually moved an inch.

When Louise had reached the cave, she'd scrambled up onto the cave ledge and then glanced back down at Serge, who she'd quickly noticed had only actually reached the mid-point. His lack of interest in the challenge, it had then quickly transpired was not due to his lack of interest in Louise at all but related more to his actual lack of experience when it came to mountain climbing and his lack of ability to actually perform the challenge they'd both been set. Clearly, Serge had never actually climbed a mountain before and his inexperience had shown as he'd lagged behind, filled with uncertainty and a lack of confidence.

"Do you need some help?" Louise had politely offered.

Serge had nodded.

Louise had quickly climbed back down to where he'd been positioned and then she'd helped him up the remainder of the rocky face. "You should have said something." She'd mentioned as the two arrived and then clambered up onto the cave ledge. "I'd have helped you."

"Thanks Louise." Serge had replied as he'd glanced at Louise's face and then smiled.

Louise had smiled. "It's nothing really, mountain climbing isn't for everyone and not everyone's done it before." She'd quickly reassured him.

Serge had smiled.

Unfortunately however, the white light that the some of the other couples had seen inside their caves, was no longer even visible in Louise and Serge's cave as the time set for the challenge had already lapsed, by the time they'd actually completed it. Despite this setback, the two made friendly small talk as they stood inside the cave and waited patiently for further instructions from Mark, not even aware as yet that they had both actually failed the actual challenge itself. Louise quietly began to notice that they actually quite a bit in common and slightly more than she actually had in common with Steven as they conversed politely and continued to wait.

A thought suddenly struck Louise like a dart that perhaps Steven hadn't actually been a great match for her in the first place as her mind began to wander and she quietly considered Steven for a moment, slightly more thoroughly. Perhaps, Louise had been caught up in Steven's charms and his flattering advances and perhaps really, she'd allowed her own emotions to run away with themselves upon Steven's caravan of romantic promises that in reality, wasn't really actually the optimal romantic relationship for either of them. It suddenly began to dawn upon Louise as she waited for the challenge to end that if she did not keep her own emotions in check, she might actually end up leaving her vacation without a suitable romantic match at all or with a very inferior, substandard romance that might self-destruct in the space of just a few months.

"Right, everyone can remove their headsets now." Mark suddenly announced as he concluded the simulation exercise.

Everyone inside the room immediately complied as they quietly removed each of their headsets.

"We'll have a short break now and then conduct the second pairing activity before lunch with your final match." Mark clarified. "After lunch, you will then be free to start considering your five final selections."

Each of the twelve men and women nodded as they listened.

Upon the screen directly in front of Mark, the results of the first pairing activities rapidly appeared as he quickly glanced down at them and prepared to load up the second pairing activity simulation. A few of the potential couples inside the room it seemed, were very compatible and thankfully, Zoe and Giovanni were actually included in that group of compatible matches which totally relieved him as Mark had actually noticed their interest in each other. They had rendered a 'Compatible Match' result and Mark smiled as he quickly glanced at it and nodded. Despite Zoe's successful match on this particular occasion, Madeline and Steven's pairing however, had resulted in an 'Inconclusive Match' result and as he scanned the screen further, he quickly noticed that Louise and Serge had also received a 'Inconclusive Match' conclusion, even though neither of them had actually completed the challenge successfully.

Due to the positive nature of the outcomes from some of the potential couples in the group of twelve attendees, Mark was somewhat pleased in that, at least there seemed to be some possible potentially successful pairings amongst the group. For the group of vacationers that Mark was actually responsible for looking after whilst they were at the resort, it was now the midpoint of their vacation and as most vacations at the love resort only tended to last a week, that meant there was a certain pressure upon him to actually ensure that his group of vacationers actually left the resort with at least one romantic coupling that could lead into a successful, long term romance. He was extremely encouraged by the first pairing activities that day as he quietly loaded up the second simulations and each of the men and women were swapped around to the second potential match that lay within the current group. Mark knew that the resort absolutely had to deliver and he was under no illusions regarding his own role in that delivery in that, he had to actually ensure that each pairing activity was conducted thoroughly. Another aspect of Mark's role was to actually ensure that each of the participants in the pairing groups that he maintained were as comfortable about participating in those activities as they possibly could be and that could at times be slightly tricky as not all participants adapted well to the virtual simulations.

When lunchtime finally arrived, once the second simulation had been performed and enacted, Zoe, Madeline, Louise, Giovanni and Steven made their way towards the dining hall. Their discussion as they walked was a mixed bag and related more to their first pairing activities that morning as they arrived inside the dining hall and then quickly headed towards the long table to serve themselves some starters. A table was quickly found to sit at that was reasonably quiet which had just a couple of other occupants besides themselves actually seated around it but since those occupants were at the other end of the table, they felt quite free to discuss their morning among themselves as the five quickly sat down.

Louise rapidly discovered that Madeline had actually been matched and paired with Steven and that knowledge shocked her slightly as she listened to them discuss it. "Really you two were matched. How strange." She suddenly said as a frown rapidly spread out across her face.

"Yeah, it was a total disaster Louise." Madeline mentioned. "I don't know why they even matched us."

"Wow, I bet that was awkward." Zoe whispered in Madeline's ear as she glanced at Louise's face which looked slightly disheartened as she absorbed the news.

"It definitely was and is." Madeline replied as she nodded. She turned to face Louise and then touched her hand gently as she attempted to comfort her. "Seriously, we were so awful in the simulation together, it was like the worst match possible."

Louise smiled and nodded.

Once lunchtime was over, the three women and two men made their way towards the poolside as they prepared to relax for the afternoon and discuss their selections which they were actually due to make that night and submit by ten, the next morning. Due to Madeline's planned date later that evening, she would not actually be around that evening as she had a very personal date with the very handsome stranger and that was eagerly discussed by Zoe, who was completely over the moon about it.

For one reason or another Callum the third male, who usually accompanied the group was not around throughout the afternoon and it was therefore assumed as the group eagerly made plans for their evening, that he would not actually be in attendance that evening either. Due to Madeline's nonattendance the night before and her clear lack of interest in Callum, unknown to everyone else, he had actually arranged a date that evening with one of the woman from his pairing activities and hence his presence among the group had gradually started to disintegrate along with his interest in Madeline.

Callum it seemed, had completely given up on Madeline, who had shown him nothing but a frosty attitude which contained not even a single speck or ray of warmth. His potential matches had shown up each day and some of them had actually even embraced his presence with very open arms and that had changed his dedication to a woman it seemed, that really didn't actually want him. He had embraced their welcome and open arms as he'd quickly hopped of the Madeline romance bus which was going absolutely nowhere, or at least nowhere with him and then jumped onto a bus of romantic optimism with a couple of slightly more engaged and cooperative passengers.

For Madeline, who really didn't care less what Callum did or didn't do, the Wednesday night ahead held beautiful, romantic hopes as for the very first time, since she'd actually arrived at the island, she'd actually met someone she was extremely attracted to and very interested in, that she actually had a date with. Excitement teased the pores of her skin and body, every single time she thought about him and whenever she was in actual close physical proximity to him, even though as yet she did not even know his name. Since the very first second the two had initially met, Madeline had been absolutely captivated and besotted by him and now it was just a matter of a few more hours before she would actually find out if there could actually be a real romantic relationship between them both at all. He wasn't even on her potential match list, so it was a huge risk for Madeline to take but due to how she felt, she knew she had absolutely no other choice but to actually take it.

On the other side of the island, there was a small funfair and due to Callum's sudden disappearance, Madeline's scheduled date later that evening and Zoe's extremely adventurous nature, Zoe quickly suggested that the other four should actually visit it later that day. Zoe had actually discovered the funfair upon the map of the island as she'd inspected her new electronic journal inside the dining hall as they'd eaten lunch together. Due to its location, she'd quickly realized that it would actually take them at least an hour to get there as it was actually situated on the other side of the island and that meant, their visit to it had to actually be planned. There were some small electric buggies that were parked in a small car park just to the right of the main resort building that Zoe had worked out they could utilize to reach it as she mentioned that to the group and they all enthusiastically agreed to make the trip, except Madeline of course who had other plans.

Wednesday evening would essentially be the last night that Zoe and Giovanni would be hanging out with the group as they'd both decided the next night and on the nights that followed it, they should follow Madeline's lead and have a one on one dates with each other. A personal date for Zoe with Giovanni the next night, was something they had both discussed and both agreed they'd wanted as they'd organized a slightly more intimate and romantic date of their own. In Zoe's mind, their one on one date was an extremely important step for them both to make as a couple as up until that point in time, the pairing simulation was the first actual moment the two had actually spent any time alone together at all and that hadn't even been in a real environment. The couple hadn't planned to get naughty and naked on the Thursday evening but Zoe knew, there would quite definitely be a lot of romantic intimacy exchanged between them that required a lot more privacy on both the Friday and Saturday night and more particularly on the Saturday night, when they would spend the actual night together before they were due to actually return home on the Sunday.

Dinner that evening was an extremely quick affair as the evening rapidly sped in and Zoe, Louise, Giovanni and Steven quickly departed straight afterwards as they left Madeline alone to prepare for her date and headed towards the funfair. Due to the lack of pairing activities that afternoon, everyone in the group had already showered and changed but Madeline still had a few things to attend to before her actual date that evening, like her hair and makeup. Madeline left the four inside the reception area as she prepared to ready herself for her date with the extremely handsome stranger, who was actually much less of a stranger now as the two had actually met three times and even had one cup of coffee together.

Just before dinner, Zoe had actually assisted Madeline to prepare as she'd helped her choose an outfit to wear for her date and Zoe had enthusiastically encouraged her to enjoy her evening, even though Madeline would not actually be spending it with her. The smile upon Madeline's face that day for Zoe, had made everything worthwhile and Zoe had felt slightly reassured that their love vacation hadn't been a complete disaster for Madeline after all as she'd accepted that Madeline finally had a real match and a potentially great match. Her satisfaction and happiness regarding her potential love interest had now provided Zoe with a tremendous sense of peace as she had been slightly anxious up until that point in time that Madeline would not actually meet anyone she actually liked at all whilst at the resort. Zoe had feared that Madeline would actually return from her vacation, well and truly single, still romantically unattached and extremely empty hearted.

In Zoe's mind, there had been two extremely positive things to celebrate about the date that Madeline had planned that evening, the man in question was definitely her type and he had a very stable job. Whether or not they were compatible as a couple was entirely another matter altogether and those finer details would definitely have to be worked out between them both as they wandered together, deeper inside the forest of love. Hopefully, they would manage to survive the stormy winds that might whip around their sapling first dates and their love would actually grow into a tree of romantic bliss and hopefully, this time Madeline's heart would not be broken or trampled upon by the thugs and wild boars that usually inflicted heartbreak so ruthlessly upon her.

Part of Zoe up until that point in time, had actually begun to feel quite guilty that she had actually met someone she liked and that Madeline actually hadn't. Giovanni had completely delighted her but at the back of her mind, the fact that Madeline still hadn't met anyone had also worried her, after all Madeline was one of the main motivations that had prompted her to book their vacation at the resort in the first place. She always met such sloppy, unworthy men and for once, Zoe had finally had a chance to change that history of disappointment. The man Madeline would be going on a date with, seemed in Zoe's opinion, courteous, responsible, stable and helpful and those were all very admirable qualities that Madeline certainly needed present in her life, though he certainly wasn't Zoe's cup of tea or type at all.

A pale pink and gold dress had finally been chosen by both women and as Madeline had slipped it on and had then stood in front of the mirror, Zoe had smiled. The dress itself, was in fact one that Madeline had actually designed herself and it was figure hugging, short but not to short and it had an elaborate crisscross design at the rear, it was absolutely breathtaking and accentuated Madeline's figure in absolutely all the right places.

"You look absolutely stunning." Zoe had quickly reassured her.

"Are you sure this is the right dress?" Madeline had asked as she'd smoothed the material gently down against her skin.

"That, is definitely the right dress." Zoe had insisted as she'd nodded her head enthusiastically. "You look totally irresistible."

Madeline had smiled.

Once the four left Madeline's side, just beside the reception, they eagerly headed of towards the funfair as they quickly collected an electric buggy like car from the resort buggy parking lot which they'd planned to use as transportation. The four climbed inside the electric, buggy like car as Giovanni quickly offered to drive it and then clambered straight into the driver's seat. Unlike a normal car, the small, black, metal framed vehicle it seemed, could not actually travel at very high speeds but it was certainly sufficient enough to transport the group to the other side of the island at a decent enough and pleasant pace as they embarked upon their journey and Zoe squealed with delight.

"Oh my gosh Giovanni, its actually like you're taking us all out on a road trip." Zoe announced triumphantly. "To explore the island."

Giovanni grinned. "You never know after the funfair, we could do a bit of exploring ourselves and find some untouched areas of the island that have never been visited before and do a bit of personal exploring of our own." He flirted suggestively. "After all, this is a huge island and there is bound to be some inches of it that we can discover together and put our love flag upon."

Zoe giggled.

In terms of the island itself, it was actually quite huge and beaches ran all around it with many small bars, eateries, several large restaurants and various facilities upon them that were spread out quite generously across its golden sandy shores. Quite close to the main resort building itself, there was actually a very large bar and a huge open air barbecue restaurant that grilled freshly caught seafood and various meats and the women had actually eaten lunch there a couple of times. Some of the food served there, differed slightly from the food inside the dining hall as it tended to be served upon very large platters and there was actually no structured menu at all and the menu changed it seemed, from day to day. Vacationers simply requested what they wanted to eat, in terms of meat, fish, vegetarian alternatives or even a combination of any those choices from what had been freshly caught and prepared that day and a large platter would then quickly be prepared and delivered to their table. In terms of organization, the resort and every inch of the whole island was beautifully and immaculately laid out and Zoe had not been bored, even for a second, since the very first moment she'd arrived.

Each evening, the funfair at the other side of the island actually hosted vacationers but up until that evening, neither Zoe nor Madeline or anyone else they had met and subsequently hung out with at the resort, had actually visited it. Due to the fact that it was actually situated around an hour's drive away from the main resort building, no one had actually bothered to make the journey or had even suggested that the group should actually do so. Since Madeline had a date however that was very individual and since Callum had also disappeared, Zoe had decided that the Wednesday evening was the perfect opportunity to actually visit the other side of the island and very fortunately, everyone else had totally agreed. A smile crossed Zoe's face as she quietly watched Giovanni drive the electric buggy through the clean, litter free island roads, at times he could be quite masterful and assertive though not overbearingly so and that actually attracted her to him more for some reason.

When the four arrived at the funfair, it seemed to welcome them with very open arms as they drove up towards the huge, open, black iron gates and then parked the electric, buggy car close to the entrance. The four stepped out of the vehicle enthusiastically and then entered inside the large, black iron gates filled with excitement and hardly able to wait to explore their very first ride. Since there was no actual rush to return to the main resort building, the four had planned to spend most of the evening there and even most of the night and there was certainly enough to do as a mass of rides, cocktail bars, food stands and various novelty experiences immediately greeted their eyes as they walked through the gates. Each delight appeased their eyes and minds as they excitedly absorbed all the fun that the funfair actually contained and discussed which ride they actually wanted to try out first.

Almost every inch of the funfair was explored as the four eagerly rushed around each of the rides and rejoiced in the many delights they found there as they consumed sticks adorned with pink, fluffy candy floss, hot dogs drizzled with spicy mustard and ketchup, burgers and bright red, sticky toffee apples until their stomachs were packed to the brim. Some bumper cars were mounted and then roughly bumped into each other as the women and men playfully enjoyed themselves and reverted back to their teenage years in terms of behavior and lack of inhibitions. Non-stop laughter wrapped it's arms around their evening as they giggled away contently and enjoyed the spectacular rides as they participated wholeheartedly.

Several times throughout the evening however, Zoe quietly contemplated how Madeline might be doing as she considered her date down on the beach thoughtfully. There was no way on earth that Zoe could possibly call her and interrupt her evening, hence there was no way to actually find out and put her mind at ease but she certainly hoped it was going well. Despite her worries about Madeline, Giovanni kept Zoe extremely occupied throughout most of the evening as he teased her playfully and kept her in a fit of giggles and that at least, from Zoe's perspective was a very welcome distraction indeed.

Despite Zoe's worries however, Madeline had actually already met the handsome stranger down by the Coconut Bar which was situated in a slightly quieter more secluded, pebbly area of the island's coastline. The bar itself was situated slightly further away from the main resort building than some of the other beach bars that Madeline had previously visited and hence was slightly less occupied than their usual evening hangout, the poolside bar which was usually quite crowded and extremely busy. Madeline had appreciated the slightly more intimate, romantic, private atmosphere and setting the venue offered as she'd met the handsome, charming stranger at the bar and he'd politely escorted her to a nearby table.

A chair had been politely pulled out for her, drinks had then been ordered and a freshly grilled platter of barbecued meat and fish swiftly requested from the small grill stand situated right next to the main bar. She'd smiled as she'd accepted her date's polite efforts enthusiastically as she'd prepared herself to get to know the man that she'd felt extremely attracted to and listened to him speak as she'd waited. Madeline had held an extremely important question inside her mind all day and she'd waited all day to actually present that question to him.

Once the food and drinks arrived, Madeline eagerly tucked in as she'd only eaten some very light snacks that evening inside the dining hall and by now, she was actually quite hungry. Bowen smiled as he joined her and they shared the large platter of food in front of them as they ate freely and simply enjoyed the pleasant ambience that surrounded them. Soft music flowed through the air from speakers situated just behind the bar nearby as they filled up their stomachs and conversed quietly amongst themselves.

"So Madeline, what do you do for a living?" Bowen asked, even though he actually already knew the answer to his question as he'd discovered that information from Madeline's profile on the resort computer system, prior to their actual date. "And what are your passions in life?"

"I'm actually a fashion designer." Madeline replied. "I have my own clothing line and boutique that I started myself, it's nothing huge though."

Bowen listened attentively as he smiled and nodded. "Wow, that's really something." He mentioned. "You built a business from scratch all by yourself, I'm really impressed."

"Yes, these are some of my designs." Madeline immediately explained as she quickly showed him some photos of dresses and outfits she'd made over the years on her phone. "And even this dress I'm wearing tonight, I designed it myself. I've built my client list for a number of years and I try to keep them as happy as possible and I have a couple of manufacturing agreements for mass produced designs with a couple of retailers, so that really helps too."

"You are exceptionally talented it seems and very smart." Bowen acknowledged as he glanced into Madeline's eyes. "And very beautiful."

"Thank you." Madeline replied.

"Not at all, you've done amazingly well." Bowen added.

"Can I ask you a question please?" Madeline asked.

"Sure go ahead. Ask me anything you want." Bowen offered.

"What's your name?" Madeline asked as she giggled softly. "Since we first met, you haven't actually told me and no one actually introduced us."

Bowen suddenly laughed. "How true. I hadn't actually noticed." He replied.

A server suddenly approached the table and delivered another large platter of food as Bowen nodded at him and then smiled. The second platter unlike the first, contained breads, slices of plantain and various other accompaniments for the couple to consume alongside the fish and meats that they had already started to eat. Due to the sudden distraction, their attention was immediately drawn away from Madeline's question and redirected towards the hot, delicious platter of food, now situated directly in front of them as Madeline's question therefore remained for the meantime, totally unanswered.

Meanwhile back at the funfair, Zoe, Giovanni, Louise and Steven had stopped off for a break from their playful jaunt as they found a small cocktail bar and then sat down for a while. For Zoe, the night had been almost totally perfect, except for the fact that Madeline of course, hadn't actually been there with her. Each minute had been filled with fun, laughter, playful antics and a very generous portion of hot sizzling flirtation with the very sexy, extremely handsome man that Zoe had now, officially actually been matched with and in Zoe's mind, it had been almost the most perfect night of her entire life. An hour or so later, when the four finally tired from all the frolics of the funfair, they opted to return to Steven's suite to watch a movie. Several cocktails and bottles of beer had been consumed and as a result all four were a bit tipsy as they made their way back towards the electric buggy car parked just outside the funfair and then clambered back inside the vehicle.

Due to their alcohol intake, the drive back to the resort was almost as fun as one of the rides they'd ridden on whilst at the funfair as Giovanni playfully swerved around and even drove over some very bumpy ground quite intentionally. When they finally managed to arrive back at the resort, thankfully in one piece after their rollercoaster journey and despite having taken a wrong turn somewhere along the way, over an hour later, they quickly parked the buggy car back inside the small carpark and then prepared to enter back inside the main resort building.

"I swear Giovanni, you didn't stick to the main route." Zoe mentioned as the four walked towards the building. "If you had, we'd have been back here ages ago."

"Well, we're not in a rush are we?" Giovanni replied.

Zoe grinned and shook her head. "Good thing we weren't really." She teased.

Since Zoe and Giovanni had actually decided to wait, until their very last night at the resort to actually spend the night together, there wasn't any rush for either of them to leave Steven or Louise's side that night and hence the four actually watched two movies together in the end, before they finally decided to call it a night. Both men, politely escorted each of the two women back to their suites individually, once the two films had ended and just before Giovanni left Zoe outside her suite door, he leant forward and then gently kissed her upon her cheek.

Passion gently bubbled away just underneath Zoe's skin as she yearned for Giovanni to hold her in his arms and kiss her lips and very fortunately, a few seconds later, he turned her face towards him and then actually began to do so. A mountain of desire seemed to suddenly form inside Zoe as her body began to tremble as she struggled to control her inner passions. Inside of her, there was a sudden irresistible urge to feel him inside her as the temptation to invite him inside her suite and make passionate love to him danced playfully across her mind. Their first passionate kiss, almost unleashed all of the passion that had been building up inside her, since the very first moment the two had actually met but Zoe somehow managed to retain her composure. Zoe quickly reminded herself that every soon, Madeline would actually return from her date as she resisted succumbing to her own urges as she really wanted to know how it had actually gone.

The sudden thought surrounding Madeline and her date, quickly cooled Zoe back down as the flames of desire that had just run rampant through her body seconds beforehand, were rapidly extinguished. Even though it would be so easy for Zoe to get carried away in the heat of the moment, Zoe knew she could not actually allow that to happen, not yet, not tonight as she still had to consult Madeline and ensure that her date and evening had gone according to plan. Zoe's vacation, was not just her vacation and Madeline's romantic wellbeing was also of primary importance to Zoe as she'd dragged her along on this holiday and she therefore had to actually ensure that Madeline was indeed, romantically catered for.

"I'll see you at breakfast tomorrow." Zoe said as she lingered for a few seconds longer by her closed suite door and gently held Giovanni's hand.

"Definitely." Giovanni replied. "Though tonight, I'll definitely be with you in my dreams, so technically we won't have actually parted."

Zoe giggled.

Giovanni turned and then prepared to walk away as he smiled. "Night gorgeous." He called out as he started to walk away.

Zoe smiled as she held up the keycard to the small panel just beside the suite door directly in front of her. "Night handsome." She replied as the suite door suddenly swished open in front of her.

After the fun and frolics of the previous night, the next morning finally arrived quite calmly and quietly as Zoe and Madeline woke up and then met with Louise inside the dining hall for breakfast. Due to the fact that the vacationers had now met all ten of their potential love matches, they now had choices to make and those choices had to actually be submitted through their electronic journals by ten that morning. From the ten men that the women had met, they had to rank each potential match on a scale of one to ten and then from those ten rankings, their final five matches would be selected. Zoe had already in her mind, nominated Giovanni to be in her number one spot and besides that ranking, she really wasn't actually particularly bothered about the other nine men she'd met but she prepared to participate nonetheless.

Each of the three women discussed the previous evening as Zoe and Louise waited with eagerness to hear all about Madeline's date with the very handsome stranger as Madeline had actually been fast asleep the previous night, by the time Zoe had actually arrived back at their suite. Even though Louise hadn't actually seen or noticed the man

Madeline had gone on a date with as she'd entered the dining hall just after their discussion the previous morning, she was still very eager to hear all about the man that had propelled Madeline into action and actually enticed her into spending a whole evening with him.

"Madeline, how did your date go? I wanted to ask you last night but you were fast asleep by the time I came back. I want to hear every single juicy detail." Zoe insisted as the three women sat around a table in the dining hall and munched hungrily on the breakfast items that littered their plates. "Was it I do or, I don't?"

"Yes, I do too Madeline." Louise urged. "Was there a sizzle between you both and did he ignite the flames of passion?"

"Or was he just a soggy, wet blanket that dampened the flames?" Zoe teased.

Madeline laughed. "It was amazing. He's so nice." She replied.

"You seeing him again?" Zoe pressed, eager to find out how this new romance would proceed and if it was actually going to.

"I'm not sure, we didn't actually make any plans." Madeline answered.

"Madeline, how could you not make any plans?" Zoe demanded in a slightly exasperated tone. "I mean seriously that is like the most important thing."

Madeline looked at Zoe as uncertainty suddenly filled her eyes. "I guess, we were just so busy talking about other things that we forgot. Do you think he'll come by the suite and ask me out on another date again?"

"Definitely." Zoe replied as she immediately attempted to reassure Madeline that the one date she'd attended, would not be the birth and death of a potential romance that she'd only just managed to actually find. "I saw the way he looked at you Madeline, he won't let you slip out of his arms that easily." She quickly reassured her.

"Have you both ranked your ten potential love matches yet?" Madeline asked.

Zoe nodded. "In my mind I have but I still have to actually put my rankings into the electronic journal. Obviously, Giovanni will get my number one spot and everyone else will just be ranked afterwards in the remaining spots to be polite and to participate." She explained.

"Naturally." Madeline teased. "What about you Louise?"

Louise smiled. "Well, since Steven wasn't included anywhere in my ten potential love matches, he won't be ranked at all and that just leaves me with the ten other guys I was actually matched with and among them, there's no clear favorite but I'll try my best." She explained.

Zoe chuckled.

"When do we go on our five dates?" Madeline asked.

"We go on those dates today, we have two this morning and then three this afternoon." Louise replied. "Then by Friday morning, we have to narrow it down to our final two and on Friday we go on two dates with those two men which are slightly longer, one a lunch date and the other a dinner date. By Saturday lunchtime we then have to submit our final selections and we spend the Saturday afternoon and evening with them."

Madeline nodded. "I'm just ranking my potential matches to go through the motions." She mentioned. "I've already got my heart set on someone else that's not even in my potential match list."

Zoe giggled. "I mean seriously, how awkward is that?" She asked.

"I know. What are you actually going to do when you have to meet your final date Madeline that could be awkward?" Louise enquired.

Madeline shrugged. "I'm not very sure, I hadn't thought that far ahead yet." She replied as she gently shook her head.

Louise smirked.

"Well, quite frankly I'm disgusted with you Madeline, you are usually so well organized, how can you not think that far ahead?" Zoe teased.

Madeline giggled. "I know Zoe, I'm starting to sound almost as disorganized as you." She replied playfully. "I'm being infected by your chaos."

Zoe smirked. "In the best possible way of course. I mean seriously he's like absolutely perfect for you Madeline." She quickly reassured her. "I mean, I couldn't have even picked out a more suitable, perfect guy for you myself."

Madeline smiled.

Inside the resort operations room, work for that day at the love resort had already begun and Samantha was busy that morning putting some last minute touches to the correction reunion that she'd scheduled. There were thirty love mismatches that had to be sorted out and Samantha had been tasked organizing the reunion where it was hoped that those romantic corrections would actually be made. The reunion was due to happen later that night after dinner, when the mismatched clients would arrive and then spend that evening and the next day at the resort. Their trip had been paid for by the resort and all the invites had been sent out and very fortunately, actually accepted immediately. A private plane had been arranged to collect everyone from a central airport and local flights to that central airport had already been booked for each attendee. Each one of the sixty guests would attend the reunion, spend the night at the resort and then be flown back home the following evening which meant, they would actually spend the night at the resort as it was simply not practical to fly them back home on the very same night that the event was due to actually take place.

At least ten resort staff had been allocated to assist Samantha in her task and Ricky and

Becky had also offered to help. There were a few issues that Samantha knew could perhaps be quite tricky, like rematching people appropriately, keeping current guests away from previous guests, in order to avoid any possible further complications arising and ensuring that there were no further disruptions to the actual event itself. An evening meal had been scheduled, just after the current vacationers dinner sitting which it had been announced that day would be slightly shorter than usual and the kitchen staff had been briefed accordingly.

Any details surrounding the problems that had actually created the need for the event had been provided on a need to know basis only and as far as most of the resort staff were aware, it was a purely one off reunion event that had been planned as a treat for some past guests. Bowen had insisted that this was the best course of action as he'd wanted to ensure that the staff's faith in Honey and the love matching system that the resort utilized, remained intact. If the resort staff started to doubt Honey and the resort's love matching capabilities, it would essentially in Bowen's opinion, be quite demotivating for them, he'd decided and hence, minimal details were provided to any staff not directly involved. A meeting had been held the previous afternoon and all the resort staff that would actually be in attendance at the reunion, had been briefed and adequately prepared.

All the guests flights to and from the central airport had been reserved and paid for, from the company's account as per Bowen's instructions as due to the fact that the error had been the company's fault, it had made perfect sense that the company Love Inc. should actually foot the bill for any corrective actions that had to be taken as a result. Technically, there was no real explanation as to how a virus had actually infected Honey's system but Bowen had accepted that the protective systems he'd put in place to guard Honey had failed to actually notice it and hence, he'd taken responsibility for those failings. The impact of the Virus had negatively affected Bowen's customers and now he'd quite simply had to foot the bill to positively correct those errors.

Since most of the vacationers that day were attending, one on one dates with their final five best love matches, the resort actually required less input from the resort coordinators which actually freed some of them up to attend and attentively orchestrate the reunion plan. The next day, when the reunion guests were due to spend their day at the resort before heading home in the late afternoon, there were again more scheduled dates planned for the current vacationers and that meant very fortunately, the resort coordinators once again would have less to do as there would be no scheduled pairing activities to supervise throughout the day.

One thing definitely worked in Bowen and Samantha's favor and that was the fact that the mismatches had actually all occurred in the past few weeks as that meant that any emotional attachment amongst the mismatched couples, would not be very established or even fully formed yet. Each invitation that had been sent out had simply stipulated that the sixty guests had been randomly selected to join a special event to celebrate the fifth anniversary of the Love Colony which had now been operation for five years and hence none of the guests in attendance would actually be any the wiser as to why they were actually there. Everything that Samantha could think of had actually been taken care of, except for one thing and that was how to actually rematch the attendees without them actually becoming suspicious or opposing any rematching suggestions.

"We can only really provide rematching suggestions by seating them beside their correct matches for dinner and perhaps by having some kind of activity groups the next day." Bowen had advised at the briefing he'd held the afternoon before. "Besides that, there's not really much else we can do. Our objective is just to try and reduce the negative impact that may have occurred but like their original vacations, it's really down to each individual to exercise their own right of choice and pursue a match or a subsequent rematch. We can only provide the opportunity but we can't force anyone to take make the most of it."

Bowen's logical approach to the issues at hand had seemed to make total sense to Samantha as he'd encouraged her somewhat, that whatever actually happened at the reunion or didn't actually happen, the resort and its staff, had done their very best and everything that they possibly could to try and rectify the situation sufficiently. No computer system was perfect and when people bought into a vacation love matching package managed by a computer, there was a chance that a small margin of error would perhaps at some point actually occur and now, that was something that Bowen had actually had to face, alongside the resort staff that had uncovered the issue and then subsequently tried to help him to actually resolve it.

Precise, intricate planning had gone into the evening that lay ahead and the Reunion Dinner and Dance, it had been planned would actually take place inside the dining hall. Everything had been arranged with precision, from the flights, suites and even the guests seating arrangements at each of the dinner tables and Samantha had done all she could humanly possibly do, to actually ensure that the night was a success. Each guest would be seated at a table of six, next to at least two matches that they should have initially been paired with and each person in attendance would also be given an individual suite to sleep in. The main objective of splitting people up at night being to keep them as far away as possible from the person they had been incorrectly matched with on their previous visit to the resort and who they had then subsequently chosen as their final match that they really shouldn't have ever actually been matched with at all.

The afternoon sped by quickly for Zoe, Madeline and Louise, who attended their final three dates from the five they'd had to attend that day and Zoe was absolutely delighted to find Giovanni at one of hers. When the evening approached, straight after dinner, the three women headed back to their suites in order to prepare for their evening ahead and Zoe's very first individual date. Zoe and Giovanni, for the very first time that week would not actually be in attendance at the poolside bar that night as they'd opted to spend some time together alone instead.

There was a couple of hours to spare however, before Zoe was actually due to meet Giovanni for her date and once she'd eaten a very early dinner with the final date she'd met that day which she'd been eager to end as soon as she possibly could, she'd opted to spend that time with Madeline. The two women had decided to take a gentle saunter around the resort as they enthusiastically searched for some form of entertainment, to occupy their minds and their time.

Meanwhile, each of the sixty reunion guests had finally arrived at the resort, just as the early evening settled in. The allocated resort staff collected them from the reception area and as they met each one, it was very fairly easy to see almost straight away, some of the mismatches that had actually occurred. Some of the couples stood beside each other inside the foyer but had very strained expressions upon their faces and their relationships seemed fragmented and devoid of any real romantic interest and commitment towards each other. Disharmony was very clearly prevalent as the ten resort staff collected each of the sixty guests and then showed them politely to their single suites.

An hour later, when the dining hall had been emptied of current resort guests, it was then quickly filled up with the sixty reunion guests as Mark attended the reunion guest's dinner service which he'd been asked to supervise by Bowen. His boss had chosen him specifically to assist as Bowen had felt that Mark was the height of discretion and Bowen knew, he could totally trust Mark to handle the extremely confidential situation that had actually arisen. The Virus had thrown a huge spanner in the works with regards to Honey's usual smooth, precise love matching processes and results and the thirty vacationer's couplings that had been affected, now had to be rectified. Each of the sixty guests had to be provided with the chance to meet the potential match they should have met the first time around and didn't meet due to the misallocations and mispairings.

Sixty people had been given at least one wrong potential match whilst at the resort and those incorrect matches they had then gone on to select as their final dates and that was the error that Samantha had been tasked with trying to rectify. All of the sixty people in attendance had one thing in common as they arrived for dinner and were courteously seated at tables, they had all been mismatched and they had all chosen the mismatched person as their final selection.

Music suddenly began to fill the dining hall as the reunion guests were seated as the resort DJ that usually supplied music to the bars at the resort, who had actually been tasked with providing music for the dance that evening, began to play some soft, soulful tunes. Each of the ten tables that the sixty guests were seated at had been placed around the edges of the dining hall and in the very center of the banqueting hall, there was a large, clear space which had been cleared to serve as a dancefloor. Servers rushed to and fro as they attempted to serve each of the reunion guests platters of food and take individual orders. Glasses of champagne, brightly colored cocktails and bottles of beer and wine adorned each table as the reunion guests started to tuck into their meal and conversed sociably among themselves.

Two tables from the ten, were filled purely with men and two with only women but the other six tables had an equal spread of female and male guests seated around each of them as Bowen suddenly entered the dining hall to assess the situation. Fortunately, he found the reunion dinner in full swing as he arrived and that all the guests who'd been invited were indeed all actually present and they appeared to be enjoying themselves as he glanced around the room and nodded with satisfaction. Samantha stood at one side of the large hall as she'd been released from her usual work schedule inside the operations room that day, in order to provide hands on assistance for the

Reunion Dinner and Dance that evening and she smiled as Bowen made his way over towards her.

"I have some work to do inside my office. I'll be back later on to see how things are going." Bowen explained.

Samantha nodded and replied. "Don't worry Mr. Logan, we'll handle things here." She gently reassured him.

Bowen nodded.

The remainder of the evening continued to saunter by quite peacefully as dinner ended and then some of the reunion attendees enthusiastically got up to dance. Very fortunately, most of the attendees actually present, danced with everyone else in attendance and they did not stick to purely dancing with the incorrect matches that they had been coupled with just before they'd left the resort, after their initial vacations. Each of the ten resort coordinators joined in as they'd been instructed to and danced with the reunion guests, in order to actually encourage everyone to dance with each other. For the resort staff in attendance, like Ricky and Samantha, despite the slightly awkward nature of the event and its primary motive, it was on the whole quite a pleasant evening as for once they actually got to mingle with the guests and actually see the faces of those they made love matches for every single working day which was a very welcome change for them indeed.

Due to the now upbeat music being played inside the dining hall, the Reunion Dinner and Dance immediately attracted Zoe's attention as she and Madeline wandered by and suddenly heard the tunes being played, sift out from in-between the now closed dining hall doors. There was still at least another hour before Zoe's date with Giovanni was due to commence and hence, she still had some very free time which she was eager to spend in a manner that was as entertaining to her as it possibly could be. The usual group meeting and activities that usually took place each evening beside the poolside bar had finally been shelved that night in the end as Louise had opted to watch a movie with Steven on their own, in an attempt to repair some of the damage that had been done by the two not being matched at all by the resort. Since Madeline would therefore be the only potential attendee at the poolside bar and since she had absolutely no interest whatsoever, in standing at the poolside bar drinking cocktails on her own, no one from the group it had been decided, would actually attend the poolside bar that evening for drinks.

There were two small, circular windows situated at the very top of the two white, glossy dining hall doors and Zoe quickly peered through them as a mischievous grin rapidly spread out across her face. Inside the dining hall, there seemed to be a very active, pleasant dance underway and a dance that neither Zoe or Madeline had actually been invited to or even notified about and curiosity suddenly tugged away inside Zoe's mind as she quickly yearned to actually join in.

Zoe's mischievous nature was instantly aroused as she gently pulled one of the dining hall doors open ever so slightly and then peeked inside. "Wow, Madeline there's a dance inside the dining hall, let's go in." She quickly urged as she suddenly turned back to face Madeline and then grinned at her mischievously.

"Perhaps it's only for certain people." Madeline quickly mentioned as a slightly worried expression suddenly crossed her face. "I mean, they didn't tell us about it and we certainly weren't invited, are you really sure we should go in there? I don't recognize anyone there, perhaps it's not for us." She added as she peeked inside the dining hall.

"You only live once Madeline." Zoe insisted as she quickly silenced Madeline and gently grabbed her arm and then led her inside. "I intend to have as much fun as I can whilst I'm here and you can either come along with me or go back to the suite and sleep. It's not like you have anything else planned this evening."

"Okay, okay." Madeline replied as she succumbed to Zoe's mischievous plans. "But if they kick us out, we leave straight away."

Zoe giggled.

Music rapidly flooded into both their ears as Zoe and Madeline quietly sneaked inside the dining hall. Once they were inside the banqueting hall, Zoe quickly found a spot to dance in, right in the midst of a group of people and Madeline immediately joined in as she danced along to the song being played, anxious not to stand out among the dancing reunion guests that now surrounded her to avoid being noticed. The two women certainly looked as if they had actually been there all evening as they quickly blended in and moved to the rhythmic beats that flowed through the air. None of the resort staff actually noticed the two current resort guest's arrival, since there were so many other reunion guests dancing around them and hence, Zoe and Madeline's arrival and presence slipped by, completely unnoticed.

For the resort staff, the evening so far had gone quite well but there had been a couple of brief sticky moments that mainly revolved around some of the reunion attendees. One of the couples that had been invited along to the Reunion Dinner and Dance, Ricky had actually found just outside the large French doors at one side of the dining hall at one point throughout the evening, involved in a huge argument and he'd almost started to flip out and panic as he'd become slightly distressed. The couple in question had gone outside due to the dispute between them both and Ricky, who had also walked out of the large doors onto the veranda for a breath of fresh air had very unfortunately, landed slap, bang right in the middle of their argument.

"I saw you staring at her. You're so annoying. You have absolutely no respect for me." Jade argued. "Seriously, I can't even believe the resort paired us, we are so not compatible. They must have made a mistake."

"You're always nagging me though. Can you blame me?" Gideon replied as he sighed.

Ricky took a deep breath and then quickly interrupted the arguing couple as he approached them both. "Hi, are you both having a good time?" He asked. "Would you like to dance Jade?" Ricky offered Jade.

Jade nodded. "Yes sure, I'd love to dance." She replied. "Since we are so obviously here to appreciate other people, I think I should do the same."

"Let's go." Ricky insisted as he gently held Jade's arm and led her back inside the dining hall.

"We're just not getting along. We don't get along at all." Jade explained to Ricky as they walked back inside the dining hall. "I think I might have picked the wrong person from my final selections."

"That's okay." Ricky advised. "We all make mistakes sometimes, if you like I can introduce you to someone else." He suggested. "And then you can take things from there."

Jade smiled and thanked him. "Would that be possible? I really think it might be for the best, thank you so much."

Ricky smiled. "That is totally possible." He quickly verified. "After all there's no point being in a relationship for the rest of your life with someone who makes you completely miserable."

Jade nodded. "I totally agree." She said as she smiled.

Another tune suddenly started to flow out of the sound system at the very top of the hall as the two entered back inside the room and Ricky quickly scoured the interior for the potential, optimal match that Jade was actually supposed to connect with whilst at the Reunion Dinner and Dance. In no time at all, Ricky had managed to identify him and then he immediately led Jade towards him.

"Hi Aaron, this is Jade." Ricky said as he quickly introduced the two.

"Oh, hi Jade." Aaron replied as he quickly offered to shake her hand. "I'm Aaron. I think we sat next to each other during dinner. Would you like to dance?"

Jade nodded enthusiastically.

"I'll just put my drink down at our table and I'll be right back." Aaron quickly reassured her as he smiled.

Jade smiled in response.

"You see Jade." Ricky encouraged her. "Some men don't appreciate what they have until it's gone and sometimes you really have to be gone, in order to find something better for you." He advised.

Jade grinned. "I think you could be right." She agreed.

"Enjoy your night and enjoy your life." Ricky whispered as Aaron suddenly returned. "I'll leave you guys to it."

Jade nodded and smiled.

Despite their lack of invitations, Zoe and Madeline had actually found a group of six men upon the dance floor that had welcomed the two women into their midst and then danced them with nonstop, almost since they'd first arrived. Technically, the women knew almost immediately that the six men were not actually heterosexual but that didn't bother them at all, since they were just there to have fun and not to actually look for a potential date. The hour passed by quickly as they two women, filled themselves up with cocktails and danced to

450

every tune that was played with the six men that surrounded them.

"Zoe, we have to go." Madeline suddenly urged as she quickly glanced down at her phone and checked the time. "You have a date with Giovanni."

Zoe nodded as she prepared to say goodbye to the six men that she'd just enjoyed a very energetic dance session with. "We'll have to love and leave you I'm afraid gentlemen." She explained to the six gorgeous men around her.

"Really?" One of the men asked. "So soon?"

"Unfortunately, the body is willing but the schedule for this evening definitely isn't, I have to date to attend." Zoe explained.

He grinned at Zoe. "Well, remember us well fair maiden and if he ever breaks your heart, we'll always be here for you." He teased just before he leant forward and then gently kissed both Zoe and Madeline on both cheeks.

Zoe giggled in response.

A minute or two later, the women slipped out of the dining hall through the French doors as they made their departure via the veranda and prepared to return to their vacation and

JILL THRUSSELL

their actual plans for that evening, or in Madeline's case her lack of plans. Their arrival, attendance and departure, went for the most part, completely unnoticed by any of the resort staff, who had by now convened at one end of the dining hall to discuss the evening and how everything was going so far.

The dining hall doors, suddenly opened as Bowen swept back inside the room and then strode across the large dining hall towards the resort staff, who were now situated at one side of the large room together. Each one of the resort staff glanced at him as Bowen approached them and acknowledged his arrival as they politely nodded their heads.

"How's it going?" Bowen asked Mark.

"It's a bit chaotic really Mr. Logan." Mark explained. "Things are a bit all over the place. Some people have adapted and started to mingle with the correct potential love matches and some haven't."

"Let's pull the plug for tonight. I have another plan we can implement tomorrow morning. It's getting late now." Bowen suggested. "Tomorrow, the reunion guests will go out on lunch boat trips in the same groups as they were seated at tables with for dinner.

Each of you will have to make a meeting point for each group around the reception area, poolside bar and the beach bars for around eleven." He instructed.

Everyone nodded their heads in agreement.

Bowen suddenly left their side and then strode quickly across the hall towards the resort DJ. "Let's call it a night." He instructed. "Turn of the music and I'll make an announcement to end the dance."

"Right Mr. Logan." The resort DJ replied as he quickly lowered the sound system and then politely handed him a microphone.

Once the music had been switched off, Bowen quickly turned to face the crowd of reunion guests as he held the microphone inside his hands and everyone in the hall, immediately stopped dancing as they turned to face him and fell completely silent.

"I'd like to thank everyone for coming along to celebrate our fifth anniversary of the Love Colony. Tomorrow, we've organized some special boat lunch trips for you all that you can attend before you leave the resort. If you speak to the resort coordinators beside each of your tables, before you leave the dining hall tonight, they will let you know where to meet tomorrow morning for the boat trips." Bowen announced. "I hope that you have all enjoyed your evening and I'd like to thank you once again for attending and for giving the resort a chance to celebrate our five years of romantic success with some of the people who have enjoyed our services." His words were immediately greeted with smiles and nods as he quickly glanced around the dining hall and smiled, what hadn't been resolved and rectified that night the resort at least, had one more chance to try to repair the next day and to provide some form of actual restitution and for that, Bowen was extremely grateful.

Just outside the main resort building, Zoe and Madeline had quickly skirted their way around the exterior and had finally arrived back at the main entrance as they'd headed back towards their suite, now in a bit of rush due to Zoe's pending date with Giovanni. Their fun filled hour, that they had spent inside the dining hall dancing with strangers had not been planned or even scheduled but it had actually been one of the highlights of their day. The two women very fortunately, had not actually encountered Bowen on their way out of the dining hall as they'd slipped out of the side doors that led out onto the veranda, whilst he'd entered through the main doors and hence their paths had not actually crossed as he'd arrived and they'd departed.

"We were so no meant to be there." Zoe giggled as she celebrated her naughty gatecrash of a party that she quite certainly hadn't actually been invited to.

Madeline nodded in agreement. "Well, at least no one noticed us." She observed as they walked back along the corridor that led towards their suite.

"Yeah because if they did, they would have definitely booted us out." Zoe mentioned as the two women arrived outside their suite.

Madeline quickly fished the keycard out of her bag and then held it up against the small panel on the wall beside the door and the door rapidly swished open in front of them. "I think you're right." She agreed. "It really seemed to be just for certain guests."

Both women rushed inside their suite and then collapsed down upon the sofa as they giggled among themselves. Their night had been filled with unexpected fun and now, they were slightly worn out but happy from their

455

unexpected deviation and jaunt. An alarm suddenly went off on Zoe's cellphone and she quickly stood up as it immediately alerted her to the time and her pending date with Giovanni.

Zoe walked towards her bedroom. "I have to finish getting ready, really quickly." She explained. "Giovanni will probably be waiting for me by now."

Madeline grinned as she followed her inside the bedroom. "You really like him don't you?" She asked.

Zoe nodded. "It's still too early to tell yet, if he's actually the man I'll actually spend the rest of my life with." She replied. "But the indicators are positive and the gut feeling I have is good. I don't want to jinx it and say I'm certain and then it all goes messy, so I'm trying to take it slowly in terms of my own emotional commitment. I do have a good feeling about Giovanni though but only time will tell."

Madeline smiled. "I really hope it works out for you Zoe, you really deserve to have a decent man in your life." She said as she gently touched Zoe's hand.

"And so do you Madeline." Zoe replied as she glanced into Madeline's eyes. "You really do. I best get moving." She insisted as she quickly slipped a slinky black dress over her head and then attached some jewel like clips to her hair. "Or Giovanni might start to think I've actually dumped him."

Madeline giggled.

SEMI FINALS

Finally for Zoe, the Thursday night had finally arrived and so too had her first one on one date with Giovanni that they'd actually planned together without anyone else's involvement. Eager anticipation began to mount inside Zoe as she walked towards the reception area with every step she took and it felt absolutely and utterly delicious. It had been arranged that they would meet each other outside at one of the beach bars which was actually situated a short distance away from the main beach area at the very front of the resort, in order to avoid large gatherings of other people so that they could both enjoy a slightly more private and intimate evening. Small, black, iron lanterns hung off small black poles that lit the pathway as Zoe walked towards the bar in question and as she approached the bar, she smiled as she suddenly noticed Giovanni at the very front of the shack like venue as he waited patiently for her to arrive.

In terms of his appearance, Giovanni had chosen to wear a sharp, white crisp shirt and a pair of very smart, black trousers and he actually looked extremely handsome as Zoe walked towards him and quietly admired his physicality. At times, when Zoe looked at him, she often wondered what their future might actually hold in their very real lives and this was another of those speculative moments. The resort fostered an atmosphere of idealistic romance but Zoe knew, their real romantic relationship would definitely be quite different in that, it would have to cope with the realities that real life bore and some of those realities could at times actually be quite tough and very difficult to face.

Inside Zoe's mind, she didn't have any huge worries or concerns about Giovanni as he certainly kept her on her toes which was good for Zoe as she usually got bored quite quickly and distracted very easily. He had somehow managed however, to keep Zoe totally captivated and interested in him and despite his more outgoing, extroverted nature which differed slightly in terms of her usual type, he seemed to be quite loyal and faithful. Over the first few days of her vacation, Zoe had actually inspected and assessed Giovanni intensely as she'd sought out any worrying signs of any possible nightmare that might actually present itself at a later date, further down the line but very fortunately, had seen absolutely none.

Giovanni certainly had a healthy sexual appetite, just as Zoe had herself but from what Zoe could see, he wasn't actually a player, so in that respective they were definitely a good match. Usually, men who were more outgoing and interesting came at a price and usually that price was that they were more outgoing and interesting with everyone they came into contact with which meant the women they usually dated had to constantly watch their backs for any possible betrayals but Giovanni seemed to be very faithful and that had impressed Zoe somewhat.

"Should we have a drink at the bar first or should we go for a walk on the beach?"

Giovanni asked as he gently kissed Zoe on the cheek to greet her.

"Let's go for a walk on the beach first." Zoe insisted. "Then we'll stop off for a drink somewhere."

Giovanni nodded.

The couple skirted around the busy areas as they walked as they avoided the busy bar areas completely and made their way towards a more solitary, isolated part of the beach, upon the coastline of the island as they found a quiet place to sit. A large, rock jutted out over the water, almost like a pier and Giovanni politely placed a light jacket down upon the edge of it that he'd carried and held inside one of his hands, so that Zoe could sit down comfortably. Their one on one date was extremely interesting for Zoe as it was the first time really that she was actually getting the chance to see how romantic Giovanni could actually be. Yes, Giovanni could certainly make Zoe laugh and even turn her on but now she needed to be sure that he could actually create, treasure and appreciate tender moments between them both too.

Just above the water, in the distance, a pink, fluffy sunset greeted their eyes as they both watched the sun slowly sink into the water. The couple started to embark upon a slightly more serious discussion as they sat and discussed what they wanted out of life and their possible future as they contemplated quietly internally, exactly what life together might actually, really be like.

"How many children do you want to have Zoe?" Giovanni asked Zoe as he turned to face her and then smiled.

"I'm not really sure, not a football team though, one, maybe two. Not loads or I'll spend my whole life working to provide for them, changing nappies and arguing about when it's bedtime." Zoe explained as she laughed. "What about you?"

Giovanni nodded. "Yep, one or two would really be enough for me too, otherwise you'd spend all your time working to provide for them which would then rob you of the enjoyment you should actually receive from spending time with them." He agreed.

Zoe smiled. "What about the distance between us Giovanni? Will it bother you that we don't actually live in the same city?" She asked.

Giovanni smiled. "Nope, your only two hours' drive away. I can come over on weekends or you can come to mine for the weekend, every single weekend and then when we're ready, one of us can move." He suggested.

Zoe nodded. "Yeah that'll be nice." She agreed.

Despite the usual sexually flirtatious nature of the couple's interactions, that evening was extremely calm, tender and less sexually charged. The sun finally departed as Zoe placed her head upon Giovanni's shoulder and simply enjoyed his presence. Romantic relationships had to endure the longevity of life and that meant physically, it would be impossible to jump into bed very single minute as they would both be totally worn out. Sometimes, if Zoe and Giovanni actually did commit to each other and did decide to take the romantic plunge which it certainly looked like they would, they would have to spend time together that wasn't focused upon the bedroom or even upon any other activity. Sometimes, they would have to relax and simply just be together and that evening proved, in Zoe's mind that they could both actually do that together and enjoy it immensely.

Darkness suddenly crept in around the island and the resort as the two made their way back towards one of the quieter beach bars where they then ordered some cocktails and a grilled platter of spicy meat and seafood. The food, much like the conversation was spicy, hot and mouthwateringingly delicious and Zoe was completely in her element. Hours had gone by and as midnight approached, the two made their way back towards Giovanni's suite to watch a movie together which they had planned to watch earlier that evening.

Later that night in the early hours of the morning, once the movie had ended, the two walked slowly towards Zoe's suite as Giovanni prepared to bide Zoe a final goodnight. They arrived outside the door of her suite and then he tenderly moved a lock of hair out of her eyes as he stared into them intensely. Giovanni suddenly leant forward and then kissed her gently on the cheek and as his warm breath pleasantly caressed her face, Zoe smiled as it was deep, raspy, heavy and sexually charged. He was definitely sexually aroused and so too was Zoe.

Giovanni paused for a moment as he quickly took a step backwards. "I can't do more than that right now Zoe, or I'll end up abducting you and taking you back to my suite for the night and then I probably won't let you leave until the morning." He whispered.

Zoe smiled as she nodded. "I completely understand." She replied and she certainly did as the passion had most definitely been stirred inside her too. Zoe yearned for his touch and his tender, sensual embrace but she knew, the more he actually touched and kissed her, the more she'd want their physical flirtation to continue and actually progress much further.

The two had made a promise to each other that they would actually wait until the final night of their stay, before they would actually engage in actual sexual intimacy and as tempting as it was to break that promise, Zoe knew it was better to be disciplined about it and actually wait. Her final two selections had already been made and Giovanni very naturally, had been Zoe's number one choice and although she hadn't made her final, official selection yet, she couldn't wait to actually do so the very next day. Her second choice that she'd had to rank in second place had been placed in that position simply as a formality but Zoe had absolutely no interest in him whatsoever.

"Did you make your final two selections Giovanni?" Zoe suddenly asked.

"Of course." Giovanni replied.

"What number was I?" Zoe enquired playfully.

"Number one, number ten and every other number in-between." Giovanni gently reassured her. "Zoe, you are my only real choice."

Zoe smiled.

Romance lingered in the air as Giovanni touched her hand softy and then kissed her tenderly on the cheek and Zoe understood his sentiments without either of them even uttering a single word. Neither of them wanted to leave each other's presence but finally after a few minutes, Giovanni somehow managed to pull himself away as he quickly turned and then walked away back along the hallway as he left Zoe alone. Despite his abrupt departure, Zoe fully understood why it actually had to be so sharp as if he didn't leave that way, it was highly likely that they would both get caught up in another moment of passion and then they would definitely be swept away by the lustful yearnings that filled every inch of their core.

Zoe quickly pulled the key card out of her bag and then unlocked the suite door directly in front of her and as it swished open she smiled, the two had spent a very beautiful evening together and that was definitely something that she could treasure and reflect upon, not only whilst at the resort but also when she returned to her very real life and world. She quickly entered inside the lounge area and rapidly discovered that Madeline was actually already fast asleep which Zoe had almost expected, due to Madeline's lack of plans for that Thursday evening, Once inside their suite, Zoe made her way quietly towards her bedroom with a content smile upon her face as she completely resisted the urge and temptation to actually wake Madeline up in order to tell her all about her night, Madeline would find out all the glorious details tomorrow and for now, Zoe's news could definitely wait.

When the next morning arrived, both Zoe and Madeline woke up at around ten as Zoe's alarm beeped loudly and woke them both up. Despite her late night the night before, Zoe had set her alarm to wake her up quite early the next morning, in order to actually ensure that she attended the first of her final two dates that day on time.

Madeline greeted Zoe with a huge smile as Zoe entered inside the lounge and then flopped down onto the sofa next to her. "How was your date?" She enquired.

"Amazing Madeline, Giovanni and I are really going to be such a cute couple." Zoe replied. "He's everything I'd hoped for and more."

Madeline smiled. "I'm so happy for you Zoe." She mentioned.

"Yep and today we go on our final two dates and then make our final selection. So if that guy doesn't come back for you and grab his chance, you can always pick someone else." Zoe quickly reminded her.

Madeline nodded.

"Do you know his name?" Zoe suddenly asked.

Madeline shook her head. "I did ask him and then we got distracted as someone served us some food and then I guess, I just forgot to ask him again." She explained as she smiled. "There was just so much going on around us."

"How funny is that? You actually went on a date with a man whose name you don't even know." Zoe teased. "How daring of you Madeline, that's just not like you at all."

Madeline giggled. "I know." She replied. "I don't know how I'll ever live it down."

Zoe laughed. "Well Madeline, you only live once and he was definitely worth the risk, he's totally your type and extremely handsome." She teased.

Madeline nodded.

"Just call him, Hottie for now." Zoe suggested playfully. "That way I'll know who you are talking about."

Madeline grinned.

For the resort staff that day, an early morning meeting had been organized as Bowen had attempted to make the most of the remaining time that the sixty reunion guests actually had left at the resort. The final step in sorting out the mishaps that had occurred due to the Virus that had attacked Honey absolutely had to be actioned that day and he'd come up with an almost foolproof plan. Each of the sixty guests were still actually in attendance at the resort and that lunchtime, it had been planned, they would spend some time in their groups of six with their optimal matches and attend picnic lunches and boat trips that the resort staff would supervise. Unlike the reunion party, the boat trips would actually totally separate the attendees from the mismatches they'd been paired up with at the end of their initial vacations. Among their small lunch groups, there would be at least one or even two more suitable matches that they should have initially been paired with upon their first visit to the island, if Honey's system files had not actually been corrupted and Bowen hoped that throughout their day, some meaningful, romantic connections would actually be formed.

One of the main objectives of the lunch was to give the attendees the chance to meet and bond with their optimal matches and give them the chance to actually keep in touch with those people, if indeed they actually wished to do so. Bowen couldn't actually change what had happened and the outcomes of those events but he had certainly tried to correct any negative eventualities as far as he possibly could. He'd selected ten resort staff to assist him that day and once again Ricky, Samantha and Becky had all been asked to attend and help him with the implementation of his plan.

Each of the other guests at the resort, who were attending their vacations for the very first time, had been provided with their date schedules for that day by Honey, via their electronic journals and that meant, there was less of a need for heavier supervision by resort coordinators. There were no pairing activities to supervise and perform and that was one small comfort to Bowen as it freed up several of the resort coordinators so that they could actually assist him. By the end of that day, Bowen hoped to have done everything he possibly could to resolve the messy situation that had resulted from the Virus's attack upon Honey so that he could finally put the matter to rest.

Coolers had been filled to the brim by the kitchen staff as the final arrangements for the boat trips were kicked into motion that Friday morning and actually actioned. Bottles of alcohol, cocktails and an assortment of soft drinks had also been prepared to accompany the grilled meats, sandwiches and vast array of consumables. Becky, Samantha, Ricky and Mark had assisted Bowen as much as they possibly could with all the preparations as he'd released them from their usual duties and assigned them solely to that task.

Meeting points had been arranged for the sixty guests the night before and the boat trips were all due to commence at eleven that morning and everything so far, had gone according to plan. Each group it had been planned would contain a resort coordinator and six reunion guests and all the resort coordinators that would be in attendance had been briefed accordingly, in order to prepare them for the lunch ahead. Every resort coordinator that was due to man and facilitate a boat trip, was instructed to encourage active engagement between the participants and to support friendly communication between the six guests that they had each been allocated to.

A few skews and errors had actually been present within the current resort guests matches but thankfully, Ricky had been able to shuffle those around and he'd tweaked the final selections accordingly and hence, there were no longer any problems prevalent in Honey's system. The resort staff had, had to provide a few awkward explanations to some guests but for the most part, the current resort guests had seemed happy enough with the results as most of them as yet, did not actually have any strong romantic leanings towards anyone they had actually met yet.

When eleven arrived, Samantha enthusiastically met her group of six reunion vacationers beside the poolside bar and then started to lead them towards the pier where the boat had been moored that she would utilize to take them for their picnic lunch. The six seemed in extremely good spirits as she escorted them towards the pier and most of the six conversed with each other quite happily as they walked alongside her. Once they arrived at the small, black, glossy pier that the boat had actually been moored to, the six stepped straight onto the boat and then quickly sat down upon the shiny, black bench like seats inside it as they laughed, giggled and filled the boat with chitter chatter.

For Samantha, despite the negative circumstances that had caused the event, it was actually a pleasant change to be outside and spending some time with some of the resort guests that she usually spent all of her working days matching. Honey's face was beautiful and very pretty but at times she did actually yearn to be around other people as Ricky certainly wasn't much of a conversationalist and as a result, her working days could often be quite lonely at times. In some respects, she was actually quite grateful for the opportunity that the unfortunate event had provided as it meant for once that she could actually have a day where a computer screen wasn't all that she actually looked at.

Samantha rarely left the operations room throughout her daily working hours as she spent most of her days simply processing love matches and ultimately working with Honey. She absolutely never, ever actually saw the results of any of those matches and she rarely if ever, actually engaged in a conversation with any of the people she was actually responsible for reviewing potential romances for which meant the boat trip for her, was an extremely refreshing change.

Each boat had already been filled with coolers, hampers and various containers filled to the brim with food, liquids and various other necessities in preparation for the picnic lunches and that meant, all Samantha had to do was actually switch the boat engine on. A programmable journey had already been charted and programmed into the boat's computer system and hence thankfully, Samantha did not even actually have to steer the boat herself which was a complete relief in her mind as she had absolutely no desire to do so at all. No matter how nice the deviation from her usual routine was, steering and sailing a boat, were quite simply things that she wasn't equipped to do and in Samantha's mind, such tasks would be an absolutely surmountable feat and extremely terrifying.

Despite the fact that none of the sixty reunion guests had actually been placed into groups with the people they had arrived at the resort with and chosen as their final matches throughout their initial vacations, absolutely no one seemed to question that at all or even mind as the reunion guests simply accepted their lunch groups at face value and participated which relieved all the coordinators tremendously. Samantha prepared to switch on the boat engine as she smiled, Bowen was right she quietly considered in that, they could provide an opportunity to correct things but they couldn't actually physically choose someone's actual partner for them, that decision was ultimately down to each individual themselves but they had at least provided the guests with ample opportunity to reselect a much more compatible partner, if they actually wished to do so.

Inside the resort, Zoe and Madeline enthusiastically prepared to leave their suite as they quickly checked their electronic journals and prepared to attend their first dates that day. They made their way towards the reception area and met Louise inside it and then had a quick chat before they prepared to separate as that day their final two dates were all very individual and all situated in very different locations.

Zoe was anxious to proceed as she wanted to eliminate her second choice as soon as she possibly could and finalize her future romance with Giovanni. Due to the fact that Madeline did not as yet actually have a second date with the handsome man she'd met at the resort, Zoe had encouraged her to participate in her final two dates with a very open mind indeed. She had discussed the matter at some length with Madeline the day before and Zoe had urged her to participate with her potential love matches, regardless of how she felt about the male stranger that had charmed her and swept her off her feet. Zoe was completely adamant that he had not yet made an actual romantic commitment to Madeline and had rightly pointed out that he hadn't even told her his name yet and that until he did, he should be not be considered as Madeline's final date.

A slightly glum expression adorned Madeline's face as the three women prepared to separate inside the reception area as Zoe glanced at her. Zoe could fully appreciate Madeline's dissatisfaction with her current status and now actual, romantic limbo. Just before the three women actually parted, Zoe once more encouraged her to participate as she gently reassured Madeline that participation was indeed the correct thing to actually do, in the current situation and circumstances.

"Madeline, just go along on your dates and if you like anyone, pick them out as your final selection." Zoe advised. "You're not in a relationship with anyone yet and the handsome stranger you went out on a date with the other night has left you hanging."

Mark was situated inside the reception actually waiting for the final six reunion guests to arrive for the lunch boat trip he was due to supervise as he quite unintentionally actually overheard the woman's conversation.

"Yeah, you came all this way Madeline and spent money on this vacation and that guy hasn't even asked you out yet." Louise agreed. "Zoe's right."

Madeline caved in as she smiled. "Yes, I guess you guys are right, if he's really serious, he'll show me that he is and make some kind of commitment to me."

"It's not playing games." Zoe insisted. "We're here for a purpose and that purpose is romance and a relationship and we are definitely not going to leave here empty handed."

Mark smiled as he listened.

Madeline suddenly noticed Mark nearby and pondered for a moment as to whether she should actually ask him about the man, he'd been standing with inside the dining hall, the second time she'd actually met the handsome stranger. "Hi Mark." She suddenly said as she smiled and nodded at him.

"Hi Madeline." Mark replied. "Are you all ready to go on your final two dates?"

Madeline nodded.

"Don't worry Madeline, whatever romance is supposed to come along your way, definitely will." Mark gently reassured her. "Our resort has a great track record for matching people successfully."

Madeline nodded.

"Yes Madeline, let's go on our dates." Zoe urged as she gently held onto Madeline's arm and then led her towards the entrance of the main resort building.

Louise smiled politely at Mark and then followed them both.

The other nine boat trips had already started and continued, despite the delays to Mark's boat trip which had been slightly delayed as some of the reunion guests were actually late. When Samantha's boat arrived at its destination, one of her group, a female reunion guest actually approached her with a question as they hung back slightly and waited behind as everyone else exited the vessel.

"If we like someone on the boat trip is it alright if we exchange numbers with them?" She asked Samantha as she sought further clarity and privately attempted to address an issue which had arisen inside her mind.

"Certainly." Samantha replied as she nodded enthusiastically. "Feel free to do whatever you want."

Despite the fact that the boat trips had actually been organized and arranged for that very purpose, Samantha had been instructed not to divulge that information to any of the attendees and hence had not actually mentioned it. The briefing Bowen had provided had been very clear, the resort coordinators were to encourage potential pairings with more appropriate matches but not to directly attempt to influence them. Part of Samantha actually felt quite relieved as she quietly observed that her own group of six were actually starting to make connections with their other potential matches and that not too much social engineering had actually been required to achieve that. In fact, it now actually seemed as if the boat lunch trips would yield more successful results than the actual reunion party itself had and that warmed her as a sense of peace gently rested inside her interior and settled her thoughts.

Two of the actual lunch boat trips were being supervised by Becky and Ricky, who had each been allocated a group of six reunion guests to look after that day and as they made their way towards the piers where their respective boats were moored, their paths crossed. The two quickly noticed, to their surprise that they had both been actually assigned groups with reunion guests solely filled with members of the opposite sex and that prompted them both to smile as they drew closer to each other.

"Wow Ricky, today you'll actually get to spend your day totally surrounded by women." Becky teased as she passed him.

Ricky laughed. "I know, life sure sucks. What more could a man possibly ask for." He replied. "I really can't complain."

"You better behave yourself." Becky whispered playfully as she suddenly drew quite close to him.

"I don't know, instead of sitting in front of a computer screen all day, I have to spend my whole day around all these women, it's such a task." He teased.

Becky laughed.

Both Ricky and Becky knew, that the women he would be taking out for lunch on the boat trip and the men that Becky would spend her day with, would not be remotely interested in either of them as they had both been assigned to supervise same sex partner groups but it still amused them nonetheless. The sixty guests had been allocated to individual suites the night before and had actually been physically separated upon Bowen's request, so that there would be no disruptions to his plans the following day and thankfully that arrangement had prevented any complex questions being asked by any of the reunion guests in attendance.

Later that afternoon, when the guests from the reunion were actually due to leave the resort and return to their homes, Bowen had hoped that most of the sixty guests would have at least had the chance to exchange numbers with one of their more suitable matches and that any errors which resulted from the Virus would have actually been rectified. His plan to rectify the mess that the virus had caused, definitely wasn't concrete, infallible or fool proof but it was certainly preferable to simply leaving the situation as it was and completely ignoring the mistakes that had been made.

Each of the boat trips had been planned meticulously and the picnic lunches were due to actually take place in various spots around the island or on small neighboring islands situated nearby. Most of the sixty reunion attendees seemed extremely relaxed and comfortable as the ten boats carried them peacefully towards their destination as the reunion guests conversed, laughed and joked with each other and fortunately, there definitely seemed to be a few romantic attractions present among each of the groups.

When Becky's group of six finally arrived at their designated picnic spot which they had been allocated to by Bowen, situated upon a neighboring island nearby, she quickly spread a few blankets out upon the ground and then invited her group to sit down upon them. Coolers, containers and hampers had been carried from the boat towards the actual picnic spot itself by everyone in the group as the reunion guests had all mucked in and assisted Becky and that had encouraged her tremendously as she'd admired the spread that Bowen had arranged and encouraged everyone to tuck in.

Each of the six men in the group that Becky was responsible had gently teased her on their way towards the picnic spot, about Becky being the only woman around and how, just for today they would all have to share her. One of the men, once he'd placed the coolers and hampers down at the chosen picnic spot had then even physically lifted her up and spun her around and Becky had squealed with laughter. Due to the fact that Becky's group were all males that were interested in same sex pairings, she'd known straight away that their jokes had been purely that, just jokes but she'd still been amused by the men's sense of humor and enjoyed the attention anyway.

"Don't worry Becky, we'll make your day more fun." One of the men had insisted. "Even though we're men's men which means that you won't get any off the action but you'll definitely get lots of attention and non-sexual satisfaction."

Becky had laughed.

Quite close to the picnic spot that Becky's group had been allocated to, there was a stream and as the group sat down upon the blankets, one of the men in the group suddenly noticed it and shrieked. He quickly proceeded to roll up his trousers, removed his shoes and then rushed enthusiastically over towards it. Laughter suddenly erupted from the other five men in the group as they sat and watched him.

"Don't worry about me you guys." He called out playfully as he suddenly jumped into the shallow edges of the water and then paddled around inside the stream. "I'm just catching our lunch."

Becky giggled as she watched him.

Unlike the start of Becky's picnic however, the beginning of Ricky's picnic with his group had not gone quite as smoothly. The six female reunion guests in his group had by now, arrived at the chosen picnic spot which was actually situated on the other side of the resort island and he'd quickly laid some blankets upon the ground for them to sit on. One of the women had actually turned up her face as soon as they'd arrived at the chosen picnic spot and had given it and Ricky an extremely scornful look as she'd abruptly shaken her head.

"Personally, I think I'd have preferred to eat my lunch inside the dining hall. I'm not really a fan of eating outside." She'd moaned as she'd turned up her nose quite snobbishly. "Being one with nature is not quite my thing."

Ricky had sighed internally as he'd quickly accepted her complaints and then simply tried to make the best of the situation as there really wasn't much he could actually do about it. "Anyone hungry?" He'd asked as he'd attempted to divert everyone's attention away from her complaints and towards the food.

Despite the rocky start to his picnic, some bottles of wine were quickly opened and then poured very generously into glasses as Ricky attempted to break the tension and encourage everyone in his group to relax and interact with each other as freely as possible. Fortunately, the other five women responded positively as they dug into the meal and drank glasses of wine straight away and the sixth women, after a few minutes of stubborn silence actually proceeded to join them.

Meanwhile, back at the resort. Zoe, Madeline and Louise had actually attended their first lunch dates with the first of the two people they were actually supposed to meet for a date that day. Each woman had been instructed to attend a bar down by the beach area of the island where they would not only meet their first dates but also spend some one on one time with them. Their first dates all started at around midday and each individual had been provided with a list of suggested topics to discuss throughout their dates by Honey via their electronic schedules.

Unfortunately for Zoe, her first date was not actually with Giovanni but as she approached the Palm Bar, where she was due to meet her first date, she politely greeted Patrick as soon as she arrived. The courteous man who she'd allocated as her second choice, greeted her politely as he kissed her upon the cheek and they both sat down beside a table. He certainly wasn't Giovanni by any stretch of the imagination, in Zoe's opinion but the list of topics they'd been provided with was quickly utilized as a conversation guide as the two ate, drank and conversed and he seemed pleasant enough. Time slipped easily from Zoe's grasp as the early afternoon came and went as the late afternoon finally approached and the two prepared to separate.

"Will you be picking me at the end of this?" Patrick asked Zoe at the very end of their date in quite a serious but frank manner.

"Patrick as much as you are a great guy, I won't be I'm afraid." Zoe confessed extremely honestly as she attempted to avoid giving him any false impressions or hopes that she had absolutely no intentions of actually fulfilling.

She could sense that he actually really liked her and right now that feeling wasn't completely mutual and she wanted to be very truthful about that as she smiled at him and continued. "I have someone else that I really like which is nothing to do with you at all, in fact I actually met him the very first day I arrived and we just really get along."

Patrick nodded as he listened. "I appreciate your honesty Zoe." He replied.

"Well, I don't want to waste your time." Zoe explained.

Patrick nodded.

Before the actual dinner date commenced which was actually planned to start at five in the evening there was an hour's break in-between which Zoe, Madeline and Louise quickly utilized to meet to discuss their first dates that day. The three women made their way towards the poolside bar as they discussed each of their dates and how each one had gone so far.

"I'll be so gutted if I'm not Giovanni's top selection." Zoe commented as they walked. "I mean seriously, he was definitely mine and I expect total dedication in return."

Madeline giggled. "Don't worry, he'll definitely be your final date." She gently reassured her. "He completely adores you and anyone can see that."

"He better be." Zoe replied.

"Well, at least your date was in your ten selections. Steven wasn't even in mine." Louise moaned as they sat down on top of some bar stools.

Due to the fact they had some free time upon their hands, the women quickly ordered some cocktails as they discussed the men they had already met that day as Thomas suddenly approached them. When Zoe noticed his arrival, she immediately politely invited him to join them.

"How are your dates going Thomas?" She enquired.

"They're going really great Zoe." He replied as he leant up against a bar stool. "A couple have been really interesting and I've definitely got my eye on someone." Thomas explained.

"You seem much more confident now Thomas, that makeover really helped." Louise observed.

"And you look great." Zoe added as she encouraged him. "Did you make it into her top two?" She asked.

Thomas nodded. "I did. There's definitely someone for everyone and I think, I've finally found my someone." He mentioned.

Zoe smiled. "That's the spirit Thomas." She encouraged.

Time flew by as the three women and Thomas waited beside the poolside bar for the allocated time to arrive for their final dates. A slight worry occupied Zoe's mind that she hadn't actually seen Giovanni that day at all as she'd simply followed the schedule she'd been sent and attended her organized date earlier that day obediently. Inside Zoe's mind, there was a slight tinge of uncertainty as the schedule had said where and when each date would be held but not who each date would actually be with and that meant technically, if Giovanni hadn't actually selected her, Zoe's second date that day might not even be with him.

"I need to get a lipstick from our suite." Madeline suddenly mentioned as she quickly stood up and prepared to leave the poolside bar.

"I'll come with you." Zoe offered. "We're a bit early for our second dates and we still have fifteen minutes before they actually start."

"I'll come too." Louise added as she stood up. "You coming Thomas?"

Thomas nodded and quickly prepared to accompany them.

"I'm going to be so pissed if Giovanni is not my second date today." Zoe mentioned as they slowly walked back towards the main entrance of the resort.

"He will be Zoe, don't worry about it." Louise quickly reassured her.

Zoe nodded and smiled. "I hope you're right Louise." She replied. "What about Hottie Madeline? Have you seen him today?"

Madeline gently shook her head. "Do you think perhaps he's forgotten about me?" She asked as the three women and Thomas walked along the glossy, white hallway towards Zoe and Madeline's suite. "It's like he came into my life like a whirlwind and now he's disappeared, almost as quickly as he arrived."

"No way. How could anyone forget about you?" Zoe asked. "You're irresistible and absolutely gorgeous. He's probably just been busy with work or something."

Madeline nodded.

"Yeah Zoe's right, he'll turn up again soon." Louise quickly agreed.

Soon it quickly transpired, was actually sooner than any of the three women could have actually anticipated or predicted and as the four collected the lipstick and then made their way back towards the reception area, Bowen strode briskly towards them. A warm, seductive smile suddenly crossed Madeline's face as soon as she noticed him and Zoe grinned. Zoe quickly grabbed Thomas and Louise's arms and then gently led them further along the hallway as she left Madeline completely alone with Bowen to have a conversation with the man that had absolutely captured and then successfully retained her attention. Flirtatious, romantic conversations were always best between two people and without any unnecessary spectators and both Zoe and Madeline fully understood and appreciated that.

"How are things going Madeline?" Bowen asked as he approached her, his white, sparkling teeth flashed between his lips as his mouth provided a charming invitation to a discussion which in his mind was long overdue.

"Fine thanks, we are just taking part in the activities they organized for us today, it's our final dates with our two final matches." Madeline explained.

Bowen nodded.

Zoe, Louise and Thomas, who were now slightly in front of the two, could still clearly hear their conversation but pretended not to as they made light conversation between themselves as they walked along the remainder of the hallway. Lipstick, perfume and makeup were quickly deliberately discussed as the two women attempted to give Madeline and her handsome love interest a bit of space, in order to facilitate Madeline's romance in any way that they possibly could.

"Anyone in particular you're interested in?" Bowen asked Madeline as he smiled at her.

Madeline gently shook her head and smiled. "Not really." She replied.

"Well, I gave you a bit of space as I wanted you to be totally sure." He mentioned as he gently touched her hand. "I didn't want to rush you."

Madeline nodded as she paused and then glanced at his face. "I'm very sure." She replied.

Bowen paused as he raised his hand up to her face and then gently moved a lock of hair away from her eyes. "Good, I'm very sure too." He quickly reassured her, his lack of attention since their date was certainly not attributable to a lack of interest and Bowen sincerely wanted Madeline to understand that.

Madeline smiled and nodded.

"Look, you better go back to your friends and perhaps we can meet up for dinner tonight, once all your dates are finished." Bowen suggested.

"Sure, that would be lovely." Madeline immediately replied as she quickly embraced, accepted and welcomed his invitation.

"Great, I'll meet you at eight at the Coconut Bar again and then we'll decide where we want to eat." Bowen verified.

Madeline nodded. "See you at eight then." She said as she smiled.

Bowen nodded.

Madeline smiled as they entered inside the reception and she returned to Zoe, Louise and Thomas's side, there was a spring in her step as she walked and it almost felt as if she was walking on a bouncy bed of grass as she made her way towards them. Her feet felt cushioned by the plush warmth and softness of a love that waited to be realized, enjoyed and fully explored.

"Are we ready to go?" Zoe asked.

"Yes." Madeline replied as she smiled.

"Right, let's get moving." Zoe urged as she gently took Madeline's arm and then guided her towards the entrance.

Louise smiled as she followed them alongside Thomas. "Thomas for your final date this afternoon, here are my tips, don't speak to much, even if you feel slightly nervous." She advised. "Listen to her speak and make sure you ask her everything that you really want to know."

Thomas nodded as he listened.

"Our vacation is almost over." Zoe mentioned to Madeline as they walked.

"I know." Madeline replied. "Soon you'll have to make your final romantic choice and then you'll have to pack that up in your suitcase and actually take it home with you." She teased. "Soon, we'll be back at work and back in our own very real lives." Madeline agreed.

"And soon, I'll have to really see Collette again." Zoe groaned as she rolled her eyes.

"At least, you'll have Giovanni to look forward to." Madeline mentioned.

"Yeah, that might just make the long working hours I have to spend with Collette each day slightly more bearable." Zoe replied.

The four gathered just outside the front entrance of the building as they prepared to separate and to attend their final date for that day. Excitement filled Zoe inside as she prepared to walk towards her dinner date that she hoped would be Giovanni, it just had to be him or she would be utterly and completely heartbroken.

"We better get moving." Zoe advised as they walked towards the beach area where some of the bars were situated. "Or our dates will think we've stood them up."

Madeline, Louise and Thomas nodded as they arrived at the beach area and then quickly split up.

For the resort coordinators, the picnic lunches were now almost over and Ricky's lunch had actually gone quite well in the end, despite its slightly unpleasant start as he'd encouraged the women to get involved in some group games and all six of the women had actually participated. The groups made their way back towards the resort as the resort staff prepared to say goodbye to the reunion guests and return to their usual actual jobs. A few numbers had been exchanged among Ricky's group and he'd felt quite hopeful as he re-moored the boat back at the pier that perhaps some incorrect love matches had actually been corrected. Each exchange of numbers was a positive sign that would provide a remnant of comfort to Bowen Logan that the attack upon Honey had not permanently damaged any of the past vacationer's romantic life. Most of the reunion guests seemed to be in good spirits as they returned, despite the negative circumstances that had actually brought them together which thankfully, they were still completely oblivious to.

Once the sixty guests arrived back at the resort, Bowen quickly arranged some small buses for them, to return them to the island airport so that they could catch their return flights home. Relief set in as thirty minutes went by and all sixty of the reunion guests were escorted from the reception area with their bags as they started to make their way home as Bowen watched them leave. In Bowen's mind, he really had done everything he possibly could within his power to correct the situation and now the rest was really up to each individual guest themselves. The Reunion Dinner and Dance and the boat picnic lunches had been relatively successful and had definitely fostered an environment where the mistakes of the past could possibly be corrected and some perhaps even actually put right.

Down by the beach bars, the second of the final two dates had already started as Zoe, Madeline and Louise found their respective dates and then sat down at a table with them. Zoe to her complete and utter joy had been coupled with Giovanni and a huge weight had suddenly been lifted from her mind as she'd welcomed him with an affectionate hug, kiss and smile and had then prepared to eat dinner with him.

"Looks like we should talk about these topics." Giovanni had suggested as he'd glanced at the discussion list upon his electronic journal that the resort had provided them both with earlier that morning. "Though I think we might have discussed most of these already."

Zoe had grinned. "Yep, how many children we both want, where we live, views on travel, career, future aspirations, how we feel about marriage, I think we have already covered most of those." She'd agreed.

"We could always discuss what we're actually going to do next weekend and where we're going to do that." Giovanni had offered.

Zoe had grinned. "I almost thought, you weren't going to come." She'd mentioned. "I'd thought for a moment that I might have to rally Louise and Madeline and send them out on a search party to come and find you."

"Zoe, no one can keep me away from you." Giovanni had replied as he'd gently reassured that he was indeed, very committed to her. "I'm here for life." He'd insisted as he'd gently touched her cheek. "Or at least, until you dump me. Let's go for a walk on the beach and make the most of our official few hours together." Giovanni had suggested as he'd stood up.

Zoe had nodded and smiled as she'd quickly embraced the tender moment between them both. "You know, I've seen a whole other side to you Giovanni this past few days, you're actually, really quite romantic, underneath that spicy, saucy exterior." She'd murmured as she'd stood up. "And I definitely like it, more than that, I absolutely love it."

Giovanni had grinned as he'd gently held her hand. "Stick around and you'll definitely see a whole lot more of it. I promise. Now, let's go catch some starfish." He'd teased. "And then we can discuss when we're going to move in together and who's going to move. I'm a private contractor for a technology company and my company has offices all over the world, so technically I can relocate quite easily." Giovanni had mentioned as he'd led Zoe towards the beach.

"Well, the beauty company I work for has salons in several large cities, so I don't think relocation would be much of a problem for me either." Zoe had replied as she'd walked alongside him. "And a reason to leave Collette would be most welcome."

"Who's Collette?" Giovanni had asked as a puzzled expression had suddenly crossed his face.

"My boss." Zoe had replied. "Sometimes, we don't always see eye to eye."

"Ah, I completely understand." He said as he smiled. "Sometimes bosses can be quite tricky. You just have to be tolerant at times and try to get along with them."

"Yes, Collette definitely requires tolerance." Zoe had agreed as she smirked in response.

"Perhaps, we could both move and pick out a city of our choice that we both want to live in together." Giovanni had suggested as they'd arrived at the beach.

Zoe had immediately nodded in response. "Now that, sounds like a great plan." She'd agreed.

The couple's romantic walk along the beach continued for another hour as the two delved and paddled enthusiastically around in some more serious areas of conversation regarding the realities of their future romance and the nearby ocean as they removed their socks and shoes and then played around in the shallow edges of the water. Their discussion highlighted and reconfirmed to Zoe inside her mind, that their attitude towards life, love and priorities seemed to be very compatible and even more compatible it seemed than even she had initially realized. In terms of his makeup, there was certainly more to Giovanni than met the eye and their discussion and agreement on certain, important issues was a great indication to Zoe that there was more than just animalistic, sexually charged chemistry between them both and more depth to them as a couple, than just a bit of lust and the few flirtatious jokes that they regularly shared.

For Madeline, her second date with the handpicked selection that the resort had chosen for her, was at least amusing, if not actually romantic but she'd attended anyway just to comply with the process, despite her heart lying very firmly at the doorstep of another man's human form that was not actually due to be in attendance. Her actual attendance was now purely a formality as Madeline knew, her actual heart had already been given to someone else, who in her mind certainly seemed to be the best possible match for her and someone, who appeared to be very interested in her.

Despite her lack of interest however, Madeline attentively participated with her second date nonetheless which was with a man called Nathaniel. He worked as a private, international investigator and even though Madeline had absolutely no interest in him in a romantic capacity, she listened to him relate some of the stories about some of the things he'd got up to throughout the course of his work, some of which actually sounded quite hilarious. Nathaniel was reasonably good looking, very cheery and seemed pleasant enough and Madeline had quickly attributed his single status, inside her mind to his chosen profession. Some women, Madeline had quietly contemplated found it quite difficult to actually be in a relationship with men that often had to travel and she'd quickly concluded that, that was probably the main reason he hadn't actually married yet.

Louise in the meantime had a date with Trey, a tall, slim, Japanese man with a very bald head, her first date that day had actually been with an optician, who she'd appeared to listen to but had not actually been interested enough in to retain a single word he'd said. She had sat through her date with a 'when will this end' expression upon her face as she'd glanced down at her phone every few seconds and had waited patiently for the hours to pass by and finally, they had and then she'd been released from her boredom. He had been absolutely boring and no matter how hard Louise had tried to actually listen to him that was one factor that absolutely could not be changed and as he'd departed, Louise had smiled with complete and utter relief. Her dinner date with Trey, the second date that Friday, had fared slightly better as they had discussed his job as an animal handler at a Zoo he worked at and Louise had amused herself as she'd listened to him speak.

"Have you ever actually been inside a cage with a lion?" Louise had asked him.

Trey had laughed as he'd shaken his head. "Nope, I've never been inside a cage with a lion but I have been in a cage with a hippo before." He'd replied.

"Are hippo's vicious?" Louise had asked.

"They can be at times." Trey had explained. "Depends on how you handle them."

Each of the three women had made an effort to actually discuss each of the topics upon the list that the resort had provided to them as that had seemed like a great way to approach very serious topics in a manner that wouldn't seem pushy or intrusive. Every topic that the list contained, seemed to be issues that were actually extremely crucial to a relationship's long term success and that gave

504

a very human perspective to the whole matching process as well as further insight into what a potential partner's outlook was on life.

The Friday for Thomas had also gone quite well as he'd met his first match, who was extremely pretty, for lunch but deep down Thomas had already known that she would not be his final selection as he actually had his heart set on someone else. In terms of physical appearance and attributes, she'd been way out of his league but there had it seemed, been some kind of intellectual attraction between them both that had warranted him a place in her final two dates and her in his. Deep down, Thomas actually preferred his second date that day however, who was actually called Dottie.

When the afternoon had arrived, Thomas had sighed with relief as Dottie had greeted him affectionately as they'd met and then eaten dinner together down by the beach. She was simple, down to earth and more intellectually astute than his first date, Trisha and she would certainly not give Thomas the kind of headache that an extremely attractive woman could inflict upon him, in the longer term. Despite his romantic shortcomings, even Thomas had realized that he would struggle to keep his very ambitious first date, Trisha happy in the longer term and therefore, Dottie was a very welcome romantic relief to that potential, long term unsuitability. Dottie seemed to be much more comfortable, just being around him and was like a breath of fresh air as she had no huge demands and aspirations in life that he, Thomas would be expected to fulfill.

Once the three women's official dates had ended, their Friday evening was full of dates, laughter and fun as they met briefly beside the poolside bar before they prepared for their evening ahead. Dates had been planned for the evening ahead for all three of them as they discussed what they would do that evening and when they would next actually meet up. Zoe had already arranged and planned her date with Giovanni, Madeline had a date with the Hottie, who's name she still as yet did not actually know and Louise was spending the evening with Steven, who was not actually an official love match for her but who she'd accepted now, never actually would be.

"Giovanni said, we'd spend our weekends together when we get back home." Zoe explained as she sat beside Madeline and

Louise and related the details of her date to them both. "He even offered to move when we both feel the time is right." She gushed as her eyes shone brightly with excitement. "Though I don't actually mind moving, just to get away from Collette." Zoe mentioned as she giggled.

"I'm so happy for you Zoe." Madeline replied as she suddenly leant towards her and then hugged her affectionately. "Well, that certainly clarifies his commitment to you, if you had any doubts at all inside your mind."

"Yep, there's no maybes, ifs or buts, he certainly seems very certain." Zoe agreed. "And very devoted to our sizzling, hot romance. I can't wait to choose him as my final choice."

"Ladies, I have to love and leave you." Madeline suddenly mentioned as she quickly stood up. "I have to get ready for my date."

Louise smiled. "Good luck Madeline." She encouraged.

"Yeah and this time Madeline, try to find out his name at least." Zoe teased playfully. "A name would be helpful, you can't be screaming 'yes, yes, yes whatever your name is' whilst he's taking you on his lovejet to the heights of passion." She joked.

Madeline grinned. "I'll make sure I do that this time and I'll remember to actually make another date." She quickly vowed as she prepared to depart.

"You only have thirty minutes to actually get ready Madeline." Zoe warned her. "You better hurry up."

Madeline nodded and then quickly departed.

A few minutes later, Giovanni and Steven suddenly appeared as they approached the bar and the two women that were seated beside it, who were actually waiting for them. The group of four decided to make their way down towards the beach to play a quick game of beach volleyball before they separated as there was no actual rush to go anywhere that evening as the next day, their final date would not actually take place until the mid-afternoon.

Brightly colored cocktails, beers and spirits were very quickly ordered as soon as they arrived beside the beach bar, right next to where their volleyball match would actually be played. Their spirits were high as they embraced the evening and started to engage in their playful volleyball match and simply enjoyed being alive and being around people that for the most part, they appreciated immensely as time slipped by and evening began to vanish.

Meanwhile, dinner for Madeline was an extremely elegant affair as she met Bowen and then they both entered inside a black, shiny jeep which he collected from the resort parking lot. Bowen was the perfect gentleman as he drove Madeline across the island towards a beautiful restaurant that hung out delicately just above the water, parked his jeep and then held the door of the restaurant open for her as the couple made their way inside. He was completely determined that, that evening he would give Madeline his undivided attention and as much time as she actually wanted or desired.

The reunion guests had by now, already left and that meant, Bowen was much more relaxed and much more focused upon his date and the woman that had caught his interest and actually managed to retain it as their evening together gently flowed through every second they shared. Bowen had certainly done his best to correct the mistakes that had been made and had provided an atmosphere where the reunion guests could find their correct matches extremely easily and now, it was entirely up to individual attendee involved to choose, who they did or did not want to embark upon a romantic journey in life with. Now, his focus could be turned back to his own love life which was practically nonexistent as he'd sought to give Madeline and himself a romantic night that they would both definitely remember.

A server showed the couple to a table and as they sat down, Madeline smiled at Bowen, several lit candles adorned the table and soft music played all around them as she embraced the heavenly night that the love resort had unexpectedly provided her with. The romance between the couple as yet had not actually been defined but Madeline felt gently reassured that at least now, it would have a chance to survive, exist, blossom and be pursued by both parties.

Bowen smiled with content as he glanced at Madeline's face peacefully, his love resort had been designed to guide, introduce and invite people into the sea of romance, yet he himself had not as yet, committed his life to any woman at all and for the first time ever, he actually felt he could be on the verge and brink of actually doing so. The Love Colony resort wasn't a complete romantic solution, in that people could accept or reject the recommendations that Honey, Bowen's system made as they wished to. He personally did not have any control over any of the romantic decisions that the resort guests could or did actually make and neither did Honey, his complex, sophisticated computer system and Madeline was certainly no exception to that scenario.

Deep within Bowen's mind however as he glanced into Madeline's eyes, he hoped that after that night, Madeline might actually forgo the ten potential matches that Honey had offered to her and actually make him, her first romantic choice. He'd strived to provide the best possible environment and love matching service that human knowledge, science and technology could actually provide but for once, he now hoped that the very human choice of his coupling with Madeline, would now be chosen by Madeline over and above the choices that his own technology, Honey had actually provided.

FINAL SELECTIONS

Dinner for Madeline that evening had been a total delight and an extremely tender, intimate, romantic affair as Bowen had literally swept her of her feet with an attentiveness, charm and dedication that she'd quite simply never, ever experienced before. He was certainly not in her list of ten potential love matches but he'd definitely won her heart as she returned to her suite and around midnight and quietly contemplated how she would have to reject all ten men she'd been potentially matched with and actually save herself for a man that she hadn't actually been matched with at all. During the course of the evening however, Madeline had now at least actually discovered that his name was Bowen which seemed vaguely familiar to her somehow but she couldn't quite remember why that was, or who he actually was.

When the next morning arrived, the Saturday was filled with sunshine and warmth as Zoe and Madeline made their way quickly towards the dining hall to meet Louise for breakfast and discussed her dinner date the previous night with Bowen, or Hottie as Zoe fondly referred to him. On their way, the women suddenly decided to take a slight detour and pass by the poolside bar first, in order to enjoy some of the very pleasant weather that had decided to actually grace their day and the resort with its presence. Very unexpectedly however, when they sauntered by the poolside bar, the two women suddenly caught sight of Steven, who was actually with engaged in what looked like an extremely intimate conversation with another female and it certainly wasn't Louise. The two watched quietly, unnoticed by Steven as they remained out of sight and hidden from view as he suddenly leant forward and then actually kissed the woman next to him, directly on the lips. In a matter of seconds, the two then started to engage in a passionate kiss that was certainly much more than a polite peck on the cheek.

"Well that's not Louise." Madeline mentioned.

"Yeah, we better let Louise know as if she was in any doubt at all, he's really decided things for her now." Zoe added.

"I thought he was very serious about her." Madeline remarked. "Guess he wasn't really that serious after all."

"Yeah, I'm really surprised, after all he did follow her around a little bit like a lost puppy dog for days at the beginning of our vacation and announce his devotion to her quite openly." Zoe observed.

"Guess, he's not quite as dedicated as he claimed to be." Madeline replied. "But he's definitely behaving like a grown up dog right now, never mind a lost puppy."

"I guess not." Zoe agreed as she quickly shook her head. "What a toad."

A few minutes later, the two women entered inside the dining hall as they prepared for breakfast and they quickly sought out Louise as they served themselves some food and then found a table to sit at. The dining hall was unusually quiet and Louise did not appear to be anywhere inside it, so they quickly ate breakfast and then made their way towards her suite to see her in person as they still had a couple of hours before their final scheduled dates were due to start that afternoon.

Once they arrived outside Louise's suite, Zoe gently tapped on the door and the two women glanced at each other slightly nervously as they waited for Louise to answer it. They had arrived but they had arrived with some bad news that they both knew, they definitely had to break to her. Any romantic notions that Louise may have held due to Steven's proclamations of love, would now certainly die a very abrupt death, despite the awkwardness of them not actually having been matched throughout their vacation which they had both somehow, actually managed to recover from. Steven was quite definitely, very firmly romantically involved with another woman and his involvement had actually gone as far as kissing that woman upon the lips in a very passionate embrace.

Zoe smiled as the door in front of them both suddenly swished open. "Hi Louise." She said as she braced herself to break the bad news. "Did you sleep well?"

Louise nodded. "Yes I did, are you going for breakfast?" She asked.

Madeline smiled. "Well actually, we've just eaten breakfast and we waited a while for you but when you didn't turn up, we decided to come and find you." She replied.

"Yes, I woke up quite late this morning." Louise explained. "I was just about to start making my way towards the dining hall now. How was your date Madeline?" She asked as she stepped out of the door and it swished closed behind her.

"Amazing, I'll tell you all about it whilst you eat breakfast." Madeline insisted.

Zoe gently held onto Louise's arm as the three started to saunter gently back towards the dining hall. "Louise, there's something I have to tell you and it's not very good news I'm afraid." She began.

Louise nodded as she listened. "What's wrong Zoe? Just tell me, it can't be that bad." She replied as she smiled. "After all, we're on vacation at a beautiful, tropical island resort full of handsome, eligible single men which has been pretty heavenly so far."

Zoe smiled and then took a deep breath. "Well Louise, it's Steven, we actually saw him this morning with another female and they seemed to be very engrossed in their discussion, in fact they were actually kissing." She suddenly blurted out as her words clumsily fell out of her mouth and tumbled into the air that surrounded her. "And it wasn't the kind of kiss that you give your grandmother."

"Really?" Louise asked as she glanced at Zoe with a very confused expression upon her face. "But I just left him an hour ago." She suddenly confessed as tears rapidly began to form inside her eyes. Louise accepted the heartbreaking news as she gently shook her head, deep down she'd always suspected that Steven might not have been as sincere as he professed to be, regarding his romantic intentions towards her but this news was a blow that even she'd been totally unprepared for. "I guess this just confirms that my suspicions about him were right." She admitted. "The worst part is, I've already slept with him a few times."

"How come you didn't tell us Louise?" Zoe asked. "When did that happen?"

"Several times, ever since the night he was actually matched with Madeline." Louise explained. "He convinced me that the resort had made a mistake and that he was extremely serious about me. I invited him inside my suite to discuss it and then one thing just led to another."

"And you believed him?" Zoe asked.

"Yes. It's really quite sordid as I didn't really want to sleep with him but I guess I'd just drunk a bit too much and was a bit tipsy and I gave in. He was very convincing." Louise explained.

"Why didn't you tell us?" Zoe enquired but as soon as she'd asked the question, she wondered why she'd even bothered to ask. "Why would you tell us, we'd only just met really." She quickly concluded as she answered her own question. "At times, even the best of friends keep secrets from each other, some for years and years."

"True, I guess you tell people things when you're ready to." Madeline agreed.

"I guess, I was just embarrassed about it." Louise answered with a rather sheepish expression upon her face.

"How do you feel now?" Madeline asked as she gently slipped her arm around Louise's shoulders.

"I'm absolutely mortified." Louise replied. "I mean, I really believed him and I thought he was sincere. Turns out he's fake as hell really, he's probably been hedging his love bets with other women around the resort all along."

Zoe shook her head. "Look Louise, it's not too late, you still have your final date today and you can take that choice very seriously." She advised.

"Yeah, you might actually spend some time with someone really nice, someone better than Steven." Madeline immediately reassured Louise as she quickly agreed with Zoe.

"Yep, Louise just move on and forget about him, he's so not worth your time." Zoe insisted. "He's probably playing with her the same way and a few others."

"True, at least I didn't actually waste any of my choices on him." Louise agreed as she slowly started to accept Steven's lack of dedication and obvious betrayal. "There's no point confronting him about it really, I'd just look stupid for sleeping with him as we weren't even in a committed relationship and we hadn't even been officially matched by the resort."

Zoe nodded in agreement. "Yeah, you'd have no grounds upon which to challenge him really." She admitted.

"I just feel so used." Louise said as she gently shook her head. "He didn't even commit to anything with me and he actually managed to sidestep that because we weren't even officially matched. I've been such an idiot."

"He's a very fickle, insincere person." Madeline seethed. "He's done you a favor really by showing you his true colors now, before you actually invested any more of your time, emotions and effort into a real romantic relationship with him."

"Yes, it's totally his loss." Zoe rapidly agreed. "You are a beautiful, kind, sweet, sexy woman and Steven definitely doesn't deserve you."

"I'm still quite gutted about it though." Louise explained as she gently shook her head.

"I know, I know, he's definitely wronged you." Zoe acknowledged as the three women arrived outside the dining hall. "Would you prefer to eat breakfast inside your suite? You can order something and we can all hang out there." She quickly suggested.

Louise nodded. "Yes, I just can't face a bunch of total strangers right now." She admitted.

"Right, let's go back to your suite." Madeline agreed as she quickly turned around and then started to led Louise back along the hallway, in the direction they had just come from.

Deep inside as the three women walked, Zoe actually felt quite gutted about what Steven had done to Louise, her heartbreak had been totally undeserved and absolutely unexpected. If Giovanni had betrayed Zoe that way, she'd have been totally cut up about it and extremely livid, especially since they had also actually been matched. The future for Zoe, now very deeply involved Giovanni, the man she'd met on the very first day she'd actually arrived at the love resort and if he'd betrayed her that way, she would have struggled just to get up and walk away from that and their shared vision of the future together. They had not yet been physically intimate but they were actually on the verge of physically consummating their romantic union and once that actually happened, she sincerely hoped in her heart of hearts that afterwards, he would not just get up and walk away from her.

For women, physical intimacy for the very first time or even the first few times with a man was always a slightly tricky issue. Every time a woman opened herself up physically to a new male partner, there was always a risk that his efforts to romance you were nothing more than a ploy to actually get you into bed. There was always a risk that once that had been achieved for the very first time, he might then disappear forever and simply just never, ever actually return. Even if there was a repeat performance and he did actually return, there would still be an element of uncertainty as to the man's motives and his sincerity towards the woman, as women would wait and watch to see exactly what happened afterwards. The reality was some men got what they wanted and then would immediately bugger off but some would stay around just to actually have what they wanted a few more times as it suited them and when it no longer suited them, then they would simply bugger off and vanish into thin air like an invisible man.

Both Zoe and Madeline, fully understood and appreciated Louise's pain as they had both been through it themselves at various times in their own lives and they both knew, such an experience was hurtful, very humiliating and extremely disappointing and the two women could most certainly relate to Louise's predicament. The three women continued to walk in silence as Madeline and Zoe affectionately held Louise by the arms as they attempted to steady her steps, though this time their actions were not due to excessive alcohol consumption but rather due to shock and hurt.

Once the three women actually arrived outside Louise's suite, they quickly made their way inside and then Madeline ordered some room service breakfast for Louise, who as yet that morning still hadn't actually eaten anything. Despite Louise's upset and the bad news surrounding Steven, their discussion quickly turned towards Madeline and her date the prior evening as Zoe rapidly steered it in that direction, anxious to hear every single, intricate detail about her date and anxious to distract Louise as much as she possibly could from her current heartbreak.

"Madeline's heart has been totally stolen." Zoe mentioned as she teased Madeline and glanced at Louise. "I mean seriously, she's absolutely in love with this guy and before yesterday, she didn't even know his name."

"Well actually, I do know his name now." Madeline announced. "I made sure I found that out, before he dropped me off back at the resort last night."

Both Zoe and Madeline, knew each other long enough and well enough, to understand and notice when love actually had actually struck one of their lives and hearts and Zoe knew, love had definitely struck Madeline's heart. The glint in Madeline's eyes, her laugh, her smile and the spring in her step, all confirmed to Zoe that this match was indeed true love, at the very least from Madeline's point of view, regardless of how unofficial it actually was from the resort's perspective.

In terms of attachment, it usually actually took Zoe slightly longer to emotionally attach to someone romantically than it did for Madeline and hence their vacation had been extremely interesting for them both as it had actually seen a reversal in their usual approach to romance. Since Zoe had been in a more relaxed, controlled romantic environment, she'd actually relaxed a bit more and had welcomed Giovanni straight into her heart with very open arms which was unusual for Zoe in terms of her usual approach to men and dating. In Zoe's mind, it had been absolutely impossible not to accept Giovanni however as they were the perfect love match, regardless of what any computer did or did not actually decide. Madeline very unusually however, had actually hung back and it had taken her some time to make an actual emotional commitment to anyone and that had amused Zoe somewhat initially, although towards the middle of their vacation it had actually started to slightly worry and frustrate her as she'd begun to panic.

A waiter suddenly knocked upon Louise's suite door and Madeline quickly jumped up from the sofa where she'd been seated to answer it. She quickly collected the tray that contained Louise's breakfast from him and then thanked him politely as he rapidly departed. Madeline carefully carried the tray that was filled with food into the lounge area of Louise's suite and then placed it gently down on top of the coffee table.

"Do you think men get hurt like women do?" Louise asked as she picked up a piece of French toast and then bit into it hungrily.

"Sometimes maybe, probably not in the same way though." Zoe mentioned. "I have three brothers and they do seem to get hurt sometimes but they also seem to bounce back quite quickly to. So I definitely think it's slightly different for men."

"Yeah, men tend to be governed more by their physical needs, whereas women tend to be governed more by their emotional attachments." Madeline agreed.

"That's why you cannot possibly allow yourself to be dragged down by your emotions." Zoe insisted as she placed her arm around Louise's shoulder. "He was the one in the wrong, not you Louise. It's like when you ride a horse and fall off, you need to get straight back up and move on and take another horse out for a ride."

Louise giggled. "That's so funny Zoe but I think I'll stay away from the physical riding part for a little while at least." She replied. "Give myself a chance to heal perhaps."

"Louise, don't waste this chance just because of a plum, you are in a love resort fruit salad, filled with lots of sweet chunks of fruit. You don't have to get naughty and naked with anyone else but please make sure that before you leave this island and your vacation, you have a romantic connection with someone who is worth your time." Zoe insisted. "Don't let Steven defeat you and waste your money, you came here for a reason and he wasn't it."

Louise nodded as she listened.

"Madeline, when are you seeing Hottie again?" Zoe asked.

"I'm meeting him just after midday inside the reception." Madeline replied as she smiled. "Just before we go on our final date today."

"Well, when Louise is finished breakfast we'll walk you along. I need to collect something from our suite before I go to my final date." Zoe offered.

Louise nodded in agreement.

Approximately twenty minutes later, the three women graced the reception area with their presence as Madeline prepared to once again meet Bowen, the man that had captured her attention and heart. Much to Madeline's surprise however, when she arrived inside the reception area, she found only Mark there and no Bowen. The three women walked quietly towards him as Zoe gently nudged Madeline and prompted her to ask him where Bowen actually was.

"Ask him where Hottie is." Zoe whispered. "They were together the other day, he might know."

Mark smiled as the three women approached him. "Ladies, just the people I was looking for." He mentioned. "Or more precisely Madeline, you,"

Madeline smiled slightly nervously as she began to fidget. "Well, I'm certainly here." She replied softly. "Just waiting to be found."

"We'll just head on down to our suite Madeline." Zoe suddenly mentioned as she gently held onto Louise's arm and then led her away. "I think he wants to have a private discussion with her about her date." She whispered to Louise as they walked.

Madeline nodded.

"Madeline, I've been asked by Bowen to ask you a very important question." Mark explained as he gently held Madeline's arm and took her to one side of the reception area.

Madeline nodded as she listened. "Sure go ahead." She replied.

"I've been asked to ask you, if you would prefer to go on your final date today or whether you would like to drop out of it and attend a date with Bowen instead?" Mark asked. "He wanted me to ask you so that you wouldn't feel uncomfortable about expressing what you really wanted. He didn't want you to feel pressured by anyone else. He'd like you to make that decision very independently." He explained.

Madeline nodded as she listened. "How thoughtful of him. I'd really like to spend the day with Bowen." She insisted. "I'm very certain."

Mark immediately smiled and nodded. "Well, in that case, whenever you're ready, he's waiting for you down by the Coconut Bar." He explained.

Madeline smiled. "Great, I'll just get ready and let the others know that I won't be back until later today." She said as she smiled.

Mark nodded. "I'll let Bowen know you're on your way." He clarified.

Once the conversation between the two ended, Madeline quickly made her way back towards the suite that she shared with Zoe, filled with excitement, joy and hope. A few minutes later, when the suite door suddenly swished open, Madeline quickly entered inside the suite and Zoe quickly rushed towards her and then grabbed her arm and led her towards one of the sofas inside the lounge.

Zoe's eyes shone with excitement as she demanded an immediate explanation. "Well, what was all that about?" She urged. "Do tell all."

"Ladies, I actually have a date today, all day." Madeline replied as she smiled.

"So you won't be going on your final date?" Louise asked slightly confused by the sudden change in Madeline's plans for the day ahead.

"I certainly won't." Madeline explained. "I've already found my match and he's extremely lovely."

Zoe giggled as she gently pulled Madeline to her feet and then began to dance chaotically around the lounge with her. "Oh my gosh, this is soooo exciting and he's so handsome, I'm so happy for you Madeline." She remarked as she giggled. Zoe paused for a moment and then stared into Madeline's eyes with a huge smile upon her face. "I can even see the babies you guys will have together, they'll be so cute."

"And on the plus side, if it doesn't actually work out since he works for the resort, he can always give you a free vacation to come back and find another love match." Louise gently teased as she smiled.

Madeline giggled. "True but hopefully this will be the guy that I spend the rest of my life with." She mentioned. "Coming back here for a second go isn't really what I actually had in mind."

Zoe gently squeezed Madeline's arm as excitement rippled delightfully through her body. "This is so exciting Madeline. So exciting." She gushed as she inspected the happy expression upon Madeline's face, he definitely hadn't let her down and he was definitely, totally interested in her and Madeline certainly deserved the happiness that his romantic interest and his commitment to her had ushered in.

Five minutes later, the three women left the suite as they headed back towards the reception area and prepared to separate, in order to actually attend each of their individual dates that afternoon. They would all be headed off now, in very different directions as their dates were actually situated at various points across the island's coastline and none of them were actually close to each other at all. Each of the women discussed their pending dates as they walked, Zoe had her date with Giovanni, Louise had opted to go on another date with Trey, who she'd chosen as her final selection and Madeline of course had a date with Bowen, who Zoe still referred to as Hottie as they hadn't yet actually discussed his name and Madeline as yet, still hadn't actually imparted that information to her. Louise's absence from breakfast, Steven's betrayal and Louise's subsequent heartbreak had interrupted and distracted them both that morning and hence as yet, they had not actually managed to have that conversation.

On the way towards her date, Zoe actually bumped into Thomas and she managed to have a quick catch up with him as he was headed in the same direction as she actually was. His final date, he quickly explained to Zoe was with Dottie, who he'd picked from his final two dates the day before and he was extremely happy that she had also actually chosen him. In terms of niceness, Zoe felt that Thomas was actually a really nice guy as he was so polite, considerate and courteous and even though he was a bit nerdy, he was actually quite a likable nerd.

"Dottie is very lucky to have you Thomas." Zoe gently reassured him as they both approached the Hulu Bar, the actual meeting point for both their dates that day.

"I'm very lucky too Zoe, Dottie is absolutely lovely and she's totally perfect for me." Thomas immediately replied.

Zoe smiled. "Well, you enjoy your date Thomas." She insisted as she quietly contemplated for a moment how ironic it actually was that the woman Thomas had chosen as his final date, had a name that was actually quite similar to the name of her beautician's chair at work. Zoe had no absolutely no desire at all to offend Thomas however, who she felt at times could be slightly sensitive, so she didn't mention the similarity through fear that she might actually insult him very unintentionally.

"I can bring Dottie along to meet you all this evening." Thomas suggested.

Zoe smiled. "That would be lovely Thomas." She replied. "I'm sure Dottie's very nice."

Thomas nodded. "She's sitting just over there." He explained as he quickly pointed towards a woman seated a table just in front of the Hulu Bar.

A slight trickle of curiosity had been aroused inside Zoe as she quickly glanced around and then inspected the table just in front of the Hulu Bar that Thomas had actually pointed towards. Throughout Zoe's entire vacation, she hadn't actually seen Thomas with any females at all and hence her curiosity had definitely been sparked as in some respects, now Zoe almost felt slightly protective towards him. Thomas seemed quite innocent, in terms of his nature and character and in some ways, Zoe almost felt as if she had to perhaps shield him slightly from any dubious women that might try to get their claws into him, just to suit their own agendas and purposes. She'd seen it a hundred times before, beautiful women would latch onto a total nerd, simply because they wanted some kind of financial security that they hoped that nerd would provide to them and Zoe certainly did not want that to actually happen to Thomas. Women at times could be so cruel and calculated and Thomas, Zoe could very clearly see had never really been exposed to that side of reality or even to that side of women.

Fortunately however, Dottie it quickly transpired as Zoe quietly glanced at her, seemed to be very much like Thomas in terms of her own appearance and mannerisms and that provided Zoe with an instant reassurance that Thomas was probably in very safe hands indeed. When she noticed his arrival, Dottie quickly stood up and she even seemed to be around the same height as he was. Thomas immediately politely excused himself and then walked over towards her with a huge smile upon his face and his arms outstretched.

Zoe smiled. "What a cute moment. All our hard work and that makeover has quite certainly paid off." She muttered to herself.

In terms of her appearance, Dottie certainly wasn't a beauty pageant queen but she wasn't unattractive either, she had mousey, brown hair, a cute smile and light green eyes that twinkled and shone gently as she spoke. A cute, pair of black glasses adorned her face and a simple beige and cream dress adorned her frame which Zoe immediately noticed was actually quite slender although she did have a few very gentle curves. All in all, Dottie was quite pleasant to look at in a cute, bookwormish kind of way and as Thomas brought her over towards Zoe to actually introduce them both, Zoe smiled politely as she greeted her.

"This is Dottie." Thomas announced as he presented Dottie to Zoe.

"Lovely to meet you Dottie. I'm Zoe." Zoe replied as she extended a hand politely towards her. "Are you going to join us for a drink later Dottie?" She offered. "A group of us get together sometimes in the evenings and have a drink and I'm sure everyone would love to meet you."

Dottie immediately nodded in response. "That would be lovely. Thank you." She replied as she warmly accepted Zoe's kind invitation.

"Right Thomas, I have to go as my date is actually waiting for me." Zoe explained. "You two have a lovely day and a wonderful date."

Dottie smiled and nodded. "You too." She replied.

A few seconds later, Zoe smiled as she walked away from the both as relief gently washed over her mind, Thomas had definitely made a good choice as he'd actually chosen a woman that would definitely stick by him through thick and thin. He hadn't picked out some high maintenance chick with some weird fetish for bookish nerds that might get bored and then suddenly dump him, once they tired of him and got over their attraction to geeks phase. Relationships like those rarely lasted and Zoe had seen it all before, many, many times. Beautiful women would pick up some nerd, use him for a while and then dump him when they became bored or when a more attractive suitor came their way. The choice Thomas had made, absolutely made total sense to both Thomas and Zoe as he certainly seemed to get along Dottie as Zoe could hear them laughing and conversing quite happily together as she walked away from them both.

Right next to the bar, a charming smile patiently waited for Zoe as she walked towards Giovanni and prepared for their final date. Today, they would spend their first whole day together and then the whole night and Zoe could not wait for the night to actually arrive, when she would spend it inside Giovanni's arms before they both actually returned to their very real lives and worlds. Their first day and night together would be filled with love and fun and memories would definitely be created which they could then pack up in their suitcases of thoughts and treasure forever.

The remainder of that day for Zoe was completely and utterly perfect as she spent the entire day with Giovanni and they visited eateries, bars and even paddled along the beach together and then built some sandcastles. In the evening they visited a quiet, intimate restaurant for dinner and once they'd eaten their meal, they quickly made their way towards the poolside bar as they prepared to meet Thomas, Louise, Dottie and Trey briefly, who they'd promised earlier that day to have a drink with that evening.

Every inch of the beach shimmered and shone as they walked as the sun began its descent and the soft, pink fading rays gently bounced of every grain upon the surface of it. Due to the fact that most people had actually attended their final dates that day, the beach area seemed unusually deserted and slightly quiet as the couple headed back towards the main resort building and the poolside bar. Zoe had by this time, actually taken off her shoes and as she walked across the golden sand in her bare feet, Giovanni very affectionately held onto her hand.

Suddenly and very unexpectedly, an argument broke out nearby and interrupted the quiet calm that surrounded them and Zoe immediately scanned the area for the offending couple. The two people in the midst of an argument, it quickly transpired were actually quite close by and as a result Zoe could actually hear every word that was spoken as their voices were actually raised. Apparently, the woman had chosen the man but he had not actually picked her as his final date and that had not only upset her but also offended her profusely.

"You promised that you would pick me Oscar." She said in an extremely loud voice as she wagged a finger directly in front of his face as she angrily expressed her disgust, regardless of any onlookers or passersby. "That's why I slept with you."

Zoe cringed as she listened.

"Please Claire, do you need to tell the whole resort?" Oscar replied as he pleaded with her to be a bit quieter. "We just weren't as compatible as I thought we would be." He argued.

"Yes but you were more compatible with someone else, I wish I'd known that before I'd slept with you." She barked.

Just on the other side of the arguing couple, Zoe suddenly noticed Thomas and Dottie and she quickly notified Giovanni and then walked around the arguing couple towards them. The couple's argument had created a slightly uncomfortable and awkward moment, not only for Giovanni and Zoe it seemed but also for Thomas and Dottie, who had also overheard the heated discussion and were slightly disturbed by it. Both Zoe and Dottie were quite silent as they simply nodded at each other and then prepared to head off towards the poolside bar as even though they did not know the woman in question, they could both certainly understand her pain and her disappointment as they empathized internally with her predicament.

Very abruptly however, just seconds later, the couple suddenly disappeared as they quickly abandoned the beach area and headed off somewhere else to finish their very heated discussion. The four walked quietly along the beach with Zoe and Dottie just a few steps in front as they internally contemplated the argument they had just actually overheard. For the two women, they could absolutely understand the woman's position as they considered how hurt they would have been, if they had actually been in her position and appreciated how lucky they were that Giovanni and Thomas were not as calculated as he appeared to be.

A minute or so later, Giovanni and Thomas sped up and then walked alongside the two women as Giovanni smiled at Zoe and then gently slipped his hand inside her hand. Between the four, there was now a slightly uncomfortable silence present that kept them company as they walked but noone it appeared was actually ready to break it.

Zoe took a deep breath and then smiled. "How awkward." She finally said.

"They slept together to quickly really." Dottie observed thoughtfully. "I'm not surprised it didn't work out, I mean there's no rush to jump into bed with each other."

"I agree Dottie." Thomas replied as he placed his hand gently inside her hand and then smiled.

Zoe smiled as she listened. "So how far away from each other do you two live?" She asked as she contemplated quietly for a moment that Thomas certainly wouldn't be getting any sexual action for a while but he seemed like the decent type that could probably handle it as he'd probably spent quite a lot of time on his own before, so it probably wouldn't be a huge problem for him to cope with.

Dottie smiled as she answered Zoe. "Thomas only lives about an hour's drive away from me." She quickly clarified. "So it'll be very easy for us to see each other on a regular basis."

Zoe nodded. "Wow, you two are really well matched." She mentioned.

Thomas nodded proudly as he smiled. "I know, Dottie is absolutely perfect for me." He agreed.

Very fortunately for both Zoe and Louise, the argument between the couple on the beach hadn't actually happened in Louise's presence as after what she'd just been through that day with Steven, such issues were still quite raw and sensitive and Zoe could fully appreciate that as she walked. The four finally arrived back in front of the main resort entrance as they prepared themselves for their evening drink together beside the poolside bar. Zoe smiled as they quietly walked along the path that led towards the poolside bar as she internally considered Thomas's match further for a moment, she absolutely had to face it, whatever Thomas lacked in terms of charm and male sexual allure, he certainly made up for with brains. His final match had been and was the absolute best possible match for him that he could possibly have found and chosen at the resort and the computer had certainly delivered for him. Sexual pressure was certainly not something that Zoe perceived Dottie would ever have to actually worry about with Thomas, he had impeccable manners and he would definitely wait until Dottie was actually ready to participate with him in a sexual manner.

Once the four arrived at the poolside bar, they found Louise and Trey waiting for them, just beside the bar and they quickly ordered some cocktails and bottles of beer. Neither Zoe nor Louise had seen hide or hair of Steven since earlier that morning which was really, actually a very good thing indeed, especially after what had actually occurred that day. His indiscretions had been exposed to Louise, who had been completely enlightened about his ugly conduct which had not been pretty or handsome at all.

A round of drinks and some snacks quickly arrived and then the six found an empty corner right beside the pool as they sat down on top of some vacant sun loungers. Each of the three unoccupied sun loungers they'd found to sit on, was placed around a small table nearby and shared as each of the women sat alongside their final dates and simply relaxed in the knowledge that they would all return from their vacations with the romantic coupling they had actually come to the island to actually find.

Interestingly a few minutes later, Dottie suddenly began to fuss over Thomas as Zoe watched them both quietly, her nature seemed sweet and very caring and Zoe could see as she glanced at his face, Thomas clearly enjoyed the attention she showed as a huge smile rapidly spread out across his face. Dottie paid attention to his actual wellbeing and that was in Zoe's opinion, totally and utterly cute. She made sure he wasn't hungry, that he had enough to drink and that he had a napkin and whilst it wasn't like she mothered him exactly, it was certainly an outward display of concern and care.

One day, when Thomas wanted to have children, Dottie would probably be a great mother and she'd probably also be a great wife to him and Thomas would in all likelihood one day actually marry her. Why shouldn't he, Zoe quickly concluded who better to do marriage and children with than a woman like Dottie. Despite his nerdy mannerisms and appearance, Dottie had totally proven that there really was someone out there for everyone and even for a socially awkward, misfit like Thomas. From a whole world full of woman, one woman thought that Thomas was absolutely wonderful and Thomas very fortunately, had actually managed to find that woman.

Zoe had rapidly discovered that Dottie spoke extremely articulately and that she also seemed to be stuffed full of knowledge and she playfully began to tease the couple as she sipped on her cocktail. "Okay you two, tell me the truth, who out of the two of you is actually the brainiest and who has read the most books?" She suddenly asked.

"I couldn't possibly say how many books I've read Zoe, more than I can even count." Dottie replied as she smiled. "Thomas is definitely the most intelligent person I've ever met though, he has a Doctorate and two Masters degrees."

Zoe giggled as she quickly glanced at Thomas and noticed that he blushed slightly. "How many do you have Dottie?" She asked.

"I just have one Master and a Doctorate." Dottie replied. "But my Masters is in the arts, whereas Thomas specialized in the fields of science."

"I don't think you can really compare intelligence Zoe, different people are intelligent in different ways." Thomas mentioned. "Dottie is extremely intelligent."

Zoe smiled as she listened to them both, her mind was completely and utterly satisfied. Their relationship definitely seemed to have a very solid foundation and a great chance of success as it was based on a deeper level of companionship and appreciation which had clearly been forged between them both throughout the course of their vacation. Hopefully, their bond of companionship and mutual appreciation would keep them both together and committed to each other whilst they sailed through each of the trials from the rocky waters of life which at some point in time would almost certainly rock their love boat, Zoe mused.

"Can you believe it, we really have to go back to work on Monday?" Zoe suddenly moaned as she glanced at the five faces all around her.

Giovanni smiled and raised his glass. "Yep, so you better enjoy the sun, sand and cocktails whilst you still can." He advised playfully.

"My cocktail, just like this vacation is almost finished, so I definitely need another one." Zoe joked.

Giovanni smiled as he quickly stood up. "I'll go and get you one. Anyone else need anything?" He politely offered.

Louise and Trey immediately shook their heads.

"I'll come with you." Thomas mentioned as he also quickly stood up. "I need to get Lottie a peppermint tea."

Zoe giggled. "What did you guys get up today Louise?" She asked as she suddenly turned her attention towards Louise and Trey.

"We spent some time down on the beach and even had a skimming competition." Louise mentioned as she smiled.

In terms of her type, Trey really was more like Louise's type than Steven had been and that encouraged Zoe slightly as she glanced him. His parents, he had mentioned were both Japanese and hence he had very dark, jet black hair and dark brown eyes and the widest smile that Zoe had ever seen in her life. Height wise, he was quite tall and quite a bit taller than Louise was and he had boyish good looks that reminded Zoe slightly of a boy band group member. He seemed very calm, relatively peaceful and extremely polite and he'd greeted the rest of the group with a warm, friendly handshake when they'd first met at the bar earlier that evening.

"Yes, I wasn't sure until the very last minute that Louise was even going to pick me." Trey mentioned. "So I was delighted when I found out that she had and that my final date would actually be with her."

Zoe smiled.

Conversation and drinks continued to flow as Giovanni and Thomas returned and Trey fully engaged in conversations and jokes with everyone around him. He had a great sense of humor and he made everyone laugh as he began to tease Louise about his culture and how she would have to actually comply with it, if she ever actually did meet his parents.

"When you meet my mother, you'll have to wear traditional clothing Louise." He explained. "You'll have to bow your head to greet people and be very quiet, unless I speak to you first."

Louise suddenly looked horrified as she glanced at Zoe's face with a shocked expression. "Really?" She asked as she considered for a moment what she might have actually let herself in for.

Trey smiled as he quickly placed his arm gently around Louise's waist and then glanced into her eyes. "Don't worry Louise, I'm just playing. My mother is an investment banker and my father runs a university." He gently reassured her. "My parents are extremely westernized and my mother has a very bubbly and sociable personality. She drags my dad around all the local shopping malls practically every weekend and even takes him to karaoke bars at times, it's totally hilarious."

Louise giggled. "Well, I can't really sing but I can try and with a few cocktails I'll probably sound slightly better." She mentioned. "And be slightly braver."

"Great, my mom will love you and especially if you do the whole karaoke thing with her, she absolutely loves it." Trey insisted. "She's always teasing me about being single and asking me when I'm going to settle down, so she'll be very happy when you actually meet her."

Zoe smiled as she listened.

"Where's Madeline?" Thomas suddenly asked.

"She's on a date." Zoe mentioned proudly. "She won't be back until much later tonight." She quickly clarified.

"Really, who with?" Thomas asked.

"With a very handsome man." Zoe replied. "I'm very impressed with her choice, he's an excellent match for Madeline." She clarified.

Thomas smiled.

"Who's Madeline?" Dottie suddenly asked.

"Oh you haven't met her yet, Madeline is Zoe's best friend. They came to the resort together." Thomas explained.

A female resort worker called Yvette, suddenly approached the group and asked them if they wanted to participate in some dance activities that she'd organized inside the dining hall that evening and the six quickly agreed to join in as they all rose to their feet. The dance activities she'd arranged she explained as they walked towards the dining hall, apparently involved a traditional dance from the island itself and as everyone followed her, they listened to her discuss the dance and the history behind the dance and the music. Masota, she explained as they entered inside the dining hall was the name of the dance movements and the music which accompanied them and they seemed to be very sensual and intimate as the music suddenly began to play and they watched her illustrate some of the movements. Each twist and turn seemed quite intricate and involved as the six stood in rows just behind her and watched her dance with a male resort coordinator, who had apparently volunteered to assist her.

Once the basic native dance moves had been fully illustrated, she then walked around the hall as the music played and encouraged everyone to reenact what she'd actually just shown them. The lesson lasted for about an hour as the music continued to play and afterwards, the couples hung out together for a while longer as they drank cocktails and beers and continued to dance until midnight actually approached.

In terms of enjoyment, for Zoe her entire day and evening had been quite simply the perfect ending to her stay at the Love Colony island resort and that night she knew, she would spend a perfect night, gently wrapped up inside Giovanni's hunky arms. They would be totally uninhibited by schedules or any kinds of plans and completely free to just enjoy each other's presence until they both left the resort on the Sunday and returned back to their lives their homes.

Although the two women, Zoe and Madeline had actually paid to attend the special Love Ball at the end of their vacation, they had actually decided not to in the end as they'd both pursued their own individual plans with their dates instead. For Zoe, it had been worth skipping the ball, which was actually being held in another part of the island at least an hour's drive away from the main resort building, in order to spend her final night with those she'd bonded with throughout her vacation as she really had no idea when some of them might actually have another chance to see each other again or if they would even ever actually have the chance to meet ever again.

Just before the six parted for the night, Zoe took Louise gently to one side as she attempted to gauge her feelings about her final date, in a slightly more private manner. Romance wasn't an exact science and Zoe completely understood that as she attempted to analyze, inspect and review Louise's date and her feelings towards the final man that she would now actually enter into an actual real romance with.

"How do you actually feel about him Louise?" Zoe asked as she searched Louise's eyes for some indications of excitement and interest. "Does he lit your fire?" She teased.

"Well, he is certainly my type." Louise replied. "He's very handsome and extremely well-mannered."

"Have you actually kissed him yet?" Zoe asked.

Louise immediately shook her head in response. "Not yet. Perhaps I will when he walks me to my suite." She mentioned.

"Make sure you do." Zoe advised. "Seal that romantic connection with a kiss but keep it outside your suite and don't invite him in."

Louise nodded. "He lives about two hours' drive away from me." She explained. "So it'll be quite easy to see him on the weekends."

"Great. He's so much nicer than Steven." Zoe remarked as she hugged Louise affectionately. "You lost a toad but were given a prince. Trey is definitely a more serious contender for your heart Louise, so give him a chance to prove himself. The tables of love have turned and this time, they're actually in your favor as he's a great guy."

Louise nodded and smiled. "He really is." She agreed.

"I'm off to enjoy my night of passion with Giovanni." She mentioned.

"Have a lot of fun." Louise said as she giggled.

"I sure will." Zoe replied. "Don't wait up for me, because I certainly won't be back tonight." She teased.

Louise grinned.

Another hug was exchanged between the two women before they separated and then Zoe quickly made her way back towards Giovanni as she prepared to spend her first ever, entire night with him. A large, enthusiastic smile pleasantly adorned her face as she gently slipped her hand gently inside his and the two prepared to leave the rest of the group. Giovanni had been one of Zoe's ten potential love matches produced by the resort computer system and Zoe, on this particular occasion definitely agreed with that recommendation as she accepted that somehow, both her mind and the computer's programming were in complete and utter agreement.

Whether the two would have actually met and connected in a different situation, circumstances, place or time, Zoe was completely uncertain, it was highly probable but actually quite impossible to actually predict. Part of Zoe felt slightly surprised as Giovanni led her down the white, glossy corridor towards his suite that they had actually managed to survive all the different dating obstacles at the resort and the alternative choices they had actually been presented with at all. Could a computer really select and make better choices about people's love lives and emotional attachments than people could themselves, Zoe pondered thoughtfully as she walked. Honey, the resort's computer had certainly got both her match with Giovanni and Thomas's match with Dottie right and so perhaps it was actually possible.

The final question danced across Zoe's lips as she walked towards her night of passion with Giovanni and she was adamant that very soon her curiosity would actually be satisfied. Soon, she would actually discover herself just how accurate a love match by a computer could actually be and whether or not Giovanni and Zoe could actually be a real love match for the rest of their lives. Due to the time of Giovanni's flight departure the next day which was actually midday, Zoe knew that the couple would only really have the actual night itself together as the next morning, he would have to pack and then leave, almost as soon as they actually woke up.

Part of Zoe was extremely excited but a small part of her was also slightly nervous as she was actually taking a risk that night and Zoe fully understood the fickle nature of human beings.   At times, people could seem so sincere and then turn out to be very insincere and there was a chance that when the two actually returned home, back to their very real lives that Giovanni might never even call her and might completely disappear. A negative eventuality could possibly happen and as much as Zoe didn't want it to, she had to prepare for the reality that it might actually do so.

When they arrived outside Giovanni's suite, he quickly touched the panel with his keycard and the suite door swished rapidly open in front of them both as they smiled. Zoe took a deep breath as she prepared herself to enter inside his lounge and his bedroom, this was the moment that they had both held themselves back from and eagerly anticipated ever since their sexually charged holographic experience inside the resort. Inside her heart, Zoe had absolutely no desire to back out now, regardless of what might happen in the future as she wanted their night together to be as perfect as their day had just been so that at the very least, she would have that perfect memory of a perfect night of romance and passion that had been completely and utterly fulfilled to keep with her.

Life could at times, be so unpredictable and no one could actually foresee what might happen the very next day, never mind the next year and for that reason alone, Zoe quickly decided that she had live for the moment and grab the passion she felt by the hand and enjoy every single second of it. Time that night was indeed very limited and Zoe knew that meant, they absolutely had to make the most of every single second before it vanished, never to return again.

Giovanni gently held onto Zoe's hand as he led her inside the lounge and smiled. "Are you really sure you're ready Zoe?" He asked. "We can just cuddle up and sleep and wait, if you want to."

Zoe smiled. "I'm very sure Giovanni." She replied as the suite door suddenly swished closed behind them both. "Surer than I've ever been about anything in my entire life."

"You're definitely going to come and see me when we get back home right?" Giovanni asked as he turned on some soft music.

Zoe nodded. "Definitely." She replied.

Giovanni smiled and then placed his arms gently around her waist as he pulled Zoe closer to him. "I just need to be sure." He said softly as he whispered inside her ear. "I need to know that this is not going to be all there is to us."

"Come on Giovanni, you can't get rid of me that easily." Zoe replied as she flashed a charming grin at him.

Giovanni smiled. "It's just you know, sometimes people say things they don't really mean and promise to do things, they have absolutely no intention of doing and I don't want us to be like that Zoe." He explained.

"We're definitely not like that." Zoe replied as she gently touched his face tenderly and then planted a soft kiss upon his lips.

Suddenly, passion gripped Giovanni's body as he frantically began to kiss Zoe's lips as he caved into the animalistic passion inside of him. His tongue and lips gently moved down to her neck as he caressed every inch of her skin and Zoe started to groan with pleasure. Desire stirred inside them both as Zoe quickly surrendered her body to him and he eagerly began to explore every part of her naked skin with his tongue and hungry lips.

In a matter of minutes, the two were inside the bedroom and Giovanni gently picked Zoe up and then placed her softly down on top of the bed. The lights were quickly dimmed and then Giovanni lay down upon the bed beside her as he prepared for the moment of passion, they had both longed for ever since the very first second they had actually met. Every part of Zoe's body tingled with excitement as she lay beside him, she wanted Giovanni, she wanted this and she had absolutely no doubts inside her mind at all that she definitely wanted to make love to him for the very first time, that very same night.

Each inch of Zoe's flesh was explored and caressed as Giovanni removed all her clothes and tantalized her body and mind seductively with his tongue and lips. Every touch and caress was immaculately and tenderly placed as Zoe's body suddenly began to arch in delight as she accepted his seduction and embraced every second of it enthusiastically. Her body was gently cushioned by the bed underneath her as Giovanni suddenly rose up above her and prepared to penetrate her. This was the moment that they had both waited patiently for and this was the moment that they had both yearned to happen, every night since they'd met that they'd actually spent alone.

Darkness flooded into the bedroom from a window nearby and Zoe could clearly see some stars high up in the sky just outside it that twinkled and shone as she wondered for a moment, if they could actually see her. How many couples had the stars in the sky watched making love, how many babies had they seen being conceived and then born and how many first kisses had they been an audience to, she quietly contemplated as she allowed Giovanni to mount her and welcomed him inside her. They were certainly not the first and no doubt, they would certainly not be the last. Zoe suddenly clung onto Giovanni's naked back hungrily as she accepted him inside her, tonight however, it was their night and this was definitely the first night, the stars had ever seen them both make love as it had absolutely never, ever happened before and in that respect, it was totally unique.

Every minute of the night was passionately consumed as the couple made love to each other greedily, hungrily and frantically and explored every wave of passion until it reached its climax. When they could both physically do no more and their bodies finally succumbed to tiredness, they fell asleep wrapped inside each other's arms peacefully as they drifted off into the dreams that eagerly awaited them. Zoe's final night at the beautiful love island resort, she concluded peacefully as sleep carried her gently away, had been utterly, completely and absolutely, totally perfect.

THE RESULT

The final day of the two women's vacation sadly arrived as the morning gently crept into the resort and woke them both up. Despite having arrived at the resort together however, they both woke up inside two very different suites as Zoe greeted the morning, wrapped contently inside Giovanni's arms and smiled. Once Giovanni stirred and woke up, he quickly got up and then ordered breakfast which was actually delivered to the suite within ten minutes and the couple then ate it in bed. When they two finished eating, they climbed out of bed and then showered together as they attempted to make the most of their morning and the remaining hour that was left. A black, solitary suitcase was quickly packed in a matter of minutes as Giovanni quickly bundled the few of his belongings inside it that remained to be packed, so that he could spend with Zoe as possible. Most of his belongings had actually been packed the previous day but a few bits and pieces had remained unpacked, simply due to necessity and required usage.

Despite the warm, bright weather and the sunshine that flooded into the suite through some French windows inside the lounge, the two looked quite downcast as they walked towards the door and Giovanni pulled his solitary case behind him. They held each other's hands affectionately as they walked and inside Zoe quietly mourned as she prepared for their pending separation.

Those final moments together were precious to them both and their silence reflected their mood as they quietly reflected upon the time they'd actually spent together at the resort as they walked. Real life was now calling them back into their very real lives and worlds and romance would now have to be placed in a secondary position as they tended to their very real life responsibilities and duties.

A large part of Zoe would definitely miss Giovanni, she contemplated as she walked down the hallway towards the reception area alongside him. He had definitely touched her heart and that piece of her heart he would always carry with him as they prepared for their pending separation and their promises of weekend visits. They would not see each other every day anymore but they would at least have something to look forward to each weekend.

Once they arrived inside the reception area, Giovanni quickly handed in his suite key card and then they both walked slowly towards the main entrance. Very solemn expressions were clearly displayed upon their faces as they walked and held each other's hands.

"I'll come and see you soon." Giovanni promised. "I only live a couple of hour's drive away, so that means we should be able to see each other most weekends." He gently reassured her.

Zoe smiled and nodded. "That'll be really nice." She replied.

Despite his words, Zoe did worry slightly inside herself that when the two did actually return home, the reality that might subsequently occur, could actually be quite different from their intended promises to each other. Words were so often spoken and exchanged but so rarely acted upon as so often broken promises simply lay abandoned and deserted in the trash heap of life and discarded dreams. Whether Giovanni's promises to Zoe would call into that category remained to be seen but she sincerely hoped that they wouldn't.

"We better go outside." Giovanni insisted as he led Zoe gently by the hand towards the main entrance and pulled his suitcase along behind him.

"Now, there will be more than just a few hallways between us." Zoe mentioned quite solemnly. "And a physical distance that can't be eradicated in the space of five or ten minutes." She added as the couple stepped outside the large glass doors.

"I'll never be that far away Zoe, always remember that. I'll always be there every night when you close your eyes, inside your dreams." Giovanni insisted as he suddenly paused just outside the front doors and then quickly turned to face her. He touched Zoe's face and then kissed her lips softly as he prepared to depart and board the bus that was parked right outside the entrance. "I'll call you later tonight, when you get back home and when I get back home." Giovanni gently reassured her as he smiled. "This is not the end for us Zoe, this is just our beginning."

Zoe nodded as she smiled. "I'll miss you Giovanni." She confessed. "I'll miss you a lot."

Giovanni stepped onto the bus and then smiled as he turned back to face her, the bus doors suddenly started to close just in front of him. "I'll miss you too Zoe." He quickly called out.

Zoe giggled and nodded.

Just a few seconds later, the bus suddenly started to move off and Zoe quietly watched as the electric, computer driven vehicle carried Giovanni away, off into the distance until she could no longer actually see the bus or Giovanni anymore. A sad sigh somehow managed to escape from her lips as she turned and then made her way back inside the resort building and headed back towards the Cuddle Wing. Now, Zoe had to actually prepare herself for her own departure and her own return to her very own real life and her very own real life.

Giovanni had really brightened Zoe's world again as he'd entered into her life, almost like an invigorating breath of fresh air and it was as if someone had actually destined their paths to cross as they'd breathed life back into Zoe's heart and provided her with a breathtakingly beautiful romance. Soon, they would adorn the walls of each other's real lives with the bright colors of joy, happiness, love and warmth and the ugliness of failed relationships, disappointments and heartbreak would be completely forgotten as Zoe basked in Giovanni's offer of love and actively pursued it. The suite Zoe shared with Madeline appeared directly in front of her as she neared the end of the corridor and quickly began to search for the key card to open the door.

Since Madeline had actually been out on her date all day Saturday and Zoe had then been away for the whole night, the two women hadn't actually seen each other for almost twenty four hours and that meant, there was a lot to discuss. When Zoe stepped back inside the suite they shared very fortunately, Madeline was actually already there and as she entered inside the lounge, Madeline quickly stood up enthusiastically as she began to greet her.

"You're finally back Zoe. How was your night?" Madeline asked.

"How was your date?" Zoe asked.

"Well, you really won't believe what happened." Madeline gushed.

"What happened?" Zoe asked as she giggled.

"I had the most amazing day with Bowen." She explained. "He took me to this restaurant on another island close by and we spent most of the day on his yacht."

"Did you say Bowen?" Zoe asked.

"Yes, that's his name Bowen." Madeline replied.

"Madeline, Bowen is the owner of the resort and the island." Zoe quickly explained as she smiled. "You are actually dating the Love Colony founder."

"I know, I found out yesterday, he actually told me. Apparently, he lives on an island nearby." Madeline remarked.

"Okay, more importantly, did you actually kiss him?" Zoe asked. "And was it good?"

"I did." Madeline immediately confirmed as she nodded in response.

"And did he past the delicious kiss test?" Zoe probed.

"He certainly did." Madeline answered.

"Oh my days, this is absolutely amazing." Zoe remarked as she giggled.

"He's going to fly down to mine some weekends and every other weekend, he's going to fly me out here to stay with him." Madeline mentioned. "He's very serious."

"Okay, I just need a moment to take this all in." Zoe replied as she suddenly grabbed a magazine from the top of the coffee table nearby and waved it in front of her face. "I mean Madeline, this is just amazing, finally you've actually found someone responsible and he seems to actually like you as much as you actually like him. I'm just so happy for you." She mentioned as she suddenly leapt to her feet and then hugged Madeline. "I could actually cry, tears of joy of course."

"I know, all those deadbeats and nightmare relationships are very firmly in the past now, isn't that amazing Zoe?" Madeline asked as she giggled.

"Definitely. No more deadbeats for you." Zoe replied as she giggled and then sat up upon one of the arms of the sofas. She smiled as she happily accepted that Madeline's life had been completely changed, in just the short space of a week. Zoe was completely certain that Bowen would now heal all of those ugly scars and the wounds of betrayal that had been inflicted upon Madeline's life for so very long. "I'm so happy for you Madeline, this is the kind of good fortune you need." She reiterated as she rejoiced in the fact that Madeline's shoulders would no longer have to carry around the heavy weight of bitter disappointment, now Madeline would know the beauty of the real love, she'd always yearned for and that she'd been denied time and time again by the unworthy love cheats that had crossed her path.

"I'm so happy Zoe." Madeline said as her eyes shone and her cheeks glowed.

"I know and I couldn't have possibly chosen a better man for you myself, he's perfect for you." Zoe replied. "I'm so glad you found him, or rather that he found you, or that you both found each other. No more kissing fake toads, finally you've met a real prince and guess what Madeline, Thomas struck gold too."

"Really?" Madeline asked as her eyes suddenly widened in disbelief.

"Yes, we met Thomas's wifey to be yesterday and her name is Dottie and she is absolutely perfect for him. I mean seriously, they are like the perfect match." Zoe explained. "He's over the moon, totally."

Madeline giggled. "Wow, I can't wait to meet her. Dottie, isn't that the name of your chair at work Zoe?" She asked. "Oh no, your chair's called Lottie."

"I know, totally funny isn't it?" Zoe replied. "I almost cracked up when I found out."

"How's Louise?" Madeline enquired.

"Well, she's actually doing quite well considering what happened and she's met someone else and they seem to be really get along." Zoe explained. "I'm just so glad she took my advice and didn't actually sit around moping over Steven for the rest of her vacation, he was so not worth it."

"Yeah thank goodness, it would have been such a waste to come on a vacation like this and then have it spoilt by some dude that doesn't even know what or who he wants." Madeline agreed.

Zoe nodded. "Exactly." She replied.

"Let's go and eat some lunch before we leave." Madeline suddenly suggested as she quickly stood up and then walked towards the door. "We still have about an hour and thirty minutes left before we're due to head off towards the airport."

"That's a really good idea as the food on those flights is absolutely terrible." Zoe immediately agreed as she followed Madeline towards the door of their suite.

"So, were the Holographic Bonking Room Suite predictions actually accurate, do tell all?" Madeline asked as they stepped out into the hallway.

"Definitely, after my night of intricate, scientific exploration and the expedition to the physical confines of Giovanni's love making universe, I can indeed confirm, they are one hundred percent correct." Zoe confirmed.

"So you had a great night then?" Madeline teased.

"Absolutely and I can't wait to venture up into the peaks of ecstasy with Giovanni my fellow explorer again, very soon." Zoe replied. "Our first expedition was a tremendous success and we'll be venturing out on our second expedition at some point, in the very near future."

Madeline giggled. "So instead of being tucked up in your bed inside our suite, you spent the entire night bouncing all over Giovanni's bed?" She teased playfully.

"I did and it was absolutely fantastic." Zoe admitted as they neared the entrance to the dining hall. "We had a tremendous amount of fun as we explored and journeyed up many peaks together and we had a lot of pleasure."

Madeline giggled.

Every inch of the dining hall buzzed with excitement as the two women stepped inside the room and prepared to eat lunch and to see Louise. They had both already showered and dressed in preparation for their flight and were in fact, actually ready to depart as they'd already packed their suitcases the previous day which meant that day, there were very few formalities to actually attend to and hence there was no need to actually rush.

Glimmers of sheer excitement, shone and sparkled inside Madeline's eyes as Zoe quietly glanced at her face as they entered inside the dining hall. She was utterly delighted by Bowen Logan and he'd really been a Godsend to them both as he'd charmed Madeline faithfully and romanced her and delicately kissed away all the ugly pain that idiots like Humphrey had inflicted upon her over the years.   Now, Madeline was actually being shown exactly what real love should look like and exactly what it should actually be.

"You really like Giovanni don't you Zoe?" Madeline suddenly asked.

"I really do and I've never been more sure about a romantic choice before in my entire life." Zoe admitted. "Giovanni is definitely the man for me." She confessed.   "There's absolutely no getting away from it."

"I'm so glad you brought me along on this vacation Zoe. It's really changed our lives and especially our romantic futures."   Madeline mentioned as she suddenly turned to face Zoe and paused.

Zoe nodded and smiled. "I'm really glad we came along too.   Now, we're both finally receiving the romantic love life, we actually deserve not the remnants and drags of a dirty dating bathtub that hasn't been emptied for at least a year."

Madeline nodded in agreement and then glanced around the dining hall as she searched for a table to sit at. "Look there's Louise and Thomas." She quickly pointed out as she suddenly noticed them seated at a nearby table.

"Let's go and sit with them." Zoe suggested as she gently held onto Madeline's arm and then led her over towards the table.

The two women quickly sat down opposite Louise when they reached the table and smiled at her. Very fortunately, both Thomas and Dottie were actually also seated at the same table and Zoe quickly introduced Madeline to Thomas's love interest as soon as they sat down. A few minutes later, Trey also joined the group at the table as Louise smiled as she welcomed his presence.

Inside Zoe, she rejoiced silently in the knowledge that someone else had actually blotted out that ugly ink splat that Steven had made upon the shiny, white piece of paper that represented Louise's delicate, gentle heart. An ugly, unsightly splurge of dirty, black ink had been placed there by his ugly deeds and then gently removed from Louise's life by someone a lot more serious and sincere and the smile upon her face very clearly illustrated that.

Lunch was quickly served and then rapidly consumed as Zoe and Madeline collected Louise, Thomas and Dottie's contact details. There was no way that the vacationers could ever be sure that they would ever actually meet again, unless contact details were exchanged and hence they were offered and collected. Some bonds of friendship had actually been created throughout that week and Zoe wanted to actually ensure that they did not simply sink and disappear into the watery depths of life as each of their realities consumed them once more.

Despite, Thomas and Lottie not being Zoe's usual type of friend, she was quite mindful that perhaps her own attitude towards friendship had to actually change somewhat as Zoe quietly contemplated her own superficiality and challenged it inside herself. Due to her work, which predominantly revolved around beauty and the perfection of outward, physical appearances, she had always tottered around life with what was admittedly, a very superficial outlook. Her attitude hadn't been formed by her work at the beauty clinic but since she'd specialized in that field, it had certainly added to it and that wasn't always a positive thing and Zoe had finally started to realize and accept that.

Both Thomas and Dottie were extremely pleasant and they had touched Zoe in a way that was quite unusual and for once in her life, she actually wanted to welcome that into her environment and embrace it. Zoe had definitely grown quite attached to them both, despite their differences and she actually wanted to retain a friendship with them that not only exceeded their vacation but that also entered into their actual real lives and worlds.

Madeline teased her playfully as the two women finished eating lunch, left the dining hall and then made their way back towards their suite. "You see Zoe, you are getting soft in your old age. You even took Thomas and Dottie's phone numbers and email addresses."

"Maybe. I guess I just like them." Zoe explained. "Thomas is kind of funny and Dottie well, she almost has the same name as my chair at work and that's definitely a sign that we're supposed to be friends or keep in touch somehow."

Madeline laughed.

"That reminds me, I have work tomorrow and I cannot even be a minute late." Zoe groaned. "Collette will not care that I've been away all week at a beautiful, tropical resort trust me. She'll have absolutely no mercy on me at all if I'm late."

"Yeah, it's been really nice to get away from the hustle and bustle of the city and the daily slog of work." Madeline mentioned. "It's actually been quite refreshing."

"Yep and the smiles on your face certainly prove that Bowen has definitely been very good for you." Zoe observed. "I'm very impressed, he seems very committed and sincere."

"Did you actually manage to sleep at all last night?" Madeline teased. "Or are you still quite tired?"

"I'm still a bit tired, I went to bed last night but that was actually more tiring than being up." Zoe replied as she giggled.

Madeline quickly glanced down at her phone. "We better get our cases and then start making our way towards the airport." She advised. "It's almost time for our flight."

Zoe nodded. "Thanks so much for coming on vacation with me Madeline, I mean seriously I couldn't have come here on my own." She said appreciatively as they walked back along the long hallway that led back towards the Cuddle Wing and their suite.

"It's no big deal. We both had fun right." She replied. "Thanks for bringing me along.

This was definitely one of your better adventures."

Zoe giggled.

Silence filled the air as the two women walked along the remainder of the long hallway and internally prepared for their departure from the resort and the weeks' vacation they had thoroughly enjoyed. Zoe quietly contemplated as she walked, how sincere Madeline actually was and how very lucky she was to actually have such a good friend. She was extremely glad that they had both chosen each other as friends all those years ago and then chosen each other as friends every day ever since. They had sauntered through life together, best of friends and each other's strongest ally as they'd formed a union which very fortunately, had never, ever actually been broken.

Deep down, the two women both genuinely wanted the best in life for each other and that was something that was very rare in female friendships that were usually littered with jealousy and petty rivalries. Madeline genuinely cared about Zoe and Zoe genuinely cared about her and that had been clearly displayed over the years. Whenever Zoe wanted to do anything very reckless or extremely outrageous, Madeline would always be the one that she would confide in and the one who would actually worry about her. She was just more sensible and cautious and in some ways, she'd actually balanced out Zoe's vices and protected her from being to wild and outrageous at times and from going too far. In return, Zoe had somehow pulled Madeline slightly further out of her shell as she'd encouraged her to be braver and participate in life in ways that she alone, perhaps would naturally never have dared to explore. They both somehow needed each other and their bond of friendship that held them together so strongly through the walk of life.

"My dates with Giovanni this week were absolutely delicious." Zoe mentioned as they arrived just outside the suite door. "I just hope we can sustain that enjoyment in real life as real life really isn't a tropical paradise."

"Isn't paradise wherever you are together?" Madeline asked as she held the keycard up against the small, square panel on the wall and the suite door suddenly swished open in front of them. "I just hope in the real world, Giovanni is everything you want him to be."

"Yeah, you're right Madeline. Don't worry, we'll be utterly spectacular together, tropical island or city suburbs." Zoe replied as she stepped inside their suite for the very last time. "We have to be, I spent a lot of money on this trip." She teased.

Madeline giggled.

Fifteen minutes later, when the two women arrived inside the reception area with their suitcases in tow, they sadly said goodbye to the Cuddle Wing for the last time as they prepared to leave the resort. Inside the reception area, they found Thomas and Dottie, who immediately walked towards them as they smiled.

Dottie fussed over Thomas as they walked. "Are you sure you'll actually be able to make it this weekend Thomas?" Dottie asked as she quickly glanced down at his suitcase and then gently shook her head. "And have you got all your luggage Thomas?" She asked.

Zoe giggled as she listened.

"Yes I can definitely make it, I'll come and take you out for a drive in the countryside on Saturday and then afterwards we'll go for dinner." Thomas immediately reassured her.

"And yes, I've definitely got everything, I checked my suite about ten times."

Zoe smiled as she watched and listened to them both, their romantic coupling was sweet and so innocent and not highly strung or sexually charged at all. She gently nudged Madeline and then whispered in her ear. "Did you realize that Thomas is not actually coughing and clearing his throat anymore?"

Madeline nodded. "Actually you're right Zoe he isn't, I wonder why?" She observed.

"Perhaps it was a nervous thing and perhaps, Dottie has given him more confidence in himself." Zoe suggested.

Madeline nodded. "I think you could be right." She agreed. "Nerves do affect some people in different ways."

Mark suddenly appeared from a door just behind the reception desk and he walked towards them both as he smiled. "Ah, you're leaving us ladies what a sad day." He mentioned. "I hope you had a great vacation."

Zoe smiled as she suddenly leant forward and then hugged him affectionately. "I really did and thank you for looking after us Mark." She mentioned appreciatively.

Becky suddenly entered inside the reception from behind a set of glass doors nearby and she quickly walked towards the Zoe and Madeline as she prepared to bid them farewell. "I'll really miss you ladies." She mentioned as she leant forward and affectionately hugged both Zoe and Madeline.

"I'll miss you to Becky." Zoe replied as she hugged her enthusiastically in response.

"I really hope we'll see you both again one day and if there are any weddings, don't forget to invite us." Becky teased. "Mark and I love a good wedding, makes our jobs worthwhile."

Zoe giggled. "Definitely, if any of us get married, you'll be the very first people we'll invite." She replied as she released Becky and then smiled at her.

Suddenly, Louise arrived inside the reception area and Zoe smiled at her as she approached the women with her two suitcases in tow. A warm smile adorned her face and Zoe celebrated her happiness, she almost looked as if she'd completely recovered from the ugly disappointment that Steven had inflicted so harshly upon her. Louise had bounced back it seemed as Trey had somehow managed to restore her faith in the male species and actually convinced her to give love another chance. They hadn't spent much time together but the time they had spent by each other's sides clearly showed as Louise's face beamed with happiness.

Very fortunately, Louise had actually discovered just in time, what an awful person Steven really, actually was before she'd attended her final date and that had allowed her to actually make the most of that opportunity, instead of being caught up in Steven's pretentious love affair. Both Zoe and Madeline had advised her that, if Steven was that bad whilst at the resort in that short space of time things would only get worse once they left the resort and returned to their real lives, if he even actually bothered to see her at all. Their advice had been received and then actually accepted as Louise had swiftly moved on and swept Steven neatly and under the rug of lovers that should be forgotten in the shelves and memories inside her mind as she'd completely buried their relationship and avoided any further contact with him. The relationship between them both had been very negative and very negative, extremely quickly and therefore Zoe and Madeline's dissuasion was extremely easy to accept and their advice easy to adhere to.

"It will only get worse Louise." Madeline had advised her. "Once a relationship sinks into those murky pits of disrespect, it really doesn't get any better, trust me I should know, I've been there myself many times. The love just starts to disintegrate until its completely swallowed up by anger, hurt and pain and then there's nothing left to like anymore."

For once, Madeline had actually been able to see through Louise's experience, what Zoe so often saw when she looked at Madeline's relationships, a woman who had been hurt, used and mistreated and it had essentially opened her eyes to the years of pain she'd actually endured at the hands of men who really didn't give a dam about her. Finally, Madeline had seen through the mistreatment of Louise, what was usually inflicted upon and accepted by herself.

A few minutes later, much to Madeline and Zoe's complete surprise, Bowen suddenly appeared as he quickly strode across the reception area towards them and then took Madeline to one side. His interruption was immediately welcomed by Madeline as she quickly smiled at him and then followed him towards one side of the reception area, in order to enable a slightly more private conversation to occur between them both.

"Madeline would you actually like me to take you to the airport?" Bowen offered.

Madeline immediately nodded in response. "That would be lovely Bowen thanks so much for offering." She replied. "I think there's three of us all heading in the same direction though and getting on our flights at around the same time."

Bowen nodded. "That's fine. I'll get the jeep ready and then I'll wait for you all outside." He replied as he smiled.

Madeline nodded appreciatively.

A sudden sense of relief suddenly washed over Madeline as internally she appreciated his efforts as his kindness would mean that they wouldn't actually have to struggle with their items of luggage. Bowen was it seemed, extremely considerate and very helpful. Once Bowen had left her side, Madeline walked back over towards Zoe and Louise and then quickly discussed Bowen's kind offer with them which they immediately, very readily accepted.

Once the three women had bid farewell to Thomas and Dottie, they quickly made their way outside and then jumped inside the jeep which was parked just on the right hand side of the resort entrance. A couple of male resort staff assisted the women as they handled their luggage and then quickly placed it inside the jeep, at Bowen's request. The three women sadly waved goodbye to Thomas and Dottie as they stood just outside the entrance to the resort and watched them leave.

Deep inside as Zoe glanced and waved at them both, she was extremely uncertain when she would actually see either of them again as they both actually lived quite a distance away from both Zoe and Madeline. Numbers and email addresses had been exchanged however, so there was some hope that it would perhaps happen at some point, in the not too distant future.

The vehicle gently rolled forward as Bowen steered it away from the main resort building and then gradually picked up speed as Zoe sighed with sadness. Her vacation was now well and truly over and although it had been the holiday of a lifetime she knew quite definitely that the two women would absolutely never, ever have a vacation like that one ever again. Now, it was time for a new beginning, a very real one without the sand, sea and tropical beauty that the love island, Zincata had actually provided. Now, it was time for Zoe and Giovanni to actually have a real relationship and a very real romance.

Their journey continued for around another ten minutes as Zoe sat quietly lost in her thoughts as she contemplated her potential future with Giovanni further. The romance and chemistry between them had been absolutely mesmerizing and she wondered if that rampant passion would actually still exist in their relationship without the beautiful, romantic surroundings they had actually met in. Perhaps in some ways, it would be slightly different, more deeply grounded in reality and slightly less magical, perhaps the island created a magical atmosphere of romance that could not actually be sustained outside it's physical boundaries.

In no time at all, the jeep came to a stop as they arrived just outside the small, island airport and Zoe was abruptly pulled back out of her thoughts as she quickly focused upon the task at hand, getting her flight home. The two women, Zoe and Louise quickly jumped out of the vehicle as they left both Madeline and Bowen behind to say their goodbyes to each, slightly more privately and without an active audience.

Unlike some of Madeline's more recent romances, Bowen certainly wasn't a loser and Madeline seemed extremely happy and very comfortable around him and absolutely radiant in his presence. Zoe's heart was touched as she quickly glanced back at the jeep and observed the couple's smiling faces for a moment, Bowen was certainly a refreshing change and not only for Madeline but also for her as she'd grown extremely tired of the unworthy men that crossed Madeline's path in life all too frequently.

On the flight home, the mood was slightly more somber as Madeline and Zoe sat in their seats and prepared for their return to reality. Louise had actually boarded a completely different flight as she was going in another direction entirely but since her flight departure time had been just thirty minutes after Zoe and Madeline's, they had made their way to the airport together. The two women took comfort in the fact however, that at least they had met some decent men, made some unexpected friendships along the way and that they had all left the island and their vacations with a potential romance that promised to be absolutely spectacular.

When Zoe had initially booked their vacation, she'd simply thought that the holiday might be a bit of fun and perhaps even a bit of a joke but it had certainly delivered. The love resort had more than exceeded her initial expectations and hence Zoe was pleasantly satisfied with the end results of their vacation. For some reason, the return flight seemed much quicker than the outward flight for Zoe but that was probably due to the fact that she actually dozed off at one point and slept some of the hours away.

Once the two women arrived back at the city airport they had initially departed from, they quickly exited the plane and made their way through the various security check points. A cab was quickly hailed as soon as they stepped outside and then Madeline was dropped off at home first. The two women hugged each other affectionately as Madeline prepared to depart and Zoe thanked Madeline once again for coming along on the actual trip.

"Thanks for coming along Madeline. I had a great time." Zoe said in a grateful tone as she hugged her affectionately.

Madeline smiled. "No thank you Zoe, if I hadn't come along, I wouldn't have met Bowen." She replied. "I'll meet you after work on Wednesday and we'll go for dinner and hang out."

Zoe nodded. "Sure but don't come before six, you know what Collette's like, she won't let me out of the building a minute before six." She advised.

Madeline laughed. "It seems a bit strange to be back home again, doesn't it?" She asked.

"It certainly does. I could have spent forever at Zincata island and not having to wake up early for work every morning was certainly something I could have quite easily become very accustomed to." Zoe replied.

Madeline smiled.

A few minutes later, the car left as Madeline turned around and then walked towards her front gate with her suitcase in tow which she gently pulled just behind her. Zoe sighed as she sat back inside the vehicle quietly and prepared to return to her own apartment, it had been an amazing resort but now it was back to her very real apartment block and her very real life.

Zoe's journey finally ended as the cab arrived outside her apartment block and she quickly paid the cab driver and then made her way inside the building. There would be no more brightly colored, shiny cocktails waiting for her consumption just down the hallway, now it would just be lattes, teas and whatever soft drinks she'd actually placed inside the fridge and perhaps sometimes, the odd bottle of wine.

Although technically, Zoe had actually arrived home early enough to unpack as it was before nine that evening which meant she actually had ample time in which to do so, she left her suitcases in the hallway just inside her apartment door and then made her way towards the lounge. There was no way on earth that Zoe was actually going to unpack her cases at that precise moment in time or even that night, she quickly decided as she totally ignored their presence and began to relax.

Before even an hour had passed by, Zoe quickly called a pizza delivery service to order some food as she surrendered to her desire for fast food and the urge to eat something without actually cooking anything or stepping inside the kitchen. The day essentially had actually been quite long and Zoe was slightly knackered as a result.

Once Zoe finished eating, she made her way towards her bedroom and then threw herself down upon her bed as she quickly made an executive decision, her unpacked luggage could definitely wait until the next day and the next evening. The next day, Zoe had absolutely no plans after work at all and that meant, when she returned home from work she would actually have the time to unpack her suitcases and wash all the dirty laundry that had been accumulated throughout her trip. Work had to be attended on time the very next morning as Collette would certainly have her guts for garters if she was actually late on her very first day back at work after being away for a week's vacation.

True to his word, Giovanni actually called Zoe that evening as he'd promised and since she hadn't actually spoken to him since that morning, she welcomed his call appreciatively as she lay down upon her bed for a few minutes and just listened to him speak. Giovanni had a very sexy voice, in Zoe's opinion and as she listened to him, she quickly realized that she was quite definitely missing his voice and him already. Their conversation didn't last very long as he also had work the next morning and he actually had a much earlier start than Zoe did but it was long enough for him to mention how much he missed Zoe and how he couldn't wait until they saw each other again, the next weekend as they'd planned.

When their conversation ended, Zoe started to drift off to sleep, slightly comforted by the fact that Giovanni had actually called her but missing his physical presence all the more. Finally, Zoe had actually embarked upon a romance that was special and had engaged with a man that seemed sincere, serious and very certain about who and what he wanted in and from life and that was an extremely refreshing change for Zoe in so many ways.

The romantic connections which had been made whilst at the resort, it now pleasantly appeared, were actually about to transcend into reality and that was a huge encouragement to Zoe as she accepted

Giovanni's real entrance into her very real life with open arms. Their coupling was not just a holiday fling and the resort had not just been filled with men just trying to get a quick leg over, though Louise had certainly met one man like that throughout their stay.

At times, singles holidays usually promised so much but were really just filled with horny participants that tried to hop into a different beds, some even hopped into as many beds as they possibly could in the time the duration of the vacation physically permitted. Zincata island and the Love Colony resort had been completely different however and in Zoe's mind, Love Inc. the company responsible for the vacation packages which was run by Bowen Logan had certainly lived up to its promises and actually delivered beyond expectations.

Tomorrow, Zoe knew she would actually have to turn up for work and then the romantic, tropical island would no longer be the place where she would actually spend any of her waking hours. She groaned as a sudden vision of Collette jumped into her mind and then quickly rejected it, there was no way on earth she was going to think or dream about

Collette after the beautiful conversation she'd just had with Giovanni. Zoe quickly tried to focus her thoughts upon the couple's possible future together as she waited for sleep to fully embrace her and carry her off in its peaceful arms. Counting sheep might help, she suddenly decided or perhaps she could count naked Giovanni's instead, that would be much sexier and a lot more soothing than the startling appearance of some mangy, greyish, manky sheep.

Fortunately, when Zoe's alarm actually beeped the next morning, extremely loudly as each piercing sound cut sharply through the air, she woke up straight away. A hand was quickly stretched out from underneath the duvet as Zoe hit it hard to silence it and then forced herself to actually get out of bed. Bills had to be paid and work was definitely waiting for her and gone to were the sun, fun and cocktails of the previous week, now it was time for very real responsibilities.

Rain pitter pattered against the windows of her apartment as Zoe climbed out of bed and then made her way towards the bathroom, a shower was definitely required and that would definitely wake her up. Once she'd showered and dressed, she grabbed a coffee from the kitchen and then made her way towards the front door, it was definitely raining outside and so Zoe quickly grabbed a jacket on her way out from the coat hooks just beside her apartment door as she braced herself and prepared for the cold, wet weather that sat waiting for her, right outside her apartment block.

When she stepped out of the main entrance to her apartment building and onto the street, Zoe suddenly winced as drops of rain immediately angrily spat onto her face as if the skies were actually insulting her. Madeline was extremely fortunate at times, Zoe quietly mused as she could work from the confines of her own home if she wanted to and that meant, she did not actually have to leave her home early every working day and brace any kind of atrocious weather that the skies had decided to inflict upon the face of the earth. Rarely, did Madeline ever actually have to attend an early morning Monday appointment or meeting as most people simply didn't organize meetings for very early on Monday mornings as most people were not like Collette. Zoe on the other hand, had to get up and actually go out to work, early every weekday morning whether it was rain, snow or shine.

Once Zoe was inside her vehicle, she quickly started the engine and it began to purr as it gently moved off. Zoe had actually missed her car, her bed, her coffee machine and her home but she wasn't quite sure yet whether or not those sentiments actually extended towards Lottie, her beautician's chair as that came hand in hand with Collette and she certainly hadn't missed her.

Collette's character was a very tough cookie without any soft chewy bits and Zoe knew her particular brand of biscuit was as tough as a pair of old iron boots and the kind of thing one only attempted to eat, if you were absolutely starving. A smile suddenly crossed Zoe's face as she quietly decided to buy some donuts on her way into work. The backstreets were quite empty as she drove along them and avoided the heavy traffic flows that usually occupied the main roads. Heavier traffic added additional minutes onto her journey time and those additional minutes would definitely make her late as it was now almost rush hour.

The box of donuts would perhaps cheer everyone at work up, Zoe quietly considered thoughtfully and then perhaps, they would forget about the rain that beaten down upon them earlier that morning on their way into work, they would forget the fact that it was actually a Monday morning and that meant their working week had only just started and perhaps they would also forget the awful fact that they all actually worked for Collette. She'd place the box of donuts inside the reception area so that her colleagues could help themselves and eat them with their morning coffees, after she'd taken out a few first for herself.

Very unfortunately, Zoe's first day back at work was just as she expected, extremely brutal and for some reason, it actually seemed to be exceptionally long as it dragged on and on and on. Surprisingly however, Collette was actually quite easy upon her that day and didn't actually cross her path much at all which was very unlike Collette. Perhaps, Collette had actually missed her, Zoe quietly considered as she waited inside her consultation room and prepared for her last client that afternoon. Before the final client of the day arrived however, someone else popped into her consultation room and Zoe quickly braced herself for the scolding she expected to follow as Collette suddenly entered inside the room.

"How was your trip Zoe?" Collette asked as she smiled.

A stunned expression rapidly crossed Zoe's face as she glanced at her thoughtfully, Collette was actually being nice and was actually attempting to hold a pleasant conversation with her and that was extremely strange and even slightly worrying. An awkward silence sat delicately in-between the two as Zoe hesitated slightly for a few more seconds before she took a deep breath and prepared to actually answer Collette's question.

"It was actually lovely Collette thanks." Zoe finally replied as she glanced at Collette's face slightly suspiciously, Collette certainly wasn't the type to make social visits or to engage in social conversations with employees simply for the sake of it and her question therefore seemed, totally weird and completely out of character.

She quietly cast her mind back over her day and her lunch break as she pondered as to whether or not she had actually returned from a lunch a few minutes late. The question posed had to be a trick question and a scolding for something was perhaps, just around the corner waiting patiently to be unleashed upon her by Collette's sharp, razor like tongue. Zoe held her breath as she waited to be lambasted and watched Collette quietly but nothing further was said.

One of surfaces seemed to attract Collette's attention and she suddenly walked over towards it and then fussed over it for a few seconds as she wiped it over with a wet cleaning wipe. A strange hum emanated from Collette's mouth as she worked which surprised Zoe even more as Collette absolutely never, ever hummed.

"You know Zoe, it was pretty quiet round here last week, when you weren't here." Collette suddenly mentioned as she finished cleaning the surface and then strode back across the room towards Zoe.

"Really Collette?" Zoe asked. "Does that mean you missed me?" She gently prodded as she bravely attempted to ask Collette a question that a month ago, she'd never have dared to ever ask.

Collette smiled. "Now Zoe, don't push your luck, your still not leaving early on Friday afternoons." She replied as she grinned.

Zoe smirked as she watched Collette leave the room. "I think she missed me." She muttered as the door of her consultation room swung closed behind Collette's back. "Yep, she definitely missed me, how strange is that?"

The two women gradually adjusted once more to their real lives as the next six months literally flew by for Zoe and Madeline. Their weekly routines had definitely changed slightly as they assimilated not just back into work but also adjusted their weekend schedules to include and accommodate the presence of their very new, extremely exciting romantic relationships. Quite often, throughout the weekdays, they would even actually spend their evenings together, whenever they actually had a chance to as their weekends quickly became filled up with travel arrangements to spend time with Giovanni and Bowen. Whenever the two met, they would often reminisce about their vacation and discuss the very fond memories the both held enthusiastically, with grins and smiles. At times, Louise even actually visited them both and then they would spend a whole weekend together and hang out as they discussed their relationships, binged on fast food and showed Louise around the city.

Despite all Zoe's good intentions, since she'd actually arrived back from her vacation, she still hadn't actually called Thomas or Dottie even once but Louise actually had and each time she saw Zoe and Madeline, she'd update them both on how the couple were actually doing. Louise had kept her promise to stay in touch with them both and according to Louise, they were still going strong as a couple and very much in love. Since their vacation, Louise had also seen a lot more of Trey and they'd even begun to formalize their romance as she'd met his parents several times and he'd also met hers.

Each time Louise visited the two women, she would tease Zoe playfully about Giovanni and gently remind her about the Holographic Bonking Room Suite and the holographic visions they had all seen inside it. Inside Louise's mind, no matter how much time passed by, those holographic visions had been absolutely impossible to forget and absolutely impossible it seemed, for Zoe to ever live down as neither Madeline nor Louise would actually allow her to forget about them.

"Yes Zoe, you and Giovanni were really at like rabbits." Louise had playfully teased her upon one occasion. "No wonder you're both still together."

"You're all just so jealous." Zoe had replied. "Yes, we have good sex and yes, I'm definitely enjoying it."

Approximately seven months after their vacation as the three women gathered to spend the weekend together in Madeline's home, Zoe and Madeline picked Louise up from the city airport and then made their way back towards her house as Madeline insisted that she had something to tell them all that was very private. When they arrived outside Madeline's home, they all quickly entered inside and then made their way into the lounge as the two other women searched Madeline's face for any possible clues as to what her surprise might possibly be but there were no obvious clues. The two women then sat down upon the sofa as Madeline quickly poured everyone some glasses of wine and then she stood directly in front of them as she prepared to make her very special announcement.

Zoe quickly glanced at her stomach. "You're not pregnant are you?" She asked.

Madeline smiled. "Bowen has actually asked me to marry him and I've actually said yes." She announced as her eyes glistened and shone with excitement. "We're going to have a very brief engagement but it will just be for a few months and then we'll actually tie the knot."

Zoe immediately leapt to her feet, rushed towards Madeline and then hugged her as excitement filled her core. "Oh my gosh Madeline, I can hardly breathe, this is so exciting. A wedding is actually coming and you, Madeline are actually getting engaged and married to a caring, decent, compassionate, kind man that really suits you. I'm over the moon." She remarked.

Madeline giggled. "I know isn't it amazing?" She replied.

Louise nodded. "I'm so happy for you both, for you and for Bowen. He's a very lucky man Madeline as you are one of the sweetest women I know."

Zoe immediately nodded. "He sure is. Bowen is a very lucky man, a very lucky man indeed." She agreed.

When Madeline's wedding day arrived, three months later, Zoe naturally attended as her Matron of Honor and as she stood next to the altar and watched her best friend marry the man that she had somehow actually indirectly introduced her to, there were tears of joy in Zoe's eyes. The two women no longer actually lived in the same city anymore as Madeline had actually moved in with Bowen and she now lived on a small island right next to Zincata, called Chinga. Despite the fact that the two women now spent far less time together due to the distance between them, Zoe really didn't mind at all although sometimes she definitely missed her. Madeline was happy and Zoe was happy that Madeline was happy and that in Zoe's mind was all that really actually mattered as Madeline couldn't put her future on hold just for a few nights of female companionship, a few glasses of wine and a few laughs, she had marriage to do, babies to make and a man to actually be a wife to.

For once, one of Zoe's strange adventures that Zoe usually dragged Madeline along to, had actually resulted in something very positive and something very permanent and something breathtakingly beautiful and something, so very real. Suddenly all those years of tolerance as

Madeline had endured Zoe's erratic lifestyle and participated in things she had absolutely no interest in at all, had paid off and she'd been rewarded with something very special and something very beautiful. A future with a man who absolutely adored her and a future with a man, who she too completely adored.

Each tear of joy slipped gently down Zoe's cheeks as the two read out their vows and Zoe watched her most trusted friend in the entire world, actually accept Bowen Logan as her husband. In one of the aisles at the very front of the church, Madeline's mother sat and cried as she watched as she rejoiced in the happiness that had very unexpectedly, actually embraced her daughter's life. Ever since Madeline's father had actually passed away many years ago, when Madeline was still a child, her mother had always feared that Madeline would never actually find anyone decent to actually settle down with and that had been a constant source of worry for her. The fact that Madeline had waded from one romantic disaster to the next over the years, hadn't actually helped at all and it had almost completely convinced her mother that her husband Harry, had in fact been the last decent man alive on the face of the planet.

Just a few rows further back from the pew where Madeline's mother was actually seated, Thomas sat next to Dottie and Trey and Zoe glanced at the three as she smiled. A tissue was quickly wiped over his brow as Zoe watched Dottie fuss over him as usual and Zoe grinned. Despite their quirkiness, their relationship and romance had actually managed to stand the test of time and it was highly likely that they too would also actually get married one day quite soon. Naturally, Louise had been asked to be a bridesmaid and hence she was actually missing from Trey's side but the couple were still very much together and still very much in love.

A few more rows further down, on the other side of the church, the resort staff Mark, Becky, Ricky and Samantha all sat next to each other with huge smiles upon each of their faces as they watched the wedding ceremony and Bowen Logan and Madeline publicly commit to each other for life. In some ways, Zoe felt the whole event had to be incredibly satisfying for them, to see real relationships and marriages actually occur from some of the matches they had helped to make and nurtured at the resort. The performance of their job had given birth to so much real love and joy and that certainly had to be a very motivating experience for all of them.

An hour later, once the service ended, Zoe quickly returned to Giovanni's side as she found him seated in a pew quite close to the front of the church and then gently slipped her hand inside his. They were both now actually engaged and he immediately squeezed her hand affectionately as he enthusiastically embraced her return. Marriage as yet, had not actually happened for them both but that was not due to a lack of desire on Giovanni's part as Giovanni had actually proposed to Zoe several times. Zoe's reluctance towards marriage was nothing at all to do with Giovanni however and she'd explained that to him several times as she'd accepted their engagement and his engagement ring but refused to commit to an actual wedding ceremony.

"Giovanni, if I ever marry anyone in life it will definitely be you." Zoe had explained upon one occasion. "I'm just not keen on the whole concept of marriage. All these people get married and within a year they're divorced and I don't want us to be like that or like them."

In some ways, Zoe had already compromised for Giovanni as she'd actually engaged him and for her that was a huge step. Marriage in Zoe's mind had always been something that people did that was a bit like a ritual, something that usually ended up in divorce and something quite negative that people usually did predominantly to satisfy nagging relatives and other married friends. Despite Zoe's negative attitude towards marriage however, Giovanni had persisted and he'd asked her for her hand several times and Zoe knew as she glanced into his eyes, their attendance at Madeline's wedding would definitely prompt him to raise the issue with her again.

Once Zoe had spent a few minutes with Giovanni, she then quickly left his side once more as she walked back towards Madeline as an organ suddenly began to play inside the church. Each of the pews that lined the church walls was filled to the brim with people as Zoe quietly cast her eyes over some of the guests as she walked and admired their elegant, smart and sophisticated outfits. Some of the guests that sat inside some of the pews inside the church, Zoe immediately recognized as they were actually members of Madeline's family that she'd met several times before, usually at birthday parties and other family related events that Madeline had invited her to attend.

A few seconds later, Zoe bent down and picked up the edge of Madeline's train which cascaded onto the floor behind Madeline as she prepared for the couple's exit from the actual church building itself.   Due to the extremely long nature of the train, Madeline had actually request Zoe's assistance, prior to the actual service and hence Zoe understood exactly what she had to do and how she had to actually do it without any further explanations. The wedding itself, had been almost like a fairytale and absolutely no expense had been spared by Bowen as practically everything that a woman could possibly ever hope for or want at a wedding service had been provided. Bowen had provided Madeline with much more than just a fairytale wedding though and Zoe fully appreciated the other gift that he'd provided to her that only she and Madeline actually knew about. He had given Madeline a reason to try to love again and he'd restored the hope that true love did actually exist and that sometimes, it could actually find you.

The couple arrived at the mid-point of the church and Madeline turned and smiled at Ricky, Becky, Samantha and Mark as she passed them in the pew they were seated upon. Several guests, by this point had already made their way outside as they'd wanted to take pictures of the bride and groom and throw confetti over their heads as they exited the church and had been anxious to secure a position just outside the church that would allow them to do that effectively. Zoe politely smiled at some of the guests as she walked past each of the pews about three meters behind Madeline as she carried her dress and escorted the couple back towards the church entrance.

"Who would have thought that our very first wedding invite would have actually been from our own boss." Samantha suddenly mentioned as she quickly dried a tear in her eye. "Isn't it just so cute?"

Ricky, Becky and Mark immediately nodded their heads in response as they agreed.

Approximately five months later, Zoe received an emergency call as Madeline went into labor and she quickly flew out to the private hospital situated upon the mainland close to Zincata, along with Giovanni to be by her side in a private jet that Bowen had actually sent to collect them both. During Madeline's labor, Zoe remained right by her side as Giovanni and Bowen waited for them inside the hospital waiting room. Bowen had actually been present inside the delivery room but because he'd panicked a bit, Zoe had actually had to send him outside as Madeline had become quite stressed and uptight as a result. Madeline wasn't really great at coping with pain and had screamed extremely loudly for some of the night but Zoe had managed to stay by her side regardless and she'd finally urged the labor nurse to provide her some kind of pain relief.

"Can you give her some pain relief please?" Zoe requested as she cornered the nurse on one of her observation visits to the delivery room.

"Well, I did initially ask her if she wanted some but she absolutely refused." The nurse politely explained in response.

"I won't refuse now." Madeline suddenly pleaded as she pushed each word out of her mouth in-between screams. "Now, I'll take everything you've got."

A few hours later, once the pain was actually over and Madeline had actually given birth to a bouncing, very healthy, extremely cute, baby boy, Bowen was actually allowed to enter back inside the delivery room, much to his utter delight. His face absolutely lit up as he glanced at his son and stood beside Madeline's bed and gently stroked her hair as she held their child inside her arms.

"I'm so proud of you Madeline." He said.

"I am to that was incredibly painful and extremely hard work." Madeline replied as she smiled at him. "Noone told me it would be as painful as that."

Zoe grinned. "I think they don't tell you about the pain as they don't want women to actually stop having children as it's too painful." She teased.

Madeline grinned.

Giovanni stepped inside the room with a hot cup of coffee inside his hand and then made his way over towards Zoe's side. "I brought you this." He offered as he gave her the cup. "I thought you might need it right about now."

Zoe giggled and nodded. "I sure do." She replied. "What are you going call him Madeline?" Zoe suddenly asked as she glanced at Madeline's face thoughtfully.

"Well, we've both discussed it a lot and we're actually going to call him, Zoen." Madeline replied. "We wanted to name him after you and we'd actually like you and Giovanni to be his Godparents, if you want to be of course."

"Oh my gosh Madeline, that is so cute." Zoe exclaimed as she quickly leapt to her feet. "I feel so honored, he's actually been named after me. Of course I'll be his Godmother, I mean I'll try my best anyway." She smiled as she graciously accepted the huge honor that Madeline had just actually bestowed upon her as she glanced at Giovanni's face.

Giovanni smiled. "Of course we both will." He quickly volunteered.

Two pale blue blankets were gently wrapped around the bundle of joy inside Madeline's arms by Zoe as Madeline prepared to give their son to Bowen so that he could hold his child for the very first time. Despite the fact that Bowen was overjoyed about his son's arrival, he was also extremely nervous as he quickly stepped forward and Madeline held out their son towards him as his arms began to tremble.

Due to his nerves, Zoe quickly leant towards him to assist him as she helped him support Zoen's neck and head properly. Regardless of Bowen's many achievements in life, it quickly transpired that he had absolutely no clue at all when it actually came to the issue of holding newborn babies. Zoe smiled as she watched him, most guys didn't have the slightest clue anyway and men seemed to be a lot more nervous around newborn babies than women were for some strange reason.

Everyone inside the room, focused upon Bowen and Zoen as a beautiful moment suddenly occurred as Bowen gazed down at his son inside his arms and an expression of pure joy, love and devotion immediately appeared upon his face. One day perhaps, Zoe quietly considered thoughtfully Giovanni would perhaps be standing in that position and doing exactly the same thing to their own son or daughter and that day she knew, Giovanni would be the proudest man alive.

Just a few minutes later, Madeline's mother suddenly arrived and some of Bowen's relatives and the delivery room rapidly filled up. News of the birth had it seemed, spread extremely quickly and had been responded to instantly as relatives rushed to the hospital to welcome the new arrive into the world.

"It's starting to get a bit crowded in here." Zoe whispered as she drew much closer to Giovanni.

Giovanni glanced at Zoe's face and then slipped his hand gently inside hers. "Let's go and get some sleep." He insisted. "And we can even practice making a baby of our own." Giovanni whispered.

Zoe smiled and nodded. "I just can't believe, dragging Madeline along for a week's vacation actually resulted in all this joy, it's so amazing." She replied as she allowed Giovanni to led her out of the delivery room. "Maybe one day perhaps we'll be doing this too."

"Indeed we will, indeed we will." Giovanni quickly reassured her. "We certainly practice the creation process enough." He teased.

Zoe giggled.

Several positive things happened after that day as Zoe finally learned and accepted that marriage wasn't just about two people but that it was also about the children the couple brought into the world and providing those children with a stable relationship and home to grow up in. Finally, Zoe agreed to actually marry Giovanni and their wedding date was quickly set. Despite the fact that the couple only had three months in which to prepare for the big day, that wasn't really a huge problem for Giovanni as he'd been saving up for a while as he'd patiently waited for that moment to actually arrive.

Time flew rapidly by as the three months quickly slipped out of their hands and their wedding day suddenly approached. Zoe and Giovanni's big day had finally arrived and as Zoe prepared to walk down the aisle with the man she loved, she knew in her heart of hearts that she had definitely made the right decision. Due to the fact that Zoe's parents had actually divorced when she was actually quite young, it had put Zoe off marriage almost completely as their divorce and custody battle had been extremely ugly and a very bitter affair but

Giovanni somehow, had managed to change that and Zoe's attitude.

"I want you to be my wife Zoe and I want you to marry me. I want you to make that commitment to me because you want to spend your life with me, not because of what other people think or expect from us." Giovanni had often told Zoe.

Finally, Zoe had believed him as she accepted his sincerity towards her and his patience as he'd waited for her 'Yes' for quite a significant period of time. Zoe had made him wait but she had made him wait for a reason as she'd wanted him to be sure that he was very sure, before she actually participated as divorce was something, she definitely never, ever wanted to actually experience.

The wedding guest list had actually been quite large in the end as so many of the couples' relatives, friends and work colleagues had been invited to attend the event. Giovanni actually had seven brothers and sisters, who were all actually married with children and everyone of them was actually due to attend, along with Zoe's three brothers and their respective families and all of their aunties, uncles and cousins had been sent invitations which they had all accepted. Madeline and Bowen had of course been invited and Louise and Trey, who were now also engaged and Dottie and Thomas had also been asked to attend.

Despite all of Zoe's negative run-ins with Collette, she had also been invited and was actually seated in one of the pews as the wedding ceremony commenced. Collette nodded at Zoe as she walked down the aisle with her arm linked to one of her brother's arms as her oldest brother, Keith assumed the responsibility of giving her away as her father had unfortunately, been unable to attend. At the very front of the church, inside a pew, Zoe's mother Cheryl sat quietly with a look of pure relief upon her face as she watched Zoe walk down the aisle.

"He's absolutely perfect for you." Cheryl had whispered in Zoe's ear, the very first time she'd actually met Giovanni. "I really like him." She'd continued. "And you really need to settle down Zoe." Cheryl had absolutely loved Giovanni straight away and she'd accepted him with very open arms as she'd encouraged Zoe to further their relationship and immediately welcomed him into her family.

Each pew seemed to filled to the brim as Zoe walked past them, all her aunties, cousins and uncles had attended, all her brother's families had come along and the church almost heaved with human bodies. Once the wedding ceremony was over, the reception afterwards which was held inside a huge banqueting hall was even more packed as more relatives and friends turned up to celebrate Zoe and Giovanni's extremely special day and packed themselves inside it. Everyone drank and ate merrily as they celebrated and discussed the couple's marital union and wished them well for the future.

"Well young lady, you took your time but you finally got there in the end Zoe." Zoe's Uncle Stuart teased as he toasted to the couple's health and then handed them a large cheque. "I've been saving up." He mentioned as he winked at Zoe.

Zoe smiled.

Once the speeches and main meal were over, music suddenly began to play as Zoe and Giovanni took to the floor for the first dance and everyone inside the room immediately turned their attention towards them. For Zoe, it was definitely a breathtaking moment as she finally accepted that now, she could no longer escape the fate that life had actually intended for her. Her life was with Giovanni and that had actually required a marital commitment from her and regardless of how much she'd tried to avoid that in the past, that day she'd finally had to give that commitment to a man that in her mind, actually really deserved it.

Later that evening as the reception continued, Collette actually approached Zoe and then gently took her to one side as she began to congratulate her. Collette had actually attended Zoe's wedding and reception along with her husband, who much to Zoe's surprise was actually quite a tall man with jagged, dark spiky hair and a very trendy appearance. Apparently, it quickly turned out, he was actually a singer and a very famous one at that and Zoe had actually been quite surprised that Collette had never, ever actually mentioned it to anyone or that she even worked at all as apparently, he was extremely wealthy and that meant, she probably didn't really actually have to. The two women stood at one side of the large banqueting hall as Collette suddenly drew much closer to Zoe as she carried on with their discussion.

"With all your wild ways Zoe, I never thought I'd actually see the day that you would actually settle down." Collette mentioned as she hugged Zoe affectionately and then raised her glass up in the air. "And I'm very, very proud that you now have. To the bride and groom and to your future together."

Zoe giggled. "You're absolutely right Collette, I never thought I'd see this day myself." She replied. "But we both survived to see this day and now that means, the whole world has been completely changed forever. There's no more wild, chaotic Zoe causing mayhem everywhere she goes anymore. End of an era." Zoe said as she sighed and gently shook her head. "Now I have to be a real grown up. Whilst we're on the topic of surprises, how come you never actually told me that you were married to the biggest folk singer in the world?" She asked. "I mean seriously Collette, all my aunties and uncles are going on about it and they're even asking me why I didn't tell them he was going to be here."

Collette giggled. "Well Zoe, he was my husband way before that happened and he's been my husband ever since." She explained.

"Not everything in life is always as you expect it to be. Sometimes there are unexpected variations, melodies and events that can take your breath away and the song of your life is not always easy to hear by someone who doesn't recognize the tune."

Zoe giggled. "How come you still work at the beauticians?" She asked. "I mean, you really don't have to."

"I like to keep busy and I like to keep my financial independence to some degree." Collette replied. "A man respects you more when you have something of your own." She advised. "Keeps them on their toes and if they ever actually do anything wrong to you, it provides you the power and ability to leave and walk away when you actually want to. Absolute power corrupts everyone Zoe, even in a marriage, remember that and you'll be more than a survivor, you'll be a victor and your marriage will be a much happier one."

Zoe nodded as she quietly accepted Collette's words of wisdom. "I don't think I ever would have even actually married anyone, if I hadn't met Giovanni." She mentioned as she smiled. "He really changed everything for me somehow."

"Well, when the right one comes along, you just know." Collette insisted as she smiled.

"I think perhaps you do." Zoe agreed. "For the first time in my life, I actually believe you do."

Suddenly, Giovanni interrupted the two women as he requested a dance with Zoe and then led her towards the dance floor as Collette smiled at him politely and nodded. Giovanni held Zoe extremely close to him as he began to whisper sweet nothings into her ear and promises that contained information about what exactly he intended to do to her later that night when they would actually be alone together. Later that night, Zoe would actually be flying out on a trip with Giovanni to a tropical paradise but this time it was a very different kind of trip than the one she'd originally taken with Madeline when she'd initially first met him, this time it was actually the couples' honeymoon. Zoe smiled as she quietly thought about her trip with Madeline to the love island where the two had first actually met, she would never, ever go on a holiday like that again, she quickly concluded but perhaps, you only really needed one holiday like that in your entire lifetime to change absolutely everything.